Mercy's Grace

DISCOVERIES

JESSICA MUNZLINGER

WESTBOW
PRESS
A DIVISION OF THOMAS NELSON

The Bible verses quoted in the story are paraphrased.
The chapter and verse are cited at the end.

WestBow Press books may be ordered through booksellers or by contacting:

WestBow Press
A Division of Thomas Nelson
1663 Liberty Drive
Bloomington, IN 47403
www.westbowpress.com
1 (866) 928-1240

ISBN: 978-1-4908-2044-6 (sc)
ISBN: 978-1-4908-2045-3 (hc)
ISBN: 978-1-4908-2043-9 (e)

Library of Congress Control Number: 2013922946

Printed in the United States of America.

WestBow Press rev. date: 12/27/2013

To Sandy,

The imagination can never run dry if you fill it with books!

w/♡ + ☺

Jessica Munzlinger

Djorites
Djorite City
Freiton River
Draken
Don Luceor River
Ashites
Landar
Tawney City
N
W
E
S

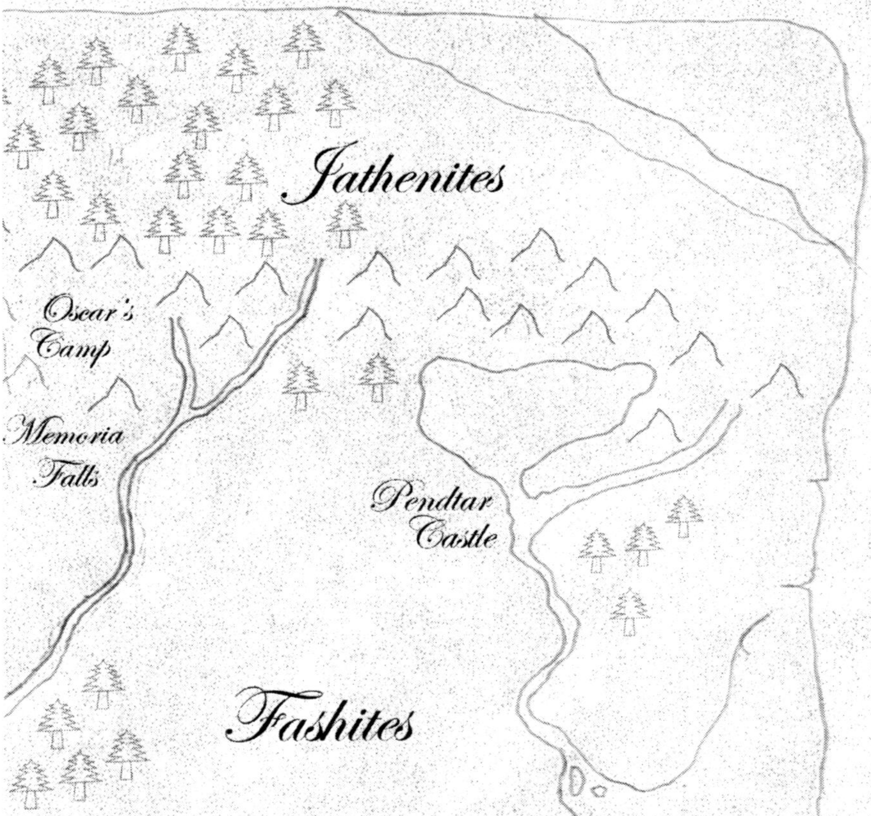
Jathenites
Oscar's Camp
Memoria Falls
Pendtar Castle
Fashites

PART I

Ashites

Chapter 1

The flat line rippled. It calmed for a moment but rippled again. As the second hand tirelessly ran another lap, the number of ripples increased. All of this went unnoticed until dawn when the nurse entered the room to change the patient's IV bag. She might have missed the movement completely if she hadn't been finishing an exhausting double shift that threatened an already stiff neck. She stretched and turned. Upon opening her tired eyes, the readings on the electroencephalograph, which monitored the brain's activity level, begged for her attention. Weariness delayed her understanding of what that small motion meant.

"How did that happen?" she whispered. She looked down at the young man. He didn't appear any different than he had for the past seven months. He looked pale. And alone. The nurse quickly left to find the only doctor she trusted.

"I'm not seeing things," she declared as they entered the room. "I know how to read these instruments. I may be tired, but I'm not incompetent."

"I know," the doctor said. "I apologize for sounding condescending, but what you're telling me is impossible." The ripples on the monitor declared it possible. They strengthened in size and frequency as the second hand continued its marathon. The doctor couldn't blink. "It's impossible," was all he could say.

"Well, I guess it's a good thing the other doctors voted down your proposal to disconnect," the nurse said tartly.

"How many brain-dead coma cases have ever woken up?" he asked. After a moment of silence he said, "I can't think of one either. So my proposal wasn't out of line. What I really want to know is why the panel refused?"

"Maybe they had hope," she offered.

"I doubt that," he returned. "You know, come to think of it, they've allowed so many exceptions to all our procedures for this patient." He paused. The gnawing feeling returned. It had come frequently during the past several months due to the mysterious actions of the presiding forum of senior physicians.

"Why don't we keep this between us for now?" he suggested.

"There will be other nurses in here," she reminded him.

"I'll just turn off the monitor. I doubt they'll notice."

"But what if he wakes?"

"We'll deal with that then," he answered. "Just do what you can to keep this quiet. I have a suspicion."

"Don't worry," she said. "You're not alone in that."

Two weeks passed with no major changes. The nurse turned on the monitor to check his progress. His brain activity increased. Color filled his cheeks, but there were no other signs to give her more hope. Then the day came when he moved. She was working his legs through some exercises when his hand twitched. She waited for more movement, but he remained still. For the first time in years, though, she felt that something good might actually happen in the hospital.

"He moved today," she whispered to the doctor hours later.

"Really?"

"Mm-hmm."

"How much?" he asked, picking up a chart.

"Just a twitch, but I have a little more hope now."

He turned to fully face her. "You know one of my biggest regrets?" he asked pensively.

Startled by his change of tone, she slowly answered, "No. I don't know, of course."

"Not asking you out on a date when we still had a city safe enough to walk down the street."

She blushed and immediately chided herself for reacting in such a childish way. Then again, she reconsidered, it actually felt nice to do something that seemed so natural.

"You're really pretty when you blush," he said. She immediately sobered.

"I'm sorry, Joshua," she whispered. "Even if we could—even if we both want to—"

"We do want to."

"Yes, but the patients won't ever stop coming. I will never stop having to come here every day. And you . . . do you ever see your home?"

"No," he answered and turned to avoid her searching eyes. "It burned down some time ago. I can't bring myself to even leave this place. You're right. The patients will never stop coming."

"We've wasted too much time now." She wiped away the only tear she couldn't hold back and walked to the nearest room.

The doctor suddenly felt old. He sat down and stared at the board full of names of patients who would live, and many who would die. The exhaustion pulled heavily at his body, taking away the desire and drive he once possessed. Finally, the futility of his efforts crept into his thoughts and he wept. All his tomorrows would be the same. Lives came and went, and nothing he ever did could affect that.

But he had already made a decision that unbeknownst to him, especially while in the depths of such dark despair, would lead to the end of hopelessness and the beginning of peace. The boy in the coma remained in his quiet room, but the stillness broke as the bed creaked when he moved.

Chapter 2

The shrill sound penetrated the darkness with great frequency. He wasn't conscious enough to wonder or question, but that noise had to stop. It pierced to his core. Every beep hit the same throbbing point of pain, making it grow and spread until his entire head ached.

"Make it stop! Make it stop! Make it stop!" he tried to scream. The pain was almost forgotten when he realized he couldn't move his mouth. He focused on his tongue and jaw. A ringing in his ears generated an excruciating response that made it difficult to concentrate. He relaxed as best he could, but the beeping continued. He wanted to weep. As his attention drifted to his eyes, he finally realized they were closed. A question found its way through the distractions: *what happened?* The pain thwarted his efforts to think once again, so he gave up trying. He eventually returned to unconsciousness.

The nurse entered the room to check the contents of his feeding bag. She stared at him for some time before she left. He had seemed different, at least in his facial expression. She laughed at herself because, in her frustration, she hoped that he would just wake up and get it over with. Exhaustion pulled her down into a seat, and she allowed the brief moment of rest. This was always dangerous, but she didn't mind tonight. Over twenty new people had been rushed in that evening.

After they were treated, many released, she had wandered the hospital until deciding to check on her favorite patient. She smiled. She'd developed a fondness for the boy, and she finally began to wonder what had happened to him before he was brought here.

That night seemed so long ago. Of course it did. Each day was a year—a year of people coming and going, a year of empty eyes and empty words. The hospital was the safest place, yet it viewed the most darkness. She closed her eyes. A tall man dressed in healer's clothing had carried the young man through the doors. The boy was extremely pale. The man didn't say how long the boy had been unconscious, just that he had fallen. She opened her eyes, noting that she didn't remember seeing a head injury. In fact, the senior physicians, who were rarely on her floor, had taken care of the matter. During the first few weeks they were the only ones to see the young man. Then they stopped coming. She had always been suspicious of that, but had she ever really wondered why? There had been no time for her to allow her curiosity to wander. Now it seemed there was.

She stood, stretched, and went back into his room. What was that song her mother used to sing to her? The words had vanished into the mist, but the melody still played. She hummed softly and turned on the electroencephalograph. There was more activity than ever. Her shock silenced the song. As the song disappeared, so did some of the activity. Thoughtfully, she looked down at the young man and hummed again. Softly and slowly, she rubbed his arms and legs. The monitor levels increased.

"Kid, can you hear me in there?" she whispered. His eyes twitched. "Come on, kid. If you can hear me, do something."

He opened his mouth a little, and she thought he said something.

"You said something?" she asked in amazement. "Say it again, kid."

Slowly, with great concentration, he mumbled, "Make it stop."

She gasped with childlike relief. "Yes, okay. Make what stop?"

"It hurts."

"I'll be right back," she said hastily. "Hang on, kid. I can help you there." She hurried to the medicine room and opened the cabinet that held the pain-suppressant herbs. It was empty. In disbelief, she opened the doors to every other cabinet. Most were empty.

"This was all stocked," she choked. "This was all stocked." She breathed deeply to calm herself before she left the room. Another nurse was nearby. "Beth, what happened to all the herbs?"

Beth shrugged. "I don't know. Ask Abigail."

"Abigail?"

"She was in there all day long," Beth answered. "The 'big doctors' had her doing some things."

"What is it now?"

"Who knows, but I gotta go, okay?"

"Bye," the nurse said. She was not going to ask Abigail anything. Abigail worked too often with those doctors to be trusted. What could she be doing in there for them? Why would they take all of the medicine? She returned to the boy's room. Yet another patient she couldn't help.

"Sorry, kid," she said. "I couldn't find anything."

When he didn't respond, she assumed he was unconscious again.

"Kid, if you keep pulling my emotions around like this—" She left to check on some patients who didn't give her hope. Emotions generated by positive events were foreign, unstable, and even painful because they didn't last. Death and dying were familiar. People getting a second chance—impossible.

She ran into Joshua late the next evening. Exhaustion had taken full effect by then, and she walked right into him. He caught her by the shoulders, but she didn't pull away as instinct encouraged her to do. She ignored the impulse, even resting her head against his chest. Weariness had captured her tears, so she just buried her face and breathed.

"You okay?" Joshua asked. Her reply didn't reach his ears. As she stayed, he slowly wrapped his arms around her, determined not to move until she did.

"Hey, you two, there's no time for that!" another doctor shouted from down the hall.

Though she didn't want to move, the nurse let the urgency of her duties return to her thoughts. Some people were still alive. Only because their wounds weren't life threatening, but nevertheless, they needed her care.

"Sorry," she mumbled.

"No, it was . . . nice," he said, smiling faintly.

"It was only a lapse of concentration," she said, hoping it sounded truer than she meant it. She finally admitted to herself that she would return the feelings Joshua held for her if he pressed her. This encounter with the boy was causing her to desire a life outside of the death. She walked away while her strength was still available and unintentionally returned to the boy's room.

"What is it with you, kid?" she asked as she approached the silent person on the bed. "You don't have any idea what you're doing to me, huh? Of course not. You know nothing. Well, I know nothing, too, so at least we have something in common." She sat down on the side of the bed and rubbed her temples. "Why won't this headache go away?"

A sharp pain coursed through her neck and shoulders, answering her question.

"Oh, kid, what I wouldn't give for a seven-month nap. That would be so wonderful," she said. "And selfish," she muttered as an afterthought. "The battles keep coming. They used to be farther away, but now they're right in our city. You know, kid, it really eats me up. And you know what ticks me off the most? When kids like you come in here. Like those morons can't tell the difference between an adult and a child. They just blow up the buildings and swing their swords at anyone breathing."

She paused to reflect. Time to reminisce was a rarity, and the memories were buried so deep that it took time to uncover them.

"I remember my mom," she said quietly. "She always sang to me. Mostly stuff she made up. And she'd read to me—a lot. But that was before all the books were banned and burned. I loved to smell the paper. You know, the fact that I can read is the only reason I have this job. It's the only job left in this area where you have to write things down, so if you can read and write, you're in. It's the safest place to be, too. That's a perk. Or an irony," she said thoughtfully. "People come here to have a safe place to die. I won't ever understand it, kid. Can I call you kid? No one knows your name, and my imagination is only so good. All I got is kid. Kid or hey you! Which is it?"

"Kid," he said raspily.

That surprised her, and she leaned closer to him. "You can hear me?"

"Nearly. You talk too fast," he said with the faintest sign of a smile.

"Are you going to stay awake this time?"

"If you make it stop," he said slowly.

"What stop? The pain?"

Slowly, and only slightly, he shook his head. "What's causing the pain?"

"What's that?"

"Noise." He released a long breath as the effort to talk took its toll.

"Are you telling me to shut up?"

He scrunched his eyes and winced.

"Sorry, kid. I'll be quiet."

"No. Not you. The noise."

"I don't hear anything," she confessed.

"It comes and goes."

She concentrated on listening, hoping to understand what he was describing. The instruments all around drew her attention. The dropping of the IV, the silent electroencephalograph, and the heart monitor. Bingo.

"Kid, I can't turn that one off without causing a lot of people to come in here and mess things up. You see, my bosses—I don't trust them. And I don't want them to know that you're awake. For some reason, you're different from the other patients."

She waited for a reply. The kid said nothing. His breathing was deep and heavy. She shook her head. Asleep again. At least this time he had been awake long enough for her to get something out of him. A new name.

Later that day, when she had time, the nurse found the doctor. "Joshua, he woke up today," she whispered.

He almost dropped his coffee. "What?"

"The noise from the heart monitor's giving him a headache. Any suggestions?"

"There's the syathia leaves. Or what about rushwood? That would relax him at least," he suggested.

"Tried that," she replied.

"They didn't work?"

"They're gone."

This time he set his coffee on the counter. "What?"

"Abigail's doing something for the big guys. I'm not going to ask around, but Beth didn't know anything."

"That's saying plenty," he said. "I was beginning to wonder if there was anything she didn't know."

"She doesn't know about kid."

"True. So she is human after all."

The nurse's confusion was written plainly upon her face. Since the boy's signs of improvement had started, she found it silly to hide her emotions anymore—especially with new ones coming daily.

"Of course she's human. What else could she be? What out there is capable of knowing everything?"

Joshua revealed nothing, but blankly stared at her in a moment of debate. If he was overheard telling her the truth, he could be killed. He released himself from the tension and looked around for any ready ear. Then he took her arm and led her into the kid's room, shut the door, and looked again for an eavesdropper. She remained confused, but alarm also grew inside her.

Satisfied after the hunt, he whispered, “There is someone who can know everything. I’m sorry, but I guess I assumed that you knew.”

The puzzled expression remained on her face, so Joshua reached into a hidden pocket of his coat to pull out a small, worn, and loosely bound book. She gasped.

“Shh,” he warned.

“Is that what I think it is?” she asked with terrified wide eyes.

He nodded.

“They will kill you,” she warned through clenched teeth.

“Not if no one tells.”

“Then they’ll kill me.”

“And would that really be so bad?” he asked softly.

She was stumped. Why did it seem like such an awful fate to die? “I—I guess not.”

“Please don’t tell anyone,” Joshua begged. “I honestly thought that you read it, too.”

“Why?”

“Because of the way you talk about hope.” He looked over at the kid.

“I don’t understand.”

He sighed and looked at the book. “This book is full of it. See, my dad was a doctor, but he learned everything from—” He paused to remember. “I can’t remember, but you know the people I’m thinking of.”

“Yeah.”

“He got one of these books from them. Except it was handwritten. I wanted to have one with me, so I typed one up and made the print as small as I could so the book could be easily hidden. A friend of mine knew how to bind books. It was finished before—before the death came to this city. I read it often, but my dad said that it was fiction, you know?”

“Every book is.”

“Yeah, but I don’t think this one is. I don’t read it as though it is. In here, there is a person who knows everything. Like I said, I just assumed you would understand. I’m sorry if I’ve put you in danger.”

She studied him for a moment before she eventually shrugged. "No problem. Maybe you can let me read it? I haven't read a book since—goodness, it's been about twenty years."

"Here. And maybe try not to think of it as fiction."

"If you say so, Doctor." She took it from him.

He returned his attention to their patient. "So, what are we going to do about him?"

She pocketed the book. "Well, I've taken over Beth's shifts for a while. She's helping her family move to Toverville Parkland. So, for a few weeks, it's just us to take care of kid."

"And?"

"We could switch patients. There's another coma down the hall, same age as the kid. Anyway, he has brain activity and the like, so he won't be dying anytime soon."

"To keep the heart monitor going," he said, quickly understanding her idea.

"Right. We take the kid elsewhere to give him a quiet room, and write on the charts that the other patient woke and went home."

"But what if that boy does wake?"

"We send him home," she answered. "Policy, right? If they wake up and can sustain themselves, we release them. We're covered for when the big doctors come looking for him. Since they won't tell us the big secret, all we have to follow is policy."

"Okay. When?"

"Tonight."

Chapter 3

The other doctors and nurses continued with their rounds, unaware of anything out of the ordinary. No one ever entered the rehabilitation room. None had reason to—there was no more time or even staff to work it. So no one noticed the bed tucked in the corner. The nurse checked on the young man daily.

The kid finally opened his eyes after a few days. The softer lighting in the rehabilitation room helped make the adjustment to light easier. The nurse never said much, but brought him food and asked how he felt. As she watched his color come back, even to his hands and feet, she allowed herself to freely accept the relief and peace that came to her heart. Life did happen after all.

"So, do you remember anything yet?" she asked, as part of the ritual she'd fallen into over the past week. It was too soon for an affirmative answer, but with this hope as a new feeling, she was going to use it as much as she could.

"No, I don't," the kid answered, but not regretfully, because he had noticed his answer never upset her. He suspected she asked for a different reason than the question suggested.

"Okay. Anything new to report?" The next question came, as well as the plate of food.

"Well, just that I hope when I get out of here, I can find a place with better food."

She laughed outright, forgetting herself and the dangerous situation in which they all were. Laughing, too, had been a long-ago memory that resurfaced when his eyes opened. She laughed softly as she thought back to that day, not even a week ago, and eventually let the feeling calm down to a smile. When he got out and the danger was over, she thought, would she keep on laughing and hoping still, or would time once again weed it out of her system? She pushed those thoughts aside. That was a future situation. She wanted to be in the present.

"Do you think I can try walking today?" the kid asked.

"You're asking the wrong person, kid."

"Who else comes down here for me to ask?"

She chuckled. "Kid, do you think you are ready to walk today?"

"Oh." He blushed. The simple act made him look years younger. "I think I am."

"All right." She pulled off the covers and quickly retrieved a walker from the other side of the room. He was already sitting on the side of the bed, swinging impatient legs, when she returned.

"Now be careful," she cautioned. "You may think you can do it, but those legs haven't moved in eight months."

His smile faded, and the color retreated from his cheeks. He lifted his eyes and his gaze locked on to hers. "Eight months?" he whispered. He dropped his head. "Eight months?"

She hadn't considered what that information would do to a person. Any other coma patient who woke up did so in, at the most, two months. Other than that, they drifted off to a deeper sleep that stopped the body completely. The latter were not the rarest.

"Yeah, kid. You were in a coma for about seven months before you started improving," she explained. "That was about a month ago, give or take a few days."

With some effort, he pulled his legs onto the bed and fell back onto the pillows. "On second thought, I don't think I can walk today."

"No. I'm not letting you do that, kid," she snapped, surprising herself too. "Everyone—everyone gives up around here. But I'm not anymore, and I'm not letting you give up either. So what if it's been eight months? You haven't missed anything! Now get your butt up and start walking."

With shock clear in his eyes, he obediently returned to the upright position. She placed the walker in front of him and held it firm as he lowered his feet to the floor and gripped it with white knuckles.

"Now let's walk," she said. She moved backward as he slowly strained to push his feet forward inch by inch. Each step brought more confidence, and he loosened his grip enough for the white knuckles to change back to their natural color.

"You're doing great," she said encouragingly. "You're doing it!"

He looked up at her and smiled. She returned it gladly. They walked for just a few minutes before she noticed weariness upon his face. "I think that will do for today. But we'll do more tomorrow, okay?"

He nodded, and after he returned to the bed, he found that he was too tired to even eat. She had been right; it was harder than he thought. He fell asleep quickly.

Every day for the next week, they worked on walking for longer periods of time at each effort. By day eight, he wanted to walk without any assistance at all. Secretly, when she had been gone, and when he was in need of something to do, he had used the walker in hopes of getting stronger faster. And the night before, he had made it slowly around the room by himself. So the moment she entered on day eight, he hopped down to the floor to meet her, laughing when she almost dropped the tray.

"You're walking!" she exclaimed.

"Of course. Don't act like I haven't been all week. Could I carry the tray?"

"Sure."

He knew he wasn't moving as fast as she was, but that would take time. He was content with the progress so far. He set the tray on the side table, crawled up on the bed, and ate everything in sight. Still hungry, he sighed but said nothing. He knew that if she could bring him more food, she would. But she had mentioned danger and not wanting others to be suspicious, so he concluded that this time was also her only time to eat in a day, and she gave all her food to him.

"Gee, that was fast," she said. "With all that walking, I bet your body's burning up more energy. You're probably still hungry, poor thing."

"I'm fine."

"Liar. Hey, I just had a thought. Can you read?"

"Read?"

"Yeah. Do you recognize that word?"

He nodded thoughtfully. "It seems familiar, but what is it?"

"Hmm—you might not be able to."

"Is that normal?"

"Well, actually, for someone your age, it is. It's just . . . there's a book I've been reading . . ."

"What's a book?" But his question, he noticed, didn't pull her out of the pensive mood she had settled into for the past few moments. She looked so tired, with deep black circles under her eyes. He was certain she was young, though. Perhaps midthirties. But her eyes were far away at that moment. He sometimes saw her like that, staring off at some invisible image. He liked to study her face. He liked to hear every word she said. He especially liked just being around her. She was very pretty, with short, choppy, blonde hair and green eyes. Her smile revealed straight white teeth and deep dimples in her cheeks. Though she was too skinny, he knew it to be from the stress and poor diet, especially if all she ate was one meal, which she'd lately been sharing with him. That thought made him feel guilty, and he finally looked away. At his empty tray.

"You know, you never have told me your name," he said loudly to pull her out of her thoughts.

"My what?"

"Your name."

"You tell me yours, then I'll tell you mine."

He grinned. "My name's Kid."

She laughed. "Mine's Dawn. Dawn Tracy Jones."

"Three names?"

"First, middle, and last. The last in case there's another Dawn in the world, and middle in case there's another Dawn Jones. But I've never met a Dawn Jones. Or another Dawn, for that matter. Oh, well. Back when I was born, there were a lot more people on this planet, I think. Either way, Ashites still give their kids three names. Traditions, I guess. In case this war finally ends."

"You've mentioned things before about a war. What's going on outside?"

"Nothing you want to know."

"But I'll be out there soon. In case I don't remember anything by then, I'd like to have some idea of what I'm walking into."

She released a pensive sigh before she faced him. "Fine. You talked me into it. Where to begin?" She settled back into the chair and stared at the ceiling. "When it comes to history, I can only help you so much. That's because there isn't much beyond my lifetime that anyone truly knows. You and me, we're Ashites. All I know about us is that we've never really worked together as a people. There's no particular reason why not. If I remember correctly, we just lived apart. Because of that, there was no way to protect ourselves from raiders. It wasn't safe to be out alone. Then the Fashites invaded." She paused, accurately reading his confusion. "I know I'll leave a lot out.

"Hmm—since anyone can remember, there have been at least four nations." She chewed on her thumbnail as she tried to remember. "All kept to themselves, but every once in a while, one would attack the other. We Ashites really attacked each other. Until about forty years ago."

"What happened then?" Kid asked.

"Henry Carpenter. I have forgotten so much in my life, but no Ashite could ever forget that name. He united the Ashites. Made it safer for everyone to live. The raiders disbanded. Many people moved to Landar. My parents came here, though. It was very small, but still the largest populated Ashite city apart from Landar. Ashites have always sailed the oceans, and there's a port just down the river. My dad was a sailor." Dawn smiled. "Which only meant he was gone for long periods of time." She shrugged. "It was a good living apparently. Mom didn't mind. Back then, the group called the Fashites had a couple of civil wars. One about forty years ago, and another almost ten years later. Hmm."

"Confusing yourself?"

"No. I just have to back up. The Fashites were ruled by a dictator after their first civil war. Their second one ended with the Pendtars as the new leaders. They are brother and sister—Claude and Leonora. And they're wicked. I only assumed that because of the world we live in now, because within a year of becoming the new dictators, they started a type of war that had never been fought before. They wanted control over the whole planet."

"Why?"

She shrugged and looked at him. "Who knows? No one had ever wanted that before. Land to live on, yes, but no one needed the whole planet. But as they marched out to fight against the other nations, one was completely destroyed. It was a shame, though, from what my mom told me. They were the most gentle and helpful. They were the ones who copied books and gave them to everyone else. But I can't remember the name of that group." She thought a moment.

"Having trouble remembering?"

"Don't tease me."

"Guess it's contagious."

"What?"

"Memory loss."

Dawn giggled. "Now you've made me lose my place in the story."

"This was a story?"

She shook her head.

"I am curious, though. How do you know I'm an Ashite? What if I'm really a Fashite?"

"Your accent gives you away. Each people group has a different accent. At least, I think so. I've only encountered

Ashites and Fashites. I suppose the Jathenites would have a different accent as well."

"Oh. Do you guys only treat Ashites here?"

She shook her head. "No. Anyone who needs help, actually. Though I don't think the Fashite soldiers would trust us."

"Have the Fashites conquered all the Ashites?"

"No. They were able to conquer a lot of land. We're part of that conquered land, though there are many people who are still fighting. The war's been fought on these city streets for decades. And there are also petty battles between different groups of Ashites living in this city. Like I said, the Ashites never were completely together."

"So . . . we're Ashites." Kid thought out loud. "I probably shouldn't trust Fashites. And you mentioned Ja-then-ites?"

"Jathenites. They live past the mountains. They're all warriors, according to rumors. A Jathenite can hold his own against a Slave. Even defeat one."

"Slave?"

"No one truly knows their purpose, but they are Fashite soldiers, of sorts. That's what I know. Except you'd probably be killed if you ever saw one. That's all they're good at."

"You mentioned books earlier. What about them?" Kid asked, more curious about them than anything else.

"The Pendtars want all books destroyed. They destroy them the moment they conquer an area. Not that the Ashites ever really had many. But we were learning how to read and write our own stories. In this place especially, writing made life easier." She stared across the room, lost in thought.

He sat patiently, wondering what she would teach him next. She finally shrugged. "I give up. That's all I can share for the day. I need to go and get a nap in before I have to get back to work. There's still tomorrow."

"Yeah, but I have only so many before I have to leave."

"But you're not leaving tomorrow." She picked up the tray. "Bye, Kid."

He sat there and pondered the history lesson. None of it made sense to him, nor did it seem familiar. But he did want to remember every detail. So he stood up and paced as he told himself the story over and over again. Then he got the idea to jump. He jumped just a few short leaps at first to get his muscles used to the movement. Then he wanted to go higher. And higher. He finally squatted and jumped from that position, surprised at how high that got him. So he did it until his legs burned and the muscles spasmed from being overworked. He ignored the pain, replaying the history in his head until his legs mutinied, no longer wanting to work.

He fell onto the floor, landing on his face, barely catching himself in time with his arms. Kid was unwilling to stop. He wanted to get his muscles strong. Looking at his arms, he wondered what to do to work them. As an idea formed, he decided to test it. He pushed his torso up and then lowered it. The motions felt natural, as though he'd done them before. As the sensation of remembering something swept through his body, he worked faster with his arms, pushing himself up and then slowly lowering himself to the floor until his arms, too, could not work anymore.

Surely there was something else to do, Kid thought as he slowly rolled onto his back. Why was he so desperate to do this, he wondered. Was it the history lesson? Why did that trigger such urgency to get stronger? As he placed his hands on his stomach, he realized that there was muscle there, too. How did one work on it? The answer came as soon as he thought the question. He worked and worked until he couldn't move another part of his body, eventually passing out from exhaustion.

Chapter 4

A loud siren shook the still air, generating panic in its wake in a town of severely raw nerves. When the wave reached Kid's consciousness, he sat upright without a thought. When he finally came to himself, he saw that his hands were in tight fists.

With great effort, as his muscles shook with pleas to be allowed to rest, he got to his feet and went to the only window in the room. It was too high to see through, except for a view of black clouds. At least he thought they were clouds. Barely enough light passed through the panes for it to even be early morning. He felt each bolt of pain as he walked to the door. His arms were almost too weak to open it, but he managed with time and effort. No one was around. To his left was a large window that he was happy to see, until he looked at the streets below. Bodies were everywhere. An army marched past. Every man moved at the same pace. Must be the Fashites, he guessed. It made sense that their army would be that professional. He retreated to his room, working to rub the soreness from his muscles.

Once he was safely behind closed doors, he noticed a baton hanging from the wall. Not tired enough to go back to sleep, and ignoring his burning muscles, he took the stick into his hands and held it like those soldiers had held their swords. He slowly swung it back and forth, then over his head. When he suddenly spun and slashed the baton in a downward strike, he paused. It had felt natural, but why? Slowing his breathing down, he closed his eyes and no longer concentrated on what to do; he decided to just let his body flow. He was unaware of what he was doing, but after an hour, he was aware that he was tripping over his feet. Sleep sounded good, despite the siren, and it overwhelmed him before his head hit the pillow.

The next day, Dawn entered the room many hours after she normally did. Kid would certainly be starving, she knew. More than triple the number of patients had arrived that day, mostly children. She fought back tears and quietly shut the door. The lights were off, but she decided to turn them on after setting the tray on the table. She almost tripped over Kid as she crossed the room. As quickly as he could, he jumped up and grabbed the tray before she dropped it.

"Sorry," he said. He hurried to the bed and sat without so much as an explanation.

"Are you okay?" she asked after flipping on the lights.

"Hungry. Eat with me."

"No. I'm not hungry."

"Liar."

"I'm not lying," she declared. She was hungry, she could admit, but after the day she'd had, food was not appealing.

"Fine," he said, though she could tell by his tone that he didn't believe her. Silence visited them while he ate. Dawn sat down heavily upon the chair, closing her eyes for a brief rest.

"I must have been hungry because that tasted wonderful," he said when he was finished.

"Sorry I was so late."

"I understand," he said softly. "I found a window to look out of this morning. You must have been so busy."

She nodded and swallowed the threatening lump. A change of subject was needed. "Why were you on the floor?" she asked.

"Can't say that I know why," he admitted. "But I'm trying to strengthen my muscles."

"Restless?"

"Extremely. But not enough to wander around and get you into trouble."

"Thank you." She stood. "I have to leave now. Work never slows."

"Thank you, Dawn, for taking care of me so well."

She left. He tried to sleep, but the deep rest he desired never came. He woke remembering dreams—or nightmares—filled with unknown faces frozen in silent screams.

Two days later, the hospital quieted down to a less than normal flow. Dawn piled the tray higher than usual and went down to see Kid. She had only had time the past two days to watch him eat before she had to leave, so she was excited to talk with him. When she entered, she saw him jumping around the room, and she just laughed. He stopped and smiled sheepishly.

"Food!" he cried. When he noticed the amount, he asked, "Are you finally going to eat with me?"

She nodded. Once they finished, he asked, "Can we play a game?"

"A game?"

"Yeah. I found a ball yesterday, but I think it would be more fun to kick it around with someone else."

"Okay."

"It's better than jumping around, I figure."

She smiled so she wouldn't laugh. "Sure. Let's play."

"Great." He ran over to where he had last kicked the ball. From there, he passed it to her with great accuracy. She, however, was less able to keep the ball rolling straight. Kid had to run over to the door to retrieve it. At that moment, Joshua walked into the room, looking frantic.

"Joshua!" Dawn exclaimed. "What's wrong?"

"Our cover patient just regained consciousness. He's in perfect health and quite impatient to leave. I have to release him, which means Kid's got to go now. Here are some of my clothes and plenty of money for you, Kid," Joshua said as he handed them to him. "Dawn, please hurry back upstairs. I'll need you by me when the senior physicians arrive."

"Why do I have to leave now?" Kid asked.

"I'd just feel safer for you," Joshua said. "If those doctors don't buy our story, then they'll come looking for you."

Kid swallowed nervously and nodded, not really knowing what else to do.

Joshua turned to leave but then hesitated. He clenched his fists and crossed the room to reach Dawn's side.

"What is it?" she asked, worried.

He embraced her and kissed her hungrily, as if he'd never be able to again. After he released her, he quickly left. She stared after him, dumbfounded, blinking rapidly.

"Wow," Kid said. "That was overdue." He chuckled, clutching the bundle of clothing Joshua had given him. "I'll go change."

Once he was dressed, Dawn handed him the book she had concealed in the oversized pocket of her apron and said, "Remember the group that was destroyed?"

He nodded.

"This book came from them. It's the main one the Pendtars have tried to burn. I guess somehow it scares them. Joshua's read this book. And he's a good man. The best. I want you to become a good man, too, so read it. Please?"

He nodded again. With that done, she led him through a maze of corridors to a discreet exit. No one was around, so she pulled Kid out after her and hugged him tightly.

"Never let anyone know you have money or that book. They'll definitely kill you to steal the money. And anyone with a book gets killed immediately if they tell the wrong people. Head to where the sun sets. Don't look back and don't slow down." The tears finally threatened to fall and her voice quivered. "And though you may want to, don't ever come back. Just know that we'll miss you."

"Okay," Kid said. "Promise me something."

She wiped away the tears. "What?"

"Marry that man." Then he turned and ran.

When he was out of sight, she rushed back upstairs and composed herself in the stairwell before she calmly returned to her floor. She went first to Kid's old room. It was empty.

Then she searched for Joshua. She found him in the lounge, getting a cup of coffee.

"Hi, Dawn. How are you?" he asked regularly enough.

"Thinking that sounds like a great idea," she answered, pointing to his cup.

"Coffee?"

"Oh, yeah. I need it."

"I'll get you a cup." He turned to the attendant. "Another one, please."

After they received their orders, they returned to the reception desk. Since no one was around, Joshua felt it safe to talk.

"Is Kid gone?"

She nodded and sipped the hot beverage.

"The other patient just left, too. But no one's down here yet."

"Oh, no!" she said in alarm. "I left the tray in rehab. And the bed!"

"It'll be fine. We'll get everything patched up tonight."

She breathed deeply and picked up a chart. "I have a promise to keep now, you know."

"Oh." He raised an eyebrow. "What's that?"

"I have to marry you."

She grabbed his cup before he dropped it.

"Kid's orders," she explained.

"I knew I liked that kid."

She almost released a laugh when she saw them. The doctors stepped out of the elevator and stared straight at her.

"Here's your coffee, Doctor," she said loudly enough, handing him back his cup. Quickly, she raised hers to hide her mouth as she whispered, "Showtime." Then she took a sip.

Realization overtook his brief confusion, and he grabbed the cup. "Thanks, I've been needing one of these."

The doctors walked right past them and into the freshly vacant room. Joshua and Dawn donned their best confused masks as they watched the scene unfurl. Not a single doctor seemed happy.

"Where is this patient?" one asked, approaching Joshua.

Joshua lowered his cup. "I released him, sir. The boy was anxious to leave."

"He was in a coma for eight months!"

"I assumed it was all right. Was I wrong?"

"Why did you release him without consulting us?"

"I was just following policy, sir. It doesn't say to consult you. It says that if any patient desires to leave, and they check out fine, then we let them leave."

The doctor breathed heavily from his anger. Dawn held the cup to her mouth, hoping the aroma would overpower the doctor's stale breath. After a few minutes, with Joshua delivering a stellar performance, she noted, the doctors left. They both sighed but displayed no more reaction.

After a safe amount of time had passed, Joshua jumped on a subject he'd long pondered. "So, when's the wedding?" He smiled.

She smiled coyly. It quickly faded as his cup fell to the floor, and he went limp. She dropped hers in order to catch him. A sharp pain went through her chest. Her eyes locked on to the eyes of death—the eyes of a Slave. Both died quickly.

The Slave removed his sword and returned to the chief physicians' meeting room.

"Those were the two with the most contact with the boy?" he asked.

The doctors nodded, too afraid to speak.

"No one else knew about him?"

Almost in unison, they shook their heads, a few gulping.

"Liars," the Slave said brusquely. "You all knew about him too."

The Slave left the room void of life.

Chapter 5

Kid ran until he eventually collapsed. He wasn't yet out of the city, but the past few days of overexerting himself proved to have been a bad idea. He had no more strength. Rain began to fall, forcing him to look for shelter. The buildings were so severely damaged that he knew it would be a stupid idea to enter them. Finally, he noticed a stairwell, covered and dry. He curled up in a corner and quickly fell asleep.

The rain had long since stopped when he awoke. The sun was shining blindingly bright, but that wasn't what woke him. Someone was poking him with a sharp object. He opened his eyes cautiously and squinted up at the intruder.

"What are you doing here?" the intruder asked sharply.

"It was— I, uh—" Kid stammered as his eyes locked on the sword hanging in front of his face.

"Come on. Out with it!"

"It rained last night. This was the only dry spot I could find," Kid finally said.

"Right. What's your real reason? Spying on us? Admit it. You're a Went, aren't you?"

"A what?"

"Now you've just proved it." The intruder moved his sword under Kid's chin. "Do you know what I do to Wents?"

Kid pushed himself up and his hand slid against a door. He wondered if he even had a chance to escape through it. *Great*, he thought, *not even a day out, and I get myself killed.*

"I'm not a Went," he spat out, edging away from the sword until he was completely pressed against the door. His hand crept toward the knob. "I don't even know where I am."

"You're in Reeve territory, that's where you are. But I know you know that. Other Wents have played this same game. That's when I know I've caught me one."

Kid fell backward as the door opened. He slid down a few steps before running into someone's legs.

"What in the world?" a female voice cried. "Charlie, what are you doing?"

"He's a Went. I caught him spying."

"Yeah? Everyone's a Went, aren't they? Can't you just bring them straight to me before scaring them to death?"

"They need to learn—"

"You need to learn!" she snapped. "Zachary, you got him?"

"Yup." Two strong hands grabbed Kid and pulled him to his feet. "You okay, kid?" Zachary asked.

Kid only stared at the tall man in amazement. Was "Kid" the universal name for someone with no name?

"Lucy, I think the cat's got his tongue," Zachary called out to her, but she was on the other side of the doorway, yelling at Charlie.

"Never again, do you understand me?" Her red face and flaming hair only accentuated her fury.

"Yes, ma'am," Charlie mumbled submissively.

"Good. Now apologize."

Charlie's head snapped up. "What?" he exclaimed.

"Apologize."

Charlie merely gaped in shock. The notion was as foreign to him as peace was to that city.

Lucy pushed herself nose to nose to him and through clenched teeth said, "Say, 'I'm sorry.'"

Out of pure fear, Charlie managed to mumble, "I'm sorry." Then he pushed his way down the steps. With him gone, Lucy turned her attention to Kid, who flinched.

"Ah, you don't have to worry about me," she said. "Charlie's just a jerk I have to rein in every so often. Thinks everyone's the enemy. Of course, he's not always wrong. So I've got to ask you: who do you support?"

"S-support?" Kid stammered.

"Yeah. You're an Ashite, right? Sound like one, anyway."

"Yes, I am. Uh, yes. Sure," Kid said hastily.

"Mm-hm. Too young to be a Fashite foot soldier." Her eyes looked him over, intently focused. Kid's nerves rattled all the more, and he fidgeted with the shirtsleeves that were too long, hanging to the tips of his fingers. "Got a mom and dad?"

"Uh, um . . ."

Zachary chuckled. "You've the same effect on every one of these kids, Lucy."

"If they're not scared of me, then I can't keep them in line."

Zachary shook his head. "I vote to take him in. Another picked-up stray. What do you say?"

Lucy crossed her arms as she analyzed Kid more thoroughly. "I suppose he's harmless. Not a Went, that's for sure. Where are you from?"

"I just came from the hospital," Kid answered.

"Injured?"

"Yeah. I—uh, yeah. Just got better, I think."

"You got somewhere else to be, then? Heading home?" she asked.

"No, well, I just need to keep heading to the sunset as fast as I can," he explained.

She placed her hands on her hips, blocking more sunlight from streaming through the door. "Oh? Why's that?"

"I don't know," he said, dropping his head and shoulders.

"Where were you born?" she continued her interrogation.

"I don't know."

"Know anything?" she asked, raising a questioning eyebrow.

He shook his head.

She relaxed. "Well, I'm Lucy. He's Zachary. You met Charlie—a quite forgettable experience, I hope. To make up for it, turn around and head down. We've got room and food to share. Stay with us, if you'd like. Zachary and I pick up you strays all the time. Doubtful you'd survive on your own. You're not armed with anything to protect yourself, scrawny thing. Just don't let Charlie talk you into joining his gang. He had brothers who called themselves the 'Reeves' or whatever. Constantly fighting with the Wents, Standoffs, and whoever else is fighting over some stupid part of this city. We fight the only enemy we ought to—the Fashites. Everyone else is a moron. Can't wait for the day when Charlie finally leaves."

"Lucy . . ." Zachary said warningly.

"Can't help it. He's bad for my heart. All right, newbie, follow the giant down, please! I'll be back in a bit, Zachary. Got to go do that thing."

"I was going to go with you."

"It'll be quicker if I go alone. Don't worry. Take care of this stray." She turned and hurried down the alleyway, disappearing around the building at the corner. Zachary shook his head. "And she calls us idiots." Turning his attention to Kid, he smiled. "Well, good morning! Hungry?"

Kid was, but was nervous to do anything. He wanted to leave and continue his journey. How far could he go on an empty stomach? He lifted his eyes and nodded. "Your lot usually are," Zachary said. "Come on down. Just don't expect anything to be warm. Or good, for that matter. All we have are restaurant scraps and rations we've stolen from the Fashites. Terrible but edible. Anyway, come on. It's at least dry down here."

Zachary led the way, and even though he was usually two or three steps ahead, Kid couldn't look over his head. The man was very tall, and that intimidated Kid a bit, in spite of how nice the man seemed. The woman, on the other hand . . . Kid shuddered.

The stairwell opened up to what had been a basement. There were no real walls—slabs of wood or hanging bits of tarp sectioned off the rooms. Kid's host led him to a large slab of concrete in the back, used as a table. Kid sat atop a bucket and waited for Zachary to return. He arrived a few minutes later with some stale bread and cold meat.

"Here." Zachary sat on a stool that was taller than the slab of concrete. "Eat. Digest. Talk. Not really in that order."

Kid nodded and looked at the sandwich. In comparison to the hospital food, it definitely was lacking in appeal. However, hunger was a great motivator. So he took a large bite and ate the meal as quickly as he could.

"I'd like to think I'm not as scary as Lucy," Zachary said. "So, honestly, tell me—what's your story? Who are you?"

Kid looked him in the eye. What was he supposed to say? He himself didn't know the answers to their questions. How much to tell, then? Would the man believe him? Could the man be trusted? Dawn and that doctor seemed to think that not everyone could. Kid swallowed and stared at the rest of the sandwich. He couldn't lie. He didn't know enough to be able to lie. He took a deep breath and decided to risk the truth.

"I just came from the hospital. I really don't know how I got there. Um, I just woke from a coma a couple weeks ago. There were a doctor and a nurse there. For some reasons they didn't really say, they hid me until I was well enough to leave. Before that, I don't remember anything."

"So what's your name?" he asked.

Kid shook his head. "No one knew my name."

Zachary leaned back and waited a moment. "You were in a hospital, in a coma, and no one knew who you were?"

"No."

"How long were you in that coma?" Zachary asked.

"Almost eight months."

Zachary released a low whistle, and Kid hung his head. He turned the sandwich over in his hands, no longer desiring to eat. He wished he had some idea of what he could do. The other young people who lived in that basement peeked at the two before continuing with their chores. Kid's eyes drifted to them. Dozens of kids moved about the place. Some were cleaning. Others looked like they were making stuff. Swords, perhaps? Kid couldn't really tell. A few sat at the other end of the makeshift table, trying to swallow their meals.

"What is this place, anyway?" Kid asked, wanting the attention off his pitiful circumstances.

Zachary shrugged. "Who knows? Lucy—well, she's got her own story to tell. We met years ago when I first fled to this city. Orphans, the whole lot of us. All the kids that you see and more. We've always got to scavenge for food. The littlest are the best. They can get in and out without being seen. Lucy and I are, well, the oldest, so we are the guardians, I suppose. In the end, it's just a safe place for these kids. It's either here or in the streets, where they'll get killed. Though sometimes we do run raids on the Fashite posts out here. Usually when we outnumber them, of course. That's where Lucy went. There was a big battle a few days ago. A couple of the local gangs got together to . . . Well, in the end, it wasn't successful. Lucy keeps trying to get all of us together. But Ashites are stupid. Everyone wants to be the leader, so we just stay apart. More die every day. Life in this city. You get used to it."

Kid picked off a piece of bread and squished it between his fingers. "I've noticed," he said softly. He shoved the bite into his mouth.

"Anyway," Zachary said loudly, standing. "We'll have to give you a name if you don't got one of your own. Any preference?"

"The nurse called me Kid."

Zachary chuckled. "All right. If you want to stick to that one. Kid. We'll see how well that works, because, I got to tell you, we kinda call everyone around here 'kid.' They're all young. Most are younger than you, I'd bet. Still handy with a dagger, though. But . . . finish eating. When Lucy returns, she'll probably interrogate you some more, so be prepared." Zachary patted Kid on the back and walked off toward a group of kids in the corner. It seemed like they were playing some sort of game. Laughter trickled from that area, breaking the silence.

After some time, Kid finished off the sandwich and decided to meander through the place. It was a large open space. The only door was in the back. When Kid approached it to inspect it, someone explained that it was the lockup room. One got thrown in there when one got out of line.

When Lucy finally returned, Kid froze at the sight of her. She was tall and thin, yet a demanding presence. One listened when she spoke, and everyone seemed to understand that rule. As she entered, the others drifted toward her. As Kid observed, though, it didn't seem like they were afraid of her as much as they were in awe of her. She spoke to one kid about something and then listened to another. Her hands were never still. They fell upon shoulders and tousled hair or balled themselves into fists to be tucked against her hips. She loved all of them. Kid realized he could stay here, maybe. Zachary whispered something to her, and she turned her eyes toward Kid. He felt himself grow tense again.

She approached, still fixing a discerning look upon him. When she stopped in front of him, she crossed her arms and narrowed her eyes. "Zachary said you don't have a name. Why?"

"What do you mean?"

"Why don't you have a name? Everyone does. You're born, and your parents give you a name. You don't remember yours?"

"No. I don't know anything. At all." Kid stared at the ground. Now he wanted to run again.

Lucy pursed her lips. "Joe," she said definitively. "How about that? We'll call you Joe."

Kid shrugged. "Okay. Sounds . . . fine."

"All right, Joe. Have you made up your mind? Staying or going? Got to know. Those who stay have to pull their weight. Only the first meal's free."

Kid inhaled deeply and looked about. All had their eyes on him, which made him all the more nervous. He knew Zachary was right. He couldn't survive out there on his own. However, was he far enough away?

"I, uh . . . would like to stay, but . . ." Kid swallowed. "I don't know. I think . . ." A sensation filled him. It felt like he had a home somewhere, waiting for him. Humming and someone squealing. The feeling was powerful, but it passed as quickly as it had come. He shook his head and looked at the floor. "I just think I have to go somewhere else. I don't know where, but it's not here. Wherever I'm from, it's not here. I can't explain it."

Lucy lifted her head and turned her eyes to Zachary, who looked confused. "You sure?" Zachary asked.

Kid nodded.

"Okay, then," Lucy said. "Good-bye." Her voice sounded strained. Kid looked at her, and she almost looked upset. She turned from him and headed back to some of the kids making arrows.

"I think she likes you," Zachary said. He looked down at Kid. "Be safe, I guess. You know where we are, if you change your mind."

"Thank you for everything."

Zachary shrugged nonchalantly. "It's what we do. Really, though, I don't like the idea of you out there unarmed. Let's get you a dagger or two, hm? Follow me."

As Kid and Zachary looked over the limited supply, a few of the older kids who had never left a small area up front by the stairs began to get agitated. The commotion drew Zachary's gaze. Kid watched as Lucy approached the group.

"What's going on?" Kid asked.

"Don't know. Those are screens. The Fashites have a network of security cameras throughout the city. Lucy managed to tap into them a few years ago. It allows us to keep an eye on them, too. Let's go over there."

Kid followed Zachary over to the wall of monitors. Each screen displayed different areas of the city. Kid found himself looking for the hospital. Everyone else was looking at a screen near the bottom. In it stood a man who wore all black clothing and a black wide-brimmed hat with a scarf covering half his face. Another man, a Fashite general, stood next to him.

"That's a Slave," one of the kids said in obvious panic. "I've never seen one before, but I know it's never good to see one. What could they want?"

"I'll find out," Lucy said. She handed all her weapons to Zachary. "If anything happens to me, you know what to do."

"Luce . . ." Zachary said softly.

"I'll be fine. Just . . . keep everyone calm." She went to the stairs and quickly ascended them. Everyone stood, tense, watching as Lucy made her way through the different screens. She would pause every so often and cup her hands to her mouth.

"What is she doing?" Kid asked.

"Pretending she's looking for someone," Zachary explained.

The Slave and the general heard her and the general made his way over to her. She shied away at first as he approached but froze as he drew closer. He handed her something. She shook her head and returned it. Then he left. He and the Slave eventually left all the screens. Everyone jumped a few minutes later when she stormed down the stairs. They scattered out of her way as she marched to Kid, grabbed him by the throat, and slammed him against the nearest wall.

"Who are you?" she screamed. Kid wanted to say something, but her grip was too tight. "*Who are you*?"

"Lucy, he can't talk," Zachary pointed out, placing his hand on her wrist. She released Kid, who fell to the floor, gasping for breath.

"What's going on?" one of the others asked.

"That Slave is looking for him," Lucy yelled, jabbing a finger at Kid. "Had a picture and everything." She squatted and, using his shirt collar, pulled his face close to hers. "Who are you?"

"I told you everything about me," Kid gasped.

"You're lying. Do you understand how much danger you just put us in?"

"I didn't ask to come here," Kid said. Lucy angrily shoved him back down to the floor. She stood and paced, fidgeting with her nails.

"I say we take him to the Slave," Charlie said.

"Then why don't you, Charlie?" Lucy snapped. "Or don't you know nothing? That Slave would kill you before you're even in sight."

"I'm sorry," Kid said. "I'm sorry. Really. I didn't know. I'll just leave. No one will know I was here."

"And within an hour, you'd be found. I can't do that," Lucy said. With a scream of rage, she grabbed the nearest object and threw it at the farthest wall. Her breathing was heavy, and it was the only sound in the room full of frozen people. "Zachary, let's get him out of the city. It's his only chance. If we can get him to Memoria Falls . . ."

"Memoria Falls?" Zachary asked. "That's weeks away."

"Yeah. But if we're going to find out who this kid is, that's the first place we need to look."

"Why? What's in Memoria Falls?" Kid asked.

"Information. On everyone who's born, everyone who's died, or anyone who's missing. We may not find anything about you at all, but it's a place to start."

Tears gathered rapidly, and Kid didn't know how to hide them. "Why would you help me?"

"If those Slaves are looking for you, then that means you're important to the Pendtars. They only target those who threaten them, though I can't imagine why they would feel threatened by you. Either way, I would love to see their end. The rest of you can hold down the fort while we're gone. Timber, you're in charge."

"Got it covered," one of the older kids said with a firm nod.

"I don't know when we'll be back," Lucy continued. "But we'll be back. And if Charlie starts talking mutiny, lock him up or kick him out, whichever seems best to you. Now we've got to hurry and pack. Let's move."

Chapter 6

Within half an hour, they were loaded down with enough gear to last a few weeks. The trio carefully made their way through a debris-filled mine shaft that eventually opened up several kilometers from the city. From there, they headed northeast toward Memoria Falls.

Silence was their constant companion as they meandered through the underbrush. Zachary paused every so often, as Kid tended to fall behind. At these moments, Kid did his best to trot forward in an attempt to keep pace, but as the day drew long, his feet became too heavy to lift. The straps of the pack dug into his bony shoulders. Kid panted and wiped off the sweat, but close to nightfall, even his arms were lead weights, flopping at his sides. He thought of asking them to slow the pace, but he had already burdened them. It didn't feel right to make himself more of a burden.

After they broke camp one morning, he decided to break the silence, hoping it would distract himself from his weariness. "So, uh, what are your stories? I mean, how did you come to be where you were?" he asked.

Zachary answered first. "Well, I lived with my family until I was fourteen. An army of Fashites invaded. I managed to get out with some other kids, but my parents and theirs didn't make it. Eventually, we went to Tawney City."

"Where's that?"

Zachary looked at him in disbelief. "That's where we just came from."

"Oh." Kid felt stupid.

Lucy smirked, but Zachary continued, "Eight years ago, I ran into Lucy. We've been together since, along with all the other orphans you met there."

"Are you two married?"

Lucy laughed out loud and Zachary chuckled. "No, Kid, we're not."

"It's Joe," Lucy said as she pushed past Zachary to take the lead. "Remember? His name's Joe."

"And your story?" Kid asked her.

"I grew up in Tawney City," she said. "That building, in fact. Well, my home had been aboveground. Now we live where we find space. And that's who we are. Not much, but enough."

"Well, I don't feel like you guys are strangers so much anymore."

"And what about you, Joe? No stories for us?" Lucy asked.

"I told you everything," Kid answered.

"Okay. Just checking."

"If you don't believe me, then why are you helping me?"

"Honestly? I don't know. It just feels like the right thing to do. And I was right; if a Slave is after you, then that means the Pendtars want you out of their way. Of course, what they would want with someone as young as you is a mystery."

Kid was grateful that that was the last statement. They said nothing more as the hours passed, and Kid mulled over all the unanswered questions that continued to increase in number. He wondered when his memories were going to return. He wondered how Joshua and Dawn were. He wondered if that Slave meant something. Could the Slave possibly have been at the hospital? Could he have harmed Kid's friends?

Lucy headed up a hill with Zachary close behind her. Kid almost missed the change in direction. His thoughts had captured him for a moment. He sighed heavily to push them away and tripped over a tree's root. A low branch helped keep him upright, and as he clung to it, he paused to recollect himself. It was an opportunity to catch his breath. At the top of the hill, Lucy and Zachary were still. Kid groaned. He didn't think he could scale this mountain, but he moved one foot at a time.

Once he reached the top, though, he saw the real reason Lucy and Zachary weren't moving. Six men were not far away, and they all had swords in hand.

"We told you the truth," Lucy was saying. "We have no money."

Kid gulped. He hadn't told them yet about his stash, but he remained quiet. One of the men stepped forward.

"Well, why don't we just kill you and find out for ourselves?" The ingrates behind him laughed. Lucy quickly shed her pack and unsheathed her sword. Zachary followed suit.

"Looks like these kids want to play," one said. At once, the group rushed them. Kid stepped backward and slipped, falling down the hill. Once he stopped, he unburdened himself and stood to watch Lucy and Zachary block and deliver blows.

One man charged Kid, wildly swinging his sword. Kid easily dodged the blows, but wondered when his energy would completely falter. Kid grabbed a fallen branch and used it to block. The man's sword became stuck in the wood. As he tried to dislodge it, Zachary came up behind him and knocked him unconscious. "Grab that," Zachary said to Kid with a gesture toward the newly ownerless sword. With a few jerks, Kid pried it free but didn't know what to do with it. It felt heavy and awkward.

Back at the top, Lucy grunted. Kid watched as her sleeve turned red. Only one man was down. The other five kept coming. Kid swallowed hard as another man came his way. Without a thought, Kid parried and blocked, finding it rather easy to determine the pattern of the man's blows. Curiosity overcame Kid as he sensed or understood how to disarm the man. A quick slap with the broadside of his blade across the man's knuckles made the attacker yelp and release the sword. Kid had it in his free hand within a moment. An overwhelming sensation possessed him. It almost felt as though he was finally somewhere familiar. The feeling caused

Kid to smile—an action misinterpreted by the attacker, who turned and fled in fear.

Kid looked up at Lucy as she began to grow slow in her movements against the two men pitted against her. Zachary had disposed of another man, but he seemed to be overwhelmed. His opponent was much quicker. And Kid saw exactly what he needed to do. In a flurry, he interrupted the blows from Lucy's challengers, setting them back in surprise for a moment before he delivered several well-placed thrusts, knocking the men back into defensive positions. They tried to regain the advantage, but Kid dodged every blow so quickly, the men exhausted themselves in their efforts to find a mark. Then Kid disarmed them, and they fled.

When the last man saw that he had been deserted, he retreated, leaving Lucy and Zachary gaping at their traveling companion. As the last man disappeared from view, Kid dropped the swords and fell to his knees, gasping for breath, yet smiling.

The sound of clapping reached Lucy's and Zachary's ears after a few moments. Kid didn't hear the clapping until the old man performing the deed patted him on the back.

"Well done, son, well done," he said. "I've been waiting and hoping for some time for someone to scare those cowards off. Had I not been an old cripple, I would have done it myself. No matter. Come with me. I have something for you."

Curious, Kid pulled himself up and followed the slow-moving man. Lucy and Zachary, finally finding their senses, grabbed the packs and followed.

"You said you told us everything," Lucy said hastily.

"I did," Kid said.

"What was that, then? I've never seen anyone move like that!"

"I don't know where that came from," Kid confessed through heavy breaths. "I didn't even think about it. I just moved."

"Thanks," Zachary said. "You saved our butts."

Kid smiled halfheartedly. They arrived at a small clearing, and the old man proceeded toward a wide, short hill. Kid was moaning at the thought of climbing up it when the old man grabbed a small tree growing from the hill and pulled it to reveal a door.

"Come in. Come in," he said cheerfully. The house smelled like damp dirt, Kid immediately noticed. A small lantern hung on a wire by the entrance, providing light to an open room with several pieces of furniture. Kid saw only the couch.

"Mind if I lie down?" he asked.

"No. Go ahead," the old man offered.

He didn't intend to, but Kid fell asleep immediately.

"Poor boy's out of conditioning." The old man chuckled. "We'll let him sleep. How about some food? And tea? Say no and you'll insult me, so take a seat. I'll be right back." He limped away slowly toward one of only two doorways and disappeared.

Lucy and Zachary exchanged cautious glances, but they eventually sat at the table on the opposite side of the room from the couch. Zachary noted intricate carving on the legs of the table and the backs of the four chairs and wondered if the old man had made them. The table was solid. The biggest surprise was how comfortable a wood chair could be.

When he looked at Lucy, he noticed her injury. "Do you want me to clean that for you?"

"Huh?" She had been lost, staring at the impossible way the walls arched over their heads.

"Your arm's bleeding."

She had to look at both of them before she noticed the gash down her upper right arm. "Great," she hissed.

"Is it that bad?" he asked, wary of her temper.

"Shut up and hand me my bag."

Before Zachary moved, the old man returned with two cups of tea and a satchel draped over his shoulder. "Here you go. I hope you enjoy it. Actually, you probably won't, so drink fast, please. And I'll have your friend drink some when he wakes. Now, Missy, give me your arm so's I can fix it up."

She didn't have time to protest. He quickly ripped off her sleeve and cleansed the wound. "This needs some stitching. Don't flinch," he cautioned. From his satchel, he produced the necessary equipment. Lucy gripped the sides of her chair as the man quickly sutured the gash closed. He spread a thick layer of herbal salve over the cut before he wrapped it with swift expertise.

"There. All better," he pronounced. "Except I have to share some bad news. All I have to eat is bread and cheese. I've been preoccupied lately and have forgotten to forage and hunt. So I hope you don't take me for a poor host because of my shortsightedness. Please, drink up, and I'll return with a snack." He shuffled to the kitchen again, leaving the pair, who sat for a moment in silence, pondering the mystery of their host.

"How many battles do you supposed he's been in to dress a wound that neatly?" Lucy asked, gingerly touching the stitches.

"Quite a few, I'd guess," Zachary said. "I've never seen anyone stitched up that quickly. Does it hurt?"

"All that's natural," she answered. "I suppose now we should be polite guests and drink up."

"Drink? Oh! The tea." Zachary lifted his cup. "He said it was awful, though."

"At least try it," Lucy encouraged.

They barely swallowed the first gulp. "Yuck," Zachary said.

"Shh, not so loud," she warned.

"He wasn't kidding. Ugh."

"At least try to drink half of it."

"Okay." Zachary drank for as long as he could stand before he set the cup down and flicked his tongue to rid his mouth of the bitter taste.

"You look like an idiot." Lucy chuckled and drank some more. She shuddered but refrained from performing Zachary's antics.

"Okay, okay, here's what I have," the old man said cheerfully, carrying a tray piled with sliced cheese and rolls. "I see you're actually drinking the tea. How do you like it?"

"It's terrible," Zachary spat out. Lucy frowned at him as the old man laughed.

"That's wonderful. A man with no guile," the old man said, then turned to Lucy. "I suppose you were going to say that it tastes fine?"

"You caught me."

"Always be honest. Don't put up pretenses in order to be polite. They cause much more harm than good. Now, let's eat."

They nibbled the food in silence. Then the old man invited them to rest by his fireplace, which was just a pit that sat in the middle of the room. After some great effort, declining every offer of help, the old man succeeded in igniting a sizable fire. He pulled a rope dangling from the ceiling that opened a flap at the top of his house so the smoke could escape. Then he sat on one of the cushioned chairs to relax. Lucy and Zachary reclined on the thick rug beside the fire pit.

"Thanks for your hospitality," Zachary said. "It's nice to be inside for a while. The trip's been pretty chilly, even with our cloaks covering us. I thought it would be warmer."

The old man nodded thoughtfully. "The weather has truly grown unusual these past few years, that is for sure. More rain. More winds. Fierce winds, too. And then the cold. When I was young, the only time it was cold was when you were on the highest mountaintop." He stared at the flames. "There's nothing so precious as warm light," he muttered contentedly. "That, and perhaps a good stiff drink now and again. When they can be found, of course. So, what brings you here? Strange place to be, I'd say. Only crazy old men live in these parts. And since you're not kin, I know your intention was not to visit me."

"We're just passing through on our way to Memoria Falls," Lucy explained.

"And what is there?"

"Answers, we hope. Joe over there doesn't remember who he is. Of course, I'm not a hundred percent won over to that story after the skirmish today."

"Aw, that was just instinct, girl. A person knows how to bite before he even knows how to think. Anyone with proper training just does and thinks about it later." He paused long enough for them to chew on that. "Well, this has been pleasant. Please, take your companion's example and get some sleep. I am influenced enough to do so myself. Lay your bags here by the fire because I only have one room with one bed, more's the pity. You're young enough to survive one night here, I suspect. So, good night."

Once Lucy was certain the old man was out of hearing distance, she leaned close to Zachary and asked, "What are you thinking right now?"

"Why did he make us drink that tea?"

She leaned away and snorted with disgust. Why wasn't he the least bit concerned about their traveling companion?

"I know what you're thinking, but the old man's right. How many times have you been too exhausted to think and still been able to fight off a half dozen men?"

She sighed in resignation. That was true. "I know. There's a part of me that really wants to help him. Right from the start. But with the Slave and everything, I wonder—who am I helping? Does he even need it?"

"He does, truly." Zachary moved as close as he dared. "He's still a kid, you know? Just because he can hold his own in a battle doesn't mean he can hold his own in life."

"I'm tired. All this stinking thinking has wiped me out more than that skirmish. Good night, Zachary." She crawled into her sleeping bag and purposely turned her back to Zachary. However, her mind was racing too much to fall asleep yet. It was a while before she heard Zachary move to his sleeping bag. That caused her mind to wander to thoughts she often forced herself to quickly dismiss. Thoughts about how she felt about Zachary. Thoughts of her suspicions of how he felt about her. Why wouldn't he say what was truly on his mind? A man without guile indeed! Of course, what would he say if she just came out and asked, "Do you love me?"

Kid was the last to wake the next morning. He could have slept longer if it weren't for the dream. It was the same unknown faces frozen in silent screams. This time, they had caught fire and burned away from his sight. He fell and fell until he hit bottom, and his body jerked him awake. The sweat that had collected on his forehead was easily removed with his shirt's long sleeve. His breath came in short, quick bursts that he fought to tame. Once he felt in control, he carefully sat upright and stretched. The movement sent tremors of pain from his head to his toes, and he nearly fell back down, unconscious. He bent forward instead, shocked at the blackness he saw even though his eyes were wide open.

The old man kept an eye on the boy. He didn't feel that it was appropriate to bring any attention to him while he was still so obviously weak. When Kid finally stood, the old man felt it safe to say something.

"Well, now, look who finally got himself up!"

Kid stretched himself to as upright a position as he could before he joined them at the table. "What's to eat?" he asked.

"I have eggs, and meat to go with our bread and cheese. Your friends have already delivered a blow to the portions, but if you need more, it won't cause me no hassle."

"Thanks," Kid said. He wanted to eat everything in sight, but the headache caused such nausea that he suspected nothing would stay down.

"Why don't you start with some tea?" the old man offered. "It'll settle your stomach."

"Thanks."

Before Lucy or Zachary had a chance to warn him about the taste, Kid had it downed in a single gulp. After pulling the cup away, he screwed up his face and shook his head. "Ugh. What is that?" he asked, peering into the cup.

"A special tea. You'll feel better soon, don't worry. Now, eat—even if you don't want to."

Kid respectfully followed instructions, nibbling on the food at first. It didn't take too long before the nausea disappeared and he was finally able to eat everything he wanted to eat. With the satisfaction of a full stomach, Kid relaxed.

"What's your name, sir?" Kid asked.

The old man's eyes twinkled. "Patrick. Yours?"

"Depends on who you ask. These guys call me Joe, but there's a couple at a hospital who call me Kid."

"I don't like either of them. They don't suit you." The old man allowed a memory to surface; a memory it seemed Kid had walked right out of. "You remind me of David."

"Who's David?"

"Someone I knew many, many years ago. I respected and admired him. That is mostly because he saved my life, but that's all I will say for now. First and foremost, though, why aren't you telling these guys that you can't keep up with them?"

Kid paled and quickly ducked his head. Lucy leaned forward, staring at Patrick before she turned to analyze Kid. Zachary merely stopped picking his teeth. Kid hoped someone would talk since the silence made him feel uncomfortable.

"Well?" Patrick prodded.

Kid was shocked to find that he had to choke back tears. "I didn't want them to think I was a burden. They've done so much for me already."

"You've got a good heart, Mr. David, but in time, you'll only put them in more danger if you don't rest more often. Until you get some stamina in you."

Kid nodded but refused to look up. The shame of being discovered burned his ears.

"Boy, get your head up. You've nothing to be ashamed of," Patrick said.

Kid slowly obeyed, casting only a quick glance at Lucy and Zachary.

"That's better," Patrick continued. "Now, in order for me to help you out, you've got to tell me when you started feeling this weak."

Kid glanced at Lucy and Zachary again and swallowed.

"Why are you so nervous?" Patrick asked.

"I—I haven't been strong, sir," Kid said. "I am getting stronger each day, but since I woke up, it's been hard to walk—"

"Woke up? What do you mean?"

"Didn't—didn't they tell you I was in a coma? For almost eight months. I woke only a few weeks ago."

Patrick sat high in his seat and directed his emerging anger to his other guests. "And what are you two doing dragging him through the woods all the way up to Memoria Falls?" Patrick snapped.

"He has a Slave looking for him," Lucy said. It was the only explanation she had.

Patrick's reaction intrigued them. He appeared afraid, but his countenance quickly shifted to excitement. He shook his head. "Daft idea," he muttered. His attention returned to Kid. "What could you have done to draw the interest of the Pendtars? Unless—Hmm."

He stood and disappeared to his bedroom. The trio sat patiently, albeit with much confusion, for his return. The longer he delayed, the more Lucy itched to leave.

"I think it's time we go," she suggested.

"Now?" Zachary asked. "No."

"Why not?"

"He's got more to say. And Joe needs some rest."

"I'll be fine. We can go," Kid offered.

"No. Go lie on the couch and get some rest," Zachary barked.

"Zachary, come on!" Lucy said. Kid decided that leaving the table at least was a good idea, as Lucy's fury began to surface. As he stood, Lucy snapped, "Sit down. Zachary, we don't know who this guy is or where his loyalties lie. He seemed pretty happy when he heard about that Slave."

"Joe, she may seem like she can tear you to pieces, but she can't. Go lie down."

Lucy slammed her fist on the table. "Zachary, when will you ever try to see things through my eyes?"

"When will you ever try to see things through mine?" he snapped, causing an end to the heightening emotions and the beginning of an awkward truce.

"I'm gonna go," Kid whispered and retreated to the couch. As he reached it, he noticed Patrick in the doorway, holding two swords. Kid gulped and rejoined Lucy and Zachary at the table. Zachary was the first to change the direction of his glare upon noticing Kid's hasty return. Alarmed, he immediately stood. Lucy spun around and drew out her sword in a fluid motion. The tension and the silence pounded each other and swirled throughout the room in a deadlock battle.

"Well, I'm insulted," Patrick said. "You honestly think I'd attack you? Of course, I could be flattered that you'd feel threatened by me even through I'm crippled. But these are for our new Mr. David. I'll never be able to use them again, and it would be a shame to let them rust away to nothing."

Patrick lowered the blades and then turned them handle out toward them.

"Try them on, Mr. David. See if they fit."

Kid didn't notice anything threatening about Patrick. There was a small grin on his face, and bemusement filled his eyes. Besides, Patrick was right: he wouldn't be able to attack. His left foot was turned inward, body leaning to the right. Patrick moved about as though his hips were crooked.

Kid approached him and took the swords. They looked a great deal heavier than they actually were. Intricate carvings covered the center of the blades, complementing the artwork of the hilt. Kid marveled how something so deadly could look so beautiful.

"I'm glad to see that you like them," Patrick said. "Good. Those are my finest work."

"You made these?"

"Sure did. Took me weeks to get the molding perfect. But, as you can see, I managed. They're strong steel that will most likely cut through anything. You wear them well, boy. Go stand over there behind the couch and try them out."

"How?"

"Wave them around. Do what feels natural. Go on. That's why I left that area empty."

Kid hurried to the far side of the room. Being closer to the wall drew Kid's attention to the support beams that curved up into a short dome shape, and to the roots of countless trees that held up the dirt in the ceiling. Kid wondered what the place was like when it rained, but he let the excitement evoked by his gift retake his attention.

Thinking back to that morning with the baton, he relaxed and closed his eyes. As his arms moved, he felt that the swords directed his motions. Again, everything felt so natural that he moved silently about, spinning, thrusting, and slicing without any consideration of time. He felt free.

Patrick watched contemplatively. The boy's skills out in the forest had looked so familiar, but he didn't want to confirm his suspicions too soon. As Kid's movements appeared more recognizable to Patrick, he allowed himself a smile of relief. The routine was too similar for it to be a coincidence. The one factor that still remained a mystery, though, was the boy's age. These exercises were too advanced for one so young. Patrick bemoaned his inability to learn from the boy how he had come to learn them.

Kid eventually stopped, smiling so broadly that Patrick knew sword fighting had been more than a necessity to the boy. It was an art—an obsession—a quest for perfection. Yet another fact that led his thoughts to David.

"Well, Mr. David, I think you like them."

"They feel so—right," Kid confessed.

"Good. Let us sit a spell and rest for the day. You can leave tomorrow. I'll make sure to send you off with some tea. And, Mr. David, I insist that you drink what I give you. It will help you recover your strength faster."

"Thank you for your kindness."

Kid joined Patrick on the couch, sinking into the oversize cushions. His muscles liked the idea, and he relaxed. Zachary, preferring to know more about their host, carried his chair across the room to set up a spot nearby. Lucy reluctantly followed.

"Sir, may I ask how you came to live here? For that matter, how did you build this place?" Zachary asked.

"What do you do when it rains?" Kid asked.

Patrick chuckled. "This hill never used to be here. I built this dome, put in the rooms, and then covered it all with thick leaves from the bampusa trees that grow out by the ocean. I figured since people use them for roofs out there, it could work here. After that, I began the long, long task of piling dirt everywhere. After a few years, it all began to stay in place, so I planted grass, bushes, and trees everywhere I could.

The rest is what you see now. A very dirty home," he ended with a chuckle. "And a very private one at that. I always get overlooked by passersby, but I don't mind. Unless, of course, they happened to all be as beautiful as you, my dear miss."

He smiled broadly, looking at Lucy, and she rolled her eyes to look away, hoping she wasn't blushing.

"I like it," Kid exclaimed. "I want one just like it one day."

"Perhaps I'll give you this house too, huh?" Patrick winked at him and Kid grinned. He was still so young, Patrick thought.

"Who is this David you mentioned?" Lucy asked.

"You've the longest memory I've ever seen. Well, I'll be straight with you. David is a man who saved my life many years ago. I would see him now and again. He taught me some skills with the sword that have, since then, saved my life many more times—until I received my last injury, which has left me as you see me now: completely unable to fight anymore with this useless leg. But I am hesitant to tell you this one thing. David was a Slave."

Lucy steeled her face and revealed nothing. She was a leader, Patrick noted. Zachary lifted his eyebrows in surprise but offered no other reaction. How did Mr. David react? Patrick glanced at Kid, who only looked confused.

"What are you thinking?" Patrick asked him.

"Well, just, mostly—how do I remind you of him? Him being a Slave and all. Aren't Slaves the enemy? And wicked?"

"What do you know of Slaves?"

"Just what Dawn told me," Kid answered.

"Who is Dawn?" Patrick asked.

"The nurse at the hospital. She gave me a history lesson one day. A very brief one."

"Oh. So you heard one person's opinion?"

"Well, the Slave that was in Tawney City caused a lot of fright among their group," Kid said, gesturing toward Zachary and Lucy.

Lucy glanced at Zachary, who shrugged. Couldn't argue with truth, he figured, though Lucy argued with anything that wasn't her truth. He watched her relax and let the comment pass. Good, he thought. *It doesn't reflect upon you at all*, he wanted to say. She pulled back her red hair and straightened her shirt.

"How is it possible for a Slave to work outside his own motives?" she asked. "They're programmed. How can you be sure he's a good man?"

"I can't," Patrick answered, staring at her challenging eyes with a twinkle of amusement in his. "If it was in his motivation to save me, then, so be it. I know at that time in my life, I was a rebel and a nuisance to the Pendtars, surely, therefore a mark for the Slaves to destroy. Why would he save me from them? It's a very curious thing."

"It is," Lucy agreed, but her tone told him that she left much unspoken, which only charmed him more. He would have wanted a daughter like her.

Kid stood. "If it's fine with you, could we leave?" he asked.

Patrick was unable to disguise his surprise. "Now? Why?"

Kid looked down at his swords and bounced them in his hands. "I think I've rested enough. I'm anxious to find out who I really am."

Patrick closed his eyes and didn't speak lest his voice betray his sorrow. Visitors never came, and he had been lonely for some time, so much as to wander through the woods in hope of finding companionship.

"Joe, are you sure? Because we're fine with staying," Lucy said.

"I'm sure," Kid answered. "Patrick, I will take up your offer of that tea."

Patrick briefly smiled and, as quickly as he could manage, went to the kitchen. Whatever food he had, he packed for them, as well as the leaves for his special tea. As he left the kitchen, he remembered the sheath.

"Wait a moment longer," he requested after delivering the bundle to Kid. "I've forgotten something important." With that, he disappeared into his bedroom. It took some time to pull it down from storage, as his swords had previously been hanging on special hooks attached to the wall. As he walked out with the harness, Kid grinned.

narrow our search. And if not, then we can still take him to Memoria Falls."

Lucy finished her food before she said, "Fine. We could change direction and head to Landar. Same difference in time, either way."

"Mmm-hmm."

She looked at him out of the corner of her eye and noticed how intently he stared at her. Could what she suspected be true? She wondered. There was only one way to find out, but she was afraid to be wrong. That would be embarrassing, not to mention complicating to their friendship. But that look in his eyes—

"What are you thinking at this moment?" she asked coyly, avoiding eye contact.

Startled by the change, Zachary acted like a child who had been caught doing something he knew was wrong. "Um, nothing."

"No. You were thinking something. What was it?"

Zachary laughed nervously and glanced at Kid, who was blissfully asleep and tantalizingly out of range of the firing squad. How Zachary wanted to be asleep at that moment. He didn't know how Lucy would react to the thoughts he had allowed himself to entertain.

"Come on," she prodded, nudging him slightly, tipping her head to finally look at him.

"I was just thinking about doing something, that's all."

"And what was that?"

He grew suspicious of the motive behind such questions. Could she have suspected his thoughts and was trying to get him to act upon them? Summoning a load of courage, and hesitating only slightly, he leaned forward and kissed her. Pulling away a little, and half expecting a slap across the face, he was surprised to receive no negative reaction. He kissed her again, grateful for this moment of privacy the two had never been able to have.

Before Zachary opened his eyes the next morning, the suspicious sounds of shuffling feet met his ears. He tensed and cautiously opened his eyes to look around. When he saw the empty spot where Kid had been, alarm sent him to his feet. The noise woke Lucy, who sat upright. When they discovered the source of the sounds, they both relaxed as their fears fled. Kid was in a clearing not too far away, breaking in his new swords. Lucy quickly got to work fixing food and breaking camp. Zachary merely stared, entranced by the art at work before his eyes.

"How can you get to be that good?" he thought out loud.

"What do you mean?" Lucy asked, unaware that his question hadn't been intended for anyone else to hear.

"Uh, well, so good that you don't even have to think about what you're doing. I mean, Joe doesn't remember a thing, but there he is—"

"Well, I think you said it best."

"Huh?" He turned his attention to her.

"You don't remember?"

The quizzical stare was her answer.

"You said that even when we're too exhausted to think, we can still continue fighting after that. You know, like Patrick said—instinct."

"You're different this morning."

Lucy shrugged and tossed him some dried meat.

He smiled. "Come over here."

"Why?" she asked suspiciously, placing her hands on her hips.

"Nope. I was wrong. You're not different."

"What?"

"You're still stubborn."

She raised her eyebrow and sauntered over to him. Once there, though, she punched him in the arm.

"Ow. And mean," he teased.

She only shook her head at the jest and turned her attention to Kid. "Hey, Joe! Come eat before we leave, okay?"

Kid stopped in midform and quickly followed instructions. He had made a small fire earlier to brew some tea. The tea was too hot to swallow in one gulp, so he had decided to practice to allow time for it to cool. When he joined Lucy and Zachary, he checked the beverage's temperature. Satisfied, he threw it back in one long drink and shuddered once it was over.

"Ugh, the old man consigned me to a few weeks of torture," he said.

"You could just not drink any," Zachary suggested.

"Yeah, but this is going to help me heal faster, so I'll go through the torture in order to come out stronger."

"I can't wait to meet the people who raised you," Lucy said. Every day at every instant, this kid amazed her more and more.

"Me neither," Kid said quietly. They ate the rest of the meal in silence. Once finished, Kid attempted putting on the harness for his swords, but the shirt's loose fabric made it difficult.

Lucy eventually stopped him. "Let me do something, okay?"

Before he replied, she pulled out a knife and cut through the seams on both sides of the shirt to just below the armpit. She cut the fabric in perpendicular strips, which she then tied together, causing the shirt to hug Kid's body.

"There. It looks terrible, but, like you said, you'll buy something when we get to Landar," she said.

"Landar? Wait, is that on our way to Memoria Falls?" Kid asked.

Lucy chuckled. "Actually, no. Now we're heading west. For you, now that we've discovered these wonderful fighting skills, it's a better place to get answers."

"Landar is the largest city," Zachary explained as he pulled on his pack. "Millions of people live there, so it's one of the few cities left that the Fashites haven't attacked. And that's where the Ashite army's training center is located. We came to the conclusion that you might have been there."

"You think I was in the army?"

"You've obviously been trained," Lucy said, glancing at Zachary. "Does it sound like a good plan?"

Kid easily pulled on the harness. Once the blades were in place, he nodded. "Let's go."

Every evening, Kid would collapse from exhaustion the moment they stopped to set up camp, and fall asleep without eating. Every morning, he awoke before the other two and brewed his tea, then practiced as it cooled. Though he concentrated on the movements, a part of his mind would wander in a tangled maze of thoughts. He could never get out of the maze. He always ended stuck with no answers to the questions about who he was and what had happened to him.

As he became more familiar with the sword and the flow of movement, each day he'd surprise himself by doing something else he didn't recognize. Because of memory loss, though, he didn't know the level of his talent. The mornings ended with Lucy telling him to eat, and he'd stop to catch Zachary watching him. His interest caused his mind to wander through other mazes with no exits. Could he really be skilled? Or was he just swinging the swords around while everyone else assumed it was deliberate aim? His frustration eventually ended the wanderings, but each morning they would start anew.

After five days, Kid noticed that the going had become easier. His legs didn't ache anymore, and the pack he carried wasn't as heavy. He joked to himself that it could have just been because there was less food in there, but when he didn't pass out that night, even managing to eat a meal, he began to feel more gratitude for the tea.

"Well, look who's joining us," Lucy teased. "You might even be able to get your sleeping bag unrolled tonight. How are you feeling?"

"I'm not sore anymore," Kid answered. "Even my arms. It's been so hard for me to do anything, but I feel great."

"Oh? So you think we could travel farther tonight?" Lucy winked at Zachary.

"No," Kid said quickly, smiling at the tease. "But I'm finally out of water. I'll need some for the morning."

"Ah, yes. Well, you could wander around in the dark, or wait until morning," Zachary said. "I'll go with you if you choose the morning slot."

"Deal."

"Good. We can also bathe then, because I'm really feeling stinky."

Lucy giggled. "Smelling stinky is a better description."

"Well, you always smell wonderful, so I suppose you won't be needing to bathe tomorrow."

She blushed and bowed her head. Kid watched them tease each other, and he realized that he must have missed a lot by falling asleep so early the past few days. Something had happened between them, but he wasn't going to pry. After they ate, he easily fell to sleep.

As Zachary prepared for bed, he noticed Lucy staring at Kid. He could tell that she was far away. He sat next to her and asked, "What are you thinking?"

She sighed deeply and mournfully. "I miss my brothers."

The answer instantly sobered him. "How long has it been?"

"Four years, three months, seventeen days." She curled up her legs and hugged her knees.

"So they would have been twelve and—" He looked at Kid. "Sixteen."

"Yeah. Roscoe was my favorite. Joe reminds me so much of him. Same spirit. Same big blue eyes. Both my brothers had blue eyes. And blond hair. I had red hair and hazel eyes. They took after Mom, and I took after Dad, in more ways than looks."

"So your dad was hardheaded too?"

"Yeah. My mom always called him hardheaded and stubborn. That's why it's never bothered me when you tease me about it. I take it as a compliment."

They fell silent for a while, and Zachary put another stick onto the fire.

"I think that's why I was so eager to help Joe, you know?" she said thoughtfully. "He's so much like Roscoe. So ready to smile. So innocent. Tate had seen more horrors growing up than Roscoe and I, so he was more reclusive—more thoughtful. Not Roscoe. He was always happy. Nothing could deter him."

"I'm curious. Why did you want to call him Joe?"

"Growing up, Roscoe's favorite teddy bear was named Joe." Her voice cracked. Zachary wrapped his arms around her, and she buried her face in his chest. He said nothing. In all the years he'd known her, she had never cried. He hoped she would now. She remained silent and still, though, so he just held her. At least she allowed that much.

Chapter 8

Three days passed with slow progress through the brush of the forest before the monotony broke and they emerged into the uninterrupted sunlight. Kid paused for a moment as his eyes widened to take in the view. Landar loomed on the horizon. This tall, stoic fortress towered over the meadows that surrounded it. They traveled for the rest of the afternoon with the city walls drawing higher.

Kid didn't notice the time passing. His eyes locked onto the awe-inspiring sight as a nervous glee overtook his system, speeding his pace. Lucy and Zachary exchanged a few looks. Both were excited, for it was their first time in the legendary city, but the youthful glee that covered their companion's face generated their amusement.

In early evening, they arrived at the wall that curved around the city. Kid peered down the length and caught the twinkling of water in the distance. Zachary told the guards at the entrance of their origin before they were allowed to enter.

"Here we are," Lucy said. The gates closed behind them as they passed several booths of vendors selling trinkets or treats. Kid seemed entranced by the lines of carts along the wall, so with a firm hand, Zachary pulled the boy along to the gate in the second tier of wall. This one encircled the entire city.

When the gates opened, Kid froze. He had not been prepared for the sight. Buildings soared to dizzying heights above him, casting shadows over the streets. Windows exposed wares from food to clothing. Blacksmiths displayed their handiwork alongside candlemakers and glassblowers. Some buildings housed tenants, while others were hospitals or banks.

The streets were cobbled and ever crowded with pedestrians or merchants pulling their carts behind them. Lampposts decorated every corner, not yet lit, since that task began at sundown. Furry rodents scampered about, causing children to give chase and women to yelp. It was overwhelming.

Lucy giggled at the expression Zachary wore. He wanted to gaze at the sights as well, but as Kid was completely hypnotized, Zachary had to continually push and pull him through the crowd, generating great frustration. Lucy pushed her way back to them and laced her arm through Kid's.

"Hey! Hey!" she snapped, finally gaining his attention. "Hi. Where do you want to go?"

"Um . . ." Kid looked about for a minute before he gasped. "A clothing store!" he cried and bolted toward it, pulling Lucy with him.

"Joe, wait!" Zachary shouted over the noise of people who quickly separated them. Lucy managed to hold Kid at the door until Zachary caught up with them.

"Hey, Joe. Joe!" Zachary snapped his fingers by Kid's ear, winning him a few moments of Kid's attention.

"You can't run off like that," Zachary said. He felt like a parent reprimanding a small child. "We could find you in the woods, but we can't find you in this city. There's too many people. So stay close, okay?"

Kid nodded. "Can we go in now?"

Lucy giggled. Zachary felt as if he'd have been better off saying nothing. He threw up his hands, decisively defeated. "Go on."

Kid entered and dropped his things at the clerk's desk before he hurried past. Lucy and Zachary actually waited to check in their items, apologizing to the clerk for Kid's impatient enthusiasm.

"Do you think it was because of the coma that he's this childlike?" Lucy asked.

Zachary shrugged. "I wouldn't know. It does affect the mind, I'm sure."

"Certainly. But I've been thinking—you could technically say he's only a month old, so to speak."

Zachary chuckled and Lucy smiled at him. It was a gracious and genuine smile. Her face seemed to glow, and Zachary wondered why he hadn't ever seen her look this beautiful before. Well, he admitted, she'd never been this happy.

"I'm going to try these on," Kid said as he ran up to them, holding an armload of clothes. Before they could respond, he disappeared again.

"Okay," Lucy said to the air. Realizing he was gone, she turned to Zachary. "Maybe we could get something while we're here."

"What do we need?"

"Nothing, I guess. It was just a thought." She looked over a rack of belts.

"Yeah, one that requires money."

"Joe's got the money. I don't think he'd mind. In fact, if he doesn't offer to get us anything, I'd be shocked."

Kid walked over to them to show off his clothes. "What do you think?" he asked.

The dark blue pants actually fit him, and his oversized shoes had been traded in for a pair of black boots. A long-sleeved, collared shirt fit nicely under a thick, dark-gray vest.

"It looks good to me, Joe," Lucy declared. "But—do you really need that vest?"

"Well, it's thick, so it'll give me some extra padding against the harness. It's rubbed my skin raw in a few places."

"I like it," Lucy said.

"Great. This is what I'm getting, with some extra socks and stuff. You guys want anything?" Kid offered.

Zachary laughed. "What a setup! You told him to say that, didn't you?"

"When did I have an opportunity to?" Lucy asked defensively.

"We were separated for a few minutes before we came in here, remember?"

"Oh. But you know me better than that!"

"Um, should I leave?" Kid asked.

"No, no, don't," Lucy said. "No, it's— Never mind. You don't need to get us anything, Joe. But thank you."

"Fine. I'll hurry up and pay." Kid was out of sight in an instant.

"You know, if I came out dressed like that, you would have laughed at me," Zachary said.

"That's because you're a big man," Lucy explained. "You don't need to cover a scrawny body."

"Hmm. Okay. I'll let you get away with that."

"Poor thing, though. After lying on a bed for that long . . . I bet he did have some muscle beforehand," she mused.

"You're just the expert on everything, aren't you?"

"Oh, hush. One of my best friends growing up had a doctor as a dad, and I loved to learn from him."

"Here he comes—the strapping lad," Zachary said loudly as Kid approached.

Kid had a permanent smile on his face.

"Time to go?" Zachary asked.

Kid nodded. Lucy ran a hand through his shoulder-length, light-brown hair and said, "You know, since you're spending your money, why not get a haircut?"

"His hair's fine," Zachary said quickly.

"Even you don't look good with long hair," she snapped.

"You're always saying stuff about my hair. I like it."

"I hate it. Well, Joe, does that sound fun?"

Zachary shook his head at Kid, mouthing the word *no*. Lucy eventually elbowed him in the stomach. Kid laughed. It was different seeing them so animated. Kid couldn't put his finger on the reason why, but he wasn't going to complain.

"Actually, I want to cut it all off. It bugs me. Sorry, Zachary."

"Why you gotta betray me like that, Joe?" Zachary made a sound of disgust and walked to the door. Lucy giggled and watched him leave.

"Let's get to an inn first so we can all properly bathe, okay?" Lucy suggested.

With a firm nod of his head, Kid followed Zachary. Walking as if he were suddenly twice his height, and feeling every bit of it, Kid looked around at everything he could see. The place didn't look familiar, but he hadn't expected it to. He found all the buildings fascinating. They were so tall and close together. They were a stark contrast to those in Tawney City, which were composed mostly of rubble.

The scents were the most enticing since it seemed every other building was an eatery. Sweet breads filled shelves in the windows, and open doors allowed the aroma to lure people. Spiced meats were stacked in open baskets; fruits and vegetables filled more stands than he could see, every item hitting him in his weakest spot—the stomach. As seductive as each morsel was, he refrained, deciding to wait until after they had unloaded their heavy packs.

"There's a place to stay," Lucy said, pointing to a shorter building down an alley.

"Okay," Kid said.

Though the place was small, it was filled with atmosphere from the musician in the corner, the loud bartender by the entrance, and every inebriated person in between the two. Lucy led the way to the desk that sat in the back. It took some time to gain anyone's attention. Impatience overtook Lucy, and she put her fingers to her lips and whistled. The room fell silent, and someone finally approached the desk.

"May I help you?" the man asked, some annoyance in his voice.

"Of course," Lucy said tartly. "We would like a room, please."

The noise gradually returned to its normal level. The man unhurriedly looked through the books for an open room. Lucy's jaw muscles twitched as she slowly clasped her fingers around her dagger. Zachary put his hand over hers and shook his head. She scoffed and walked to the entrance to wait.

Finally, the man led the trio to a room on the second floor. Zachary positioned himself between Lucy and the clerk until the man was at a safe enough distance. The room had a washroom with a tub, only two beds, and not much else. Zachary pumped the water up and was happy that Lucy wanted to bathe first. Zachary had volunteered to go last, so after they had finished, Lucy and Kid stretched out on the couch waiting for him. It was then that Lucy noticed the small bag hanging from Kid's belt.

"Hey, I didn't see that on you earlier," she said.

"What?" he asked.

"That bag there."

"Oh, this? It was an add-on."

"What's it for? I mean, I saw you put your money in your pocket, so why do you need that bag? What's in there, anyway?"

"Oh, nothing," he said lightly, hoping she'd give up the hunt. He wasn't good at changing the subject as there was nothing he could think of to discuss.

Her eyes narrowed as she contemplated him. "No. What are you hiding?"

At that moment, Zachary joined them. "Okay. So, nasty haircut, then the Arena, or nasty haircut, food, then the Arena?"

"The second one," Kid said quickly. "I'm starving." He was out the door without another word. Lucy glared at his back but remained silent. They walked through the streets; the crowds thinned as darkness loomed. Zachary and Lucy found it hard to keep up with Kid at that point.

"Is it just me, or is Joe moving exceptionally fast right now?" Zachary asked.

"He's hiding something," Lucy answered.

"Must you always pry? If he wants to tell us, he'll tell us. He's entitled to some secrets, don't you think?"

Though frustration usually fueled her stubbornness, Lucy agreed to drop the investigation for the moment. Kid ducked into the first barber shop he saw. Lucy and Zachary waited outside for him until he emerged some time later for their seal of approval.

"Well?" he asked, rubbing his hand over the cropped locks. Lucy noted that he didn't look at her.

"It's good," Zachary said. "Makes you look older, anyway. Now, food!"

Finding a place to eat proved to be no problem. Choosing one was. Fish eventually won, and the three found a place that wasn't too crowded. Kid maneuvered the seating arrangement so as not to sit by Lucy. His palms sweated at the thought of another question from her. He regretted not finding a more clever hiding spot for the book, but he didn't think the bag would even draw any attention. He did observe that Lucy avoided the topic altogether, but he could tell she was upset. That fact caused him discomfort, remembering all she'd done for him. He had, however, promised Dawn not to tell anyone about it, and he really wanted to keep that promise.

After asking for directions, they found the Arena. It was the largest building in the city. Kid wanted to just run the whole way there; his hopes of finding his identity were almost palpable. The lamplighters went about their jobs, while those still on the streets had to move to avoid them. Vendors with carts pulled them back to storage, and all these events caused a slower pace than Kid could endure. He wanted to just scream at everyone to move.

Eventually, the trio arrived at their destination. Disappointingly, the guard at the door would not let them through until the next morning. The doors shut to the public at noon, he informed them. Kid almost broke down in tears.

"It'll be okay Joe," Lucy said soothingly, rubbing his short hair. "We'll just come back tomorrow morning."

"Easily said," Kid stated. "Let's go."

Silence filled their room that night. Lucy and Zachary relished sleeping on featherbeds. Kid insisted that he would much rather sleep on the wood floor. Once the arrangement was established, it wasn't long before Lucy and Zachary were fast asleep. As time slipped away, Kid gave up trying to sleep and sat by the window, watching the streets below.

Kid's thoughts reverted to Patrick and what he had said about David. Kid hadn't asked why he reminded Patrick so much of David. Perhaps when they were finished at the Arena, he'd return to Patrick's hill to ask him.

Kid pushed away from the window and went to his bed on the floor in order to give sleep another attempt, but it still evaded him. Kid marveled that it didn't come easily. Of course, gaining knowledge of his identity wasn't as tangible before, he realized. Here he was, less than a day away.

The swords came to mind. Kid picked them up and quietly cleared a place on the floor. He hoped he wouldn't wake the inhabitants of the two beds against the wall, but he knew that he had to do something. He performed a few techniques that he remembered. After an hour of practice, the exhaustion came, and he finally fell asleep.

Breakfast didn't arrive early enough. Kid woke long before dawn and furiously paced the room. Surprised that he wasn't waking the other two, knowing his antics would result in a severe teasing, he began to worry that they'd never wake. Dawn finally tickled the windowsills. Zachary rolled over and opened his eyes. Kid froze and stared at him. Zachary lifted his head and nodded sleepily. Yawning first, he reached over to Lucy and nudged her.

"Hmm?"

"Joe's staring at me," Zachary muttered. "How do I get him to stop?"

Lucy turned her head to look at Kid, who fidgeted with his harness straps, fighting with all his strength to remain quiet.

"Hold on, Joe," she said softly. "Let me go splash some water on my face."

Kid nodded, sucking in his lips to refrain from speaking. Lucy slowly got to her feet and stretched as she made her way to the washroom. After she was inside, Zachary rubbed his eyes before he shook his head.

"What time is it?" he asked.

"I don't know," Kid answered.

"How long have you been awake?" Zachary fought another yawn.

"A long time," Kid said meekly.

Zachary released a small laugh before he sat upright and stretched. Lucy exited the washroom and caught Kid's eyes.

"I guess now is when you'd like to go."

"Please," Kid begged.

"I want to eat first," Zachary mumbled, barely awake enough to speak loudly. Kid tossed him some leftovers from the pack.

"You can eat as we go. Now hurry," Kid said excitedly and was out the door before they could react.

Zachary looked at the bit of dried meat and fruit that had landed next to him. "I was hoping for some real food. Warm food," he muttered.

"Don't whine. Just be understanding." Lucy grabbed some dried fruit after pulling on the belt that held her sword and knives. She nearly ran over Kid as he paced in the hallway.

"What took you so long?" he cried.

"Sorry, Joe. I did just wake up."

"Sorry. I'm sorry." He hung his head. "I'm just tired of not knowing."

Zachary managed to run into them. "Oops," he apologized. Lucy grabbed Kid's hand and led him down the street. Few people were out that early, so it took less time to get to the Arena than the day before. This time they were allowed to enter. They went straight to a table they were told was the registration center.

"Hello, sir," Lucy said to the officer there. "We're hoping you can help us. You see—"

"You have to sign in," he said brusquely, regarding none of them.

"But we're not here to sign in," Lucy informed him.

Her words at least generated a response. "Why are you here?"

"To see if he's been here before," Lucy pulled Kid forward.

"I wouldn't know. The general would. He has all the paperwork. Name," he said, looking at Kid.

"Uh, um—"

"Speak up, boy," the officer barked.

"Could we at least see the general?" Zachary intervened, reading the desperation on Kid's face.

"No one can see the general except soldiers or new recruits."

"O-kay. Can we be new recruits, then?" Lucy asked.

"You need to sign in. Once you pass, then you go on to phase two."

"Pass what?"

The soldier pointed to the wide-open area to his left. It was a training ground, covered with dirt, yet open to allow in the sunlight. Half the Arena held soldiers performing training exercises. The other half was filled with younger hopefuls sectioned off at different stations. "Qualifications."

"There's no other way to see him?" Lucy asked.

"Nope."

"Where do we sign up?"

"Write your name and age to start," he answered, pointing to a paper and quill.

"Um, where?" she asked.

The soldier pointed to the paper. She stared at it for a moment and then leaned closer to Zachary and whispered, "Can you write?"

He slowly shook his head.

Kid desperately shifted his wide, alarmed eyes from face to face, watching his only opportunity slipping away. He looked down at the paper, unable to discern what the lines on it meant, and gulped.

The officer muttered as he took up the pen and asked, "What are your names?"

"I'm Lucy Zariah Morntego. twenty-three. He's Zachary Dominic Taylor. Twenty-eight. And this is, uh, Joe. Joe—David Kid. And he's sixteen."

Kid furrowed his brows, but she gave him a warning look. After the officer wrote their names, he said, "Go to that area right there. If you can pass through the qualifications today, then there will be a meeting tonight with the general. If you fail, you must undertake six months of training before you can participate in the qualifications again."

"Thank you," Lucy said.

As they walked away, Kid stepped close to her. "Joe David Kid?"

"It's the best I could do on short notice. Besides, we'll breeze through this, talk to the general, and explain everything to him tonight."

"Brilliant," Zachary said sarcastically.

"You got a better idea?" she snapped. He knew better than to encourage her wrath.

They approached the first qualification station on their left near the perimeter wall. The officer in charge asked them to disarm as he inspected their weapons.

"What is this place anyway?" Kid asked.

"This Arena houses the Ashite army. Anyone who wants to join has to come here," Lucy explained.

"Oh," Kid replied.

"Now," the officer said, gaining everyone's attention. "Here we check your skills at hand-to-hand combat."

Kid followed his companions, feeling nervous. How was he to know how to do this? Of course, how did he even know how he was able to wield the sword? Perhaps these qualifications would uncover new skills, but he didn't want to assume too much yet.

An officer randomly chose the opponents from the crowd of hopefuls. Zachary was paired with someone close to his size. Kid craned his neck to watch. The opponent threw punch after punch. Zachary dodged the barrage of blows before finally delivering a solid jab to the man's abdomen, causing the man to double over and stagger back a few steps. The officer intervened at that moment and separated the fighters. The man said a few things and gestured. Zachary and a few other people moved toward another station. Zachary's opponent was led to a place by the exit.

The officer in charge motioned for Kid to enter a ring. Several bouts were happening at once, as the area had many large hay bales blocking off the sparring areas. Kid looked about as he tried his best to breathe steadily. If just one of them made it through, then perhaps he could still have an opportunity to meet the general. Kid relaxed a bit more. Surely, Lucy and Zachary would pass all of the trials if he couldn't.

His opponent entered and brought fists up to his chin, ready to spar. The muscles in Kid's body tensed. He felt completely unprepared. The officer signaled them to begin, and Kid awkwardly lifted his fists and swallowed. The opponent threw a swift kick at Kid's side, and Kid's arm jerked to block it. *Huh*, Kid thought. *I might be okay at this if I don't think too much.* The young man struck again, throwing a combination jab and hook. Kid blocked both, while managing to land a quick uppercut before sidestepping to the young man's right to throw a knee at his exposed abdomen.

The officer halted the joust. Kid waited as he and several other people watched the officers converse. After a minute, Kid and a few others were sent toward the next station. Kid allowed his eyes to peruse the other candidates in the Arena. Most looked young, probably as young as he knew he must look. Several were dejectedly walking toward the exit. Rejected, Kid concluded. He swallowed nervously. Rejection meant no audience with the general. With a heavy sign, Kid continued his observations. *One of us has to pass.*

As he neared the next destination, a man passed through the Arena. He was dressed differently than the other officers, who saluted him as he passed them. Kid strained his neck and squinted in hopes of getting a better look. The man spoke with the soldiers doing combat drills on the far side of the Arena. He didn't seem the least bit interested in the recruits.

Zachary had managed to get to the back of the line when Kid arrived. "Who's that?" Kid asked, gesturing.

"Judging by the uniform, I'd say it's the general," Zachary said.

Kid inhaled deeply. The man was so close.

"Hey, watch it!" someone said contemptuously.

"Bite your tongue," Lucy snapped as she pushed her way to Zachary and Kid's position. "Well, that round was easy."

"Not this one," Zachary said with a smug look.

"Why?"

"Oh—it's your favorite sport."

Lucy looked beyond him and saw the targets. She moaned. "Archery."

"Yup," Zachary said.

"Why is that bad?" Kid asked.

"Lucy can't aim for nothing," Zachary said.

"Forget you," Lucy snapped. "I'll hit anything you point at with my dagger."

"Little good that will do now," Zachary replied.

"Might not make it past this one, Joe. Sorry," Lucy said.

"We just need one of us," Kid said meekly. Zachary rubbed his head.

"You," an officer said, pointing to Kid. "Get to that marker."

With a nervous nod, Kid moved, eyeing those already in front of the targets. He noted how they held the bows and nocked the arrows. His eyes shifted toward the target. *I guess I hit the middle,* he assumed. He took the bow he was handed and lifted an arrow from a quiver that hung from a pole. His breathing steadied as he nocked the arrow and lifted the bow, observing the other contenders from the corners of his eyes. He mimicked how they lined up their shots.

A breeze glided past, kicking up some dust. That would affect the arrow's path, he realized. *How did I know that?* Without a second thought, he adjusted the aim and fired. Near bull's-eye. He stood there stunned for a moment before he finally heard the officer's voice sending him on to the next round. Everyone else used up more of their three chances. Kid just moved his feet forward, dazed. Due to his snail-like pace, Zachary easily overtook him.

"I thought you would want to hurry," Zachary said.

"I'm in shock, that's all."

"Better off than Lucy."

"Why?"

"All her shots went wide. She's been sent to the exit. Oh, and I'd hate to be the men there. She is scorching mad." He put his arm around Kid and rubbed his head. "It's down to just you and me, Joe." Kid pushed Zachary away.

The general was staring at them, Kid noted. That sobered him. Why was the general staring at them? Kid shook his head and looked away. Another no-answer question. Besides, he reasoned, why wouldn't the general be out surveying potential recruits?

"The final skill is swordsmanship," another officer briefed the group gathered at the last station. "You are all privileged to be facing our best soldier today."

A younger man entered the larger ring of hay bales, smiling at the nervous faces around him. Kid watched as challenger after challenger entered the ring. Not a single one was able to touch the soldier. Overhearing a discussion among some of the recruits, Kid learned that the soldier's name was Smatt, and he had been fighting with the sword since he was seven. An expert by nineteen and now twenty-two, the army took advantage of him for training purposes.

Kid could tell that Smatt loved every minute of it. The smile never left his face as he humiliated those who hoped to scrape by, swatting them frequently on the rump. Smatt also fought with a sword in each hand, which he used to defend against careless swings. The challengers used their own weapons. There were no blunt instruments to be seen.

The first group of hopeful challengers was unceremoniously sent to the exit. Disqualified—and therefore unable to meet the general. Kid watched as the young men and women slowly trudged through the door onto the street. He swallowed nervously. He thought some of them were pretty good. Why had they been rejected?

Finally, Zachary entered the ring. Even though he obviously had the advantage in size and strength, he in no way allowed that to overrule the respect Smatt should be given. Not cocky, and therefore not careless, Zachary fought the fight he had to—defensively, attacking only when the opportunity presented itself. Smatt approved Zachary very quickly, the first of the morning, and sent him through to finish his application process. Those disqualified who were still within viewing distance seemed confused. Many of their duels had been longer, and a few felt that they should have been allowed to remain. They grumbled and scratched their heads as they continued to the exit.

Kid cast another glance at the general before it was his turn. The general had his arms crossed, watching everything. Kid shrugged off his last bit of nerves as he entered. Smatt was calm and composed, showing not a single sign of having just fought a dozen jousts that day. Kid understood that the men he had met in the woods were more like the kids who had failed today—amateurs without skill, swinging their swords around in hopes of landing a few blows.

Kid drew his swords and patiently waited for the officer's mark.

"Begin."

Unlike anyone else who had fought before, Kid remained still, calmly staring at Smatt's smiling face. Kid breathed deeply, even considering closing his eyes. He had done so every time before that day. The moment he did, he heard Smatt charge, so Kid brought his swords up and blocked both blows perfectly. When he opened his eyes, he saw that Smatt's smile was gone.

Kid pushed him away and began an attack that obviously put Smatt on unfamiliar territory. Slash down, up, quick thrust, feint a blow, and spin with both swords separated to hit the head and torso. Smatt couldn't even guess where the blows were aimed; he began to perspire from the effort of barely blocking the blows. Kid knew that he was instinctively holding himself back, so without warning, he disarmed Smatt, stopping the swing of his weak hand just below Smatt's throat. Kid held it there for a moment, and then quickly sheathed his swords.

Smatt couldn't believe he had lost. That fact alone was written all over his face. Kid retrieved his opponent's weapons and held them hilt-out to Smatt, who slowly took and sheathed them. He extended his hand to Kid.

"Today I am in the presence of one greater than myself," Smatt said quietly for only Kid to hear. "If one day you are ever in my position, please, be humbled and not humiliated."

"I promise."

The smile returned to Smatt's face. "I don't know if this one qualifies," he said loudly. "I'll let that decision rest upon the general's shoulders."

The general lifted his head. "Send him to my office." Then he crossed the Arena and disappeared into the nearest building. Kid looked at Zachary, beaming. Mission accomplished. As an officer approached Kid, he asked, "Can my two companions join me?" The man paused before he nodded. Kid waved Zachary forward and turned toward the exit.

"The redhead," Kid said, pointing. "Her name's Lucy."

The man's face grew tense with impatience, but he lifted his wrist to his mouth and said, "Bring the young lady named Lucy to the general's office." Then he addressed Kid and Zachary. "Follow me."

He escorted them through a series of doors and hallways until they finally reached one with the name *General Malkam* painted on it, though none of them could read the words.

"Wait here. It will only be a moment before he can see you."

"Thanks," Kid said. When the door to the anteroom opened again a moment later, it revealed Lucy, who was surprisingly beaming. After they were alone, she caught Kid in a big bear hug and laughed. "Wonderful duel, that was!"

"I've never seen swordplay like that in all my life!" Zachary said. "But—what did he say to you?"

"He said," came a deep voice from the other side of the room, "'If you are ever one day in the presence of one greater than yourself, do not be humiliated, be humbled.'"

The three quickly grew embarrassed as they saw the general standing by the open door to his office, which he promptly shut.

"Are you proud of what you did out there?" General Malkam asked rather harshly.

"Sir?" Kid asked stepping forward.

"You know full well what you did out there. Your friend understood the routine. That was just a test to show what you know—not to show off! That stuff may look great one-on-one, but it will wear you out during a battle. So I want to know: are you proud of what you did out there? Now all those new recruits are going to remember that the man who will train them to be their best is someone who was defeated. These kids are going to have it in their heads that even if they work their hardest to become as good as Smatt, there is still someone out there who can defeat them. Tell me. Are you proud of that?" General Malkam said the last sentence loudly, and Kid felt it to the bone. He bowed his head and swallowed nervously, wiping his damp palms down his legs.

"S-sorry, sir," Kid said weakly. "I didn't know."

"Didn't know what?"

"I didn't know that I could defeat him, sir. I thought he was going to easily beat me."

"Don't give me those stupid lines, Payden. You know as well as I do that you're ten times better than any soldier."

Kid instantly lifted his head. Lucy and Zachary grew alert too.

"What did you say, sir?" Kid asked softly.

"When did you start calling me 'sir'?" General Malkam asked angrily.

"Sir, did you just call him Payden?" Lucy asked.

"Is that his name?" Zachary asked.

Kid began to breathe quickly.

General Malkam calmed down and straightened himself. "What do you mean?"

"Please, sir, do you know me?" Kid asked hopefully.

General Malkam sighed deeply and released the tension in his shoulders. He sat heavily upon his chair and took off the helmet to rub his temples.

"Sir, please—" Kid said, stepping forward, desperately fighting back his tears.

"That explains a lot," General Malkam said. "So I apologize for my outburst."

"Sir," Kid said. "Is my name Payden?"

General Malkam looked him in the eye. "Yeah. That's your name."

Lucy and Zachary kept their relief silent as they watched the kid they had grown attached to slowly release his breath. *Payden*, he thought. *I have a name.*

"Thank you," he said.

"Do you remember anything?" General Malkam asked.

Payden shook his head. "No. I woke up maybe a month ago."

"Woke up?" The general leaned forward. "Are you telling me— How long were you out?"

"Almost eight months."

General Malkam silently swore. Not wanting to cause Payden any more stress, he pushed aside his angry thoughts. "Welcome home," he said.

"What else do you know about me? Please, tell me everything," Payden pleaded.

Malkam stared at him thoughtfully. "It's been a long day already. Why don't we talk over some food? You can introduce me to your new friends here, okay?"

Payden could only nod his head. They followed the general out of his office to a back exit. His favorite eatery was a few minutes away. Payden didn't want to even ask a question. He waited through the walk and the meal for the general to speak.

After they finished their last bites, Payden hoped the general would finally say something, but he remained silent. Feeling as though he had waited long enough, Payden finally cleared his throat and asked, "So, sir, I mean, General—"

"Watcher," General Malkam said. "You always used to call me Watcher."

"Watcher?" Payden asked. "Is that your name?"

General Malkam chuckled. "No. Not hardly. My name's really John Alan Malkam. But you called me Watcher."

"Are you my dad?"

Laughter was the answer. General Malkam shook his head. "No. No. I never had time for a family. Regrettably. No. I was an old friend of your father's. A very old friend."

Payden leaned forward. "Where is he now?"

That question finally settle General Malkam's doubts about the thoroughness of Payden's memory loss. He directed his attention to his empty plate.

"Your dad's dead." General Malkam didn't wish to see the reaction to the news, but he figured he should anyway. What he saw was pure defeat in Payden's eyes.

"Oh," Payden muttered. He had suddenly lost all his desire to regain his memories.

"It was quite some time ago. Hmm—it's been twelve years." General Malkam paused at the realization. "The village where you lived was near Jathenite territory. One day, they attacked. You were the only survivor."

Payden looked up at him. "So, my whole family—"

General Malkam sighed. "I think I've told you enough. See—"

"What?" Payden cried, hitting the table with his fist. The reaction startled Lucy and Zachary, who had silently agreed to let Payden alone talk with General Malkam.

General Malkam leaned back to study Payden. He had never respected irrational emotional outbursts. They rubbed him the wrong way. "I understand the situation you are in, Payden, but that gives you no right to yell at me or interrupt me. Do you understand?"

Payden fought hard, but he kept his response to a firm nod. General Malkam stood. "You have enough to process for one day. I'll tell you more tomorrow, maybe. Now go get some rest."

"What do you mean by 'maybe'?"

"When someone has an injury that results in memory loss, it's not always best to tell him everything. Perhaps a little, but a person's got to hold on to that part of them that wants to know. It'll pull him out of the darkness until all his memories return. I fear I've told you too much already. I don't want you to stop wanting to remember. You do need to give this kind of injury time to heal. Sometimes it takes a lot of time."

"What if my memory never returns?"

"Then we'll wait until never comes before I will tell you more."

Payden stood, visibly angry. "Maybe I'll just wait until then before I talk with you again."

He quickly left. Zachary and Lucy hurriedly stood, intending to follow him, but General Malkam restrained them.

"Payden's got a temper. Let him cool down."

"But he doesn't know this city," Lucy protested.

"My men do. They're everywhere, and I've already sent word to keep an eye on him. So relax. He'll come around."

"Really?" Lucy snapped. "Was it your theory of waiting until he comes around that got him in this situation?"

General Malkam didn't even bother reacting to her accusations. He merely said, "No. Anger did. Excuse me."

As he left, Lucy sat back down, fuming. She bit at her nails as her impatience would not allow her to remain inactive. "We should go find him."

"Maybe, but it's the general who knows him," Zachary said. "We could actually try his advice."

She sighed with stubborn resignation. "Fine. But if he doesn't show up by tomorrow morning, I'm after him."

Chapter 9

The next morning, Lucy angrily stormed back to the Arena, shoving everyone aside until she was face-to-face with General Malkam.

"Where is he?" she demanded. The soldiers nearby suppressed chuckles; they knew their general. True to his character, he didn't even acknowledge the outburst but continued his conversation with an officer.

Noting the obvious, Zachary stepped forward. "Excuse me, sir, but can I ask you a question?" he asked calmly.

General Malkam turned to address him. Lucy scowled and crossed her arms.

"You know, I never did get your name," General Malkam said.

"It's Zachary, sir. The redhead's Lucy."

General Malkam inclined his head toward her. "Good morning, Lucy."

She delivered her most venomous stare, wanting to carve that look off the general's face.

"What's your question?" General Malkam asked Zachary.

"Well, Joe—uh, Payden didn't return to our inn last night," Zachary explained. "We were wondering if you knew where he was."

General Malkam looked over to the entrance, where an officer was looking through several files. "Mikal," General Malkam said loudly. "Where's Payden?"

Lieutenant General Mikal held up a remote transmitter and asked the soldiers in the city the same question. When an answer arrived, he shouted, "In the square by the fountain."

"Thank you," General Malkam said, and turned his gaze to Lucy. "He's in the square. By the fountain."

Too angry at him to show any sign of gratitude, she spun on her heel and left an apologetic Zachary to follow not far behind.

"Don't say a word," she snapped when he reached her side.

"Not used to not being feared?" he asked anyway, too entertained not to smile.

She snorted in disgust. "Who does that man think he is?"

"Well, the general of the Ashite army, a position demanding respect considering his success at keeping the Fashites away from these parts."

Halting her rapid progress, she turned to face him, hands finding their defiant positions on her hips. "What have I done to you?" she asked.

He grabbed her and quickly kissed her. "Let's go to the fountain."

He darted away quickly to avoid an attack and headed for the square without as much as a backward glance. It felt unusual to him to act that way around her, but for the past week, he'd felt more himself than ever—relaxed, even, knowing that he no longer had to watch what he said or withhold his actions around her. He knew the biggest reason that he felt so free was the fact that she returned his affection. She was his Lucy, the hardheaded woman he loved.

Payden was sitting on the fountain's ledge when Zachary entered the square. He stopped to let Lucy catch up. She angrily hit his arm before storming past him, and Zachary chuckled. Payden didn't seem to notice them approach. He stared at his reflection but displayed no signs of emotion. Zachary took his stillness to be a bad sign from the otherwise animated individual.

"Hey, Joe, uh, Payden," Zachary said. "Where've you been? Lucy's been worried."

"Like a mad heifer," she snapped. "Don't ever do that to me again!"

He offered them no reaction or greeting. His attention remained on the water. Lucy looked up at Zachary, more frustrated than worried. She grew impatient and sat next to Payden. There were no more maternal instincts left in her. What she really wanted to do was grab Payden's head and thrust it into the water. That would snap him out of it.

"You know," Payden said softly. "I guess I was supposed to be with you guys all along. I'm an orphan too."

"So? Everyone's an orphan," Lucy said.

Zachary hit her on the back of her head.

What? she mouthed at him, which caused him to roll his eyes.

"Hey, Payden, let's go eat," Zachary said. "I'm hungry with no money for food."

Payden reached into a pocket and pulled out all his money. "Here," he said and held it up to Zachary, making no other movement.

Zachary glanced at Lucy. She flashed him a wicked grin, then scooped up a handful of water and splashed it into Payden's face. Her gesture generated a startled look.

"Oh, good, you're not dead," she said.

Payden used his sleeves to wipe off the water as Zachary picked up the money he had dropped.

"Joe, if you sit here and dare to think that you're the only person with a sad story, you're kidding yourself. I've lost family, too. Zachary's lost family. Charlie lost family. Remember him? He drove me nuts because all he could focus on was what he'd lost. Every day I just wanted to kill that kid and put him out of my misery. And you saw how bitter and cruel he was to you. Imagine being around that every day. I like you too much to let you end up that way. So you've lost your memory? So you lost your family? Don't lose yourself too! I want my happy, innocent Joe back."

Payden stared at her, hardly able to process what had just happened. She didn't realize that at the moment he thought he would gain everything, all he got was empty hands. It wasn't the fact that he had lost something; it was the fact that there was nothing to gain. Knowing she wasn't at all sympathetic enough to listen, he stood and looked at Zachary.

"Where do you want to eat?" Payden asked.

Unconvinced of his bravado, Zachary hugged Payden tightly for a few minutes. He was feeling respect for the young man at being able to handle so much at once. Lucy was right to encourage Payden not to brood over his sad state, but he did have a right to mourn. Lucy had never understood a person's need to mourn.

"Okay J—Payden. I want pancakes. I haven't had pancakes since I was a kid. So let's go find a place to eat breakfast," Zachary said after he released Payden. They let their noses lead them, for wherever bacon was, pancakes were sure to be also.

Though Payden couldn't find the strength to act cheerful as they ate, he did manage to join the conversation. He told them that he stayed awake all night wandering through the city. What he didn't mention was his disappointment at not finding any shops that sold books. He would have felt safer mentioning his own book if he had seen another, but the widespread lack caused him to guard his secret even more.

"Do you think you could come back with us and talk with that general again?" Lucy asked. Though she hated the idea of returning to that man's presence, she knew Payden needed to go.

At the suggestion, Payden froze. "No," he answered quickly.

"Come on, Payden," Zachary coaxed gently.

"No," was the reply.

"There is absolutely no way that you are more stubborn than me," Lucy said. "You're going back with us."

"No, I'm not."

"Yes, you are, and that's final! Stubbornness and stupidity may look the same, but they're not. And right now, you're being stupid."

Payden set down his fork. "I'm through eating."

"Well, I'm not," Zachary said. "So wait for me, okay?"

"How did you guys find me so easily?" Payden asked.

"The Watcher is watching you," Lucy said with a giggle. "There are soldiers all over the city keeping an eye on you." She concentrated on finishing the last of her eggs. Zachary had stopped eating, focusing on Payden. He was up to something. Anger twitched his jaw muscles. It had obviously ruined his appetite, for half the food remained on Payden's plate. Zachary silently hoped Payden would not do anything rash—or stupid.

On the walk back, Payden lagged behind, much to Zachary's concern. The crowds grew larger and harder to maneuver through, so Zachary grabbed Payden's arm to ensure he wouldn't take advantage of the situation and run. Zachary released him the moment they reached the Arena.

"Please, at least try to talk with him again," Zachary pleaded. Payden shrugged. Lucy hurried inside, and Zachary did his best to make some form of eye contact with Payden before turning to go inside too.

The Arena was deserted. Lucy looked around in disbelief. "Where is everyone?" she mused.

At that moment, three heavily armed soldiers appeared, followed by General Malkam.

"Did you find him?" he asked.

"Yeah. Right by the fountain," Zachary answered, thoroughly confused.

"Then where is he?"

"He's—" Zachary turned. Payden was gone. "We walked him right up to the door."

"Stupid, stubborn kid," General Malkam growled. "Find him!" he bellowed to the three soldiers, who quickly exited.

"What's going on?" Lucy asked.

"My men saw three Slaves today, but there are probably more. First time ever." He spit as if the very mention of them generated a foul taste.

"He couldn't have gotten far," Zachary said. "Like I said, he was with us right up to the door."

Lucy paled. "But—he could hide from the soldiers."

General Malkam looked at her. "You told him, didn't you?" he asked.

She nodded.

"You couldn't have just trusted me and let him be, could you?"

She bowed her head.

"Why are the Slaves after him?" Zachary asked.

"I don't know. I can only guess. But that's too long a story for right now. You two come with me. There's a spot no one would think to check, but it was Payden's favorite spot."

"What makes you think he'd go there now?" Lucy asked softly.

"Instinct. Payden's governed by pure instinct."

Though General Malkam could admit that he didn't know the boy too well, he knew at least that water had always fascinated Payden. He remembered sailing with Payden down the great river Don Luccour, which began at the Aflan Mountains, gathering streams and small rivers to its heart before dumping those collections into the Myriad Sea. Landar nestled just several kilometers from the delta. The river was sufficiently deep, which made shipping a major part of the city's livelihood. Payden had often begged fishermen and sailors to take him out to sea, even to the south where other Ashite towns were hidden away along the shorelines. It was to the docks that littered the river that General Malkam led Lucy and Zachary.

"Look everywhere," he ordered.

They searched every ship, under every pier, and in every shack along the waterfront, but didn't find Payden, so they returned to the street that overlooked the docking area.

"It was a good idea," Zachary said.

"No; it was just an idea," General Malkam muttered. He turned to head back to the city gates but froze. Heading their way was a Slave. With a slight flick of his wrist, General Malkam activated a thin but strong shield that instantly formed, covering the length of his body just in time; he heard a dart deflect off it.

"We're fish out of water," he said. "Get under cover."

He raised his wrist to his mouth, which held the receiver he used to communicate with his highest ranking officer.

"Mikal, send fifty men to the dock road immediately. We've got a Slave one hundred meters away."

He motioned the others back. "Get your backs up against the wall in case another Slave decides to show up," he ordered.

"I thought they only worked alone," Lucy said.

"The Pendtars must be getting desperate, then," General Malkam said. "If only we could keep Payden underground for a while longer."

"Is that why he was in that coma? To be kept underground?" she asked hotly.

"Why don't you direct your fighting energy where it needs to go, lass, and maybe you'll get to overhear us grownups talk later."

Zachary placed his hand over her mouth and pulled her back to the wall. General Malkam remained between them and the Slave, unwilling to even blink so as not to miss a movement.

"Get armed," he said. "'Cause I don't plan on dying until his head's rolling down the road."

Lucy did her best to steady herself, but the sword quivered anyway. Zachary wrapped a protective arm around her waist, willing some peace to flow into her.

The Slave continued his steady pace toward them, but then redirected his attention past them, farther down the road. General Malkam dared a peek, and it was just as he feared: Payden was approaching, but his swords were drawn, and there was a hint of blood on one.

"He's already been fighting," General Malkam said. "Has that boy gotten better these past five years?"

They watched as the Slave raised a dart gun. Lucy wanted to scream a warning, but the dart was released. Payden, seemingly knowing it was coming, managed to roll away, escaping the path of the poisoned barb. The Slave, showing no emotion, merely replaced the gun in his cloak and marched toward Payden, drawing his sword. Just before they clashed, the soldiers arrived and fired arrows upon the Slave, who successfully dodged and deflected them. The distraction had been enough for Payden to deliver the lethal blow. The Slave collapsed without a sound, and Payden solemnly wiped off the blood with the Slave's black cloak.

"Joe!" Lucy screamed. She ran to him and hugged him. The soldiers hurried over, their shields up, and surrounded them, eyes searching for any more threats. The officer in charge of the unit pulled General Malkam to the side.

"We've found three other dead Slaves," he said. "Smatt couldn't kill one, and this kid's got four now? Who is he, sir?"

"My friend's son," General Malkam answered. "But his training doesn't come from me, and you wouldn't believe me if I told you the true source."

General Malkam pushed past the officer to reach Payden. "Good job, Payden. There's still more in the city—"

"I'm leaving," Payden interrupted.

"What?"

"Every city I've been in has attracted a Slave. I don't want to be blamed for anyone's death, so I'm going to leave now before it's too late."

"We can keep you safe," General Malkam said.

"You sure couldn't stop them from coming in, and you sure couldn't stop this one now," Payden retorted. "Obviously, I can take care of them on my own. So just let me go."

"No," General Malkam answered. "Not again."

Payden slightly lifted a sword. "You can't stop me from leaving."

General Malkam locked on to Payden's angry glare with determined eyes. "You can't stop me from going with you."

A murmur of shock and confusion passed through the troops. General Malkam lifted his receiver and said, "Mikal."

"You all right sir?" Lieutenant General Mikal asked, only slightly inaudible due to some static.

"Yeah. Change of orders. From now on, you give them. Congratulations, General; you've earned the promotion. I resign." Malkam tossed the receiver to a dismayed officer before returning his attention to Payden. The boy let his anger divert his attention away from Malkam, but Malkam bowed his head in order to regain eye contact. "You with me, Payden?"

he asked. Payden's eyes moved to lock on to Malkam's. "Where are we going?" Malkam asked.

Confusion, Payden figured, was what he felt. At least, he wanted it to be confusion, because he almost felt some relief, which was unsettling. His last hope was to have the former general as a traveling companion.

"Well, I want to head upriver. Figure I could hide in the mountains. I would like for a small group of men to escort Lucy and Zachary to Tawney City."

"Uh-uh, no way," Lucy said. "I don't need an escort. Besides, I'm not leaving you, Joe."

Payden looked at her with knit brows.

"I've got to fulfill my promise."

"You fulfilled it," he said.

"Well, I'm not satisfied yet," she said. "Zachary and I will return on our own when I am."

"I don't want to leave you yet, either," Zachary said.

Payden, once again overwhelmed by their kindness, choked back tears and nodded. "Okay."

He put his swords back into their resting place.

"Okay," he said again.

"General, but—" the officer began.

Malkam put his hand on the officer's shoulder. "I'm not the general anymore. I know you can't understand, but it's just something I have to do. General Mikal is more than capable. I'm sure the Slaves will leave as soon as they realize their target is no longer in the city."

"But it's suicide."

"No. It's duty. I made a promise years ago; I don't want to break it again. Good-bye, men."

The soldiers parted to let them pass. The four kept a watchful eye out as they went down to obtain a boat and fuel. In a short amount of time, they were heading upriver. Malkam watched until the city disappeared from view.

"I'm going to miss it."

"No one invited you," Payden snapped. He could only guess why he dared to hate the man. He had no legitimate reason why, Payden figured. He knew it was because the man had robbed him of an opportunity to regain his memories. As unfair as it was, Payden hated him for it.

Though the tension surrounding them remained heavy, Malkam didn't feel bothered by it. Payden always came around, he knew. He was a good kid at heart, and his reasoning eventually won him back over to Malkam's side. He figured that even though Payden couldn't remember who he was, it wouldn't stop him from *being* who he was. He had, after all, made his way to the river.

The boat's engine fought the rushing waters northward, and Payden avoided everyone as much as possible. He had hoped to go alone. As the sun warned them that the end of the day was fast approaching, Malkam steered the boat to a secluded area and anchored it to several trees. Payden remained by the railing, watching the sunset. Before he realized it, his emotions and worries were gone as the fading light shifted through the sky's various colors. A feeling he couldn't understand or describe stirred deep inside him, and he focused more intensely on the horizon. Another question formed in his mind, but the elusive answer didn't discourage him as it had previously. What was out there? And why did he suddenly, desperately want to get there?

Chapter 10

They remained silent for days as the boat's motor churned them upstream. The trip was mostly calm. Though the river was deep and wide, fed a fattening diet of many small streams, she seemed motherly enough to rock her guests gently, perhaps even to try and soothe any gaping wounds.

Payden remained by the railing, staring down at the changing currents, not letting the tilting boat or jumping fish ease his mood. At least being on the water felt right to him, he thought. But the wall that stood between his present and his past taunted him, and even the peaceful rocking seemed a cruel prank.

Eventually they spent all the fuel and had to abandon the craft. Payden didn't know exactly where he wanted to go, but his instincts led him toward the mountains in the distance. Without so much as a spoken word, they fell in line as Payden cut a path through the thickening underbrush. After climbing yet another hill, Payden needed to rest. He turned and was shocked to see the others so far behind him. Finding a log nestled amongst the moss and leaves, he took advantage of it as he waited.

"Gee, Joe," Lucy called to him as they trudged up the hill. "Was this how you felt a few weeks ago when you were dragging behind us?"

"What I want to know is what's fueling his momentum?" Zachary wondered.

"Rage. Pure rage," Malkam answered. They crested the hill, and Malkam looked at Payden. "Things would be different if I weren't here, wouldn't they, Payden?"

Payden answered none of their questions. He turned on the log with his back toward them. "It's getting late," he said. "Here's a good spot to stop."

"Easily defensible," Malkam noted. "Good choice."

Though Malkam didn't expect a reply, he waited for one nonetheless. When his expectations were met, he sought out a decent place to bed down for the night.

"What I wouldn't give for our packs right now," Lucy lamented. "It's too itchy sleeping on the forest floor."

"I just miss our food supply," Zachary joked. He stepped closer to her and lowered his voice. "If it would help, you can sleep by me."

"Shh. In a minute. I'll come over when they've gone to bed."

Payden remained stationed on the log, and Lucy stared at him thoughtfully for a few minutes. "Joe, you gonna sleep?"

"I figured I'd keep an eye out for a few hours. Then maybe I'll sleep."

"Okay." She turned to Zachary and whispered, "I'm going to go talk to him. Don't wait up."

"Okay," Zachary said, knowing that it would be hard for him to fall asleep until she was next to him.

Payden hadn't expected anyone to talk with him, especially after they'd given him his space on the boat, so he wasn't pleased to see Lucy sit next to him. He could barely understand himself at the moment, so what possessed her to think that she understood him at all? Unexpectedly, she sat silently and watched the sunset with him. Payden relaxed and returned to his thoughts. As the sun plunged into the mountains, Payden's thoughts drifted to the future. What was it about the horizon? After four days on the river, each sunset seemed to curl her finger at him, asking him to come with her. This pulled at something inside of him, and his frustration only grew as that wall seemed to grow higher and thicker.

Would something from his past help him explain the allure of that horizon?

"Can I barge in?" Lucy asked softly.

"Depends," Payden muttered. "But I'm pretty sure I already know who you want to talk about."

"Yeah," she said. "You're right. But it depends on you how long this conversation will be."

"What do I need to do to make it brief?"

"Listen with at least enough integrity to consider doing what I have to say."

Payden scratched his head. Consider what? Not being angry at the mute general? Despite how well the man claimed to know him, Payden still saw only a stranger. Of course, the man had just walked away from his life to—what? Babysit him? He shook his head. The more he thought about things, the more discouraged he became.

"I'll try," he said dejectedly.

"Good. First, I need to apologize for a mistake I made. When we first met, I instantly liked you and knew that I could trust you no matter what. But then I let things cause me to doubt. For a while there, I didn't completely trust you."

Payden finally turned to face her, and she smiled. Good, she thought, at least he was listening.

"That was a mistake," she continued. "I should have trusted my instincts and just stuck to it."

"Okay. So you've just come to apologize?" Payden asked hopefully, though he knew better.

"No. I came to make a point, Joe. Do you mind me calling you Joe? Or would you prefer Payden?"

"I don't care," Payden muttered. "I don't think it matters, really. Until I know who I am, how do I really know which name is right? Anyone can call me what they will. Dawn can call me Kid. You can call me Joe. And Patrick can call me David."

She shook her head. "I don't know about that. I don't like the idea of you being named after a Slave."

Payden shrugged. "I don't care."

"You choose to be defeated, you know that?"

He shifted, making a sound of disgust as he turned away from her.

"You said you'd listen," she pointed out.

"I said I'd try," he sneered.

"You're not even doing that. I'm serious, Joe. Whenever I go into a battle, I choose from the very beginning to win. And even if we have to retreat, we leave having dealt the enemy a big blow in supplies and men. That is a win. When you choose to be defeated, well, you never make it to the battlefield. Then what use are you?"

"You're not even trying to understand."

"You're certainly not trying to explain."

Annoyed, he stood and walked several steps. Hearing her follow, he walked until he was halfway down the hill before he stopped.

"Listen," he said, turning abruptly to face her. "Yeah, okay, so everyone's lost a lot. And, sure, I need to get over it, but you've had years. It's bad enough to have lost my family the first time, but now I've lost them twice! More than that—all hope of gaining anything died with them. I don't want you to feel sorry for me. I don't want you to say, 'Poor baby.' What I want is for you to leave me alone and let me try to figure out how to feel right now. I don't have any memories, remember that? I don't know what I'm feeling right now. How did I handle this before? Did I cope with it? What if I didn't? Add a bunch of Slaves and no real rest for weeks, and I get dizzy. I keep—I'm trying. I just have to know who I am in order to know what to do next, and there's no answer for me. Throw as much advice as you want at me. It's not going to help."

"It must be hard, then, using a lot of energy being angry at someone when you don't have to be."

Payden shook his head, not even believing she hadn't understood a thing. "You don't get it!" he cried.

"No, I get it," she said angrily. "But what you don't get is that you're making your problems harder by being stupid. I just want you to consider relying on your first impression of the general. He was honest, at least. And he cares about you, Joe. He'd have to in order to do what he just did. So trust him. He's been right about everything so far, as much as I hate admitting that. So just drop the anger because he was right. You've already given up wanting your memory back, haven't you?"

She turned sharply and climbed back up the hill. Payden pulled out one of his swords and hacked off a few branches before he realized how stupid the idea was. He slowed his breathing and closed his eyes. The only thing that seemed to help him focus and clear his head was when he worked on his swordsmanship. So he drew the other sword and hunted for a clearing. For hours, he danced under the rising moonlight with curious night creatures as his audience. A cold breeze stirred the leaves, which the moonlight gently kissed.

Serenity filled Payden; he stopped, allowing himself to enjoy the feeling. He would choose to win—to release his anger into the night so the sun could melt it away in the morning. He chose to trust the general completely. For that matter, he chose to trust Lucy and Zachary completely. The book, another weight to bear, he decided to show them and face what consequences might come.

Once the decisions were settled, he breathed deeply and relaxed. He was surprised to feel lighter. Even the headache was gone, another victim that met its end in the moonlit grass. Sheathing his swords, he decided it was time to rest. He quickly returned to the top of the hill, unaware of the eyes that watched him—not the eyes of foxes or owls, but of another hunter. Eyes that many claimed were the eyes of death.

Malkam awoke first the next morning. Immediately, he noticed how quiet the forest was—unusual. He noted where the others slept before leaving to find something to eat. He happened upon a berry bush, and then a few rabbits. After collecting some edible forage in hopes of making a stew, he returned to the camp. There, the lack of cooking equipment dawned on him. After building a fire, he went hunting again, this time for some large stones to heat in the flames and then use to cook the meat. Successful with that endeavor, he had much of the meat done before the others woke.

"Good morning," he said as he saw them stir. "Food's almost done. There's a stream not far from here if you wanted to get something to drink and maybe splash your face."

Lucy and Zachary took him up on the suggestion, but Payden stayed behind. Malkam was greatly surprised when Payden made his way over to him.

"Mind if I join you?" Payden asked.

Malkam analyzed the boy for a moment. Noticing a great deal of difference in him from the day before, he said, "I don't mind."

Silence settled upon the camp. Payden was relaxed, Malkam noted, only feeling slightly suspicious and overwhelmingly curious. The boy had never come to his senses that quickly. Malkam decided to let silence have its way as he turned the meat.

"You never explained why I called you Watcher," Payden said.

Malkam grunted as he dredged up the memory. "It was mostly a joke, but one that stuck. You see, I may not have been your father, but I am the man who sort of raised you. As best as I could, anyway. But I am, er, was a general first." Malkam sighed. "Anyway, when you were eight, you asked me why I was called your guardian. I answered, 'Because I promised to watch over you.' And you laughed and said that my name should actually be Watcher. It stuck."

"I never called you Dad or anything?"

"Nah. Your dad was too great a man for his name to be given to anyone else."

"What did he do?" Payden asked. He grabbed a handful of berries in hopes of settling his stomach.

"Ah, well, he did a lot. Mostly he traveled and taught a great deal about peace and uniting the Ashites. Stuff our people really needed to hear and understand. In fact, he worked really hard at building up areas where everyone worked for each other and not against each other. He single-handedly did the impossible. He brought the Ashite people together. And he founded Landar, working to build that city up to what you see today."

"But you told me my father lived in a village."

"Oh, well, he built Landar long before he met your mother. In fact, they met in Landar. But he wanted to raise his children in a much simpler place. And we all thought the location was safe enough. Secluded. But—" Malkam poked at the fire.

"Can I ask for you to tell me more now? Maybe about my family?" Payden's tone betrayed his pleading. Malkam looked at his eyes. The hardness was gone. The more innocent Payden he remembered seemed to be back.

"You had a mother, of course. A brother. There was also an uncle, but I don't think you ever really knew him," Malkam said.

Payden bowed his head.

"Hey, come over here," Malkam said. Payden immediately stood and sat next to him. Malkam put his arm around Payden's shoulders, and that act of mercy caused Payden to cry a little. He turned and wrapped his arms around Malkam's waist.

"It'll be okay," Malkam muttered awkwardly.

Seeing Payden next to Malkam when they returned caused Lucy to stop midstride. She certainly hadn't expected anything she had said to produce results in that form, but she gave them their space. Zachary, on the other hand, noticed the meat about to burn and rescued it from an ill fate, preparing portions for everyone.

"Thank you for the food, sir," Zachary said quietly.

Hearing that they had returned caused Payden to sit upright and wipe his eyes. "I'll be back," he said and headed for the stream.

"Well," Lucy said after Payden disappeared down the hill. "Seems like you two made some progress."

"Yeah," Malkam said. "He's never come around so quickly before."

"Really?" Lucy asked.

Zachary rolled his eyes. “Before you get too proud of yourself, Miss Lucy, it’s a greater credit to his character that he actually took your advice than it was for you to give it.”

“I know,” she said demurely, fidgeting with her food. “But it was still my hard-learned advice.”

“Thank you, Miss Lucy,” Malkam said.

Payden had some trouble finding the stream. Birds, startled by his noisy descent, directed his attention to the sky. Crystal blue welcomed him. As he was no longer crashing through the underbrush, the stream’s whispers could reach his ears. Grateful for the water to cleanse his face and quench his thirst, Payden was tempted to jump in for a quick indulgence. However, his stomach complained after being teased with the berries, so Payden drank what he needed and stood.

Something wasn’t right. The hairs on his neck rose, and Payden quickly flattened himself onto the bank. He strained for the faintest sound that would betray an intruder’s whereabouts. Nothing but the wind stirred. He realized his breathing was too loud and focused on deep, slow breaths as his eyes scanned the trees. Still nothing, but something was out of place. The woods were too quiet.

A pebble rolled down the bank to his right, and Payden rolled to his left and ducked behind a tree. Someone was approaching. He sat there waiting for signs of the sword. It hadn’t been drawn yet, he knew, because the clear skies would have made the sun his ally, reflecting light off the object. Payden all but held his breath as he waited for the Slave to draw his weapon.

Faint, extremely muffled, he heard an unnatural sound from his right side. The Slave was not too far away. Payden slowly gripped a large rock with his left hand and readied himself. Not even a leaf crunched. Payden closed his eyes and poured all his efforts into listening. There was another sound. A soft, shifting sound. The Slave had stepped in sand.

Getting a more accurate assessment of where the Slave was, Payden relaxed slightly, which helped him control his breathing.

"I know exactly where you are," Payden said, "And I'm going to kill you in two minutes."

The sound of the Slave's foot pushing against the sand told Payden that he was undeterred and growing closer. Payden slowly counted to ten as he pushed himself up to stand. When he hit the last number, he spun around the tree and brought the rock down upon the Slave's head. The Slave collapsed. Payden grabbed him by the shoulders and dragged him up the hill.

When he burst into the camp, he caused a flurry of reactions. Lucy gasped as she reached for her sword. Malkam shot to his feet and spun around to scan the underbrush. Zachary just calmly stared, munching on his meat.

"He's the only one. Don't worry," Payden said. "Must have followed us from Landar."

"How did you kill him?" Lucy asked, picking up Payden's harness.

"A rock," he answered.

Zachary dropped his jaw, and Lucy nearly dropped Payden's gear.

"I might have actually believed you if you had said with his weapon, but a rock?" Lucy asked.

"I guess I picked a good spot to camp."

Malkam crossed over to him and swiftly decapitated the Slave. "Just in case," he said. "I wonder how long he'd been here, and why he didn't kill us before he attacked you."

"We'll never know now," Payden said. "My blow might have just knocked him unconscious."

"He wouldn't have said anything anyway," Malkam informed him. "Every Slave undergoes what's called *programming.* Over time, they completely lose their own wills. Nothing he would have said could have been trusted. It's good that there are a lot of rocks here. Let's give him a cairn, since we have no way to dig an appropriate grave."

"I say leave him to the animals," Lucy suggested.

"This man was human once," Malkam said. "He at least deserves a decent burial." Malkam looked at Payden. "That was something your dad was always keen on observing. Fashite or not, they are still human."

After piling rocks over the body, they buried the embers of the breakfast fire and continued the trek toward the mountains. Everyone gave Payden distance because as he walked, he practiced drawing and sheathing his swords as quickly as possible.

"That boy's pretty focused," Zachary observed.

"Humph, *obsessed* is more accurate," Malkam said. "Ever since he could hold a stick, that boy has had only one thing on his mind. I taught him everything I knew, but by eight, he could beat me easily. I never could figure out how a child could disarm a man three times his size. But he could. Others in the Arena raised him as well, teaching him what they knew. He was able to find a few who were better than I am. Within a few years, he had them beat too. When I asked him how he did it, he said it was because all those men were predictable. Training only taught them how to fight one way. That's why he can kill a Slave. He's already experienced their training. He can predict what they'll do. Come to think of it, Smatt mentioned something like that too. If a person's been trained, then you know what they know. Who he fears most are people with no training."

"Hmm. Well, Lucy and I have no formal training. What we have is our own style plus experience."

"Yeah, but Smatt figured you out pretty easily, didn't he?" Malkam asked. "Smatt's fought all sorts of men and studied many sorts of styles."

"So why couldn't he figure out Joe's style?" Lucy asked.

"Joe?" Malkam asked, glancing quizzically at her.

"I'm still going to call him Joe," she said.

"That's the name we gave Payden before we came to Landar," Zachary explained.

"Ah. Well, to answer your question, Smatt would never be able to figure out Payden's fighting style, even if they fought all day."

"Why's that?" Lucy asked.

"Have you ever watched Payden practicing?"

"Yeah," Zachary said. "Several times."

"Have you seen others practice?" Malkam asked.

"Yes. Many different people."

"I bet there's one obvious difference that even you could notice."

Lucy and Zachary exchanged glances. When they realized Malkam was not going to explain until they tried to figure it out, they thought back to their trip to Landar. Zachary mostly considered when Payden first held those swords in Patrick's house. Every movement flowed like a liquid. Then he thought back on every soldier he'd ever watch train. The answer was obvious.

"Soldiers swing their swords," Zachary said. "They are very aware that it's in their hands and what they need to use it for. They're always thinking and analyzing how to use it."

"And?" Malkam prodded.

"Payden doesn't think. He flows. It's as if the sword moves him, or the sword is part of his arm. He doesn't pause to consider what he needs to do in order to win. I don't think it's about beating or disarming or even killing the opponent. It's like—I don't know."

"It's like Payden's whole reason for existence is just to fight," Malkam offered, "Not to survive or exist. Nothing like the rest of us. He's here to fight a war, and he won't stop fighting until the war is over."

"You two are weird," Lucy said. "How can someone exist just to fight? It's stupid."

"Well, I can't claim that idea as my own," Malkam confessed. "See, there's another man who also trained Payden and who seems to understand him better than I ever will. He had to explain it all to me. It's destiny. Payden's father was great. Payden will be too."

"Who was his father?" Lucy asked skeptically.

"You might have heard of him even in Tawney City. His name was Henry Michael Carpenter."

Lucy stopped walking. Zachary gaped at Malkam, then looked at Payden, then looked back at Malkam, completely unaware of Lucy's disappearance.

"Go back and get your girlfriend," Malkam said. "I'm afraid she's forgotten how to walk."

As Zachary disappeared, Malkam hurried his steps to reach Payden.

"Payden!" he yelled. Payden stopped, swords in hand, and turned.

"Yeah?"

"Find someplace to stop so we can eat."

"Okay." He went on ahead, quickly finding a shady place by a stream. When he met up with the others to take them to the spot, the looks on Zachary's and Lucy's faces alarmed him.

"What happened?" he asked.

"Nothing," Malkam said. "I could only give you a brief history of what your father did, but these two obviously grew up hearing stories about him. When I told them his name, it kind of floored them."

"What was his name?" Payden asked.

"Henry Michael Carpenter."

"Carpenter," Payden said thoughtfully. That sounded familiar. Dawn had mentioned it, he realized. Before he allowed himself to worry about her, he asked, "What's my middle name?"

"You weren't given one," Malkam said.

"Why?"

"Can't say for sure. Your dad just didn't want you to have one."

"Oh."

Malkam unhooked his bow from his quiver. "I'll be back shortly. See if there's any fish in that stream while I'm gone, just in case there's no game nearby, okay?"

When Payden caught Lucy and Zachary staring at him, he blushed and looked at the forest floor. "Stop it, you guys. I'm not my father."

"You'd stare too if you knew about your dad what we do," Lucy said. "He's our greatest hero, even though he never fought in a single battle."

The smile fell from Payden's face. "What do you mean? He never fought in a battle? Or used a weapon?"

"No," she answered, but upon noticing Payden's growing uneasiness, she said, "Hey, Joe, that doesn't mean that your fighting is anything he'd disapprove of. Before you jump to conclusions, put your head on straight, okay? Don't beat yourself up."

Payden rubbed his head. "Okay."

Malkam returned in a hurry. "I heard screaming. Someone's in trouble. Let's go."

With the memory of the Slave still fresh, they moved quickly and cautiously toward the sounds of distress. The forest faded away to reveal a village among the foothills. Smoke rose from several buildings, and they could make out only a few figures.

"It's the Fashite army," Malkam informed them.

"Are we heading toward the Fashite lands?" Payden asked.

"No; those are farther southwest. They swept through this area decades ago, and no one's occupied it since, which makes me wonder how that village even got here."

When they were only a few hundred meters away, Malkam stopped in order to form a plan of attack, but Lucy surged ahead without a word.

"Stubborn hothead!" Malkam hissed. "Come on," he said to the others. "Stay close. Idiot. She doesn't even know how many are here."

Lucy had already hewed down a few unsuspecting soldiers. Zachary quickly disposed of those who intended to get her from behind. Payden held himself back, jumping in only when needed. There were only a few soldiers in that part of town, and in half an hour, no more live Fashites were in sight.

Lucy panted, more out of rage than shortness of breath. Malkam hurried over to her.

"What were you thinking, girl?" he roared. "Do you really think they'd send an army this far north with only five men?"

As if to prove his point, a rally horn sounded, and they saw a large group form at the other end of the village. Payden stepped forward as Malkam activated his shield, backing up toward the nearest wall. A barrage of arrows came their way. Payden manipulated his blades at such a fast pace that

As they nodded consent, Payden pushed open the door and ran, striking wherever convenient. Not a sound issued from any man, and each moved unnoticed to the other house. After a brief moment, the fresh bodies were discovered outside, and a cry of alarm was sounded.

"They're going to find us," Lucy said.

"No," Payden said. "They're going to start burning every building in the village. There's too many out front, so let's find another way out."

"I've got twenty out here," Zachary said from a window.

"There's only a few in back," Malkam said. "But there's so much smoke—hmm. It could give us cover for a while."

"Great," Payden said. "Lead the way."

They went to the back door, and Malkam eased it open. While heavy smoke poured in through the open door, they crouched, practically crawling to their next destination. They heard the soldiers that were nearby wheezing, but there were no other sounds.

More men suddenly came around the building, and Payden cried, "Run!"

When they reached the nearest house, bursting through the door, Payden turned to deal with the few who had reached them. Lucy and Zachary, who had gotten inside first, were looking for a quick exit when some soldiers broke through the large window by the entrance.

"They're overwhelming us!" Lucy cried, receiving a blow to her abdomen while pressuring the intruders back. Blood ran down her side and forearm.

Payden noticed her favoring the injuries. He and Malkam had been trying to force the door shut, without much success, but Payden didn't want anything worse to happen to her.

"Malkam, why don't you take Lucy's spot?" Payden said. Without another word, he pulled open the door and dove through the men. Most were startled enough to not strike. They recovered their senses only after Malkam shut and barred the door. He quickly pulled Lucy back.

"I'm fine," she protested.

"Even so, bandage those wounds," Malkam snapped.

"Toss me your sword!" Zachary cried to Lucy. He caught it and quickly slashed down at an arm. Though it felt awkward in his left hand, the sword helped block enough blows for him to be grateful for it.

Lucy angrily tore off the bottom half of a pant leg and cut the fabric into strips. Hastily, she wrapped her forearm and put pressure on the wound on her side. Then she used her knives to dispose of three men, hitting the marks perfectly.

After some time, the Fashite men pulled back, clearing the area completely. Once he caught his breath, Malkam cautiously opened the door, suspicious of the hasty retreat. Seeing no movement, he exited. Lucy straightway retrieved her knives.

"Where do you think Joe is?" she asked.

"Let's follow the path of dead bodies," Malkam said. The closer they were to the village square, the more noise they heard.

"I hope he's still alive," Malkam muttered. "Daft thing he did. No one's that good."

"He's fine. You'll see," Lucy said quickly. "But I want to stock up."

She pulled knife after knife off every body she saw. She pulled off her cloak to hold the quantity, and it quickly became full as they continued closer to the square. Once they came around the last building, they saw Payden alive but surrounded by about thirty men. Not one was moving.

"What do we do?" Lucy asked.

"You start with the knives," Malkam ordered. "Zachary, grab that man's arrows. Gather as many as you can, set yourself up behind those barrels, and use them to get up onto the roof when they charge. Keep shooting. I'll head over there with my bow. You start your attacks after I fire the first arrow. Got it?"

Upon receiving their nods, he said, "Let's go."

Payden stared at all the men around him. They weren't moving, and he couldn't understand why. Running through the village had helped him avoid being cornered, but he hadn't planned on an open square. He hadn't counted on getting into the present situation, and therefore didn't know how to get out of it. Not a single plan formed in his mind that didn't result in death. Still, no one moved.

The man he guessed was in charge of the troop stepped forward. Several men approached him, speaking in hushed voices. The man in charge pulled something that looked like a piece of paper from his pocket, studied it, and then looked at Payden. A smirk slowly spread across his face.

"It looks like we've caught you," the man said with a heavy accent. "It depends on what you do now that determines how we're going to treat you later. If you surrender, we may even feed you. If not, trust me; we know how to make a man wish for death. Your choice."

"Choice?" Payden asked. "I've already made my choice. I choose to win."

The man chuckled. "Suit yourself."

A commotion from the outside of the circle drew the man's attention. His men were breaking off, charging in three separate directions.

"What's going on?" he yelled.

"We're under attack," someone answered.

"Kill them!"

He turned and saw Payden contending with those near him. The man returned the picture to his pocket and pulled out a dart. After dunking it into a vial of poison, he loaded it into a gun and aimed it at Payden. One of his men jumped into his line of fire, and the leader swore.

Payden was relieved to know that the others were alive. He knew that he had to make it over to them. No opportunity presented itself until he saw a Slave standing in the shadows. What effect would such information have on his opponents?

"What's the matter?" he yelled. "You guys can't take me down, so you brought a Slave to do it for you?"

Many of the men became visibly agitated. Once they spotted the Slave, some retreated. The mental distraction the Slave caused gave Payden the edge he needed to burst out of the circle. He ran as fast as he could to the roof of the house where Zachary stood. Using his momentum, he ran up the barrels, landing next to his friend.

"Nice of you to join me," Zachary said.

"Where's Lucy?"

"Down there," Zachary nodded his head in her direction, without breaking his rhythm. "She'll need your help."

"Thanks."

Payden ran to the edge of the roof and jumped, knocking over three men to break his fall. His swords were swinging before he regained his footing in order to race to the front of the crowd. The men were forcing their way into a house. Payden dove through the window, coming up quickly to block Lucy's blow.

"Oh, Joe! I could have killed you!" she cried.

"You would've had to try harder," he said. "This way."

He pulled her to the back of the house, but men had entered through that door, so he cut his way across the room and up the steps. After entering a bedroom, he shut the door and shoved the bed against it as Lucy broke all the glass out of the window and evaluated their situation.

"I don't think we can make it to the roof," she said.

"Sure we can," he said with a grin. "How many knives do you have left?"

"Half a dozen."

"Think that'll do?"

She handed them over, and he sat on the windowsill. With all his strength, he shoved a few knives through the wood, and then used the hilt of a sword to beat them in farther. He stood and did the same with a few others as high up as he could reach. Then he crouched down.

"Well, let's see if this works. Do you want to go first?" he asked.

"Of course."

He helped her out, and she carefully placed her foot on one of the handles. She held her breath and put all her weight on it. When it remained stable, she reached her foot up for the next one.

"I need another one," she said. That one was thrust and beat in before she pulled up to the next knife. By then, the roof was in reach, and she easily swung herself onto it. Payden climbed more quickly because he was less confident that the knives would support his weight.

"Well, that was fun," Payden said. "Let's see if we can find Watcher."

"Okay."

Staying low, they walked across the roof. Only when they were sure no one could see them, they jumped from roof to roof until they reached a house containing a heavy concentration of men.

"How many are left?" Lucy asked.

"I don't know. Not many, I suppose. Zachary was doing a pretty good job with that bow."

"Showoff," she scoffed. "We certainly have dealt a heavy blow, though."

"Well, I did choose to win." He winked at her.

"So, what's your plan now?"

"We can find a window to climb through and go downstairs to help."

"That might be hard to do."

"Do you trust me?" he asked.

"You've proven trustworthy thus far despite how daft your plans seem," she answered.

"Come on."

They went to the back of the house.

"Hold my feet," he said. He leaned out and looked for a window. Then he pulled himself back up.

"Okay, I'm going to swing you through the window. You go find Malkam and help him. Oh, and here's the last knife."

She took it and placed it in one of the holsters strapped to her thighs.

"And what are you going to do?" she asked.

"You told me that you trusted me."

"Okay. Let's fly."

Driving one sword through the roof to use as an anchor, Payden held one end of her cloak as she crashed through the window. After she was inside, she crept through the place. The building looked like a restaurant with a living area upstairs. She peeked through the doorway that led from the kitchen to an alley. With no one in sight, she felt calmer knowing about this option of escape. She went to the dining part of the restaurant where Malkam, red-faced, sat on the floor, pressed against the door.

"What's this, Malkam?" she asked. "Keeping our guests out when they so obviously want to come in and eat?"

"Find a way to help, girl! I don't need any jokes."

Lucy quickly looked through the cabinets. Malkam released a few grunts as the task of holding the door shut became more arduous.

"We could turn the tide on them," he said loudly.

"How so?"

"They tossed some fire inside these houses. Why don't we send some outside?"

The search didn't take long. She found a container of kerosene in the storage room. Lucy grabbed a bottle of wine and emptied it. Once she had it refilled with kerosene, she ripped the tattered left sleeve off her shirt and stuffed it into the top of the bottle, tipping it to soak the whole piece of fabric. She found a piece of wood that was still burning in the stove and carried her new weapon back to the dining hall.

"Okay, chef, let them in," she said, lighting the fabric. Malkam dove to the side. Once the door opened, she threw the flaming bottle. It burst when it hit the lead man, spraying fiery liquid onto several men behind them. Malkam dropped his shoulder and pushed the men back while they were distracted with putting out the flames. Lucy shut and barred the door when Malkam returned to safety.

"Let's get out of here before they get some more torches to burn this place down," Lucy said. "Follow me."

They left carefully so as not to draw attention to themselves as they wove between buildings. They made their way to the square and had a vantage point to witness all the action. Zachary and Payden were on the ground, finishing off the last men standing.

"I think it's safe enough for us to walk over there," Malkam said. "How's your wound?"

"It's just a scratch, really. I've had worse. It just aggravates me if I twist, you know?"

"I do."

"You injured?" she asked.

"A bit tired actually. Maybe a few scratches here and there. But I'm still going strong. That's what the breastplate is for anyway. I'm not young anymore."

They walked across the square, picking their way through a maze of bodies. Once they reached Payden and Zachary, the fighting was over. Payden was bent over, breathing heavily but grinning broadly.

"Well done, guys," Malkam said.

"We'll be here for weeks burying everyone," Payden said.

"Or we could pile them up and burn them," Lucy suggested.

Malkam shook his head. "I'd prefer to give them the decent burial they're due, but Payden's right. That'll take weeks. There may be more men here in days."

Payden straightened himself. "Did anyone see where the Slave went?"

Malkam jerked his head up to look at him. "When did you see him?"

"Back when I was surrounded. I saw him right as you three began to attack."

Malkam turned about, but the square was vacant.

"Do you think he might have left?" Payden asked.

"Just what's given you that idea?" Malkam asked.

"Hope," Payden answered. "I'm not too worried about him."

"Regardless of that, we should stay cautious." Malkam said. "Let's look for any surviving villagers."

They found a large group of people not far from the village. Many were injured, and all were frightened. When they reached the villagers, everyone looked confused. Malkam understood why. They were expecting a rescue army, not a rescue group of four.

"Where are the others?" someone asked.

"There are none," Malkam answered. "We're it."

"Were the others killed?" another person asked sorrowfully.

"No. We're it," Malkam repeated.

"How can that be?" asked the first questioner.

"We were just too smart for them," Malkam said, smiling at the person, who was an old man with deep brown eyes.

The people spoke with an unfamiliar accent. They weren't Fashites. That was one accent Malkam knew very well. So—were they Ashites? A few Ashite towns were farther up the river, but their people surely wouldn't sound that different from those in the south. Malkam kept his thoughts to himself, allowing the group to murmur among themselves. Malkam noted that the injured didn't seem to be too badly off, but he checked their wounds anyway.

"We can take care of our injuries, sir," said a young woman. "We're quite capable. And we thank you for your help. They would have killed us all."

"You didn't need to tell me that," Malkam said. "Now, can I please have everyone's attention?"

He was amazed at how quickly they complied. Even his own soldiers didn't react as quickly.

"Thank you. I know everyone here has had a hard day, but could you help us carry all the bodies out of the village to an open space? We need to give these men as decent a burial as we can while still being able to leave quickly. There seems to be enough people here that I think we can bury them and be done before nightfall. I don't expect more than fifty men. Would you be willing to help?"

"Of course," the old man said loudly. "It is the decent thing to do."

Chapter 11

As Malkam had predicted, it took until nightfall to gather and bury the bodies in shallow graves. The villagers were exhausted, but they insisted on serving their rescuers a decent meal and offering them beds for the night. A young woman shyly approached Lucy.

"Would you mind some new clothes?" she asked.

Lucy had been busy cleaning her knives, which she had gratefully recovered. She looked down at her tattered apparel. She smiled at the young woman.

"I guess I can't say no, huh?"

The young woman smiled. "My name is Mary. What's yours?"

"Lucy. So, where are these clothes?"

"In my room. Follow me."

She led Lucy to a house on the edge of town that had not been damaged by any of the fires. Once safely behind her bedroom door, she went to a wardrobe. When the poor girl pulled out a skirt, Lucy balked.

"I'm sorry, but I need a pair of pants," Lucy said. "Any of those in there?"

Mary shook her head. "Sorry. Maybe my brother has a pair that'll fit. You seem to be as tall as he is, anyway."

Lucy was much happier with that selection, and she quickly stripped down to change.

Later, they found everyone else gathered in the square. The villagers were burdened with items they were taking with them. They wanted to leave that evening.

The old man, who Malkam guessed was the leader of that village, approached the four.

"Thank you again for your help," he said. "You'll find plenty of food here for your journey, so feel free. We feel that we should go as soon as we can, so we're leaving now."

"Where will you go?" Malkam asked.

"To the city in the mountains," the old man answered. "We'll return there."

"A city?" Lucy asked. "It must be very small."

"Oh, no," the old man said. "There are thousands of people there. But it's hidden from the world. You see, we came here from that city, hoping to regain the lands that had been stolen from us. Alas, we'll return with news that war is still covering the land."

"Wait a minute. Are you saying—" Malkam couldn't finish the sentence. He was too full of disbelief.

"What?" the old man asked.

Payden gasped, finally understanding what Malkam suspected. "Are you part of that group that was destroyed?"

"I suppose we are," the old man answered.

"What's your name?" Payden asked.

He chuckled. "My name is Quinn, my dear boy. It amazes me how youth can fight such battles and still have so much eagerness and energy at the end of the day."

The man turned to walk away. Payden opened his mouth to explain what he really meant to gain by the question, but Malkam stopped him.

"Let him go," Malkam said. "They're tired, and they have a hard trip ahead of them if they're going into the mountains."

"No, but—"

"Good night, Quinn," Malkam called.

Quinn paused and turned. "Oh, Malkam, isn't it?"

"Sure. Or you could call me John if you prefer my first name."

"I've always liked John," Quinn stated. "Come here. I want to share something with you."

Payden watched Malkam leave, and he felt his frustration rise. He just wanted to know the name of that people group. The nurse, Dawn, had been unable to remember their name. He'd been curious ever since she told him about all the groups. He knit his brows in thought. When that man talked, his voice did sound a bit different than everyone else's. That group had to have had a different accent as well. Lucy approached him and pulled at his arm.

"Come on, Joe. Let's go find somewhere to sleep, okay?"

He kicked at the ground, feeling reluctant. "Okay."

Payden managed to sleep well, so deeply that he woke midmorning, surprised to see the sun so high. Groggily blinking his eyes at the light as he exited the building, he managed his way through the village until he found Zachary in the square. He hurried over to him.

"Don't worry," Zachary said, clearly reading Payden's expression. "Malkam and Lucy are gathering up supplies. And we've all bathed. We'll wait for you to eat and wash up, too. You fought so hard yesterday that no one had the heart to wake you. That old man gave Malkam instructions on how to get to the city, so we're probably going to head there now. I'm curious to see it, anyway—that is, if you think it's a good idea."

Payden nodded. Then he remembered the Slave. "But what if we're followed? The Pendtars can't know that there are any survivors. The villagers might be leading that Slave there now!"

"All the more reason for us to go. So hurry up. I'll even take you to the bath house."

"Bath house?"

Zachary led him to an open area where the villagers had directed a small stream to flow through a pool they had dug and lined with sanded planks of wood. They heated the water with the rocks piled next to the pool in fire pits. Once hot enough, the rocks were tossed into the pool. Payden was more than grateful for the heat. When he picked up his clothing to dress, he noticed bloodstains. Gulping as the reality of the previous day's battle settled on him, he quickly found a bar of soap and a small bucket and frantically scrubbed the stains until long after they were clean. He then inspected his body. He saw some nicks and bruises, but no injuries like the ones Lucy had. Payden quickly worked to dry his clothes.

When he finally returned to the square, he was lost in thought. Fresh graves were just outside the village, many of whose occupants he had put there. It caused a deep feeling of guilt. Why did that weigh so heavily upon him? The others didn't seem to be as affected. In fact, Lucy and Zachary were getting pointers from Malkam. Payden shook his head. Maybe he could get some suggestions for dealing with this new feeling.

Swallowing his anxiety, he yelled as jovially as he could, "Where's my food?"

"We ate it!" Zachary yelled. "You were gone so long that we got hungry again."

"Sorry," Payden said.

Malkam tossed him some fruit.

"What took you so long?" Lucy asked.

"My clothes were covered in blood," Payden said as steadily as he could. "I wanted to wash them."

"Well, that's good, I guess. We wouldn't have wanted you to smell like dried blood anyway."

Payden smiled weakly and lifted the fruit for a bite. Before he could sink his teeth in, he froze. His eyes looked past them to the Slave.

"He's still here," he whispered.

The others followed his gaze, and Malkam instantly activated his shield. The Slave walked toward them, confidently and at a steady pace, half his face hidden behind a black scarf.

"Payden, take him out quickly," Lucy said.

"Here," he said as he handed her his breakfast. "I still want to eat that."

He drew his swords as the others, hidden behind the shield, backed away. Payden didn't let the Slave's intense stare deter him. It would be just like the five before, Payden thought. He relaxed, bouncing the swords in his hands so they wouldn't get too sweaty. Yet the Slave didn't draw his sword. The others had as they had neared him. This Slave only moved closer without displaying any intention of unsheathing his blade. Once the Slave was too close for comfort, Payden made the first move. The Slave's sword was out, blocking the blow without Payden even seeing the movement.

"Careful, boy," the Slave whispered. "That could have been a death blow."

Payden pulled back and waited, severely alarmed. The Slave stood patiently.

"What do you want with me?" Payden asked.

"I want to see how well you fight," the Slave answered.

Unease filtered through Payden's system. This Slave was different. Bothered, Payden didn't have the slightest idea what to do.

"Come on," the Slave said. "Fight!"

The Slave attacked, and Payden parried and blocked, striking at any opportunity; with every move, the Slave was there. Payden had grown accustomed to predicting his opponent's actions. That had weakened him for this duel because this Slave was not easy to predict. His blows came from many directions in patterns that surprised Payden, breaking his concentration.

"You'd better fight better than this, because you're almost dead," the Slave taunted.

That meant certain death for the others too. Payden stopped thinking. He stopped analyzing. He'd been focusing so much on how the Slave fought that he'd forgotten to fight his own way.

"I choose to win," Payden growled and went back on the offensive.

Their blades spun and slid through the air, hissing at each other and angrily clashing. The Slave's single blade was almost too much for Payden's two, but Payden ignored the obvious and let his swords wink at the sunlight as they maneuvered.

Payden sped up the attack, but the Slave compensated with acrobatic dodging and spinning, elusively beyond reach.

Malkam collapsed the shield. "We may have to help," he said.

"But Joe's got him," Lucy said.

"No," Malkam said. "The Slave's got him beat. Come on. I'd rather die fighting."

They walked over to the battle, armed and ready. When the Slave saw them approaching, he stared into Payden's eyes. "Don't worry. Your friends are coming to help you," he said.

"To help me bury you."

When the trio got as close as the Slave wanted them to, he switched from the defense he had been playing. In thirty seconds, Payden was disarmed with a sword at his throat. Malkam and the others froze. Payden gulped. He had let himself get too cocky. As he stood there, he thought of what that soldier Smatt had told him. Payden didn't feel humbled or humiliated. He admitted he was afraid because he didn't want to die.

The Slave then sheathed his sword, much to everyone's surprise.

"Well, Payden," he said. "You've kept yourself good enough to survive a battle, but I was expecting excellence by now." The Slave looked at Malkam. "Hey, Malkam. I'm surprised you didn't recognize me. It must have been a long week for you. Come on. It's never good to be seen with me, and we should get to some shelter before it rains."

He turned and headed straight for the mountains without pausing or looking back.

Payden was still frozen in fear. Lucy and Zachary were shocked, but Malkam chuckled.

"He's right," he said. "I should have recognized him. Come on. Let's go."

After Malkam was several meters away, Zachary looked up at the clear skies. "It doesn't look like it's going to rain."

They followed the Slave in silence as he continued his deliberate pace. After several hours of hiking, they passed behind a waterfall to the entrance of a small cave that contained the embers of an old fire.

"Ah, so you stayed here last night?" Malkam asked.

The Slave nodded. "I'm sure you've heard rumors that I do sleep from time to time."

"Well, you're only mortal."

"No," the Slave said. "I am immortal."

Malkam chuckled. "You're going to die just like the rest of us."

"Maybe. I have food if you're hungry."

"I'm actually just thirsty, and since my pouch needs to be refilled, I'll go down and get some water from the stream."

"Why? You don't trust mine?" the Slave asked.

"I know what you put in it, that's all."

Malkam left and the Slave concerned himself with rebuilding the fire. Once Lucy was sure he no longer noticed them, she pulled Zachary and Payden closer to the exit.

"We need to get out of here," she whispered.

"Why?" Payden asked.

"Malkam's working with this Slave," she hissed.

"So?" Payden countered.

"So?" Lucy repeated. "Have you not been almost killed by enough Slaves to forget what they do?"

"This one's different," Payden said. "I mean, we're all still alive, aren't we?"

"You don't understand. Slaves don't think for themselves," Lucy explained. "They do exactly what they're programmed to do. Maybe Malkam's one! And he's working for the Pendtars. If they've been searching for you, well, you're caught now."

"Lucy, you told me to trust my instincts, remember? I'm going to do that. These guys pose no threat."

Knowing she would gain no further ground, Lucy pulled back and paced, gnawing on her nails. The situation troubled Zachary, but he did trust Payden. Fighting his own instincts, he reconsidered his usual responses and relaxed enough to think clearly. Though alarmed, he didn't sense any danger. Since the only experience he had with Slaves was recent, this one did seem different from the others.

When the Slave noticed that their discussion was finished, he stood and studied them.

"So what's the verdict?" he asked. "Are you staying or going?"

Lucy glanced at him, but otherwise ignored him. Zachary decided to push his own limits of hospitality.

"We're staying," he said. "My name's Zachary. She's Lucy. And this is Payden."

"I know Payden," the Slave said. "I'm surprised that he didn't tell you all about me."

Lucy stopped her pacing. "What do you mean?"

The Slave directed his gaze at Payden. "Payden, is there something you need to say that will explain why you haven't the slightest idea who I am?"

Payden swallowed. "Sir, I— Well, I've forgotten everything. My memory's gone. Something put me into a coma, and I woke knowing nothing."

"You're wrong about one thing," the Slave said. "Some*one* put you into a coma. It seems that you have fallen into the hands of the Pendtars once before." He took off his hat to run a hand through his hair. "If only you hadn't run away," he mumbled. He sighed and tossed his hat aside before he sat by the fire.

Lucy approached him, eyeing him suspiciously. "How can they put someone into a coma?"

"The Pendtars know more about herbs and poisons than anyone," the Slave explained. "They have the ability to drug people so they'll sleep, even appear dead to most, for days, weeks, or months, as long as someone is around who will administer the drug periodically. Anyway, they also know how to block people's memories so that when they finally wake, they won't remember anything, and therefore not know that they're in danger. You woke when they wanted you to, and they sent a Slave to retrieve you a few weeks later. What I want to know is how did you escape?"

Payden paled. "You mean they sent a Slave to the hospital?"

The Slave nodded.

"Do you think— I mean, would he have harmed anyone?"

"Like the people I'm guessing helped you get out of there?"

Payden nodded.

The Slave looked away, thoughtfully considering the flames. "I don't like being the bearer of bad news, but I also don't like to give someone false hopes. If that Slave suspected that they helped you—" He left it unsaid.

Payden dropped to his knees, suddenly exhausted. "I would like somewhere to lie down," he mumbled.

The Slave eyed him curiously. "There's plenty of room in this cave, Payden, but what are you running from?"

Payden looked at him, confused. Everyone seemed to know him better than he could even try to understand himself.

"What are you running from?" the Slave repeated softly.

"I don't know," Payden answered.

"That's a safe answer," the Slave said. "But it's still an answer that runs from the truth. Why don't you start talking by rattling off the list of thoughts going through your head?"

"I don't know you," Payden said angrily. "Just because you said you know me doesn't erase the fact that I don't remember you. So don't start ordering me around, expecting me to obey. I may trust Watcher, and he may trust you, but I don't trust you enough yet to do anything you suggest."

The Slave stood. "Get to your feet, boy. Now!" he snapped.

Payden stood, but defiantly held his head up and clenched his fists. The Slave walked to him, glaring, locking eyes with him.

"I know you don't remember me at this moment, Payden, but I do expect the decent boy you are to dictate how you speak to those around you. Your father would have expected more. And I expect more out of you. You've never disappointed me before, and I would hate for you to start now because of sheer stupidity. And yes, I know I may seem like a stranger to you right now, but I was involved in your life long before you were even born, and I have sworn to do whatever I can in order to protect you."

The Slave rolled back the sleeve of his shirt to reveal a few inches of his forearm. Payden gave in to his curiosity and looked, but then almost gasped. Scars from many cuts covered the man's skin. There were even scars on top of scars. Payden wondered where this was going, and he looked up at the Slave's face. Hastily, the Slave covered his arm, and Payden thought he saw tears in the man's eyes.

"No one ever knows what people do for them," the Slave said in a low voice. "Nor why. I just want you to know that these scars will remind you of the life I have lived with the sole intent of keeping you safe."

Payden stared more intently into the man's eyes, wondering if he could discover something that would help him remember him. All Payden could see was an intense look, but he couldn't determine what else was there. He gulped and lowered his head. He had made a mistake with Malkam; should he repeat it with this man?

"Will you answer my question and tell me what you are running from?" the Slave asked.

Payden thought, hoping to give a decent answer. No; a correct answer. But he couldn't grasp anything. There was just a notion. A dream.

"I've had this dream a few times," he said. "And in it, there are so many people, but I don't know any of them. They are all screaming in pain. There's a fire that burns them all."

"And what does this mean to you?"

"I-I think I'm afraid that everyone I meet, everyone I know and love, will be killed because of me. I guess, right now, I just want to run from everyone so that I don't have to lose them—so they can live."

The Slave placed his hand on Payden's head. "I have that same fear," he confessed. "Many whom I have loved and fought so hard to protect have been killed, including your father. But this life is a game with rules that we're never told and must figure out as we go along. The first rule that we learn is that we are never supposed to go through any experience alone. We're born into family and friends. We don't find them or make them up. Everyone you know will die. But each life is empty without the people we are meant to meet. Don't empty people's lives by running. That's a choice of defeat. You lose before you even play the game. Now, there's a good spot to lie down farther back in the cave. There's a lot of dirt, so it's softer. And drier. Go get some rest."

The Slave turned him and shoved him in the right direction. Payden walked slowly, weighted down by his conscience and fears. He remembered something he had forgotten to do, so he turned.

"Oh, by the way, I wanted to ask you something," he said. "What's your name?"

"David," the Slave answered. "My name is David."

Chapter 12

While Payden was sound asleep, the others huddled around the fire for warmth. The rain brought with it a deep chill. Lucy shuddered and pulled her cloak closer around her body. Zachary instinctively wrapped his arm around her, and she naturally leaned close. Her thoughts held her captive. Since earlier, she had not been able to say a word. The part of her that knew so much battled against the part of her that wanted to believe David. *He's a Slave*, her intellect argued. *He's wicked and programmed to do only what is wicked.*

But why hasn't he killed us? Why do I want to believe him? her instincts countered.

Because he's a good liar.

She shook her head and stared at the flames, trying to throw her arguments into them. Burning the thoughts out of her mind would settle her nerves; if she didn't settle them, sleep would never come.

"David," Malkam said. "Do you think you could figure out what drug they used on Payden so we could bring his memories back with an antidote?"

"I don't know," David answered. "There are a couple to choose from. If I give him the wrong antidote, I could cause more harm than good. Since they gave him the drug so long ago, it would be impossible for me to figure it out."

"What do you mean?" Zachary asked.

David shifted so he could look at him. "Some drugs work best when injected at a specific point: say, the neck or straight into a vein. If I know the injection site, I can get a better idea which drug was administered as well as the antidote. The same is true of poisons. By taste, I can identify most of them, but others by where they inject it. Some have to travel through the whole body before they kill, so they're put into an arm or lower leg. That spot heals quickly, so timing is everything. Typically, one only has a few hours."

"You know a lot about the Pendtars," Lucy stated, sitting upright to stare at David.

"Of course. I am a Slave," David said.

"Why?"

Malkam chuckled. "Have fun trying to get him to answer that one, lass."

David shook his head.

Lucy furrowed her brows and looked at Malkam, then David. "What can you tell us?"

David stared intently at her for a few minutes until she shifted with nervousness, though still too stubborn to take her eyes off him.

"Technically, I am a Slave; really, I am not. I don't work for the Pendtars."

"I thought Slaves were killed the first day they defected?" Lucy asked.

"That's because a Slave is programmed with two things before anything else, and those are a desire to kill the Pendtars and an intense hatred for their uniform. Then those commands are hidden. When a Slave wants to think for himself, those programs are activated. The Slave thinks that they're his own, original desires, so he takes off the uniform and heads off to kill the Pendtars. Poor guy gets caught before he knows what's happened."

"Why didn't that happen to you?" Lucy asked.

David leaned back and stared more thoughtfully at her. "When the young men left to become Slaves, they had no expectations. Many Ashites came with the intent of being trained, then leaving to use that training against the Fashites. They didn't come prepared for the programming. Years passed before that was discovered, and no one volunteered after that. I was one of those young fools who entered before we knew."

"That should tell you how old he is," Malkam interjected.

"Yeah, I'm fairly well worn," David said. "But that army you guys took on had a lot more men before you got there. That's why they became scared at the sight of me. That was smart of Payden."

"What did he do?" Zachary asked.

"He pointed me out to the men. Many were eliminated through their fears alone. And I got to those trying to escape, in case you were wondering. So much for the detriments of aging."

Malkam chuckled.

"Where was I?" David mused.

"How you escaped the programming," Zachary said.

"Oh no, I didn't escape it," David said. "They programmed me all right. One day, I thought it was time to leave. I had learned what I thought I needed to learn. Then my next thought was to kill the Pendtars. It sounded like such a good idea, but before I acted upon it, I wondered, where were they? Their castle was huge. What if they weren't in it? And what about the other Slaves more advanced than myself? I knew I was better with the sword than twenty men, but hundreds of Slaves stood between the Pendtars and me. No way would I have made it. As I contemplated, I suddenly remembered my first week of training—which I had completely forgotten. You see, they perfected their programming several years later. Since I was now fully aware of their methods, I was able to consciously fight them. Every man who's been a Slave even half the time I have been is mindless. They have absolutely no knowledge that they can think or act on their own, so completely have they been murdered."

"Do you think the Pendtars suspect you?" Zachary asked.

"Maybe," David answered. "So I still dress as a Slave because they won't look for their own. I can still find out information this way to keep one step ahead of them."

Lucy contemplated the new information. It all seemed plausible. If only it weren't for that gnawing feeling deep in the pit of her stomach. Her eyes found their way to Payden's sleeping frame. If this man was correct, and therefore a part of that young man's life, maybe she could do the unthinkable and trust a Slave, since her little Joe was such a decent person. She shook her head, knowing better. This type of trust would take more time.

Malkam stood and stretched. "I'm going to go for a brisk walk."

David chuckled. "I've secured the area. It's safe to sleep here."

"But I haven't. I'm more thorough."

After Malkam exited, Zachary shuddered. "Why would he go out in this weather?"

"He's military. He has to go and find escape routes, anything out of the ordinary to be suspicious of. Or, more likely, nature's calling and he needs a private spot." David chuckled. "Of course, if he knew I said that—"

Zachary nodded. "Probably should have thought of that." He inhaled deeply and stretched his arms over his head. "Could I ask you a few questions?"

David shrugged. "Can't promise a lot of answers."

"No, I'm just curious about you and Payden. Well, everything. Henry Carpenter is his father, right?"

David nodded, eyes intently locked on Zachary.

"Okay, so, Malkam raised Payden. What did you do? I mean, you know Payden fairly well, right?"

"Yes, I do. Knew his father, too, since I was much younger than you. I worked with Henry in his efforts to bring the Ashite people together. We met the general later. And Malkam is the one who solidified Henry's attempts."

"What do you mean?" Lucy asked, too curious to keep quiet.

David eyed her. "Well, Henry wasn't a fighter. Didn't even try to pretend to act intimidating. But when Malkam joined the efforts, people were more apt to listen. Not that he did anything aggressive. Just his presence encouraged people to pay attention."

"He is a freakishly large man."

"You're a freakishly large man," Lucy quipped.

"Yeah, I know. So I understand what you mean. Makes me like him even more."

"Humph," Lucy snorted and rolled her eyes.

David shook his head. "Don't disrespect that man. He's saved more lives than can be counted. When the Pendtars attacked the Ashites, I think they assumed they would have another easy victory. They didn't count on Malkam. He held them back, knowing what areas to sacrifice and what areas to hold and defend. His efforts have maintained our borders for twenty years now. He's brilliant. Payden will tell you that, when his memory returns. Since Malkam raised Payden, that boy has seen that man at work over the years. Everything Malkam has done, in Payden's eyes, was brilliant."

"Malkam seems so tense around Payden, though," Zachary observed. "Were they close?"

David chuckled and shook his head. "No. Not all the time. Hot and cold, those two were." David's gaze drifted to the back of the cave. Payden was still sound asleep. "I never knew if they were in the middle of a heated battle or finally agreeing on something. Their relationship was strained at best. That's why Payden left."

"Left?" Lucy asked, leaning forward for more information. None would come, as Malkam returned at that moment.

"Man, it's wet out there," Malkam said as he entered. "Wasn't expecting this much downpour."

"Area secure, General?" David asked jovially.

Malkam nodded. "You did a good job. I was satisfied."

"I'm relieved."

Malkam settled in his previous spot next to David, though he preferred to sit on top of the log while David rested against it. Once seated, he finally unclasped his breastplate and set it to the side with his weapons and helmet. "I always forget that I have that thing on until right when it's time for bed."

"It looks a little more dented since the last time I saw you," David said.

"This one's new, actually. The last one you saw broke."

"How?"

Malkam grunted. "I fell off one of our experimental catapults."

David laughed. "Sure. I'll buy that one for your pride's sake."

Knowing that David might not be as forthcoming with information while in Malkam's presence, Lucy decided to drop her curiosity for the time being. "I think I've finally decided to cave in," she said as she stood and stretched, uncovering a yawn.

"Cave in?" Zachary asked.

"Joe's idea. I'm going to go sleep."

"I'll come with you."

They went to the back of the cave, and once settled, David leaned over to Malkam.

"Joe?" he asked, his blue eyes sparkling with amusement.

"Before they knew Payden's real name, they took to calling him Joe. She's never stopped."

"And I noticed that Payden calls you Watcher."

"Well, I did tell him that much."

"Hmm." David gazed into the fire. Time passed, slowly killing the flames. David retrieved more wood to add. While he was up, he checked to see if Lucy and Zachary were asleep. Satisfied that they were, he dropped the fire's new fuel into the pit and quietly asked, "How much have you told Payden?"

"Not anything much, just about what happened to his family."

David returned to his former position, leaning against the log, waiting until he was settled before he continued the conversation. "So, when was your last drink?"

Malkam spit into the flames yet remained silent.

"That long ago, huh?"

"You keep your secrets; I'll keep mine."

David knew the shame Malkam felt about his great weakness. Malkam described it as his 'Curse of the Thirst.' Many times over the years, Malkam would spend long periods of time drunk every evening. Then he'd come to his senses and forgo the habit for a few years. Eventually, he'd fall back into his old routine. David crossed his arms and decided to give his friend some good news. "He doesn't need an antidote for his memories to return, just to let you know. It'll take some time, but they gradually come back."

"That's good to know."

"I just wanted to warn you, in case some memories come back before others."

Malkam raised his arms to place his elbows on his knees. His gaze continued to remain on the growing flames as he leaned forward. "I yelled at him."

"Oh?"

"After the past five years of wondering if that stupid kid was even alive, the first opportunity I had to speak to him—" Malkam shifted his weight and looked at the dirt. "I saw him in the Arena, going through the qualifications. And I became angry. What was he doing? Instead of just walking up to him and welcoming him, I assumed he was playing some game on me, so I let him continue. And when he beat my soldier—"

"Which one?"

"Smatt," Malkam answered.

David released a soft laugh. "That didn't help his ego."

"Smatt took it well. I didn't. I entered my office and yelled at that kid. As if no time had passed. Just picked up right where we left off."

David rested his head against the log and shut his eyes. "You two always made up before—"

"I hit him, David. I smacked him across the face, and he left. That I didn't tell you. That's what I'm afraid he'll remember first."

David opened his eyes briefly before closing them again. Then he chuckled. "Don't feel so guilty, old friend. Payden wouldn't hold it against you, even if it is all he remembers about you. He had too much respect for you. He was probably just being stupid."

"No. Both of us were being stupid," Malkam admitted. "I think I've finally decided to apologize when he remembers everything."

"Finally?"

Malkam shook his head. "Don't even start. You know how hard his leaving has been on me."

"Will you actually tell him that?"

Malkam shrugged and picked up a thin splinter of wood to pick his teeth. "Maybe."

"You both are just too stubborn." David chuckled. "Payden got something from you after all."

Malkam laughed softly. "I swear sometimes you're Henry's ghost."

"Don't compare me to him," David mumbled. "He was a much better man." He sat up and reached for his hat. "Now if you'll excuse me, I'm going to go."

"Where?"

"I was up here for a reason, and I need to go take care of that."

"Why don't you travel with us for a while?" Malkam asked. "You haven't seen Payden in five years, either. Despite his memory loss, you know he'll want to talk with you."

"I don't know," David said, shifting uncomfortably. "I've never been able to understand that."

"What?"

"Why he prefers me."

Malkam chuckled. "I don't think anyone could. Just a few more days, David. It won't kill you, you know. Besides, we're heading up into the mountains. You won't believe who we just saved today."

"What do you mean?" David asked. "Wasn't that an Ashite village?"

"Nope. Djorites."

David sat upright, staring at Malkam in disbelief. Then he looked at the ground, swallowing deeply. When he realized he was holding his breath, he released it slowly.

"Wow. Wow."

"Mmm-hmm." Malkam crossed his arms and stared at the fire. "They're still alive."

"So where did they go?"

"There's a city in the mountains. One of them gave me directions. We're heading there tomorrow."

David slowly nodded his head. "I guess I could stick around for a few more days."

As silence fell between them, the ramblings of the small waterfall filled the void. The steady drumming relaxed Malkam enough to allow his thoughts to succumb to the idea of sleep. He crept to an empty spot near the others.

David remained awake. His mind rarely slowed its race, thus caging peaceful slumber. This night, it wandered through his dark forest of memories, the ones he wanted to forget yet never could. Djorites. Alive. He couldn't regain the memory, but something stirred deep within. He feared he would regret the discovery.

Chapter 13

Before sunrise, everyone was up and walking. David fell to the end of the line as they hiked single file through most of the trek. Malkam led, with Lucy and Zachary remaining close to him since they hadn't yet fully given their trust to David. Payden realized an inclination inside him drew him closer to David. He felt more comfortable now that David was around, less stressed and worried, even. When the hike became easier, Payden worked his way beside David, trying not to stare up at him, yet unable to help it.

"What do you want?" David asked.

"Oh, nothing," Payden answered, ducking his head to keep his eyes on the path.

"Really?" David asked skeptically. Payden quickly noted his tone.

"Sorry," Payden mumbled. "I just wanted to walk by you."

He looked up at David, whose eyes were narrowed.

"Why?"

Payden shrugged. "How am I supposed to know?"

David looked ahead, concentrating on the land. It was growing steeper, with fewer trees and more loose rocks, a terrain that increased his vigilance about keeping everyone safe from falling.

Payden pulled at his shirt and messed with the zipper on his vest, trying to figure out the best way to strike up a conversation with David. He had no ideas, just desire to know his past. Where did David fit into it?

By late afternoon, they stood on a ledge that overlooked the city.

"It's beautiful," Lucy breathed.

The city sat comfortably in the valley, encircled by a thick covering of trees: a barrier between it and the tall mountain peaks. A whitewashed stone wall restricted those leaving or entering the city to a single gate. White buildings with green roofs were set near the walls, facing an open square in the middle. A hint of color suggested numerous flower gardens.

"Even in my dreams, I never thought a place like this could exist," Lucy said.

"It'll look better up close," David said. "Come on. We still have a long way to go."

"At least it's downhill," Zachary quipped.

Halfway down the steep slope, they entered the forest. There, David felt the presence of eyes upon them, but nothing betrayed the positions of the watchers. When they neared the gate, a group of men met them. They were dressed in dark-brown pants and tan shirts and bore short sabers in their hands. Before exchanging any words, David quickly removed the belt that held his sword and tossed it to the ground. Malkam had also begun to do the same. Lucy and Zachary were more reluctant, and Payden had trouble removing his harness as neatly.

Once they were all disarmed, they stood silently. A man in more formal attire—black pants with a buttoned shirt under a light-purple vest—approached them from behind the guards. After glancing down at the weapons, he studied each of their faces. His eyes rested lastly upon David's, whose face was half-covered by a black scarf. After considering him for a moment, the man spoke, "My people have had dealings with your kind many times. Slaves, aren't they?"

David nodded once, not taking his eyes off the examiner.

"How did you expect us to react to you?"

"I expect nothing," David said. "I would gladly enter bound and go straight to a holding cell for the duration of our stay if you would prefer."

"We have no holding cells and no need for any," the man explained. "I simply ask that you uncover yourself."

"I cannot do that."

"Why?"

"For present company's sake, I decline to answer that as well."

Payden knit his brows and turned to look at David, who cast him only the briefest of glances. Just as Payden suspected, he was the cause of David's silence.

"If you would prefer I leave so that you can enter the city without being tied up, I will," Payden offered. David actually seemed surprised as he looked down at Payden, causing Payden to marvel. He thought he saw the faintest hint of tears again.

The man took his attention from David and thoughtfully studied Payden.

"You may stay long as you need," he finally said. "Follow me." His eyes returned to David for a brief moment before he turned to lead them to the gate.

Payden quickly retrieved David's sword and held it up for him. David took it from Payden, ruffling his hair.

"Thanks."

Payden then gathered Malkam's numerous items.

"Thank you, Payden," Malkam said.

They followed the guards past the gate. The city was indeed more beautiful than the first view had promised. Zachary actually had to watch over Lucy, as her eyes never left the simplicity that surrounded them. Flowered vines crawled up white walls, and tall trees provided shade to nearby buildings.

"I want to live here," she whispered to Zachary.

"And the kids at Tawney City?"

"They can live here too."

The man led them to a large estate at the northeast end of the city. Numerous windows covered the face of the building that stood taller than the rest. It too was white with a set of wide marble steps leading to the entryway. A young woman with brown hair and wearing a dark-blue dress ran out of the front door to greet the man. When she reached his side, he dismissed the guards.

"We welcome you to stay at this estate," he said. "We were informed there would be some visitors. So I thank you for the service you provided in saving my people. My name is Samuel. This is my daughter Jordan. Please, would you do me the honor of introducing yourselves?"

David stepped forward. "My name is David. This is John Malkam, general of the Ashite army."

"Former general," Malkam inserted.

"Oh, really?" David asked, turning toward Malkam.

"Happened over a week ago."

"I see," David said. Then he continued the introductions. "That tall man is Zachary. The beauty to his right is Lucy. And last of all is Payden."

"Or you could call him Joe," Lucy quipped, winking at Payden, who blushed. His attention had been focused on Jordan, and she smiled sweetly at him, which only generated a deeper reddening of Payden's ears. He bowed his head to hide his embarrassment, but he heard Jordan giggle, and he wanted to disappear.

"Come. We were preparing for our evening meal," Samuel said. "After we eat, we can take you to your rooms."

Samuel led them up the wide steps through the double entrance doors. Marble pillars held up a portico that cast a shadow on the doorway. Inside, the group followed the hallway to the right, through a towering archway that opened into a generously spacious room furnished with a long, wide table surrounded by purple cushioned chairs. Several servants were there, curious about their guests. A woman approached the servants, who immediately ducked through an archway to a separate room in the back. Payden heard some orders shouted, hissing sounds, and clanging of metal and glass. He guessed it was the kitchen, though he wasn't close enough yet to know for sure.

During dinner, Payden ate as much as he dared, but only when he was certain Jordan wouldn't see him. They all sat at the rectangular table that stretched the length of the room. It looked like it could seat at least fifty people, maybe more. Jordan sat near the far end by her father. Throughout the meal, Payden stared at her secretly, hoping no one noticed. Every so often, he'd glance at David or Lucy, hoping they wouldn't catch his discomfort. However, Lucy was seated halfway down the table and seemed to be engaged in a lively debate with other guests—over what, Payden wasn't close enough to discover, but her red face betrayed a heated discussion. When Payden glanced across the table at David, he had no way of reading his thoughts. He didn't appear to be eating, so what could he be doing? Payden couldn't tell if David was observing him or not.

Deciding not to be frustrated, he looked back down the long table at Jordan. She was staring at him. He blushed and quickly focused on the food on his plate. Goodness, she was really pretty, he thought. He had noticed her features earlier when she had first come outside to greet her father. She had light-brown eyes but dark-brown hair. Her freckles made her look young, but the way she carried herself made her seem older. Her heart-shaped face that carried an easy smile caused his heart to race and palms to sweat.

He really wanted to talk to her, but how could he? He could talk of nothing but death and wickedness. She was too pure to taint with such information. His hands drew his attention. Swallowing hard, he rubbed them feverishly against his pants. Surely she could see the blood staining them. He would avoid her, he decided, lest he taint her purity.

"Excuse me," someone said, pulling him from his thoughts. He turned toward the speaker and paled to see Jordan addressing him. She stood behind his chair with her hands clasped in front of her. Payden hadn't seen her approach.

"Yes?" he struggled to say, gulping at the effort.

"You're Payden, right?"

He nodded, afraid to make a sound and risk betraying himself.

"I'm Jordan. It's a pleasure to meet you."

She extended her hand. He stared at it, painfully aware of her clean, white skin. He rubbed his hands even more frantically down his pants.

"It would help conclude the introduction if you would take my hand and shake it a bit," she said lightly, unsure what he was thinking.

"Yes, sorry," he muttered. He finally shook her hand briefly, then quickly put his own back under the table.

"Why are you so nervous?" she asked. "Is the food not good?"

"No, no, the food is delicious," he answered quickly. *Please go*, he begged silently, remembering the smoothness of her skin in his hand.

"Oh," she said. "Then is it me?"

He had tried to swallow a gasp, which only caused him to choke and cough. Water helped quell the storm, but when she giggled, he turned red with much more embarrassment.

"If you're feeling all right, I would like to escort you to your room. My father asked me to."

"Oh, uh, well, sure," he stammered. "Now?"

"Or later. I've just finished eating, that's all."

"Oh. Um, I'm not hungry anymore, so now would be fine. Where should I take my plate?"

"Leave it. The servants on duty today will take care of everything. Let's go, friend."

She smiled broadly. He weakly returned the gesture and stood. Thinking he would just follow her, he was surprised when she looped her arm around his.

"Come with me," she said.

Payden felt trapped and did his best to hide his alarm, but his face betrayed an emotional battle. David, grateful at present his smile was hidden behind his black scarf, watched the two as they left. Payden was of age, David knew, and even the greatest warriors became the least when faced with a woman. That Jordan was an exceptional beauty was evident. Her nobility generated the gravity that had clearly captured Payden. David returned his attention to the table. The young couple had left completely unnoticed. *Young couple*, David mused. If Jordan could see Payden the way he obviously saw her, perhaps they could be a couple. Payden would be safe in this hidden city.

David let his thoughts wander. Since Henry's death, David had tried to determine where Payden would be safest. In the heart of Landar was a given, but Payden proved to have the wanderlust his father had possessed. If Payden had a reason to stay in one place . . . David leaned back to change his thoughts. He did not dare to hope too much too soon.

Jordan led Payden down a long hallway to a grand staircase in the center of the estate, across from the entrance. It curved up to the next level. She took him up the stairs to a room across the hall.

"Does your father own all this?" Payden asked after finally conjuring up enough courage. Her voice was soft with the subtle lilt of the Djorite accent, which made him wish she'd never stop speaking.

"Oh, no, our people do."

"Okay, but, um, I mean, is this your house?" Payden hoped he wouldn't offend her.

She giggled. "No. My house is nearby. This place is for whoever wants to stay here. Everyone serves each other, and we all built this manor as a retreat. We never have guests, really, but many years ago, before the war began, every city had a place for guests to reside during their stay. Those guests were primarily Jathenites. I think you are the first Ashites ever to visit us. Welcome."

"Um, I have money if you need us to pay."

She knit her brows and tilted her head, clearly confused. "Pay?"

"Yeah, don't you guys— I mean, uh, at Landar, when we stayed at the inn, we had to give money to the owner or he wouldn't have let us stay there. We had to pay him."

She shook her head. "You don't have to pay us. We don't mind serving."

"I don't understand."

Smiling, she explained, "My father was elected to be the leader, or judge, of our people. He hears their complaints and helps settle disputes. He does that because he wants to do it. In this building, each week, different people are assigned to serve. We take turns, I should say. I suppose it's difficult to understand if you've never lived like us before—where you have to pay in order to be helped. I apologize if you are still confused."

"No, I think I understand."

"Thank you for being polite anyway. Let's enter your room."

The large door rose about a meter over Payden's head, and he looked up to stare at it. The wood was thick and solid, and his gaze traced the patterns of mountains, rivers, and wildlife carved cunningly upon it. When Jordan effortlessly pushed it open, he marveled that it was not heavy. The door quickly lost his attention to the interior. The bedroom was hardly that. It was larger than anything he would have considered a bedroom to be. Remembering Patrick's house, Payden compared the two, realizing that this room seemed to be the same size as the house.

White walls were backdrops to an array of colorful paintings perched in intricately carved frames. The paintings were of peoples and places, and Payden wondered if, when his memory returned, he would recognize any. Next to the doorway stood a small, though tall, round table with two taller chairs to match. The lip was decorated with raised engravings of vines with what looked like bunches of berries on them.

A large window on the far side of the room let in the light of the setting sun. Thick, dark-green curtains curved around the frame, drawn back to introduce light into the room. The sunset alone drew his attention, and he quickly crossed the room to watch it, mesmerized at its beauty from this vantage point. Lost for a moment, he finally came to himself and turned to find a desk neatly tucked against the wall. It was a darker wood with no special decorations, but Payden could only continue to gape at the workmanship, especially that of the bench, which had a padded top the same color as the drapes.

Lastly, though he was surprised he hadn't already noticed it, Payden saw the bed. It sat neatly in the middle of the room, with its tall headboard pressed against the wall. Large poles grew from the four corners up toward the high ceiling. A white, delicate fabric draped from pole to pole, tumbling down around the headboard. The vibrant blue of the blanket made the bed look like the sea. How could anyone make such things? He carefully pushed on the mattress. It was soft. The pillows were large and numerous. His hand absently stroked the nearest one as he took in the size of the bed. He, Lucy, and Zachary could easily fit on it, he observed, with room to spare.

"It's beautiful," he whispered. Other items he wasn't surprised to have missed came into view. A small table beside the bed held a vase of fresh flowers. A cushioned couch stood against the wall right beside the door. As his eyes moved to the left of the door, he saw a large wardrobe made of the same dark wood as the desk. Just beyond, a smaller room abutted this one. He crossed over to it and opened the door. Inside were a large tub and a basin. Of course each room had its own washroom.

"It's large," he said, turning as he remembered his company, also hoping he hadn't appeared a gawking idiot.

"Yeah," she said and pulled herself up onto the bed to sit. "The designers wanted the rooms in this place to be like this. Large and beautiful. It was just how things used to be. I have never seen the old cities. They're all destroyed now, as if we had never existed. A few of the people who first came here still remembered who we were and wanted to keep our ways the same. No one wants to forget who they are."

Payden lowered his eyes and nodded solemnly. He understood that.

"Well," she said jauntily, hopping off the bed. "Hurry and change so I can take your clothing down to the laundress."

Payden stared at her for a brief moment of shock. "Uh, wait—what?"

"Don't you have a change of clothing?"

"No. All I possess is what you see on me."

"Oh. Not a problem!" She crossed the room to the wardrobe, quickly pulling it open to reveal a variety of clothes. From it, she procured a linen shirt and cotton pants, both white.

"Here," she said. "And I would give you some undergarments, but I know that I would blush. They're in the drawers you see in the wardrobe. I'll step outside. Let me know when you've changed."

She handed him the clothing and quickly headed to the hallway, pulling the door closed behind her. Once it was shut, Payden stared at the fabric in his hands. He opened the drawer full of undergarments, finding one his size before changing. The lighter clothing felt better against his skin, but as he rubbed the fabric between his fingers, he remembered his bloody hands. He wondered if he should ask her about taking a bath.

He opened the door with ease and peeked out to see where she was. He noticed a large blue vase filled with purple blossoms by the stairway. Jordan was beside it, arranging the flowers, patiently smelling each one. He held his breath as he watched. With each graceful movement she made, he became more enamored by her very essence. How could any person be so beautiful? When she looked his way, he quickly shut the door, hoping she hadn't seen him. A knock soon after confirmed that she had, and the embarrassment of being caught overwhelmed him. With a heavy sigh, he pulled it open.

"You look good," she said as she entered, heading for his pile of clothes. Once she had gathered them into her arms, she turned to him and offered, "I can send someone up to prepare a bath for you if you'd like."

"Sure. Thanks," he said, holding his hands behind him.

She eyed him curiously, amused as he fumbled to avoid any eye contact. He was desperately cute, and his shyness only caused her to like him more. Most other boys her age approached her boldly, knowing that they would be a good match. She knew that too, but a part of her wanted someone different, someone she could trust with all her heart to protect her and cherish her. Those other boys might, but they didn't have the look in their eyes that she saw in Payden's. She greatly liked that look.

"Is there anything more I could do for you?" she asked.

He shook his head and swallowed nervously.

"Okay. I'll see you in the morning. Your clothes will be dry by then, so I'll bring them up before breakfast."

As she walked past, Payden realized that she had the pouch that held the book. He had forgotten to set it aside. Before he thought about what he was doing, he cried, "Wait!"

He snatched it from her arms, pulling the rest of his clothing free with it. As it all hit the ground, he quickly knelt down to gather the articles together, careful to hide his undergarments from her eyes.

"Sorry," he mumbled.

She knelt in front of him and placed her hand over his so he would stop moving.

"It's okay," she said softly.

He dared to look up at her. When his eyes met hers, he quickly looked away. Grabbing the pouch in one hand and the clothes in another, he stood, holding the clothing out to her.

"Here," he said. "Sorry for being so clumsy."

"Why won't you look at me?" she asked as she took the clothing.

"What?" Using all his strength, he looked her in the eyes.

"Oh, so now you can? But only because I pointed it out."

His strength faltered, and he looked down at his bare feet.

"What is that anyway?" she asked, pointing to the pouch.

"Nothing." He pulled it behind his back.

"Why are you hiding it if it's nothing?"

"Because I— It's just— Can you keep a secret?"

"We don't keep secrets here."

He scratched his head, wanting desperately to tell someone. His eyes found hers again, and he stared intently. "Fine. I'll tell you. It's a book."

"A book?"

He nodded.

"Is that all? We have dozens of books in this city."

"You do?" he asked.

"Sure. But I don't understand why it has to be a secret."

"Because there are no books anywhere else. They've been destroyed. In fact, if I were caught with this one, I could be killed."

She dropped the clothes. Her eyes threatened to tear up, which upset Payden. He shouldn't have said anything.

"Don't cry, please," he begged.

"Is it really so bad out there?" she asked. "So bad you could be killed over a book?"

He nodded, resisting the urge to hold her. Why did he feel such a desire to protect her?

She gathered up his clothing and headed for the door. "I'll send someone up soon for the bath," she said dully.

"Wait, don't go, please. I'm sorry. I shouldn't have said anything."

"I'm glad you did. I've heard rumors. I've known, but you never understand until reality is right in front of you."

"I didn't mean—"

"Shh." She placed her hand over his mouth. "Thank you." She quickly left.

He shut the door and placed his hand to his lips, drawing it back to stare at it as if expecting it to change because of her touch. He looked at the pouch and went over to the bed, finally pulling out the book to inspect it. He fell onto his stomach and opened it. The pages were filled with neat lines of letters, but they held no meaning for Payden. Dawn had said that she suspected he could read, but as he flipped through more and more pages, he discovered, to his great dismay, that he couldn't.

Before Jordan deposited Payden's clothing with the laundresses, her curiosity lured her back to the dining hall. The rest of the guests were still at the table. She paused in the doorway to view the scene. The oldest of the group claimed to be a soldier. He sat near her father. During the meal, he had seemed nice. Her attention had been elsewhere, though.

The next man she looked at was the man who had sat across from Payden. The black clothing he wore clearly informed anyone what kind of man he was. She shuddered. Why would her father allow such a man into their city? When the Slave turned his eyes toward her, she backed out of the room and pressed herself against the wall of the hallway.

"Spying?"

"Huh?" She turned to the doorway, where an older woman stood.

"I saw you. Don't deny it."

Jordan hung her head. "Sorry, Salina," she said. "I'm just curious."

"Aren't we all?" Salina glanced back at the table before she crossed the threshold and stood next to Jordan.

"The war is still raging out there," Jordan said softly.

"So I figured."

"The young man—the one I just took to his room—"

"Payden."

"Mm-hm. He said that the punishment for even possessing a book could be—death."

Salina took a deep breath and placed an arm across Jordan's shoulders. "The things we take for granted, hm?"

Jordan remained silent. So many thoughts raced through her head. Salina would know all of them, of course. She always did. For many children in this valley, Salina had become the only mother they'd ever known. Jordan lifted her eyes to Salina's. "I suppose I should go somewhere I'm not intruding."

"I suppose. Or you could do what you really want to do."

Jordan knit her brows, ever suspect of Salina's intuitive guesses. "And that would be?"

"Go back upstairs and continue talking with that young man."

Jordan inhaled sharply, blushing as she averted her eyes. Salina laughed softly. "He likes you, too."

"Surely not," Jordan denied quickly. "We've just met. We're too young, and Father would never . . ."

"Yes, thank you for showing me how much you listen to your father. But why don't you go find out what your mother would say? I think you'll find that everything's going to be okay."

Jordan pulled at the long sleeves of her dress. "I haven't read her journal in a long while."

"I thought so. Go on. It's late anyway."

Jordan nodded and headed toward the exit. Then she remembered the garments she carried. "Oh! And, Salina?"

"Yes?"

"Uh, these need to go to the laundresses. And also, Payden requested some water so he could—bathe." She averted her eyes, a bit embarrassed to think about that request.

"Go to bed. I'll take care of it."

"Thank you. Good night."

"Good night." Salina smiled warmly and watched until Jordan left the estate. She stepped back into the dining hall and contemplated their guests. Quinn and the others had left this city about five years ago. Over the years, many in the valley had grown tired of hiding. Her smile fell. However, it seemed the timing was premature.

At the table, the other guests began to rise as Samuel asked several of the servants to escort them to their rooms. Salina had assigned one servant to each member of the party the moment the guests entered the estate. It was her job, among other responsibilities.

Before they reached her position in the doorway, she turned and walked down the long hallway. She passed many large rooms before the hallway curved at the end, becoming a short corridor with smaller rooms on either side. At the end of that corridor, to the right, was a door that opened to a small servants' stairwell. Down these steps was an open floor plan where much of the building's work took place. The food was cleaned here before going up to the kitchen. Laundry was washed and bath water warmed.

Among the many wonders this valley held, the most beneficial was the abundance of aquifers that bubbled just beneath the surface. If one dug deep enough around these mountains, one always found a pool of water. She crossed over to one they had discovered when digging the foundation of this estate. Its water level never lessened, and they didn't dip into the contents too often. The candlelight winked off the water's surface, rippling light rays about the room and across the ceiling. The simple beauty enthralled her.

"What brings you here, Salina? I don't often see you down here," an older gentleman inquired.

"Oh, well, you know me, Ralf. I abhor you," she teased.

The man smirked. "As I you."

"One of our guests requested a bath, and I suspect the others might want one as well. Can I count on you, Ralf?"

Ralf gave a slight bow of his head as a reply.

"Well done." She patted his arm as she passed to the exit. It felt nice to be in the cool underbelly of the large building, as much of her time did pass in the heat of the kitchen. Ralf was in charge of the workers and their various duties down below. Solomon, the head chef, was in charge of what was prepared in the kitchen. Salina managed everything else. In all the years since their arrival in this valley, and in the years since the last detail was finished on this estate, they'd never had any guests to validate the necessity of it. She knew that Ralf and Solomon must feel as she felt at that moment: vindication, for those three had fought so hard to convince everyone to erect the large building. As her feet climbed the steps, returning her to the warmer main level, she beamed even more.

Jordan stood in her bedroom and stared at the small desk by the bedroom door. A few books sat on the shelf above it. Only one of them terrified her.

When her mother discovered she was pregnant, she had begun a journal. The journal ended the day Jordan was born. Her mother was not able to write any more.

As Jordan stood there, eyes transfixed on the book containing the last thoughts of her mother's life, she could barely breathe. When she discovered the book as a child, hidden in the lowest corner of her father's study, she had craved reading every word. Halfway through the reading, though, she had stopped and could read no further.

Salina was the only other person who knew she possessed the journal. Salina was the only person who spoke of her mother. Torah. Jordan had always liked that name. Samuel and Torah Herder.

Hesitantly, she lifted her hand to the shelf, and her fingers gingerly clasped the leather cover. Carefully, breathing deeply, she pulled the book down and cradled it in her arms. It had been a long time.

She sank onto the side of her bed and reverently opened the book. Inside were her mother's secrets, the outpourings of her heart to a child she knew she would never meet. Jordan had dared over the years to read small parts in the latter half, but they didn't make much sense. They scared her. Sadness caused her to pause.

The only thing she knew about her mother—the only definitive thing—was her slip at the end, when reality disappeared. The book contained not just the beauty and poetry of her mother's soul, but the evidence of a mind becoming crippled. Many Djorites seemed to go that way at the end, the stories went. After facing so much loss, many just couldn't cope.

Jordan shook her head and laid the book flat on her lap. Salina knew her mother, and would not have advised Jordan to read this journal if she felt its contents were inappropriate. So Jordan opened the book to a page near the middle and read.

> My dearest little one,
>
> I hope when you are able to see these words that I am there beside you. As I write, though, a chill grips my heart. I have long felt that we wouldn't meet. That is beginning to feel more of a certainty. The doctors do not want me to leave my bed. My head aches with fevers, but I do not want to waste my time talking about that. I want to leave you with my hopes. I hope that you will not live in the fear that engulfs this place. It is plain on so many faces. They are like the dead, walking. That scares me more than

> anything else one could fear. That you would move and breathe, but not be alive.
>
> Know that I have lived! When the trees move, I do not hide, thinking someone is there. I feel the wind. I see the animals. Everyone else sees the ghosts of our enemy. My darling, please do not feel the fear! It's not who we are. It's not who we've ever been. We Djorites have always lived! Now I see how we have changed. Read these words, and think of us dancing! Oh, how we danced. And sang. And were not afraid to shout with joy when two were married or when a child was born. Music rang throughout the day and night. The world knew we lived! Now the world believes us dead. The few who wish to retain our essence—I hope you know them. Live with them. They are the best of us.
>
> Please, please, my precious child—*do not be afraid.*

Jordan paused. This was the moment in her mother's journal where the tone changed. She no longer implored her unborn child to act upon her wisdom. The rest of the writing seemed desperate— as if Torah needed the reader know things that didn't make sense to anyone but Jordan's mother. On the page, the lines of ink blurred in one spot. One perfectly round spot. The paper rippled slightly there, and Jordan's fingers touched the small circle. The evidence of her mother's tear. Jordan shut the book and hugged it against her chest.

She inhaled deeply. *Do not be afraid.* Salina was right. Her mother would certainly have encouraged her to follow her heart.

Jordan stood and reverently set the journal on the desk. In spite of what she knew her father would say, Jordan decided to visit Payden tomorrow. That decision felt right. Jordan giggled. That decision made her feel—alive.

Payden paced about the room, waiting for a knock at the door. He didn't know what else to do. He'd prefer to leave and explore this building a bit, but if they were going to bring up some bath water, he should at least remain in the room and wait. Of course, that was if that was how things were done here. Or did he need to go somewhere to fetch the water himself? An inspection of the washroom had revealed no faucets or spigots, leaving him to assume the water had to be brought to the room. That was a lot of work, he pondered as he continued strolling about, absentmindedly touching the soft covers of the bed or the cool wood of the desk and wardrobe.

Finally, someone knocked at his door, and Payden hurried to open it, grateful that someone had finally come. It wasn't who he expected.

"Hello," David said. "May I come in?"

"Uh, sure," Payden said, stepping aside.

"Thank you." David strode in and surveyed the room. "Your room is different from mine."

"Is that bad?"

"No. It's just an observation."

He walked over to the bed. At that moment, Payden realized he had left the book there. David picked it up.

"What's this?" he asked, holding it up for Payden to see.

Payden opened his mouth, but no answer came.

"Why aren't you answering?"

"Because I—um," Payden stammered.

"Someone told you that you would now be in trouble?"

Payden gulped as David reached inside his cloak. Instead of a weapon, he pulled out a book. Payden remained speechless.

"Don't worry," David said. "I have one too."

Payden let out a deep sigh of relief before rushing to David's side, overwhelmed by excitement. "It was the doctor's at the hospital. But the nurse, Dawn, gave it to me before I left. I haven't really had an opportunity to read it until now. See, I promised Dawn not to tell anyone about it, but Jordan saw it and said that they have books here. Would you read some of it to me? I don't think I can read."

David chuckled. "You need to calm down, first of all. Second, you can read. I taught you how. We just need to work on getting you to remember, that's all. And third, of course there are books here. This is where they all come from."

"Really?" Payden took his book back from David.

"Yes. These people are the Djorites. For hundreds of years, they've kept the old books alive, carefully copying them and circulating them around the planet. They are most known for this book," David said as he held up his. "I suspect yours is the same one."

David sat on the edge of the bed and flipped though his copy.

"Why this one?" Payden asked.

"It's unique. Other books tell full stories following the same people from beginning to end. They are fun to read, but no one really wants to read them over and over again. This book, however, doesn't even have a title. It's just called the Book. And it's full of stories that begin and end, but then they are referenced to later. This book also teaches a lot of things that, though I've read it dozens of times over the years, I still don't understand. So I keep reading it, and each time I discover something new. I learn more."

"So, does it matter where we start?" Payden asked, flipping it open.

"Not entirely. Let's read my favorite part first. I don't think it will take long for you to regain your reading abilities."

Before they could begin, another knock disrupted them. The servants had arrived to prepare the bath. Payden watched with great sorrow as David hid himself from view, stepping out unnoticed by the servants once they had cleared the doorway.

"Thank you so much," Payden said, choking down the disappointment.

A bath would feel wonderful, he knew, but relearning how to read would have been more satisfying. After the servants left, Payden remembered Jordan's promise to return before breakfast. His heart palpitated quickly at the memory of her soft smile. He could ask her to help him read.

After he tore off his clothes and climbed into the tub, he noticed his hands again. No. He had to stick to his original plan of avoiding her. *"What are you running from?"* David's voice echoed through his head. Payden bowed his head. Fine, he thought, grabbing the bar of soap. Tomorrow, he would ask her.

Chapter 14

The knocking at the door was so soft that Payden almost didn't hear it. For more than an hour he had been up, awaiting Jordan's return. He passed the time the only way he knew how—with his swords. When the knock came, he at first thought he was imagining the sound. He opened the door to check but did not expect to see anyone. Jordan was there, holding his freshly laundered clothes.

"Good morning," she said.

He quickly hid the weapons behind his back. "Hi," he said.

"What are you hiding from me today?" she asked as she entered, placing the clothing on his bed. "Did you sleep on the bed?"

"Yes," he answered, shutting the door.

"Oh, and you even slept under the covers?"

"Yes. Why?"

"I've never seen anyone make their bed the exact same way we do," she admitted. "It looks exactly as it should."

"Only Djorites would have stayed here, right? Why are you surprised if—"

"Oh, well, see, in our homes, people make their beds however they may," Jordan explained. "But here in this building, beds are made in a specific way. I'm sorry, but this is exactly right. Not even all the Djorites know the correct way. Forgive me."

Payden shrugged. "Maybe I just had a good memory of what it looked like yesterday."

"Perhaps. But you need to answer my first question."

He bowed his head and reluctantly revealed his swords.

"Why are you so ashamed?" she asked. He looked up to meet her eyes.

"I like you," he said, shocked at his own forthrightness. "That scares me a little because you live in a world that's so clean and mine is so very dirty."

For the first time since they met, she appeared to be shy. She even blushed as she said, "I like you too, Payden."

He clenched his fists with excitement, which caused him to remember his swords. Quickly, he hid them in their sheath.

"Let's sit," he suggested. He sat on the couch, and she gracefully joined him.

"Our world is not that clean, you know," she said pointedly. "We have to constantly run patrols and keep guards in the forest to warn us so we can flee again if anyone comes looking to destroy us. A part of each of us lives in fear of the large army that may one day come."

"Yes, but have you ever killed anyone?"

The question leveled her, and she looked at him, unable to hide her startled expression. He was just sitting, staring at his hands. How could someone so young be capable of killing anyone, she wondered.

"How old are you?" she asked.

"I'm not sure. Apparently I look fifteen or sixteen, but I haven't thought to ask Malkam or David for sure yet."

"Why don't you know?"

"Someone stole my memories," he answered heavily. "All I know about myself is what I've learned over the past month."

"That must be hard."

"It is. But I'll remember everything soon enough."

"That's a great show of faith," she said.

"Faith?" he asked, shifting his body to face her.

"Yeah. Are you familiar with that word?"

"I honestly don't know how I understand all the words I do know, but I have no idea what that word means."

"Well, it isn't used too much anyway," she explained. "It's just my favorite word, so I try to use it when I can. It means believing something even when you can't see it or really know it will happen."

"Oh."

Jordan waited for Payden to say something else. He seemed to be having a private debate. She tapped her fingers and waited for him to let her join the conversation. His facial expression kept changing with a slight twitch of his mouth every so often, but he didn't speak.

"I'll go wait outside so you can change before we go down to eat," she said.

He grabbed her arm. "No, please. I have something I want to say to you," he said. Then he got up and retrieved his book from the table by the bed. "I can read, but I need help relearning. Could you help?"

"Sure."

He returned to his seat next to her. "I don't know where we should start. Apparently anywhere's a good spot with this one."

Curious, she gently took the book from his hands. Flipping through a few pages, she paused to read. "Oh," she said softly. "It's this one."

Payden wanted to ask her so many questions, but he thought it best to remain quiet at present. He watched her small hands flip through the pages as if she was looking for something in particular. When she stopped, she held the book to him.

"Start here," she said, pointing midway down the page. He took the book and stared at where she had pointed.

"I can't do it," he said. "I tried yesterday, but couldn't. Maybe you could read it to me? I might pick it up that way."

"Okay." She scooted closer to him so they could both see the page. "I chose this spot because it's my favorite."

She began to read, following with her finger for Payden's sake.

"'There was a man who had great wealth. This man had two sons. One day, the youngest asked his father for all of his inheritance. After he received it, he left and traveled to a far country. There, he spent all that he had received unwisely on a riotous and selfish lifestyle. Then, a severe famine overcame the land. The son found himself with nothing. He found work tending pigs, and he hoped he could eat the food given to the pigs, so great was his hunger.

"'One day, he thought of his father and the servants he had. He remembered that those servants never wanted for food . . .'"

"'So he decided to return,'" Payden said slowly as the letters turned into words that he suddenly knew how to pronounce. Jordan handed him the book, and he continued. "'He would tell his father that he wasn't worthy to be his son anymore, but he would live as his servant. But when the son was still very far away, his father, who had been watching for him, saw him. The father ran to his son and embraced him, kissing his face. The son delivered his rehearsed speech, but the father would not hear of it. He told his servants to bring clothes and a ring for the son's finger. He had them kill the fatted calf in order to celebrate the son's return.'"

"And then his brother became jealous," Jordan whispered. "I don't like that part. Skip to here."

"'Your brother was lost, but now is found. He was dead, but now lives.'"

"I love the idea that even if you do absolutely everything wrong, your father will still wait for your return, even ignoring what you've done just because he's so happy you came back."

"Do you think such a father exists?" Payden asked, closing the book.

"Maybe," she said, wondering if she should tell him the real reason she loved that story.

Payden turned the book over and over in his hands as he sat deep in thought. His hands drew his attention again, and he thought about his father. His father, the man of peace. What would he have thought of his son, the killer? He set the book aside and sat on his hands.

"Do you really think a father could love a son who lived life so differently than he did?"

"What's really bothering you, Payden?" She tilted her head to get a better view of his face. He looked ill.

"Malkam told me about my father," Payden explained. "He was a man of peace who never killed anyone. I really don't think it's been a month, and I've killed—" He stopped, not wanting to give her a true number.

"Are you your father?"

He looked her in the eyes. It had become easier to do that. He had also become more comfortable in her presence.

"No," he answered, confused as to where she was going.

"Of course not. So why do you think that you have to live your father's life? Despite what you might think, he would be very proud of you for living your own life by your own choices."

Payden looked away from her and crossed his arms. "But my choices have landed me here: I have no memories, I live with strangers, and wicked men are hunting me for reasons no one knows."

"I'm very happy for that because I got to meet you." She gave him a small nudge.

"Yeah." He looked at her again. "And I got to meet you."

"That's better. Now, I'm starving. Let's go eat!"

When Payden and Jordan entered the dining hall, David noticed that Payden wasn't as rigid around the girl as he had been yesterday. He wasn't the only one more comfortable. Jordan had been a polite but reserved hostess yesterday, but she was snuggled closer to Payden with her whole arm hooked through his instead of just her hand.

"Good morning, Payden," he called. "Jordan." He tipped his hat toward her. The smile faded from her face, but she quickly recovered, though losing her genuine warmth.

"Hi, David," Payden said. "How are you?"

"Fine. I was hoping to talk with you for a moment. Would you mind delaying breakfast?"

"No."

"Good," David said. "I found a private place outside in the gardens. Let's go."

David sent a quick glance at Jordan and noticed her mouth grow tight. He would have to leave soon to give Payden a chance with her. He'd known his presence would be a hindrance to their welcome from the beginning. With the hope of a safe haven for Payden perfectly laid out in front of him, the choice was easy.

Jordan watched David lead Payden outside, and she wondered if the Slave had noticed her discomfort. It wasn't intentional, but she didn't know how to act around him. Every Slave her people had encountered brought death. Curiosity defeated her sense of respect, and she quietly followed them. Noting the direction they were heading, she knew exactly where the Slave was taking Payden. She knew a different and shorter route. She hurried to find a good hiding place. After a few minutes, the sound of footsteps betrayed their arrival, and she hoped she wasn't visible.

"This will be a good spot to talk," David said.

"It's beautiful." Payden walked around and inspected the flowers. "I've never seen colors like these before."

"You have; you just don't remember." David sat down on a bench.

Payden turned to look at him. "Where have I seen them?"

"Your mother's garden. Her name was Leislie. She loved flowers, and the house was full of fresh flowers every day, though you could hardly catch her inside. Even when it rained, she'd be outside barefoot and laughing. I remember one time, I was stopping by for a visit. You were about three. I had traveled for three days in nothing but rain. I was depressed, frustrated, soaked, and angry. I came over the hill and saw her with you and your brother, just spinning and playing. You were all covered in mud, but no one seemed to mind. I forgot all my problems at that moment and joined you guys. It was the best medicine I've ever had. Malkam may talk about Henry a lot, but it was your mom who deserves the admiration. You're a lot like her. You have your father's temper, but you're everything like your mom."

Payden crossed over and sat on the ground by David. "Could you please tell me more stories? Ever since I left the hospital, I've been running, and I've really wanted to hear more from Watcher, but he didn't want to tell me anything at first. And then there just wasn't any time to talk. It feels nice to rest, you know?"

"It does," David agreed and ruffled Payden's hair. "I'll tell you what I can. But I do reserve the right to say no."

"Fair enough. My first question is how did you and my father meet?"

"I can't answer that question," David said quickly.

"Why?"

"My right to say no."

"But what could have—"

"No, Payden."

Frustrated, Payden sighed. That had really been the only question he could think of at the moment, but there was something else about David that irked him.

"Why do I want to be around you more than Watcher?"

"I can't answer that one either."

"Why?" Payden cried.

David chuckled. "If I could, I would, but I only know of events that I witnessed happen to you. I haven't the slightest idea what goes on inside your head."

"It seems like everyone knows what's going on inside my head."

"That's because you're unaware of the faces you make when you think. Maybe you should practice thinking while holding still."

Payden smiled sheepishly. "Do I look funny when I do that?"

David nodded. "But it's like I said, you're like your mother. She could hide nothing."

"My mother. Was she pretty?"

"Beautiful. Blue eyes, like yours. Similar nose. She had these big lips, though. Your father's were like yours—very thin. But you have her smile. And she lit up the room with her presence. Every man wanted to marry your mother."

"Were you ever married?"

"No. I had other obligations." David concentrated on his hands.

"In love?"

"Nope."

"Why not?"

David looked Payden in the eyes. "I had no time."

"Why?"

"I was a Slave," David answered. He leaned back and closed his eyes.

"Why did you become a Slave?" Payden asked.

"The truth?"

"Of course."

Jordan leaned forward a little and concentrated on breathing even more quietly.

"I joined almost thirty-five years ago. The war with the Fashites had not begun for us Ashites, but when the Fashites began attacking the Djorites, many felt that we would be their next target. Your father, Henry, was struggling hard to gain unity. The Ashites were so disjointed back then. Due to his success, though, he eventually became a threat to the Pendtars, who had just begun training their Slaves. I had the brilliant idea of joining. At that point, I was fairly confident of my fighting skills, so I wasn't worried about getting caught. I thought that if I could be in there long enough, I'd get close to the Pendtars and learn their plans. But years passed. I got menial task after menial task. Of course, then there was the—" He paused and clutched his wrist. "Never mind."

"Why did they hurt you?"

"Who knows? Part of the programming."

"What's programming?"

"It's when someone says something to you enough times that you believe it's true. Before long, you no longer think for yourself. You stop existing."

"Why didn't you leave?"

"Your uncle William was captured just a few years after the Fashites started the war with the Ashites, so for years I sought to find him. It took me sixteen years to find him."

"Sixteen?"

"Yeah. We all knew he was still alive somewhere. When I found him, they had drugged him like you were. I never did find out exactly why they kept him alive. Well, they were trying to draw Henry out of hiding."

Payden didn't want to ask any more questions. He could tell from David's tone of voice that these weren't topics he wanted to discuss, but Payden couldn't help himself from wanting to know everything. He leaned against the bench and felt David place his hand on his head. Payden closed his eyes. Why did he feel more comfortable around David?

"Did you teach me how to fight?" Payden asked.

"Yup. But it was you who pleaded with me to teach you how in the first place. I don't remember if you were three or four, but you followed me everywhere, begging for some instruction. I made you a little blunt sword, and the obsession began. If I picked up anything new, I had to teach you."

"Where did you learn everything? From the Slaves?"

"No. I learned some, but most of it was just a style I envisioned in my head. I would wake up and somehow know a new way to do something. Then I'd practice until I perfected it. You picked up on that system of learning without me even telling you."

"That's why Patrick said I reminded him of you."

"Patrick?" David looked down at Payden.

"Do you remember?" Payden asked as he turned to look up at David. "He's an old man I met some weeks ago. He saw me fight and said I reminded him of a man named David who was a Slave. I assume that he meant you. You had saved his life. And he had this really nasty tea."

"Oh, yes, Patrick. He's still alive? My, my. With as battle crazy as he was."

"He's crippled now."

"That would slow one down."

Silence claimed the conversation. A slight breeze sailed through the trees and bushes that surrounded them, bringing a chill while breaking the pockets of shade that had begun to bend toward the visitors. Jordan shivered slightly and hoped that her breathing wasn't too loud. She just knew the Slave would be able to hear her. She wondered why she couldn't refer to the man as anything other than "the Slave." His name was David.

Then David said something that startled her and made her wonder if he did, in fact, know she was there.

"What do you think about Jordan?"

She fought not to gasp.

"She's really pretty," Payden answered. "No; she's beautiful." He grinned up at David.

"And do you know why she's beautiful?" David asked.

Payden didn't answer, but his quizzical expression was answer enough. Jordan was all ears. She wanted to know too.

"She's beautiful because she doesn't rely upon her physical beauty. You see, your mother was beautiful because of who she was and not of how she looked. The moment I laid my eyes on Jordan, I could tell she was the same way. Her beauty begins in her heart. Because of that, she will always be beautiful."

"Yeah," Payden said thoughtfully. "I really like her."

"I like her too."

"I don't think she's very comfortable around you."

"No one ever is," David said.

"I am."

"You're different."

"How so?" Payden asked.

"I can't answer that."

"Another no?" Payden smiled mischievously.

"No. Another 'I can't think your thoughts.'"

"Does it bother you when people treat you that way?"

"I'm used to it," David muttered.

"That's not what I asked."

"Then I'm using another no."

"It does bother you," Payden observed. "I'm sorry."

"Not your fault."

"But I did treat you wrongly at first," Payden said.

"And you've more than made up for it."

"Why don't you wear different clothes?"

"This is my uniform. I have to wear it."

Chapter 15

Payden looked for Jordan when he returned but assumed she had already eaten and left. Her schedule didn't revolve around him, he knew, and he had been gone for some time. He ate alone, partaking of the wide variety of fruit and yogurt. Once full, he wondered what to do next. Not many people were in the dining hall. He leaned back in the chair to analyze everything. That's when he noticed the large chandeliers over the long table.

"Wow," he whispered.

Three of them were evenly spaced above the table and had more arms than Payden dared to count emerging from the core. Each arm bore a long white candle at its tip. How did they get up there to light those, Payden wondered, staring at the flickering flames. For that matter, where did they get the gold? Gold overlaid each arm and candle holder, reflecting the light and twinkling as the flames danced.

The chair tilted backward, and Payden quickly grabbed the edge of the table. Hoping to find no witnesses, he sheepishly glanced about. Two girls who were collecting plates giggled.

"Hi," he said weakly, giving them a wave. One of the girls blushed and looked at the other, who only giggled more. Not much liking the attention, Payden stood to go wander. Perhaps he could find Lucy and Zachary.

The dining hall had two exits. One set of open doors led to the hallway. The other doors were shut, so Payden avoided them and exited, looking around as he walked. The tall ceilings captivated his attention. Instead of the normal perpendicular meeting between ceiling and wall, an arch made them fluid. Clouds that looked so real Payden thought he was outside hovered in the ceiling murals with an occasional bird flying through the sky. Mesmerized by the skill that had done the work, Payden bumped into one of the servants washing the floors. Water sloshed out of the bucket across the floor.

"Oops, sorry," Payden said.

"It's fine," the man said. "That water was going on the floor anyway."

"Do you need any help?"

"Nope." The man chuckled. "You like the ceiling?"

"Very much. How could anyone do that?"

"Scaffolding and plenty of skill. An old man who lives in the center of the city painted it. Everyone goes to him to learn. It keeps the skill alive."

"I want to learn."

"Well," the man said, picking up the brush to begin scrubbing the floor. "Learning is easy. Practicing, however, separates the artists from the imitators."

"I understand that."

"Do you now?" The man dropped the brush into his bucket and wiped the floor with a rag. Payden waited for him to say more, but the man continued scrubbing.

"Yes. I do," Payden said slowly. He crouched down beside the man and picked up the rag. The man did not hinder Payden as he followed along, drying the area the man finished washing. They worked for a while. Payden didn't mind passing his time that way. After they found a rhythm, the work seemed relaxing.

As the motions no longer needed his concentration, Payden analyzed the movements and imagined how they could apply to sword fighting. Nothing came to mind immediately, and he continued the circular motions. Once the rag was too wet, he dropped it in another bucket half-full of wet towels and pulled a dry one from a small stack next to it.

As he turned, his mind saw two men. Both were within arm's reach: too close for him to block their blows. So he turned his swords in his hands and pressed the blades against his forearms. The distinct clang of metal on metal was almost audible.

Payden jerked back a bit. The hallway surrounded him, empty except for the man scrubbing the floors. Where had the image come from? He wondered. David had said—what was it? His ideas came from his dreams. *Didn't he say that I did, too?* Payden asked himself. Was that what he meant?

"I've lost my helper," the man said, pulling Payden out of his stupor.

"Oh, sorry."

"You're a wanderer, aren't you?"

"I suppose. I was just—I don't know."

"I'm almost done. Why don't you go wander. I've appreciated your help."

"Sure." Payden handed the rag to the man, though he was still lost in his thoughts. "This has helped."

The man laughed softly. "I'm glad."

Those faceless men, charging him, kept Payden's mind racing as he walked. The meticulously arranged flora and colorful paintings that he passed were not noticed. Several of the servants voiced greetings but received no reply. His mind raced as he tried to conjure anything familiar. Nothing came.

Finally his feet stopped. His eyes saw what was around him, and he was surprised to be by the entrance. The stairs were to his right, but he didn't want to ascend. He turned to the entryway. So much detail went into this building, he noted. Dark cherry wood framed the entrance—two large doors with a picture in the center of each made from dozens of pieces of small, colored glass. Stained glass, hadn't someone said? The knobs looked like flower blossoms, and the wall around the door bore a deep green color. Tall, oval mirrors with frames of the same cherry wood as the door flanked it, and candles sat atop tables in front of the mirrors. At present, sunlight filled the entryway. The candles were only lit at night. For a place that received no guests, why had they gone to such lengths?

He looked straight to the long hallway before him. Jordan had explained that the place was common to the Djorites—an estate for guests had been in every city. So long ago, though. The war took it all away. If these few here could do this, Payden marveled at what the other cities might have been. Landar impressed him, but it lacked the refined attention to details.

Deep down, a familiarity rose. His mother had kept flowers in the house, David said. Payden turned to look down the hallway he'd just walked. So many flowers. Tall vases were bunched around the stairwell with some on random steps all the way to the top. They were everywhere.

Oh, well, he thought. He returned his attention to the hallway that was yet unexplored. He followed it, no longer feeling impressed by all the decorations. A large painting of a lone individual hung at the end of the hall. It startled Payden. The expression on the man's face drew him closer, and he read the word that had been engraved at the base of the simple wood frame: Djorard. The man's eyes watched Payden, it seemed, and for some reason, Payden thought the man looked familiar. He took a few steps back for a better view. No, not familiar. The eyes looked like the same eyes that had stared at Payden from the mirror that morning. Curious how a painting could look like him, he wandered back to the others. He realized that if he looked at each with enough scrutiny, all of them had similarities to him, though there was not a single weapon in any of the paintings. Many displayed games in fields, or portraits of simply dressed people wearing peaceful smiles.

Payden held his hands behind his back so that the paintings of people who had never known violence would not see the blood that bore witness to his violent world. He decided he had had enough exploring for the day. He needed to find company he was more comfortable with, people who came from his world.

He saw a large set of doors in the middle of the hallway to his left and stopped, wondering what was behind them. Many closed doors had filled these halls, but these were grander than all the rest combined. Laughter trickled out, and he thought it sounded familiar. Easing the door back, he stepped inside. Lucy and Zachary were within. But what were they doing? Lucy was doubled over with laughter while Zachary stood in the oddest position—head held high, arms crooked in front of him.

Payden laughed. "What are you doing?" He shut the door and crossed the long floor between them.

Lucy was unable to answer as she fought to breathe.

"This is a ballroom," Zachary said. "We've been practicing our dance positions."

"I don't really understand," Payden confessed. "It doesn't look like fun."

Lucy, finally composed, walked over to him. "Here, I'll show you."

"Okay. Just don't hurt me."

"Don't worry. Now, hold your arms like this."

She held her right arm bent in front of her, parallel to the ground, with her palm facing her. Her left arm was bent up, perpendicular to the right. Payden, not sure why he should do such a funny-looking thing, felt ridiculous mimicking her. No wonder they had been laughing. He glanced away and noticed the murals on the walls. White pillars protruded from the walls, bordering each mural as if the pillars had been cut in half to be used as frames. In several of the murals, he saw men standing in the same position Lucy had shown him but with ladies wearing colorful and extravagant dresses in their arms.

"That looks good," she said. "Now the lady, who would be me, does this."

She slipped into his frame, placing her hands in their proper positions, Payden noted from the ladies in the pictures.

"Now, watch my feet and mirror what I do," she said.

He concentrated, and after a few steps, he picked up on the pattern. Gaining some confidence, he lifted his head to smile at her, but he overstepped and landed hard on her foot.

"Ow!" she cried.

"Sorry," he said, stepping back as she hopped.

"I guess you're not a dancer," she said, limping over to a chair by a small door on the side.

"How did you know how to do this?" Payden asked.

"My parents. It was their favorite thing to do when they were young. You know, before there was no safe place to dance anymore. This is what I remember from watching them, but I may not be doing it right."

"Maybe the Djorites know how," Payden suggested. "They could teach us."

"Is that the name of this people?" Zachary asked. "Djorites?"

"Yeah."

"Who told you? Jordan?" Lucy winked at him.

Payden looked at his feet. "No. David did."

"Oh," Lucy said, not disguising her disappointment. "Him."

Hurt, Payden looked up at her. "What's wrong with him?"

She rolled her eyes and looked down at her foot, unaffected by the intensity of Payden's scrutiny. Once he realized she was not going to give him an answer, he looked at Zachary, who merely shrugged.

Payden wanted to say something, but a strange sound suddenly ravaged the still air. Lucy jumped to her feet, forgetting the pain. The three exchanged looks before they ran out to the main entryway.

"Wait; let's get our weapons first," Lucy said, turning to head up the stairs, Zachary right behind her.

Payden hesitated, but then followed them. He rushed into his room and grabbed his harness, pulling it on as he ran out and down the stairs, close behind Lucy and Zachary, who were belting their swords. Lucy finished buckling the straps that held knives around her thighs as they reached the crowd gathered in front of the estate.

Samuel was in the middle, next to a man blowing into a curved horn. He stopped, placing the instrument under his arm. Greatly agitated, Samuel took to pacing as more people gathered. He wrung his hands, then held one to his face before repeating the cycle again. He was shaking terribly.

"What's going on?" Lucy asked.

Samuel glanced her way, not even recognizing her at first. When he realized it was one of the guests, he swallowed his nerves before answering.

"Jordan is missing."

"Why the alarm?" Lucy asked.

"Wh-when . . ." Samuel tried to explain, barely able to breathe. Malkam and David finally arrived.

"What is it?" Malkam asked.

Samuel paled even more, and one of the guards led him to a bench. He sat, fighting to breathe air deep into his lungs.

The captain of the guards approached them. "We suspect that some of those Fashites avoided capture by disguising themselves to look like us. A few men in the city have been hanging around the exit too much these past few days, and we—we don't think like the rest of the world. It's not a real excuse, but no one suspected anything unusual until Jordan ran out of the city earlier today. Those men followed her. That's when we finally thought something was wrong. I had a few men follow them. They took her—"

"What?" Payden cried. "How? When? Where did they take her?"

"There was a group of Fashites at the base of the mountains," the captain answered. "They took her to them. Now they're heading east. We're found out. And they're going to—we think they're going to—"

"We have to do something!" Payden snapped angrily. He stepped forward, and David grabbed him by the wrist.

"How many men do you have?" David asked, gripping Payden even tighter as he tried to pull away.

"Why does it matter?" the captain asked.

Samuel crossed over to them, red faced, and pushed Payden aside to stand face-to-face with David. "What do you want?" he cried. "I'll give you everything. Just leave my daughter alone! She doesn't have any answers. She doesn't know anything."

"Anything about what?" David asked, keeping a grip on Payden's arm, who continued his attempts to pull away, growing angrier as his efforts became increasingly futile.

"Let me go!" he cried.

"What are you hiding?" David asked softly, pushing his face closer to Samuel's. "I thought you had no secrets here."

Samuel buried his face in his hands and sobbed. The captain pulled him back and handed him off to several of the guards. He then swallowed and looked at David. "I apologize. Obviously he's taking this hard."

"How many men do you have?" David asked.

"I still don't understand why that matters."

"Can your small group take on the entire Fashite army?"

"It was fewer men than that, and they're heading away from us," the captain said. "We could be out of here in days."

"Maybe, but I've recently come from the east. The entire Fashite army was preparing to sail up the Great Sea toward the mountains. I doubt they're trying to invade the Jathenites. What are they going to do?"

The captain swallowed nervously and looked at Samuel, who was clearly not able to answer, so the captain looked back at David. Somehow, he couldn't see beyond the black uniform. This was a Slave.

"How did you come to be here?" the captain asked.

Payden, who had been hitting David's arm and kicking him in the leg, bent his face forward and bit David's hand. This only generated an annoyed glance from David's otherwise stoic posture.

"Let me go!" Payden cried. "We're taking up too much time. We've got to go get Jordan."

"Payden, enough!" David snapped. "You'll be killed if you tried to reach them during the daylight because they're sure to have a proper amount of men—three times more than the number in that village. Stop acting like an idiot. They're not going to kill her anytime soon, so hold still. Apparently, the captain believes there was another reason the Fashites were up here. Please, tell us. No secrets here."

The man sighed heavily. "That is our undoing, then, because those men asked about the instrument. The tool. It is a very dangerous weapon when in the wrong hands."

"Don't tell them anything!" Samuel cried, breaking free from the guards. "They'll use it to destroy us all. There won't be any safe place for us to go to now. It'll be our end."

David shut his eyes. With Payden pulling and fighting on his left and Samuel yelling at his right, he was losing his composure. Already on edge just from being around people, it became harder to keep himself controlled so that he wouldn't snap.

Malkam leaned toward Zachary. "Help David out by restraining that boy, please," he whispered. Then he stepped between David and Samuel, pushing Samuel back to a more respectful distance.

Zachary pinned Payden tightly between his arms and chest. Payden twisted and squirmed, yelling out in rage. Lucy tore off the bottom of her shirt and shoved the fabric in Payden's mouth. He snapped his head around to glare at her. She scowled back unflinchingly.

"We're here to help," Malkam said. "Think of David what you want, but he's here to help, too. So back off! Now me and those three young pups risked our lives to save some of your people a few days ago. David helped in that struggle, but in his own way—without anyone knowing. We buried close to sixty bodies; ask that man named Quinn. I only counted forty during the battle. Had me and the kids not arrived, those villagers would probably have been rescued by this man alone. So stop badgering him, okay?"

David crossed his arms and lowered his head. Though he was grateful whenever Malkam helped him with crowds like this, he hated the way Malkam spoke of him—as if killing those men had been a good thing.

"Now what is this weapon?" Malkam asked, staring down the captain.

A stronger man might have been able to handle Malkam's ferocity, or at least been able to hide any signs of fear, but this captain was a Djorite. They couldn't hide anything. The captain trembled, swallowing nervously.

"Many years ago, we were given these instruments—tools. They were all destroyed, except one. That must be why the Fashites were here. If they think Jordan knows where it might be—but no one does. That's all. I swear."

Malkam turned to David. "What do we do?"

"Turn Payden loose on them."

By then, Payden had spit out the rag. He remained silent, seething with anger.

"What?" Malkam asked, alarmed by such a suggestion.

"Look at him, Malkam."

Malkam stared suspiciously at David for a moment before he turned to look down at Payden. Though trapped in Zachary's large arms, he was defiant, eyes narrowed and jaw muscles twitching. Malkam had seen that face before, but on a much older man.

"Goodness," Malkam whispered. "He looks just like Henry."

"Yes, he does."

Malkam stepped back and returned his attention to the captain. "How many Fashites?"

"My men said fifteen—twenty."

Malkam glanced again at David before staring at the fury he saw before him. Payden's anger was nothing novel to Malkam, but this was far worse than anything he'd seen. "Fine," he said at last, turning again to David. "As long as he promises to be smart!"

"Just let me go," Payden snarled.

"Let him go, Zachary," David said.

Hesitantly, Zachary released Payden and stepped out of the way of any potential blow. Payden, slightly suspicious, continued to glare at the two older men.

David looked at the captain. "You're missing part of that story."

The captain furrowed his brows as he thought.

"How did they get to the bottom of the mountain so quickly? It took us more than half a day."

"This mountain range is full of tunnels," the captain said. "They discovered one."

"Take me there," Payden said.

"Josh," the captain said. A tall guard stepped forward. "You and Stephn show this kid the tunnel where you saw them take her. Block it off once he's through."

"Okay," Josh said.

The captain looked at Payden. "Jordan knows these mountains well. She'll show you another way back."

Payden followed Josh and Stephn to the gate. Once they left, Lucy looked up at David with furious eyes. "Why did you let him go?" she asked.

"Isn't it obvious?" David asked. "The boy's in love. That troop won't know what's hit them."

"Then what do we do?"

David surveyed the small band of men in front of him before directing his gaze at Malkam, who nodded.

"We get ready for a fight," Malkam said.

The men led Payden to the tunnel and even went with him to its exit. Once there, Josh turned to Payden. "Thank you for doing this," he said.

"What do you mean?" Payden asked.

"Jordan means the world to Samuel. She's all he has. I don't think he'll recover if anything happens to her."

"Nothing will. I promise."

"Good. Now hurry. It shouldn't be too hard finding them. Their thick boots leave large tracks in the mud."

Payden quickly left. Josh was right; they were easy to track. Even though they had a few hours' head start, David's warning kept Payden at a slow, steady pace. He would reach them by nightfall. Without knowing their exact number, Payden realized he should proceed with caution. If the Fashites thought they were under attack, they might do something to harm Jordan. Payden didn't want to do anything that would risk her life.

After Payden's departure, Malkam surveyed the group around him and shook his head. Civilians. They all had belts strapped on to carry their knives and swords, but each one was as useless as an untrained civilian. He snorted in frustration and looked at David, who he assumed thought the same thing. Samuel's sobbing irritated Malkam, and he glared at the man's back for a moment before he finally stepped forward to take control.

"I've heard you talk of escape so many times that I know you must have plans. Or routes, yes?"

A few nodded, casting furtive glances in Samuel's direction. Malkam growled with frustration. "Well, just get me something, then. A map of these tunnels! Anything!"

The captain cast one more look at Samuel before he cleared his throat. "I have a map, at least. I'll retrieve it."

"Good. Bring it into the dining hall. We'll do what we can to get you ready. But we're not leaving until things are sorted! Fleeing could be just what the Fashites want. Especially if you go the wrong way. And gather all the men you can, now!"

Without hesitation, the Djorite guards disbanded. Malkam watched as Samuel moved away from the estate and shook his head. The man was worthless at this point. He turned to the others. "Well, David. Any bright ideas?"

David shook his head. "You're the better man now, Malkam. I'm useless with people like them."

"What can we do?" Lucy asked. "Why can't we go with Joe? What if something happens?"

"Payden will be fine," David said.

"But what if he's not?"

"Just trust me, girl—" David began.

"Never!" She stepped forward, pressing her face in his. "If anything happens to him, I swear I'll kill you!"

"If something does, then that would be a mercy for me."

She knitted her brows. "What do you mean? Why would you send him if you think something bad could happen?"

"Payden had to go. We had no choice in that. But if anyone—you, me, Malkam—had gone with him, then he wouldn't have had his head on straight. He's careless in a group! Didn't

longest stretches of tunnelways. "Set up posts along these. One man every couple hundred meters, close enough so you can pass signals quickly. Put a couple at the exits to watch for anything suspicious. Then we'll discuss what to do with the rest."

The captain eyed a group of men, and without a word, they left. Malkam turned toward Lucy and Zachary. "Could I ask you two to go check out this tunnel?" He gestured to the one that exited by the Great Sea. "I want people with experience at this point, if David's report is true."

"All right," Zachary said, then looked at Lucy.

"You'll let us know when Joe returns?" she asked.

"Of course," Malkam assented.

She inhaled deeply as she nodded pensively. "Fine. But we'll return immediately if there's no danger."

"Thank you," said the captain. Lucy barely acknowledged him as she and Zachary passed with several Djorite guards.

"That's one problem gone," he said as he studied the map—evidence of an even greater problem on hand.

Lucy remained silent as she hurried behind the Djorites guards. The path at this portion of the mountainside seemed more treacherous than the other areas. Rocks tumbled past her as the men ahead fought to find their footing. Her eyes drifted to the south. Payden was down there. Pain surrounded her heart, piercing it. She wanted to run after him. She couldn't trust that Slave. Why was everyone not on full alert around him? Why did they even listen to him? She refused to believe that that man had been a part of Payden's life.

They found the tunnel's entrance, and a guard lifted the hatch, climbing down into the darkness. A few minutes later, light trickled up the ladder.

"All right, I've got a torch lit."

The other guards descended with Lucy next and Zachary bringing up the rear. "This way," said the man bearing the torch. They traveled for several minutes before coming to a halt.

"I suppose one of us needs to stay here, then," someone said.

"Right. I'll do it."

"Thanks, Harvey."

"I'll scout for more firewood. We'll need to maintain light at these posts. Don't think any of us will want to stay here in the dark."

"Good. Guess it'll take some time to work out the kinks."

"Can we hurry, please?" Lucy asked. "How long is it going to take us to reach the other side?"

"Most of the day," answered the guard holding the light.

"So then, move," she ordered, rubbing damp hands down her thighs. The darkness around her grew more oppressive.

The man nodded as the others exchanged glances. Harvey turned back toward the entrance as everyone else fell in line and pressed ahead. Lucy wanted the man ahead to go faster as her nerves quaked more. The light from the torch wasn't bright enough, and the darkness around them seemed to hide sinister fears. At one point, they entered a large cavern where several tunnels branched off in different directions. A pit stood in the middle with some wood inside a metal ring.

"Chester, you want this spot?" asked the leader before he approached the pit to light the wood.

"Thanks, Andrew," Chester said to the leader. Zachary glanced at the man, whose damp forehead shone when he stepped into the light. Zachary suppressed a chuckle. He couldn't understand why darkness or small places caused others to be so afraid they'd sweat in spite of the chill. His eyes briefly fell upon Lucy. She seemed to be doing better than he expected, but her fidgeting increased, and he dared not approach her.

"Now which way?" Lucy asked, eyes darting between the four exits.

Andrew pulled another unlit torch from the pack on his back and lit it, as the previous one was mostly spent. "We go down the third one."

Chester drew close to the fire pit, avoiding the darkness, and began to breathe easier. The two guards not yet positioned at posts followed Andrew, quickly disappearing into the gaping darkness. Lucy hurried after them as the torchlight grew too dim with the distance for her comfort. Zachary again found his spot at the rear, listening to Lucy's erratic breathing. He wondered how much longer she'd last.

The trip continued in grim silence, only interrupted as the last of the guards found their positions in the tunnels. Lucy thought of all the guards behind her, standing in the dim silence. She felt glad not to be one of them.

Before fear of being lost and trapped in the tunnels completely paralyzed her, they finally reached the end. Andrew handed the torch to Lucy as he tested the ladder bolted to the rock. He ascended to unlatch the hatch at the top.

Zachary took the torch from Lucy the moment he heard the door open, knowing her panic would cause her to scramble. She scaled the rungs quickly, then rushed toward the sunlight peeking into the shallow cave. Fresh air washed over her face, and she inhaled deeply. A musty scent permeated the air, and she moved forward cautiously, eyes darting for unwanted guests. Small, furry rodents scuttled through the underbrush, easing her apprehension. If anyone else were nearby, the rodents wouldn't be there at all.

Trees thick with needle-covered branches, stood haphazardly around the exit, darkening the land beneath their tops. She carefully wove a path through them until small, leaf-filled trees appeared, woven among the taller growths. Then, as the woods thinned, more bushes sprouted from the dirt and rocks covered the ground.

When Lucy reached the tree line, her eyes followed the underbrush as it grew along a steep slope, ending at the bank of a wide sea. No ships were in sight. In front of her, the land continued, ending at a dropoff. The rocky terrain piled high into a small mound at the end of the cliff, slopes falling down either side. Her feet carried her closer to the cliff's edge, just to look downstream. No small dots in the horizon, either. The imaginary army ready to sail upstream had proven to be a myth. Why did anyone believe that Slave?

"Lucy?" Zachary called softly.

"All clear," she said, and turned to face him. "Where's the Djorite?"

"I told Andrew to stay in the cave. You know, just in case."

"Andrew! Come here. It's safe," she shouted.

"Lucy," Zachary warned, approaching her.

"The Slave lied. There are no Fashites here."

"Maybe not yet." He shook his head. "We'll go back and tell Malkam."

"Yup."

Zachary returned to the cave, shaking his head. Stubborn woman, he almost muttered. Andrew passed him, casting a questioning glance at Zachary, who shrugged. As much as he knew Lucy and tried to understand her, he didn't always know what she was thinking or feeling. That frustrated him, and he entered the coolness of the cave, feeling warmer there than he did around her at the moment.

"Yes?" Andrew asked. "What do you want me to do?"

Lucy approached him as he emerged from the trees, eyes fixed on the distant waters. Lucy kicked at a rock, and Andrew watched it roll down the slope.

"Keep out of sight, I guess," she said. "If anyone comes this way, information will get back to the city quicker with you guys in this tunnel. Try to find a place close to the cave mouth that still gives you a clear view of the sea, okay?"

Andrew nodded, eyes returning to the waters.

"I guess you should head back into the cave, then," Lucy said, turning back toward the cliff. She froze. What was that? At the edge of the cliff, where the pile of boulders had been, stood a tower. It was not as tall as most of the buildings in Tawney City, but at the top, inlaid in the stone, was an unbroken line of windows. She squeezed her eyes shut. That building hadn't been there a few minutes ago. Could the stress of the long journey through the tunnel have gotten to her? Or, more likely, was it the dread of returning to its small space and lack of light?

After several deep breaths, she opened her eyes. The pile of rocks had returned. She released an audible sigh and looked behind her. Both Andrew and Zachary were gone. Neither had mentioned a tower. She shook her head and cautiously returned to the cave, glancing over her shoulder a few times before the cliff's edge quickly disappeared from view. The cave was suddenly appealing. At least she hadn't hallucinated while inside it.

Time elapsed slowly. The wind stirred the trees, and the birds ruffled their feathers, beaks pecking their wings. A few rodents returned to the settling area, noses rutting through the piles of leaves and needles for insects.

The hunter emerged from his perch, effortlessly crossing the terrain. No sound did he produce, nor did the smallest pebble turn under his feet. Time trekked as he made his way to the pile of rocks at the cliff's edge. There it was. His eyes turned to the trees that covered the cave's entrance. He could go there and kill that Djorite and all the others he'd surely find. His eyes turned to the waters, flowing south to the sea. His masters had searched years for the information he had just discovered. It was more important than a few more dead Djorites.

The Slave descended the steep, rocky slope. The bank provided sturdier footing as he turned to follow its path. The trip to the castle would take four days, pending no unforeseen delays. He wouldn't pity those who would try to stop him. He never had before.

Chapter 16

Jordan was exhausted and hungry. The ropes around her wrists had worn the skin raw, and she was bleeding. Her knees ached from the countless times she had fallen, and her back stung from the blows she had received from the men, urging her to walk faster. She wanted to cry but hadn't the energy. What did these men want? Worse, what were they going to do to her? She looked about fearfully and fell again.

"Stupid girl," the man who guarded her muttered. He grabbed her by her hair and pulled her to her feet.

"Go forward," he growled and shoved her.

She fought to stay upright, but with her strength drained, she tripped again. He hit her with the stick he had picked up earlier, and she yelped.

"Get up," he bellowed.

She hurried to her feet and jogged ahead to get out of his reach. His chuckling reached her, and another blow crossed her back. She fought to strangle another cry. These were the kind of men Payden had killed. At that moment, she no longer cared and was even grateful he had. Part of her fought against that thought, but she was too tired to argue.

The sun had long set before the group finally stopped for the night. From where she sat, Jordan was painfully aware of every hungry pair of eyes on her. She curled her knees to her chest and avoided eye contact with all of them. After the fires were lit, a pair of boots stopped in front of her.

"Get up," the man said.

Hesitant, she stood, keeping her head bowed. The man grabbed her face and turned it up so he could look at her. He sneered and shoved her down to the ground.

"Take her to my tent," he told her guard. "The men don't need this distraction out here. They may manage to attack us tonight. Them or the Jathenites. Everyone needs to be alert."

"Yes, Captain," the guard said. "But, see, not all the men are needed to keep guard."

Without a word, the captain hit the man across the face with the back of his fist. The guard fell, sprawled out upon the ground. Dazed, he shook his head, trying to get rid of the stars he saw.

"Do what I ordered you to do," the captain said low with a voice full of venom. "We'll still have her once we're out of this area. Think with another part of your body for tonight."

He left, making sure to speak with each of the men. Jordan observed their countenances change after the brief exchange. The men stopped looking at her, and many took off to the perimeter of the camp. A few snuffed out the fires. Relief rushed through her for a brief moment. For at least that night, she had been spared.

The guard regained his footing. He roughly marched her to the captain's tent and shoved her into the corner, taking off her shoes before tying her feet together. He left without a backward glance. Fear gripped her, making it difficult to strategize a way out of her situation. Did anyone even know she was gone?

Payden crouched deep within the thick leaves of a bush. The firelight outlined the men in the camp. He quickly counted seventeen before the fires began to be snuffed. He sank lower, and once his belly touched the dirt, he slithered forward, staying behind the tree line as long as he could. When it became apparent that he had to escape the cover, he waited. The moon shone too brightly overhead. It helped him find the position of every soldier, memorize their movements and count their paces. They would see him just as easily if he moved from out of the shadows, so he waited. Some time elapsed before a series of clouds passed overhead. Darkness quickly enveloped the land, and Payden moved.

"Can you see anything?" one soldier hissed to another.

"Just the trees. You?"

"I think I see something."

"Then shoot it."

Payden froze, listening. An almost inaudible whistle headed his direction, ending with a soft thump several body lengths to his right. He held his breath and remained still.

"I guess it was nothing," the first soldier said. Payden waited until he heard their footsteps moving away before he continued his crawl. Finally, he breached the boundary of the camp. More soldiers moved about, eyes straining against the dark black night. The clouds began to thin, and Payden curled next to the base of a tent, flattening himself into the grass.

"Something's not right," someone muttered.

"What's the matter? Are you scared of the dark?" The sarcastic question was followed by a few chuckles.

"Quiet!" came a shout from farther in the campground. Several murmurs escaped a few lips as the men fanned out to their posts. One man passed by Payden, who, with a quick glance to confirm there would be no witnesses, quickly jumped and delivered a deathblow, pulling the man to the ground. Payden took the man's cloak and helmet, donning both as he stood. Without pausing, he headed to the man's post and waited for the clouds to return.

The men shifted their weights, nerves rubbed raw from tension and weariness. Payden listened carefully to a man to his right. He fidgeted more than the others, frequently taking deep breaths. When another thick layer of clouds soared past overhead, Payden moved quickly to that soldier, removing him from sight before the clouds disappeared again. Once the cloak was removed, Payden hunkered out of sight near a pile of large rocks and listened for any conversation about Jordan.

Terror, not the cold, shook Jordan's frame as she sat in the silence of the tent. Why had their leader asked that she be brought here? What was he intending to do to her? How was she going to escape? Her eyes searched through the interior, discovering the few items that covered the floor of it. She shut her eyes and tried to calm herself. Then someone entered. Fearful of the captain's intentions, she tensed. The figure approached her, crouching due to the low height of the tent, and placed a hand over her mouth. At the same time, he pulled the cloak off his head. Payden. She wanted to weep.

"Shh," he whispered. "There are too many for me, and most are archers as well. We have to get away quickly to outrun the arrows. Do you think you can?"

She nodded, and he removed his hand. When he cut off the ropes, she hugged him tightly.

"I'm so scared," she whispered hoarsely.

"It's all right." He pulled away and wiped her tears. "I'm here. They're not going to hurt you anymore."

She smiled faintly and retrieved her shoes, lacing them tightly.

"I'm ready."

"Good." He handed her a black cloak. "Wear this. I don't think the original owner will need it anymore."

"You killed him?" she asked, surprised that she felt more relief than shock.

He bowed his head. "We need to hurry. This way."

He led her to the back of the tent, where he cut a slit through the fabric. Listening for any noise that betrayed a presence, he paused. No one was nearby, so he exited and helped Jordan crawl out after him.

"Stay close," he whispered. "They don't have fires lit, so they won't be able to see us if we can get to a good distance."

He led her toward her city, angling to get close to the mountains and thicker growths of trees. Only a few moments passed before there were sounds of alarm.

"Not yet," he hissed. "Run!"

Fires quickly lit up the camp. "There they are!" someone shouted.

Payden heard an arrow glide past his ear.

"Whatever happens, don't stop running!" he said. Jordan scurried ahead as Payden fell in pace behind her. They had not made much progress when an arrow hit him in the hamstring. He cried out in pain.

"Payden!"

"I said run!" Payden yelled. Jordan hesitated but obeyed, sprinting toward the trees.

Payden almost toppled forward, but caught himself on a bush and hobbled behind it to pull out the arrow. Adrenaline filled him with the strength he needed to yank it out, but he couldn't contain his scream. The pain coursed through his entire body, and as he ran the best he could, the pain increased, delaying him all the more. The sharp point of another arrow hit its mark, piercing his back. He fell forward then, struggling to breathe. Someone grabbed his arms.

"Hurry and stand," Jordan said.

"I said run," he gasped.

"We're almost to the trees. Just a little farther." With all the might she could muster, Jordan got him to his feet. He leaned heavily upon her. When they reached the forest, she pulled him behind a thick growth of trees, where he fell to his knees.

"Could you—could you pull it out?" he asked.

She whimpered but nodded. He gritted his teeth as she tugged, but it wouldn't budge.

"It's not coming out," she said.

"Try again."

"I can't, Payden. I can't. Don't make me do this."

He gasped for breath. "Fine. But can you break it so it won't snag on any branches?"

Hesitantly, she put her hands back on the arrow. She closed her eyes and quickly snapped it in two. Payden moaned.

"Come on," she said and pulled him to his feet. The trees thickened quickly, but Jordan knew exactly where they were. Every Djorite knew these mountains. They all had to learn how to escape. And she knew that these trees grew thickest in areas near the caves.

"Leave me, Jordan," Payden struggled to say. "They'll be upon us in no time."

"No, they won't," she said. "It's too dark. They won't see us."

"But they'll hear us."

"So? We're going up to that cliff. If we can just make it up, we'll be fine."

Without another word, they slowly made their way up the rock face. Payden slipped many times, sending rocks falling. They could hear the shouts of men following them.

"They're getting closer. Please, Jordan, just go."

"But we're almost there."

"Where?"

"The cave."

Several minutes later, she half carried him deep inside a cave.

"They'll find us here, Jordan." Payden sank to his knees, too weak to stand.

"No. My people have lived around these mountains for hundreds of years. In fact, they lived inside them. Every mountain in this range has caves that we made. And every cave—" she paused and grunted, "—has an exit."

He could barely make out the trapdoor.

"I know this will hurt, but you need to jump down here. They won't find us, trust me. Because once we're inside, I can lock this so they won't be able to open it even if they do find the latch."

Payden stumbled to his feet and hobbled over to the door. Carefully, he sat down and swung his legs into the hole. Holding his breath, he jumped, nearly fainting with pain when he landed. Jordan followed, pulling the door shut and twisting the knob to lock it into place.

"Let's go," she said. She put his arm around her shoulders and helped him walk. The farther they went, however, the heavier he became.

"Come on, Payden. Stay with me," she said.

At her urging, he pulled himself up, but it wasn't long before he fell, completely unconscious.

"Payden," she whispered. "Payden, wake up."

She smote his face, but gained no response.

"Payden!" Her voice cracked. "Payden!"

She choked on her sobs.

"Don't make me go one step without you. Don't make me do that!" She shook him and pulled his arm, but nothing roused him. Finally, she pulled off her black cloak and wrapped it around him.

"I'll go get help. Hold on. I'll be right back."

Her weariness and pain forgotten, she stood up and ran as fast as she could, stumbling over rocks that littered the ground. She knew the forks this path could take, and could navigate through them blindly. All the Djorites could. In her exhaustion, she felt grateful to be at this point. All she needed to do was keep her hand on the left side, and she would easily find the exit near the village. The forks along the right took a longer route.

It didn't take long before her legs burned and begged to stop. Her lungs too caught fire. She fought every step of the way, running the whole night until she finally reached the exit of the tunnel. Her legs wobbled as she climbed the ladder, straining to retain her grip on the rungs. Desperation gave her the rush of adrenaline she needed to push open the trapdoor. Scrambling out of the hatch, she reached the city gates at dawn.

"Open up!" she screamed. "Open the gates."

The guards hurried to open them, and once they were wide enough, she pushed her body through the gap and struggled even more as she ran through the wakening city to the estate, unable to hear the guards' questions or offers of assistance. When she neared the building, she screamed out the first name that came to mind.

"David! David! David!"

Chapter 17

The dreams were always what woke him. Never were they filled with pleasantries. It was always a myriad of memories or could-be memories, latent fears or fears that had come true.

David's eyes opened. Rest again remained elusive. He never complained of it. He'd grown accustomed many years ago. His body had a will of its own.

Dawn carried with it a peculiar scent. After all these years he had spent sleeping under the skies, his senses were attuned to the subtle nuances of nature. Just before light touched the land, as the night creatures settled and the rest awoke, a scent coursed through the air rising from the east. The smell was subtly like the fresh-cut harvest, as if the plants released a sigh that the night was over.

David rolled to his side and stared at his surroundings. Very little light touched the sky, just enough to lighten the hue. He rubbed his neck a bit before he got to his feet.

Then he made the mistake of inhaling deeply. All those roses. His eyes made out the shape of the nearest one. He'd explored these gardens the first night of their arrival and discovered this spot. Immediately, he recognized it received the least amount of attention, and thus it appealed to him. If it weren't for the roses. With a quick thrust of his sword, he hacked off the nearest bloom. It fell to the ground, tilting slightly as it landed.

Djorites. Everything reeked of them. Who else but the Djorites would use marble bricks for their garden walls? He noticed the few exposed areas and shuddered. The stepping-stone paths that meandered through the gardens, surrounded by thick moss, were all distinctly Djorite. He paced around the fountain, straining not to topple it.

Kill them. Kill them.

Already? He gripped at the hair by his temples. The programming never stopped. He'd give anything for just a few minutes of respite.

He unsheathed his sword and slashed at the air around him. Many times, he found it easy to deal with the unwanted thoughts by training. Then he would envision an opponent and joust. Oftentimes, he'd compete against two or three. His focus eased his mind and cleared his head. The opponents were faceless, usually Slaves.

He fought as the sunlight finally winked over the mountainside. Birds fluttered overhead, and the insects hummed. David feinted, dodged, and parried through the emerging dawn. The faceless opponents began to change. Gradually, their faces resembled some of the Djorites. David moved to deliver a deathblow, but he froze before quickly dropping the sword. Once again, he pressed the palms of his hands against his temples.

As much as he tried to control his thoughts, sometimes he failed. Thoughts would invade that he couldn't dismiss, or memories surfaced he couldn't block. The memory that emerged was a day he hated to remember.

Henry was alive. Not just alive, but young. So was David. Landar was only a few years old, but already booming with life—trade and travelers, many new residents. Henry still chose to live in his large tent outside the city. It had become a symbol by which people recognized him.

David arrived, immediately entering Henry's tent, always so eager to see him. Henry had such life, determination, and commitment. No one left his presence unfazed. Of all the people Henry met and befriended, only David knew his secrets.

"Hey, David, you're back!" Henry said, surprised. The table he used as his desk held piles of scrolls and other paperwork. Many times, he'd hold classes to teach the Ashites how to read. It was a successful endeavor.

"Are you busy?"

"Not at the moment. What is it?"

"Nothing. Just didn't want to interrupt."

"You couldn't ever." Henry stood to greet him.

The next words out of Henry's mouth, David could never recall. It had been a time when many Ashites went to the Pendtar castle for military training, but none knew about the programming. The next memory David had was of being on the floor with Malkam pinning him down while Henry, on the opposite side of the tent, was doubled over, gasping for breath as he rubbed his throat.

Many Ashite Slaves were sent to kill Henry Carpenter. David had been the first.

David sank onto the nearest bench and breathed deeply. This was the very reason why he could not have gone with Payden. The control he easily maintained while on his own lessened around others. Worse still was being around Djorites, because the main desire programmed into any Slave was the desire to kill Djorites.

"David."

He lifted his eyes. Henry stood in front of him. A ruse, he knew. The words *Kill this man* crossed his mind.

"David!"

The image wasn't talking to him. David looked about the garden spot. The voice was a woman's.

"David!"

Jordan's voice! He leaped to his feet and sprinted to the exit, rushing along the narrow path until he broke free of the barriers. The estate was not far away, and he saw Jordan running up the steps. Where was Payden?

David's legs moved faster, beating Jordan to the top. When she finally saw David, the relief of finding him added another layer of emotions she wasn't ready to handle. Her tears of fear and panic gave way to hysterics, and David wrapped his arms around her tightly.

"You can help no one unless you take three deep breaths," he said gently. She obeyed, and then he let her go. "Where's Payden?"

"In the tunnels," she said between tears. "I don't know if he's still alive. We need to hurry. Please!"

"All right."

The commotion drew a small crowd. David and Jordan ignored them. He knew she was exhausted, but she was the only one who knew where Payden was.

"I'm going to give you something to help," he said. "Then you'll lead me to Payden."

She nodded and took the herbs he handed to her. She led him through the city and back up the mountain to the entrance. A few guards followed, concern clearly motivating them to help. The dawning light was enough to reveal the trapdoor, still open.

"He's down there?" David asked.

"But it will take all day to get to him," she said and hiccupped. "And—and the tunnel! Keep your right hand on the wall at all times, or you'll get lost and never find him!"

"Do you trust that I will bring him back?"

She nodded.

"Then go get the care you need. I'll return with Payden when I can."

She nodded again and collapsed against him. He caught her and gently laid her down on the cave floor, covering her with his cloak.

"That herb was supposed to give you some energy," he whispered. He glanced up at the guards. "Please, get her home. And fix these wounds. And have someone waiting for my return." He didn't wait for them to respond as he dropped through the trapdoor and ran, worry pressing heavily upon him. The lack of light concerned him, but he hadn't taken the time to make a torch, though he knew he could pass Payden and never know it. After several hours, he was wondering if he had done just that when he tripped. Feeling around for the object responsible for his fall brought him to Payden.

"How are you, boy?" he asked.

He pressed his ear against Payden's chest. "Well, you're hanging on."

He took off his glove and touched Payden's face. The icy coldness he felt increased his worry. Gathering Payden in his arms, David headed back to where he had left Jordan. Though he felt the need to rest, urgency overpowered his sense of comfort and stamina. Hours passed, and the burden taxed him, causing his arms to quiver as the muscles spasmed. Knowing he was close to dropping Payden, David knelt and laid him over his shoulder. At least it relieved the pressure on his arms. David continued his slow pace; he hoped Payden would survive.

Malkam had heard Jordan's voice from where he stood in the dining hall. The interruption heightened the tension in the room.

Malkam wasn't as focused as he knew he should be. Payden kept entering his thoughts. Throughout the day and night, he'd plotted and planned, only to encounter objections at every turn—from the villagers themselves. As terrified as they were, they objected greatly to the idea of an outsider leading them. The captain did his best to convince them, but the arguments fell on deaf ears. These people, already raw with fear, were panicked. Malkam couldn't think straight, unused to being challenged so blindly.

And then that moment came. Jordan's words carried over the din. Malkam went to the entrance and saw David with her. When the pair quickly departed, uneasiness settled in Malkam's heart. *David, you'd better be right.*

Malkam returned to the room full of people and surveyed the scene, reading the emotions so plain on everyone's faces. He couldn't show his emotions now. With all the strength he could muster, he pushed his concern for Payden aside and shouted, "I'm trying to help!"

The outburst shocked everyone to silence. With assurance that he had their attention, he leveled them with a fiery glare. "My people have been at war these past thirty years with the Fashites. And it is because of *me* that we are still standing! So enough! You have objected enough!"

He paused to catch his breath as he approached the map. "These tunnels need to be removed!" he said pointedly, blackening many with the ink-covered quill. "And I no longer care about your objections. Reality is clear. So face it! Now go; block these off. And I'll find your respected leader," he spat, sarcasm ripe in his voice as he threw the quill onto the table and marched out of the estate.

It was easy to find Samuel's house—it had several Djorites camped in front of it. The man had cut himself off from everyone, apparently. Malkam could excuse David for doing that. Not Samuel. Not someone who was supposed to be in charge.

Without even the courtesy of a knock, Malkam let himself into the man's shelter, kicking open the door.

"Samuel!" he cried loudly, not desiring to hide any dislike he currently felt toward the man. Any man who deemed himself a leader had no right to indulge in this type of breakdown. This isolation, wailing about his inability to help his daughter, made Malkam want to wring his neck. "Samuel, I am not at this moment a patient man!" Malkam roared, ascending the steep stairwell to the right of the entrance.

He found the man sitting at his desk, his head in his hands. "Your daughter's returned," Malkam said flatly, fighting the storm of emotions raging within. Samuel's head turned abruptly.

"Jordan? Where is she? How is she?" He stood and crossed the floor.

"Unknown, sir," Malkam said, hands opening and closing in fists. He fought to deepen his shallow breathing. "She is alive. For how long depends on you."

"Me? Wh-what—?"

"If there is any sort of a man under all this blubbering I've been seeing, then he needs to emerge now," Malkam said through clenched teeth. "Your men told me that you have possession of the escape plans made by those who first entered this valley. Give them to me now."

Samuel's eyes widened. No one had ever spoken to anyone in that city in such a way. As his mind processed the request, his eyelids fluttered. "Yes. Yes. Here." He returned to his desk and retrieved a leather-bound booklet. "This is it. It details every contingency—even where to go if we feel it best to flee to the Jathenites. How much food to take. Everything."

Malkam snatched the book from the man's hands.

"Now, where's Jordan?"

"I don't know. She came for David, then left. Which means something happened to Payden."

Samuel paled. "Oh, no."

"Follow me. Your people won't do as I ask. They need someone they trust. Can you pull yourself together and be that man?"

Samuel lifted his eyes to Malkam's. He inhaled deeply and answered, "Yes. I can."

"Good. I'm glad to hear that. Now let's return to the estate. There is so much to be done, and I'm exhausted."

It was dark outside when David emerged. Guessing dawn to be hours away, he worried more about the lapse of time.

"I've got him," the guard said, pulling Payden through the hatch. David finished the climb, yet paused as his arms quivered from overexertion. He knelt beside the boy. He felt dizzy, but shook the sensations away, quickly attending to Payden.

"I brought some light earlier," the guard said, gesturing toward a fire. "Let's get him closer."

They lifted Payden and laid him on his side near the warm light. When the guard finally noticed the broken arrow protruding from Payden's back, he gulped.

"He needs a doctor."

"Yes," David said. "Have you got a knife?"

"What?"

"I can't carry him any farther. And you're right, his wounds need attention now. I'm going to have to cut this arrow out of him. So—knife. Please."

The man nodded and handed David the blade. "I'll return with a doctor. A-and . . ."

"Water. Rags. Blankets."

"Of course." The guard ran, cautiously descending the rocky slope to the gates.

David removed Payden's harness, setting the swords aside, before he cut off the shirt to assess the wound. The arrow was buried deep. Fashites were very good shots.

David tried to pull it free, but it wouldn't budge. A lack of a reaction from Payden drew David's eyes to his face. It was white, completely drawn. David removed his glove to check for a pulse. It was very weak. David fought tears as he thrust the blade of the knife into the flames. After he pulled it from the heat, he had to steady his hands, allowing the blade to cool before he focused on the opening. After several deep breaths, he cut and pried open the wound as he finally removed the arrow. Then quickly, he placed his hands over the opening to stave off the bleeding. More evidence of a wound covered one of Payden's hamstrings. The pants were darker, and David pulled at the fabric, finding a hole that revealed the wound.

"Oh, Payden," David whispered. "She's worth it, right?"

While he tied a piece of cloak around the leg to cover the wound, the guard returned with several more men and a stretcher. One knelt next to David and placed his hand over David's arm.

"Allow me," he said. "We'll take good care of him."

David lifted his eyes to the doctor, but he couldn't speak. He simply moved out of the way as the doctor did his work: irrigating the wounds, stitching them closed, and dressing them. The guards gingerly placed Payden on the stretcher and departed. At that point, David could barely move his head to watch them disappear into the darkness outside the cave.

The doctor knelt next to David and studied him. "You need some rest."

"Will he be all right?" David asked, eyes pleading for affirmation.

The doctor paused and offered a comforting smile. "The wounds, though deep, were in the muscle. The arrows didn't hit any major arteries or organs. He obviously lost a lot of blood, but he's breathing. One of the wounds is infected, so I'll keep an eye on it. Now we wait. That's all I can promise."

David sobbed. He could contain himself no longer. "I should have followed. Why didn't I? I—I couldn't . . . but I should—" He fought to breathe. Words and images played through his mind. Fires. Screaming. He shook his head to collect himself and found one of his hands tightly gripping the doctor's shoulder, right at the base of his neck. David gasped and jerked his hand away, using it to cover his face.

"Sorry. I'm sorry."

The doctor rubbed at his neck as he leaned out of David's reach. He studied David all the more, watching as the Slave tried to catch his breath. When David finally uncovered his eyes, the doctor shifted so the firelight could illuminate David more clearly. There was something very familiar about those eyes.

"My name's Roman. Do you know that name? Roman Truse?"

David shook his head.

Roman pursed his lips as he thought some more. "I remember when, as a child, the Slaves came to destroy us. They preceded the Fashite army's bombs and fires. But I remember the Slaves. They were chilling. Cold and heartless. We'd run away, terrified, and they'd pick us off as we fled. Like it was sport. My sister fell on one side of me. My dad on the other. I kept running. I wanted to live. And here I am, sitting face-to-face with a Slave. In a dark cave. I've done that once before. Except I was the one crying. A little boy, was I. Just barely nine years along. Crying in a cave. And a Slave knelt in front of me, dried my eyes, and carried me to a family of Djorites who brought me here. That family never saw the man. And I never told anyone that information. We say we don't encourage secrets in this valley, but everyone has theirs."

David was finally calm, staring at the man's face. "Why are you saying this? To me?"

"I told the man my name. As terrified as I was of Slaves, I recognized the man's kindness. A paradox—sure. A kind Slave. I'm telling you this because, well, he never told me his name. But I remember his eyes. Won't ever forget them."

David sat upright. That would have happened thirty years ago—that part of his life he never could seem to remember.

Roman stood and offered David his hand. Reluctantly, David took it and got to his feet. He felt the exhaustion, but he knew he needed to go a bit farther to the estate. He didn't want to stay in the cave any longer. Roman moved to the fire and kicked some dirt over it. The cave didn't darken too much once the firelight vanished. Dawn threatened. David stared out of the cave at the gray skies. It had been two days and two nights since he told Payden to hunt down the Fashites. It felt like much longer.

"Jordan's in the infirmary beside the estate," Roman said. "In case you wanted to know. She's resting. I gave her some medicine to help her sleep. That was obviously some time ago. She might be awake now. I was asleep in the barracks by the gate when the guards came about Payden. Wanted to be readily available. Wasn't certain which tunnel you'd be in. It's such a maze in these mountains."

"I know," David said softly.

"How do you know?"

David squinted as the outlines of the buildings below gradually became clearer. "Past few days, there's been a lot of talk about tunnels."

"How old are you, if I may inquire?"

David shrugged. "Maybe fifty. Can't really remember exactly. Old enough, though. Old and tired."

Roman nodded and began the descent to the valley. David followed, cautiously finding his footing. The growing light helped. When they reached the gates, the guards had them open already. They walked through the still-sleeping town until they reached a building near the square.

"We'll part here," Roman said. "It's my house." He extended his hand. "Pleasure to meet you, sir."

David shook his hand casually, turning to leave. The doctor held on longer than normal, causing David to pause and look at the man. "You're old enough to be that man, you know. You're about ten years older than I am, anyway. I never said thanks."

"Shouldn't have been expected to. Have a good day."

"Get some rest."

David nodded, and the man released him. David hurried forward, grateful to finally be alone. A kind Slave? If it had been him, what had he been doing around the Djorites at that time? He only remembered being with Henry and Malkam, organizing defenses for the Ashites. David pinched the bridge of his nose as an unfamiliar headache throbbed.

The guards carried Payden into the estate. Malkam watched as the stretcher crossed the hallway and was carried up the stairs. He looked at Samuel, whose focus was on the numbers sketched in the book before him. A few townspeople had arrived earlier, waking him as he slept on the floor of the dining hall. Samuel apparently hadn't been asleep. His eyes were bloodshot from hours of figuring the numbers, which had to be adjusted to accommodate the population increase over the past twenty years. When the other Djorites arrived, Samuel had quickly encouraged them to prepare to leave. However, these were people not wanting to budge. The noise of the debate was what woke Malkam.

The cook, Solomon, brought everyone food and drink. Malkam ignored the food. It was at that moment Payden arrived.

Without a word, Malkam left. When the guards cleared the bedroom, Malkam entered. He stared without any feelings for a moment. He had not understood why David believed Payden should go alone. David trusted Payden's training more than Malkam did. Where was David?

Malkam approached the bed and stopped when he was as close as he dared to be. He felt at that moment, more acutely than ever before, how much he had failed his best friend.

"Henry, I'm sorry," he whispered. "How could you think I could ever adequately replace you?" He took a few more steps and held Payden's hand. Biting down every emotion that threatened to surface, he whispered, "I'm sorry for being a terrible guardian. You always deserved better. You deserved your father. I just wish that you had known him so that you would have wanted him in your life, too. I never could understand why you hated him. You're so much alike."

When David reached the estate, he saw Jordan leaning against the pillars by the entrance, sound asleep. He wondered why she wasn't where she should be. He sat next to her and waited, watching the sun's rays spray themselves across the horizon. He knit his brows and lowered his head, hoping Jordan would wake soon. He studied her. Bandages were wrapped around her wrists. He wondered how else she fared. No longer frightened, he hoped.

As Jordan opened her eyes, she sensed someone near and sleepily looked around, relieved to find David next to her. He was contemplatively looking at the city. When he noticed her stirring, he turned, lifting his arm to drape around her as she clung to him, sobbing hysterically.

"I'm sorry," she pleaded. "I'm so sorry."

"Shh," David replied gently. "Shh. Calm down and take a few breaths."

"But this was all my fault. This wouldn't have happened if it weren't for me. I . . ."

"Jordan, calm yourself, please," David said firmly.

She nodded and squeezed more tightly to his chest as she tried to collect herself. Since waking in the infirmary, all she'd felt was panic. Only after a great deal of begging did Salina allow her to leave, but only on the condition that Jordan stay at the estate. So she had sat at the doorway and waited, falling asleep as the night drew long.

"How's Payden?" she asked. She felt David's hand squeeze her shoulder.

"We'll see," he answered, though she could tell it took some effort.

She sniffed and sat upright to wipe her eyes with her sleeves. "I'm so sorry. I shouldn't have done what I did."

"And what was that?"

She hung her head. "I was the one in the garden listening to you and Payden. I didn't trust you. There was really no legitimate excuse, but I should not have done it. I had to get out of the city—and those men grabbed me." She shuddered and wrapped her arms across her chest.

David rubbed his neck, surprised that a small part of him wanted to laugh. Such a silly reason to be in hysterics. "Jordan, I think you're overreacting . . ."

"No, I—"

"Please, listen. You were at fault in the garden, yes. But the events that followed had nothing to do with it. This whole incident—you're not to blame for it. So please, resolve it in your heart completely right now. It's not worth carrying the guilt."

She whimpered a bit as she continued to stare at the marble. After a few moments, she inhaled deeply and lifted her head. "Thank you."

With a moan, he got to his feet, turning his back to the breaking dawn. "I'm not sure where they put Payden, in the infirmary or his room. I'm going to check. But, if you could, do me a favor."

"Anything."

He pulled out a bag of leaves. "Use only two or three leaves per cup, but brew Payden two cups of tea a day and do whatever you can to get it down his throat."

She knit her eyebrows but didn't ask the question. She took the bag and inspected it.

"Good night," he said, but then glanced up at the sky, which brightened with the first touches of dawn. "Or good morning."

When David reached the top of the steps, he saw Malkam leaving Payden's room. Malkam stood still for a moment before he finally closed the door. "He doesn't look too good," Malkam said.

"It'll just take time now."

Malkam nodded solemnly. "Someone should have gone with him." David remained silent. Malkam fixed him with a venomous glare. "Did you not hear what I said?"

"I heard you, Malkam."

"Someone should have gone with him," Malkam repeated pointedly.

David lowered his gaze to the ground.

"You knew that, didn't you?"

"Malkam . . ."

"You did? And you stayed behind? To—to hide!"

"I know him, Malkam." David lifted his head, looking at his friend though his tears. "I knew he'd come back alive."

Malkam raised his hand, gesturing toward Payden's room. "And that condition is okay with you? He's alive, then? That makes it okay?"

"Payden knew the risks . . ."

"He's a boy!" Malkam stepped closer, clenching his fists. "He's not Henry; he's a boy!"

"Oh, and Henry would have fared better? I knew Henry well, and I know Payden well."

"Better than me?"

"Yes."

Malkam stood erect and pulled at the bottom of his shirt. "When will you ever tell me the truth of you? You and Henry—all those years you spent with him, only to become this. This Slave! You should have gone with Payden. Henry would have wanted you to go with him!"

"No. Leislie would have wanted me to go with him. Henry would rather have had both of us stay. Stop arguing for the man! You didn't know him!"

Malkam almost charged. "Don't you dare!"

David stepped back. "I'm sorry, Malkam. I'm sorry. Fine. The truth? I couldn't go with Payden. I . . ." The tightness in

David's throat cut off the sentence, and he lowered his head. "Please," he whispered hoarsely, "may I see him?"

"Don't act as if I'm treating you like everyone else does." The tension left Malkam and he stepped closer. In all the years they'd been friends, he'd never seen David like this. David never cried.

"Habits, Malkam. Sorry." David lifted his head. "Too often, in all these years we've known each other, you've been the one person who's never forced me to feel anything. Even when you pry, it's more in jest. So if you are going to force me to feel anything or say anything right now, then you're not acting like the Malkam I know. You're acting like everyone else." David looked at the ground at Malkam's feet as he continued, "Forgive me for retreating. I don't have the energy to act any other way." David lowered his head further. Malkam studied him for a moment.

"I think this is the first time you have ever been truly honest with me," Malkam said. "In the thirty-five years I've known you." Malkam passed him and headed down the stairs.

David waited until Malkam's footsteps faded to silence before he moved. The doors opened, and David's gaze fell upon the young man on the bed. The dread—that deep, dark fear that was always so close to David's heart—held him still for a moment. Was this it? The moment he would witness the death of the last Carpenter? The memories of twelve years ago were still so fresh. The remains of the burned houses. The graves. The fresh, neatly lined graves. Four markers bore the last name of Carpenter. Henry. Leislie. Little Egan who was barely three. And William. David had just returned William not a week before.

With several deep breaths, David approached, struggling to maintain his composure. He slowly removed the glove from his hand before placing that hand on Payden's chest. The heart beat steadily. David rested the back of his hand against Payden's neck. He was warmer than before. David sighed and sat on the bed.

"You'll live," he whispered. "You'll live."

The release finally exposed David's exhaustion. He stood and went to his own bedroom, stripping himself of his dirty, sweat-drenched clothing—removing the hat and scarf as well. The cool air touched his skin, but he barely noticed as his eyes focused on the sunlight breaching the windowsill. He shut the curtains in a hurry before crossing to the wardrobe. With the fresh clothing covering his bare skin, he crawled onto the bed. Though he couldn't remember the last time he'd slept on a bed, he decided to indulge at this time. He felt he'd earned it. He just hoped he would mercifully have no dreams.

Malkam paced about the dining hall, staring at all the paperwork strewn across the polished wood. Samuel was doing a great job delegating tasks, but Malkam knew that there was still much work that remained to be done.

Malkam's mind wandered to something Samuel had mentioned earlier about running to hide among the Jathenites. At the very least, if the Jathenites remembered the good relationship they once had with the Djorites, then the Djorites feasibly could head farther north, deeper into the mountains. It should be an option—the last option, though. It had been nearly thirty years since an outsider went into Jathenite territory. Strangers might no longer be welcomed.

PART II

Djorites

Chapter 1

The bird perched atop the highest branch, scanning the underbrush from its vantage point. Its hunting instincts, heightened from years of survival in the dense highlands, made it stand alert yet patient. A meal always came.

Far below, just as stealthy, a man clad head to toe in black shifted his weight from foot to foot. No noise echoed through the forest, so the natural inhabitants continued their daily routine without pause. A shorthaired rodent sniffed the winds around it before cautiously taking a few steps out from its shelter. After another brief inspection to test the safety of its exposure, the rodent moved a little farther. Talons closed around the prey before it had time to react. Patience was always on the side of the hunter.

The movement only caused the man to pause in curiosity. Then he continued forward, listening. He knew someone was watching him. A thorn pierced his foot, and he flinched. No, it wasn't a thorn, he observed. His vision blurred, and he staggered a few steps before he fell into a bed of damp leaves.

"Got another one," a Jathenite warrior said. "He made it too far, though."

"Mm," a second man assented. "We'll have to inform Rick at the gathering."

"Agreed. If only we could determine what they're looking for."

"Or who," stated a third, rising to his feet to check the body.

The first warrior stood and shifted his gaze to the treetops. Fog rolled steadily through the branches above them, dimming the light of the late afternoon sun. "Do you think they believe any Djorites escaped to here?"

"Maybe," answered the warrior by the corpse. "Whatever the motivation is behind these scouting missions, I wonder when they will ever realize the futility of them."

The last of the trio finally stood. "Something big is about to happen. That's the fourth Slave that has come through here in a week."

His comment was met with casual glances and a shrug. "Like I said, we'll tell Rick at the gathering. I doubt the Fashites are planning any attack in the next two months."

Silence fell as they left the body to the scavengers. Their feet moved confidently through the dense underbrush as they returned to their camp. After removing the evidence of their presence, they went back to their village without another thought of the man or the future.

Chapter 2

Petrified, Jordan stood outside the door to Payden's room for almost an hour. No news had come of any change in his condition, and she trembled at the memory of his pale face. She fought the guilt that threatened to overwhelm her. She couldn't believe David in order to come to peace with the consequences of her decision, at least not yet. She shut her eyes. *Just push the door and enter,* she commanded herself. With a sigh, she obeyed.

It opened easily as always. The curtains were still open, and the soft light of the sun made the room less intimidating. She relaxed slightly. The smell of the tea wafted to her nose, and she shuddered. It was repugnant, and she felt no temptation to even sip it. Slowly, she made her way to the bedside and swallowed deeply. He was so still. Determined not to shed a tear, she set the cup on the table by the bed and faced Payden. She needed to get him to drink the concoction. But how?

Her gaze fell upon the pillows. She could prop him up, but she would need help doing so, and she didn't want to talk to anyone at the moment. Hopping up onto the bed, she crawled over to him, gingerly reclining next to him. Her back felt so stiff. The welts and bruises that covered it stung with each movement. Her thoughts went to Salina, the woman, who, in many ways, was the closest Jordan had to a mother. Salina would not have approved of this. Jordan could almost hear her voice, encouraging her to rest in order to heal. A stray tear slid down Jordan's cheek, and she quickly wiped it away as she sat upright to look at Payden.

Her actions didn't seem to disturb him. He even looked peaceful lying there. Her hand slowly crept up to his face. His skin was surprisingly soft. Carefully, she scooted closer. The impulse had already taken root before reasoning and a sense of propriety could stop her. Slowly, she leaned forward and lightly kissed his lips.

Pulling back quickly, she whispered, "I love you. I always will. I want to go with you wherever you go."

Suddenly nervous, she retreated and hopped off the bed to cross to the other side. The initial problem of getting the tea down his throat had to be solved. No ideas came quickly except to make him smell it. She held the cup beside his nose for a few moments. It seemed to work; he moved his head a little.

"Payden, are you awake?" she asked, setting aside the tea.

"Hmm?"

"You are!" she cried and hugged his neck. She remained there for a while as his arms gently made their way around her.

"Jordan," he said, smiling.

Reluctantly, she pulled back as she remembered her duties. "I have to make you drink some nasty tea. David's orders," she said.

"Where am I?" he asked, finally opening his eyes.

"Your room."

He looked around. "How did I get here?"

"David carried you."

"Carried me? All the way?" he asked in disbelief.

"Mm-hmm." She nodded uncomfortably. She had to tell him that this was all her fault. Could he forgive her?

"Where is he?"

"In his room, I suppose. But you have to drink this." She stiffly handed him the cup.

He sniffed it. "Oh, this stuff."

He quickly drank it all in one gulp, shuddering once it was down before he returned the cup to her.

"You've had this before?" she asked.

He nodded. "It's not so bad once you get used to it. But the trouble is getting used to it."

She sighed with relief that he drank it. Her attention went to her hands. How was she to tell him?

"Where's David's room?" he asked.

"It's down the hall."

"Which way?"

"To the left, two doors down. Malkam is one down from that, Lucy's to your right, and Zachary's between you and David."

"That's good to know," he said with a mischievous twinkle in his eye.

"Well, I'll let you rest. My father wants to spend some time with me today, so I won't be back until tonight with another cup of tea. I'll let everyone know that you're awake so they will bring some food later."

"No—stay. Please." He reached for her hand and grasped it tightly. "I don't want you to go."

A shiver ran over Jordan's skin as she looked in his eyes. How she wanted to stay, curled beside him. However, her father's request brought her out of the trance. Her father, who never showed any emotion when addressing her, had looked desperate earlier, when she finally entered the dining hall to find him there. He needed her presence more now than Payden did. She swallowed to abate the tightness in her throat. The truth was, she needed to be with Payden more than her father.

Her eyes slid shut, and she placed her free hand on top of Payden's. "I have to go," she said softly. "I'll return later this evening. As soon as I can. I promise."

He didn't release her hand. She dared not open her eyes. Denying his request was easy when she wasn't looking into his eyes.

"Jordan—" He finally let her go.

"I'm sorry. My father just . . ."

"I understand. He was—well, very overwrought when he thought you were— I mean, when you were gone, I, uh—" he swallowed deeply, wishing she'd open her eyes, "—I'll see you tonight."

Her eyelids fluttered open. "A-and Payden?"

"Yes?"

"I want to tell you—should tell you that, um . . ." She struggled to control herself. "It's all my fault. This whole thing."

"What?" Payden felt the weight of confusion cloud his thoughts. "It's not—"

"It is!" she interrupted. "I was afraid of David at first and thought he was going to take you away when you two went for your walk the other day. I overheard everything. It was wrong. And David knew I was there. Or not that it was me specifically, but that someone was being disrespectful. I was so ashamed that I ran. I'm so, so sorry."

Payden chuckled. "It's not your fault, Jordan. You made a mistake. But to carry the blame of what the Fashites did as well is, to be frank, stupid. Don't worry about it."

She nodded soberly. "You're right. You are. David said something like that as well." She narrowed her eyes. "Except he didn't call me stupid."

Payden beamed at her, and she fought to contain herself. "I'm leaving. My father's expecting me."

"Then go. I'll be here waiting for that next cup of tea. Yum."

She rolled her eyes and left. Payden pulled back the covers and gently lowered himself to the floor, careful of his injured leg. He made his way around the bed, using it for support and then hopped to the wardrobe, which only aggravated his wounds. Pausing for a moment, he waited until a dizzy spell passed before he began his search for something to help him walk. He found a cane and leaned upon it as he quietly headed for the door, pausing to listen for sounds of life. Hearing nothing, he slowly opened it and gingerly walked down the hallway until he reached David's room.

Another dizzy spell delayed him. He shook his head to regain his composure before pushing open the door to enter. Since he didn't expecting David to be inside, he intended to wait for the man's return. His plans changed when he saw

David asleep on the bed. For a moment, he froze and stared, assuming David had heard him and would rise. He was unaware that David had only fallen asleep just a few hours ago. When he realized that David wasn't moving, Payden sneaked over to the bed, grateful for the thick carpet that dulled every sound.

The only thing Payden noticed was David's uncovered face. He knew that David would be upset, even disappointed with Payden if and when he discovered Payden's inability to withstand the temptation set before him. But Payden wanted to see David's face, and not just his eyes—those intense blue eyes that severed all pretenses and saw only the truth. They were hidden safely behind closed lids.

Payden swallowed and drew closer, his eyes never leaving David's face. Nothing seemed abnormal, until he was close enough to see thin pink scar lines. Line after line stretched across David's neck and down his cheeks. A symbol Payden couldn't recognize was branded into David's jawline.

Payden closed his eyes. How could anyone endure such treatment? And for what? Why? "These scars will remind you of the life I've lived with the sole intent of keeping you safe," Payden remembered him saying. Why David, he thought. Payden couldn't think of a single reason.

He made his way to the empty side of the bed and climbed onto it, still amazed that David hadn't woken yet. Payden curled up beside him and eventually drifted off to sleep.

Several hours later, David awoke at a knock on his door—the midday meal, he assumed, before he then wondered why they had brought it up to him. He got himself dressed in his usual clothes so quickly that he was unaware of Payden's presence. He opened the door and thanked them for the tray of food, which he set on the table. After asking for some water for his basin, he shut the door and turned, finally spotting the body on the bed. Unable to guess who it was, and for that matter, not knowing how the person got there without his knowing, bothered him. Of course, he had been beyond exhaustion that morning. He hadn't slept so deeply or for so long in thirty years. With trepidation, he took a few steps to discern the person's identity.

Upon discovering Payden, his legs weakened and he sank onto the couch. Why hadn't he slept in his uniform as usual, or even on the floor as was his habit? He might not have slept so deeply and therefore might have heard the boy enter. His heart pounded as his mind raced. Payden had seen what no one ever saw. Ever.

At one point in his life, David had confided in one person about his injuries but had never shown them. For others to see the scars was—traumatic. An acknowledgement that they were indeed there.

Another knock on the door startled David to his feet. It was water for the basin. As the servants brought in the pitchers, David pressed himself against the wall. After they left, he hurried to the washroom and shut the door. David felt the panic rise and his chest hurt. He needed to do something.

His eyes saw the water. Why was it here? Oh, he had asked for it. Why? He looked down at his black uniform, noticing the dirt clinging to it. His clothes needed to be washed. David removed the items and paused. No, he had asked for water to cleanse himself. The panic wasn't disappearing, though. Water burned his skin, he remembered. He grabbed a rag anyway, dunked it, found the bar of soap, and scrubbed. He needed to be active—to do something.

Once he was clean, he took to his clothes, harshly scrubbing the fabric. Then he hung the clothes but didn't feel any better. It felt as though he were being strangled, so difficult was it to breathe.

What else to do? Dry clothes. He should wear some dry clothes. A towel was handy to drape around his body, and he peeked out of the small washroom to see if Payden was still asleep. The boy didn't move. David quickly crossed to the wardrobe and grabbed the first items his hands touched.

Safely back in the washroom, he dressed and searched for some fabric to cover his face. Though Payden might have seen what he oughtn't have, David wasn't going to subject him to it anymore.

As his gaze finally found the mirror, he paused. He couldn't remember the last time he had looked at his face. Generally, he avoided the act. On his jaw was the brand, the mark of a Slave, that he had received twenty years ago. The scars on his face appeared faded, more so than he had thought they would be. Repulsion eventually set in, and he covered the evidence. He wanted to scream with rage knowing Payden had seen him that way. Instead, he sank to the floor and silently wept.

Chapter 3

Though Jordan loved her father, she was not used to his attention. The affairs of the city usually occupied his time and consumed his thoughts. She had been but a footnote in his life. For him to suddenly want to have her beside him was unusual.

Even more unusual was the fact that he spent the day at the estate. He usually stayed in the study of his house. Every person who had a say in the preparations came and went from the dining hall. The commotion was dizzying, but Samuel consistently looked about for her. By the end of the day, she was surprised at the relief she felt in having a legitimate reason to leave him. Samuel almost didn't let her, suggesting one of the servants take the tea to Payden. Salina stepped in, sending Samuel home with the excuse that he needed rest after the past few days. She winked at Jordan as she escorted Samuel out of the dining hall, and Jordan sighed before heading to the kitchen to prepare the tea. It was just after sunset when she finally entered Payden's room.

"I'm back," she called. No answer came. She looked around the room but found no evidence of him.

Before she became alarmed, she remembered him asking where David's room was. She set the tea by his bed, and left.

Once outside the room, she glanced down the hall toward David's. With every fiber of her being, she wanted to go down there just to see Payden, but she restrained herself. Instead, she went back downstairs to find a private place where she wouldn't be disturbed for a while. The endless day had exhausted her, and she wanted a quick nap.

The ballroom rarely had any activity, and she knew several chaise lounges occupied some space there. She stifled a yawn as she made her way to fulfill her plan, welcoming the idea of a nap.

When she awoke some time later, the darkness of the evening surrounded her, stirring up a bit of fear. The darkness of the other night haunted her. Hunger quickly overtook the fear, and she returned to the dining hall.

Most days, she didn't feel uncomfortable entering that room. Her father rarely came to the estate, and she was never forced to spend much time in his company. After today, and the constant attention given to her by her father, Jordan felt a little wary about entering the dining hall. Her relationship with her father was more like two strangers under the same roof. For reasons she hated to think about, he generally avoided her. It was painful, but she was used to it. Today, however, being constantly in his presence drained her, pretending they had what they really didn't. So she surveyed the area before finally entering the dining hall, satisfied that he was absent. After all these years of wanting him to look at her twice, why did she want to avoid him now that he had noticed her?

The candlelight from the chandeliers warmed the air. She stood in the doorway and waited. It always felt nice to watch the activity of the estate. Salina kept everyone moving. However, the hour was late, and most of the servants had already returned home.

At the far end of the table sat Malkam, Lucy, and Zachary. They didn't seem to be talking. All three were still, just absorbing the events of the past few days. Most of the table still held all the paperwork of the plans. Now everyone was home, performing the tasks they had been assigned. She walked toward the three.

The movement of her approach drew Lucy's attention. She smiled faintly and then returned her attention to her half-empty plate. Though the three were not talking, Jordan felt she was intruding upon an intense conversation, one she wouldn't understand.

"Hi," she said softly. "May I join you?"

"Sure," Zachary answered. "Sorry, we're poor company. The past few days have been exhausting. Well, excuse me—sorry, Jordan." He stood and approached her, realizing who she was. "How are you feeling?" He gingerly hugged her, and she guessed that some information had gotten around, since her back still ached from the lashing.

"I'm fine. Rested, you know."

"Yeah. Sit down."

Lucy remained silent, her eyes shifting to focus on the activities in the kitchen. Solomon, the cook, was singing while the others washed the dishes. This was nothing new, but Jordan sat beside Malkam, leaving Lucy alone on the other side of the table.

"What have you guys been doing?" she asked lightly, finding the tension unsettling.

"Well, Lucy and I've been running through a lot of your tunnels the past few days," Zachary answered. "Blocked some off today. Oh, my arms are sore. I've never felt like this in my whole life." He returned to his seat and sat with a soft moan.

Lucy finally turned her full attention to Jordan. "Do you know where Joe is?"

"Um," Jordan began.

"Lucy," Malkam said warningly. "Leave her alone."

"You can shut it!" Lucy snapped, almost snarling at Malkam. Jordan gulped and fixed her gaze on the table.

Zachary leaned forward to look around Malkam at Jordan. "These two are on the outs right now. Might want to move down here—if you want to talk to anyone, that is."

Jordan nodded and changed her seat. One of the servants approached her with a plate of food. They all knew her favorites. Tonight, it was basil chicken with a fruit salad. At the moment, it didn't look too appealing. Her stomach was tied in knots.

"I've never had chicken like that," Zachary said. "I liked it."

"It's my favorite," Jordan confessed. "Don't feel like eating too much right now, though."

Zachary glanced at the cold war to his left. He leaned close and whispered, "It took an hour to get my food in. Of course, that's because I had to keep Lucy off the former general."

Malkam scoffed and dropped the piece of bread he'd been clutching. He leaned back and wiped his mouth with a napkin and threw it on his plate, his gaze fixing itself on the redhead across the table. She remained frozen, jaw muscles twitching.

"And, uh, Payden's probably with David," Jordan said softly.

Malkam dropped his head. "You didn't."

Lucy's head snapped around. "What?" she exclaimed, half standing. "He's where? I'll kill him!"

Jordan leaned back, hands clutching the armrests.

"Here we go again," Zachary muttered.

"You mean, he's *with* the man who almost got him killed? *With* him?"

"Lucy," Malkam growled, rising to his feet.

"And so where is this brave man, then?" she cried. "Hiding in the rose gardens? 'Cause he's certainly not shown his face since he told Joe to go off on his own!"

Jordan felt her breath quicken. She'd never seen anyone's face turn that shade of red. And no one had ever yelled at her. What to do? She couldn't think of anything.

Lucy stood completely, lifting her fists. "I'll kill him."

Zachary shook his head. "Luce—"

"Oh, you can shut it, too! That monster has done nothing! Nothing! And we're supposed to trust him, when he lets Joe go and . . ." Her breathing became too erratic to continue the sentence. With a low growl, she picked up her fork and plunged it into her untouched meat.

"Jordan, do you think you could lead us on a tour?" Malkam asked lightly.

"A . . . tour?" Jordan was caught off guard. Why would he want that, especially after Lucy's outburst?

"Sure. Give us a chance to see the beauty of this valley. I'd like a look around."

"Um, it's not very pretty in the dark, though."

"Sure it is," Malkam said jovially. "It'll be romantic. These two need a good, romantic date, I think."

"Excuse me?" Lucy asked.

As Lucy and Malkam exchanged verbal blows, Zachary leaned close to Jordan and, in a hushed tone, said, "And now her anger's back at Malkam." He winked at Jordan. "She's wanted to kill David all evening, since we returned. Malkam sent us away pretty quick when you were gone." Zachary sobered. "So we've been busy. But now that your dad's in charge, the three of us don't seem to be so necessary. Lucy went to check on Payden. And when he wasn't in his room, Malkam and I had to keep her out of David's. Malkam's been doing a great job keeping her anger directed at him. He doesn't seem to mind her fury. In fact," Zachary paused as he glanced up at Malkam, "I think he's enjoying it."

Jordan's eyes went from Lucy to Malkam. Lucy's wrath was obvious. Malkam's face carried a subtle grin.

"Eat up," Zachary suggested. "Before your food gets cold."

Jordan nodded and cut into the chicken. Lucy's sharp comments almost caused Jordan to gasp a time or two, but she forced down as much food as she could. When the battle seemed to have ended, Jordan's eyes again went from Lucy to Malkam. He seemed a bit more agitated, while she seemed worn out, finally.

"Okay then," Jordan said weakly. "I can take you around. Show you stuff. The torchlight should be enough. Just to get a feel of the grounds, anyway."

Lucy looked down at her and Jordan weakly smiled.

"Lead the way," Malkam said. Jordan nodded and rose to her feet.

"This way." She walked quickly to the exit. Once outside, she took a deep breath. The indoors had been extremely confining today. The air smelled sweet, as always, thanks to the abundant flower gardens. A waft of smoke tinged the air since the torches and candles were lit at sundown. Yet the air was cold. Very cold. She shivered and rubbed her arms.

Zachary stepped beside her and placed his arm around her shoulder.

"You okay?" he asked.

"It's just colder than I expected."

"Well, I thought it was supposed to be this cold in the mountains. Here." He removed his cloak and draped it around her. The bottom of it dragged on the ground. "Huh," he said, noting how much fabric rested on the marble walk. "Guess I never stopped to realize how tall I am."

She looked down and giggled, lifting the excess folds to wrap over her arms. "Maybe I'm just really short."

He grinned and turned his head to watch Lucy approach. Her arms crossed her chest, and the temporary scowl still marred her face. He chuckled. "I really don't know why, but I love it when she's like this. So aggressively stubborn."

"Why is she so angry?"

"David told us to let Payden go get you by himself. She felt that David at least should have gone as well. I mean, maybe he should have, but who knows what would have happened?"

"Yeah."

Malkam stood beside Jordan. He surveyed the town. The torchlight illuminated the buildings, which glowed white in the night. Jordan led them down the steps and turned right. "This is the way to my house," she explained. "I'm only taking you there first because the rose garden is right behind it, and it's the most beautiful of them all. I get to wake up and smell them every morning."

"Sounds nice," Zachary said. "Anything's better than smoke and—stuff," he said, stopping himself from saying "charred remains." He figured Jordan could only handle so much of the outside world at a time, but he couldn't help but think of Tawney City. It was so unlike this place. The kids would enjoy it here, he knew. Anything was better than the battles that constantly raged there.

"Has it always been this chilly?" Malkam asked. The night winds picked through the area, accosting them. He shrugged his shoulders and looked up at the stars.

"It's supposed to be cold in the mountains, right?" Zachary asked.

"Nah," Malkam answered. "The Jathenites deal more with that. The mountains are higher farther north. It shouldn't be this cold around here, if I remember correctly."

"It does seem to be getting colder each year," Jordan said. "In fact, we lost a lot of flowers last year when something unusual happened. The older Djorites called it 'frost.' Nothing like that's happened since, though."

"Hm," Malkam said simply, looking about as if he only brought up the subject out of curiosity. Jordan wondered if she should continue to explain her worries. The weather had always been warm when she was a child. It began growing colder only a few years ago. No one seemed concerned, but it bothered her.

"Do you know how long ago the Djorites came here?" Malkam asked her.

"Um." Jordan thought. She glanced back at Lucy. She seemed calmer, but she walked far behind them. Probably couldn't even hear the conversation, Jordan assumed. She stopped walking and gestured toward the building in front of them. "Here's my house. My dad's inside, I think. He knows for sure when the first Djorites arrived. I can only guess."

Malkam laughed. "Let's keep walking. The night air is just the perfect temperature to cool tempers." He looked back at Lucy, whose eyes were fixed on the roses growing behind the house. Lucy plucked one and tested the texture of the petals.

Zachary finally approached Lucy and whispered to her. She didn't respond much, but it seemed like she finally had calmed. Malkam continued down the path, and Jordan followed him.

"Thirty-two years ago," she said, to answer his question. "All those tunnels you destroyed today actually saved lives."

"Back then, sure. Now, they're unnecessary."

"I guess."

The crunch of gravel behind them spoke of followers. Jordan pulled the cloak tighter as she mustered her courage.

"Can I ask you about Lucy? Why is she so upset with David while no one else is?"

"Oh, I'm mad at him too," Malkam said. "I think he knows his mistake. I just can't figure him out. So she has every right to be mad. It's just better for her to lash out right now, and since David isn't around, I'll be her target."

"I see."

"Something's wrong with her. She, uh— Well, it's more polite if I keep those concerns to myself, I suppose."

"I understand." They walked silently until they reached the edge of the gardens. No more torches lit the area, and Malkam looked up at the moon. The light revealed the large field that stretched out before them. Jordan leaned against the wood fence that surrounded the field.

"So, what stays in here?" Malkam asked. Zachary and Lucy reached them. A flower was tucked behind Lucy's ear. Zachary looked upset. So did Lucy. Jordan didn't want to stare at them, so she turned to Malkam.

"This is the field for cattle and sheep. The swine are farther south of the city. Near the chickens."

"Which were a great dinner," Zachary quipped, trying to move past whatever had upset him. "Right, Lucy?"

"Sure," she answered softly. "I'm tired. Let's go back."

The two left. That girl needed more help than she realized, Malkam mused as Lucy and Zachary gradually disappeared from sight. It was regrettable that Lucy didn't want to be around David, because he'd be the best person to help her. Malkam decided to at least mention the situation to David in the morning. Something needed to be done.

"Do you think we're still safe here?" Jordan asked.

"Hm? Oh, sure," Malkam said hastily. "We're ready, either way. It's just—your dad's keeping some information from me. Everyone is. And I hope they realize soon enough that they should take advantage of us. David and I are willing to help. You Djorites aren't alone anymore."

"Thanks," Jordan said. Her mind drifted. The information her father was hiding. "We typically don't keep secrets, you know." She wanted to defend her father. "But there's one thing we shared in the past, and it was used to destroy us."

"That weapon? The thing the Fashites want?"

"Yeah. It's not really a weapon, but there isn't too much anyone knows about it. I'm sure my father will explain it in time. We want to trust, but we're not as able anymore."

"Don't blame you. Oh, it's late. Let's head back. My old body needs some rest."

Jordan walked beside him. His pace was slow, and she glanced up at him occasionally, trying to determine his age. Definitely older than her father, she figured. When they reached her house, she paused. "I'll go home too, then. Good night, Malkam."

"Good night."

Candlelight spilled out of the window at the top of the house. Jordan swallowed nervously. Maybe she could get in without him hearing her. Or should she allow her father a chance to tell her good night? Once she crossed the threshold, she shut the door noisily and heavily walked to her bedroom. She paused in the doorway for a few minutes, waiting for any sign that he would acknowledge her return, but nothing happened. She hung her head and entered her bedroom. It hadn't taken him long to return to normal, it seemed.

Chapter 4

When Payden woke, he noticed the darkness outside. David was missing. Payden propped himself up on his elbow and looked around the room. Hoping to see or hear some sign of David, Payden grew disappointed when all he discovered was an empty room. Unable to ignore the pleading of his empty stomach, he decided to go to his room and see if they had delivered his tray.

The tray sat on the table by the door, and he took advantage of the chair at the table as he quickly ate. Satisfied despite the cold food, he wanted to search for Jordan, when he remembered her promise of a visit. The cold cup of tea by the bedside told him he'd missed her. He drank it quickly and cringed more than usual. It was less offensive when warm.

Leaning heavily upon the cane, Payden left the room to find some signs of life. No one was in sight, not even a single servant. By the time he reached the bottom of the stairs, he had to sit. A tall couch invited him, and he crossed to the wall by the entryway so that he could relax. Sitting in any position other than upright aggravated the wound in his back, which began to throb angrily, protesting his being up and about. Payden was desperate to find David. He stood and went into the dining hall. It was clean and empty. No one had been in there for some time.

The set of doors that still remained shut bothered him too much to let them remain so any longer. He looked at the exit to the hallway, then at the archway that separated the kitchen from the dining hall. With no witnesses present, he turned the handle and pulled.

Like all the other doors in the building, it opened with ease despite how heavy it seemed. It was dark inside. Payden followed the wall, which was quite short before it met another. His hands then found something soft. A closer inspection revealed curtains, which he drew back in hopes of getting some light to seep through. The moon became a coconspirator in his plot to uncover the secret of that room. As he pulled back more and more curtains, the light increased enough for him to properly see.

He laughed. He hadn't even thought to ask where all the books were kept, but here would have been his answer. They filled shelves that reached all the way to the ceiling. Ladders were attached to these shelves on every wall. Tall and fat books stood next to short and stocky ones. In the middle was a pillar topped with a glass case, with a large book that looked far more worn than the others. It stood open, but the pages were so faded that he couldn't make out a single word. Perhaps he could when there was more light. He reverently touched the glass before deciding to undo the signs of his disturbance and leave.

Sweat dripped from his brow by the time he made it to the top of the steps. He couldn't understand why everything was so difficult, but he also felt as though he was going to retch all over the place. His skin felt warm. He hoped he wasn't ill. The railing provided the extra support he needed as he paused to catch his breath before the last leg of his journey to the bedroom. Just after letting go, he watched as the door opened and David emerged.

"David!" Payden said without thinking, feeling that if he said nothing, David wouldn't see him.

"Payden, what are you doing?" David asked. He quickly put his arm around Payden's waist and held him up.

"I was looking for you," Payden answered.

"You have less sense than a rock," David quipped. "A rock knows when to stay put when it's not supposed to move."

Payden looked up at David. "I'm sorry," he said soberly, hoping David understood for what offense.

"We'll talk once we're inside."

Payden admitted that it felt nice to sink into the mattress. His throbbing back no longer taunted him, though his leg didn't feel any different.

"I wanted to change your bandages," David said. "But with your running around everywhere, I hope you haven't broken the stitches. Now lie on your stomach."

Wincing as he moved, Payden carefully rolled enough for David to easily remove the bandages. David shook his head. The doctor, Roman, had been right about an infection. David set the bandages he'd borrowed from the infirmary onto the bed so he could get his herbs out of his cloak. The wound needed a potent ointment to fight the infection.

"I want you to stop walking around and give this one a chance to heal," David said and tapped Payden's hamstring. "There's still an infection in the other one, but at least your body's fighting it. Just rest so your body can, all right?"

"All right," Payden mumbled.

After he removed his gloves and cleansed and redressed the wounds, slathering them with the balm, David pressed a hand against Payden's forehead and throat. "You've got a fever as well."

"Why didn't you come with me?" Payden analyzed David's face, looking for an answer.

David sat on the edge of the bed and picked up his gloves to give him something to focus on so he wouldn't have to look at Payden. This was the question. It had taken David all day to find an answer he could tell. Being in that washroom had tortured David beyond his capacities, so he finally forced himself to escape it, avoiding everyone until he'd settled himself in the most secluded area of the gardens. It was hours before he could finally even remember who he was, let alone explain to himself what had happened the past few days. Once he regained his composure, he had returned to the estate. It was empty. He nearly panicked again until he heard Payden call his name.

Why hadn't he gone?

"One reason was the Djorites would have needed me more in case the Fashites had an army already heading up to attack. Another is—your father. He was—" David paused. He tilted his head slightly and studied Payden. No. He couldn't know that yet, so David swallowed nervously and returned his attention to the gloves.

"Your father was a great man."

Payden didn't know what David had meant to say, but he did notice that David was apprehensive. Payden could only guess why, and he felt more guilt than he had imagined he would feel. He moved to sit next to David and reached out his hand but pulled it back.

"I'm sorry, David. I'm so sorry."

David said nothing, but he stopped fidgeting with the gloves. Payden felt guilty about having seen him earlier, David realized. That untempered panic began to creep into his thoughts.

"David, I—"

"Don't talk about it. What's done is done," David said curtly.

"Can we talk about it?"

"There's nothing to discuss," David said.

"But can't we—"

"There's nothing to discuss!" David snapped harshly, finally looking at Payden, who shrank back.

Frustrated, David stood and headed for the door.

"What are you running from?" Payden asked loudly.

The question caused David to pause with his hand reaching for the door handle. Still the same Payden, after all these years. Any advice David used to encourage Payden to do something he didn't want to do, David knew he'd hear echoed again later. Payden never forgot a word David said.

"What are you running from?" Payden asked again.

David dropped his hand to his side. "Using my own weapons against me, huh?"

"They're effective, so why not?"

"There are some things that I'd rather not tell you, boy."

"Who's asking? I just want to know why you're still running." Payden was amazed at his own boldness, but David seemed to be allowing it.

David turned and stared intently at him. Payden refused to show any signs of backing down. Stubborn boy, David thought.

"Payden, what I ask of you, I ask because I know from experience. I can offer you no advice other than that which I've learned. Trust me and do what I ask."

"But what kind of an example do you give me when you don't follow that advice yourself?" Payden asked, feeling his impatience rise.

"Because when all you've done in your life is run, it becomes harder to stand and fight than if you'd never run at all. I want you to be a stronger man than I am. I want you to stand and fight."

"Why won't you talk to me?"

"What more do you want me to say?" David asked, reminding himself to keep calm. This was Payden.

"I want you to tell me some hard truth," Payden answered. "I'm not a boy anymore. I may not remember anything, but I deserve to know something. Why would anyone put themselves through all that torture? You said it was for me, but have you ever really told me why?"

"No."

Payden waited for him to say more, but David only shifted enough to grasp his wrist. He would offer no more information, and Payden's temper flared.

"Fine. Choose your silence," Payden said. "Keep me in the dark. Ever wonder, though, if the only reason I run is because I learned it from you?"

Payden angrily fell back onto the bed, crossing his arms and ignoring the pain the rough movements caused. He stared at the ceiling, unable to handle the racing thoughts that only tormented him, fueled by anger. He didn't even know what he was running from, but he certainly felt that he would fight it.

What was so terrible about David that he refused to do the same? Payden heard the door open and then close.

Fear surfaced. He really, truly didn't know David. He wondered if all that David said was truth or a lie. He wondered if his own desire to remember his past overwhelmed his reasoning. Then again, who could he trust? Maybe his emotions were playing tricks on him.

Knowing that he wasn't going to get any sleep, he got up and found his book. Returning to the bed with a lamp, he stayed awake all night reading.

Chapter 5

Malkam woke early that morning and quickly went to the dining hall. Samuel paced the length of the table while people came and went. The activity attracted Malkam. As a young man, Malkam had always found himself in the middle of things. Back then, he formed a small army. The Pendtars didn't exist at that point in time, but the Ashites were a cancer unto themselves. After several villages near his were attacked by raiders, Malkam talked the other young men into forming means to protect themselves. It took only a few years for the endeavor to become successful. The raiders avoided their little corner of the continent. Trading evolved into a stronger life source, bringing in goods as well as news—news of a young man named Henry Carpenter traveling through the north, trying to bring the Ashites together.

As Malkam watched Samuel pore over the maps, trying to see something no one else could, he couldn't stop himself from reminiscing. In the old days, they had never stopped helping people. He missed it. Things ended with Henry's death. Malkam tried to keep moving forward, but the Fashites fought on too many fronts, and Malkam's age limited his abilities. Therefore he remained in Landar, relying on the young men who fought for him to maintain the boundaries. Giving up his position as general hadn't been as hard on him as everyone thought. At least now he was out again. Active. It felt good.

Samuel finally noticed Malkam standing in the doorway. He motioned the man over, and Malkam quickly approached. "Good morning," Samuel said.

"Samuel," Malkam assented with a nod of his head. He still didn't respect the man too much.

"No one wants to leave," Samuel said, eyes fixed on the list of supplies. "The elderly ran years ago. They don't want to do it again. The younger generations feel the same way. We made this place. It's full of our histories and art. When the Fashites first attacked, our ancestors immediately took our finest works to the tunnels. We hid so many things. And when we found this valley, we brought our treasures with us. Not only should we survive, but so should our culture. It's here, now. It would take a generation to rebuild another place for us. And we've already lost so much from previous generations. If we move again, then the Djorites might truly become extinct. You can understand this, right?"

Malkam nodded. "Of course. Stand and fight; that's my motto. Fight smart, of course."

"Yes, of course. Except we are severely disadvantaged. There's no real fight in us. We built this city before we forged a single sword. I'm not sure we even did that correctly. And we've certainly no real knowledge of how to use one."

Malkam shifted his weight, his hand finding the hilt of his sword. That young man from so many years ago, with all his ideals, still lived inside Malkam. He had taught himself to fight back then. He taught everyone around him how to fight, too. Excitement still coursed through his veins every year when new recruits arrived for training. He loved doing it. "You know, you now have a source of knowledge to take advantage of."

Samuel nodded. "I am aware. But I didn't want to assume too much."

"I'll volunteer, then," Malkam said. "If your people want to stay and hold their ground, then I will gladly do everything I can to prepare them."

"Thank you," Samuel said. "My captain has requested an audience with you several times. He'll be eager to speak with you, as soon as you're ready."

"Where is he?"

"Probably up in the tunnels, positioning men as you suggested."

"I'll find him, then. Get a training camp set up."

"And there is something else," Samuel said hesitantly.

"Yes?"

"I suppose I should tell all of you, together, if anyone else is willing to stay to help."

"I'll talk to them. Let's meet this evening. That'll give me time to convince everyone to stay."

"I appreciate that."

Malkam paused. "I wonder, though: how much I can trust your ability to lead if the Fashites do descend upon this valley?"

Samuel clasped his hands behind his back and nodded. "You feel that I would be terrible?"

"You weren't the leader your people needed once Jordan disappeared."

"No, I wasn't. But that was—personal."

Malkam knit his brows. "And your people fighting for survival isn't?"

Samuel shook his head and sat on the nearest seat. "Yes, I suppose that didn't make sense. What I mean is, you see, Jordan is all I have. And I've never told her how I feel about her. I don't know how. I'm a man who's always in my head. I prefer to be alone than in company. She—she's like her mother." Samuel fell silent and studied his hands. "I lost my wife so many years ago. Lost her long before she died, even. The war took its toll on many. Some lost their minds. My wife stopped making sense." He sighed heavily and looked up at Malkam. "The thought of losing Jordan took me back to when I lost my wife. I had never let her go. With Jordan around, I never really lost her. I wasn't prepared for how much it would hurt to lose both of them. It won't happen again. I can guarantee that."

The man looked Malkam in the eyes as he said that. Malkam always appreciated a man who could give his word without blinking. "Good. As long as you're with me. Where should I have everyone meet tonight?"

"In the study. Jordan or Salina can show you the room."

"I haven't been introduced to Salina yet."

"Yes, well, Salina believes that if no one has seen or met her, then she's doing her job well." Samuel stood, smiling. "She should be in the kitchen with Solomon. She goes over the day's menu with him each morning before breakfast. Of course, I have a few moments. I could take you there myself—"

"No," Malkam interrupted. He nodded toward the paperwork. "Keep doing your job. I'll just go introduce myself."

He left Samuel and went into the kitchen. Cooks were already busying themselves, prepping the eggs and meat. Malkam saw a man he recognized only because the man always seemed to be in the kitchen at every meal. He assumed the man was Solomon. A woman stood next to him, talking more actively with her hands than anything else. Solomon nodded, and smiled at her as she turned to depart.

"Salina?" Malkam asked.

The woman froze, obviously disliking being acknowledged. "Yes?"

Malkam hesitated for a moment. She was an attractive woman, about his age, he guessed. She instantly reminded him of someone he had lost long ago. Someone he couldn't choose only because of the war. He shook away those thoughts and did his best to smile as he approached. "Sorry if you're busy. Samuel just mentioned you were here. He wants to meet with me and members of my party this evening in the study. If you wouldn't mind escorting us there, I would appreciate it. Also, one of the young men will need special accommodations . . ."

"Yes, Payden," she said quickly. "I'll have a bed set up for him. Some of the servants will help him down as well. That boy shouldn't be up and about."

"Seems he already is," Malkam said lightly.

"So I've heard. I'll have to remedy that. If you don't mind, sir, I'll need to go adjust my schedule."

"Oh, yes. Please." Malkam stepped out of her way. She cast him a small smile as she passed.

"She sure is a pretty woman, isn't she, sir?" came a question from the back of the kitchen. Malkam's head snapped around, and he found Solomon smiling broadly at him. Before he became too embarrassed, Malkam stepped out of the kitchen, hearing stifled giggles behind him. Now, on to the impossible task of finding David.

The table in the dining hall stood empty, free of all paperwork and evidence of preparations a few hours later, as people entered for their morning meal. Zachary paced between the dining hall entrance and the top of the stairwell, waiting for Lucy. She finally emerged from her room as he started to ascend the steps. When he spotted her at the top, he froze, nervous about her attitude. Last night, she had practically told him she wished they'd never met. He hadn't taken it literally, knowing how she liked to wound whenever she felt wounded, but at this moment, he wondered what her mood was. When her eyes found him, she smiled, and he sighed with relief.

"Good morning," he called up to her.

"Hey," she replied weakly, reaching his side. He scooped her into his arms, embracing her tightly. "Let me go!" she protested.

He laughed and released her. "Hungry?"

She punched his arm. "Idiot. That was uncalled for."

"Yes, it was. You shouldn't punch anyone. That's rude."

"Not that. You are such—an idiot! What . . .?" She snorted in frustration and passed him.

He fell in step beside her, grabbing her hand. "Feeling better?" he asked.

"If I am, will you stop acting like an idiot?"

"Nope. This is what you've got this morning."

"Wouldn't every girl like to be me?" she asked, voice full of exhaustion.

"I certainly wouldn't be hanging around them."

"Oh, to be another girl, then!"

Zachary squeezed her hand.

She rolled her eyes. "What am I going to do with you?"

"Marry me."

Her heart fluttered at the suggestion. "Don't tease about that."

"I wouldn't."

"I'm hungry. Don't talk to me about anything until after we've eaten."

"Fair enough."

More people trickled through the doors, keeping the servants busy taking orders and cleaning empty spots. Malkam sat beside Zachary and Lucy, arriving just as they finished their breakfast. He spoke to them of his conversation with Samuel, and they agreed to stay and listen to what Samuel had to say.

Malkam sat as still as he could, doing his best not to glance at the entrance too often. One of his personal tasks this morning was to talk to David about Lucy. The longer she held her anger, the unhealthier the situation became. Malkam waited patiently, doing everything he could to keep the couple at the table.

The room had maintained a low hum of noise from the various occupants. The level dropped, though, when David entered. Lucy noticed the volume decrease immediately, and she quickly looked at the entrance. Zachary tensed. Malkam eased his chair back in case he needed to rise quickly. Before another moment passed, David backed out of the room.

"Oh no, he doesn't," Lucy hissed, getting to her feet.

"Luce!" Zachary cried, jumping out of his chair.

"Leave me be!" she cried.

Malkam grabbed the young man's arm. "Let her go after him. It needs to happen. This way, David will make sure it's somewhere private."

"She'll kill him," Zachary warned.

"We'll worry about that if it happens, then. It's okay. Let's talk."

David knew the gardens well enough to know which spot was the most secluded. Malkam wanted David's assessment of Lucy, so David would make sure she got a chance to tell him everything on her mind. It could all be nothing but anger because of what had happened to Payden. Whatever it was, he wasn't looking forward to the encounter. Not because of what she would say, but of what he could do.

He found the spot and turned to wait for her. Sounds of frustration and the occasional curse made their way to his ears. If he hadn't been apprehensive, he probably would have laughed at her, but the past week had drained him of life. He stood, silent and stoic.

She entered the small grotto surrounded by rose-covered walls. The way he stood there, patiently waiting for her arrival, only caused her to hate him more. This evil, wicked, bloodthirsty man! The murderer! The bile that walked about in human form. She slowed her approach, stopping across from him, cut off from everyone else. Whatever happened, there would be no witnesses.

Her hand went to her side, but her sword wasn't there. All her weapons remained in her room. No matter. She would kill him with her bare hands. He wasn't armed, she noted. At least the fight would be fair.

A bird lighted on the top of a wall, chirping away in its song about the morning. Another bird flew past it, squawking at the first, which quickly rose in chase. Beyond that, nothing disturbed the setting. David waited. If she wanted to fight, then she had to be the first to attack.

What did he want, she wondered. What was he waiting for? For her to do something? Say something? Why wasn't he moving? Her fury rose with each breath. She didn't want to make the first move; that's what he wanted. Of course—he was a Slave. They could wait forever.

Time passed, and she felt her breathing regulate as the adrenaline subsided. A few furry creatures scuttled through the grotto, squeaking as they went. Finally, when all seemed calm, David took a small step forward.

"Oh, so that's your plan? Wait until the fight's out of me?" Lucy snapped, clenching her fists as she took a few steps toward him.

"I'm sorry," he said softly.

She laughed deliriously. "I hate you. If it weren't for men like you, this world would be better. All of you—we're better off if you're dead!"

David nodded slowly. "That's fair."

"Hm, nice strategy. Gain my confidence by agreeing with everything I say?"

"No. Just honesty. I'm testing you."

Those words pierced her more than any insult could. "Testing me? Why? You monster, leave me alone!"

"I thought you were mad at me because of Payden. But that's not really it, is it? You've mistrusted me from the beginning." He paused. "That's fair."

"Don't patronize me, villain! Don't you dare!" She began hyperventilating. Images flashed though her mind. Screaming. Little Tate, hiding in a closet. She saw his eyes looking through the gap at the bottom of the door. She wanted to scream. Tears filled her eyes as they fixed on the Slave before her. David analyzed her every move. Malkam was right to suspect something.

She stepped back from him, swallowing deeply. David guessed that she had stopped being angry with him and started feeling fear about something else. He took a few steps closer. When she saw the movement, she gulped and ran. He didn't follow.

Jordan didn't take the time to eat breakfast that morning. She didn't even fix the tea she knew she should bring, because she wanted to see Payden. She just hurried up the stairs and into his room without even knocking. He stood by the wardrobe, half-dressed. She gasped and covered her eyes. His laughter reached her ears, but she was embarrassed. She kept her eyes closed even after he wrapped his arms around her.

"You still have your shirt off," she said.

"So?" he asked. "Or would you prefer I put one on?"

"Yes, please."

He let her go and gingerly pulled a shirt over his head. "I'm dressed."

She opened one eye first, and then felt relief as she opened the other.

"That's better," she said. "Now you can hug me."

He obeyed with a smile, gingerly placing his arms around her. The bandages that remained on her wrists reminded him that she should still be treated delicately. Before he allowed his anger to rise, he calmed himself with a deep breath. This brought in the scent of her hair, which reminded him of the flowers in the garden nook where he and David had talked days ago. He closed his eyes and held her tightly. When she began to hum, he laughed softly.

"Could we just stay like this for days?" she asked.

"No," he answered. "Because I need to rest my leg."

"Oh." She pulled away. "I forgot."

He sat on the bed and pulled his injured leg up carefully. The pillows were piled high against the headboard, and he leaned back against them and stared at her. Feeling herself growing shy under his gaze, she coyly made her way around the bed. Desire to be next to him guided her to his side, where she leaned her head against his chest, content. She hummed again.

"What's that song?" he asked.

"I don't remember the name, but it's an old one. My favorite."

"Huh." He sounded far away.

"What are you thinking?"

"I know where your name came from."

She lifted her head to look at his face. "How?"

"I was up all night reading. But I wonder—where is the Jordan River?"

She returned to her former position. "Don't know. It may not even exist. I mean, if it does, it's certainly nowhere we can go. But it's still an interesting story."

"I think it's more than that."

"How so?"

"Well, do other books describe unnatural occurrences as natural? Like water turning to blood?"

She pondered the question for a moment. "No. I don't really recall."

"That's what I thought. The book last night—I read so many things that I couldn't understand. But then I turned the page, and it was if whoever wrote it knew that I would be reading it, so they said something that I really needed to hear last night."

"Like what?"

"Well, there was a poem about David. I mean, I know it was meant for a different David, but it described our David in a way. It said that he would be strong and his enemies would not be able to defeat him. But then it spoke of him being rejected and mocked. I don't know."

"Go on."

"Well, I flipped some pages, and the very next thing I read was that there is no greater love than to die for your friends. I got to thinking, and in a way, maybe David's done that." He paused, feeling a bit of sorrow. "And I just want to know why."

She could think of nothing to say. She rolled and put her arm across his waist. As he fell silent, she knew that he was lost in his thoughts, but she didn't mind. He absentmindedly ran his fingers through her hair, down her arm, and back up again. The song once again filled her thoughts, and she hummed as she listened to his heartbeat.

Goodness, Jordan, what are you doing? she thought. She still didn't know him well. What was going on?

There are proper ways to begin a relationship, and this certainly isn't one of them. That was her father's voice, she knew, but she couldn't ignore it. The humming ceased. She should leave, she concluded. This wasn't right. But it was, she argued. He wasn't a stranger. He was—

She sat upright and looked at him thoughtfully. The movement distracted him from his thoughts.

"What is it?" he asked.

"I should probably go."

He leaned toward her, concerned. "Why?"

She tried to speak, but she couldn't think of a convincing enough excuse. His face went from concern to realization as he sank back into the pillows, but she wondered what he was thinking.

"I get it," he said.

"Get what?"

He looked away from her to his hands, which he slowly moved down to his sides. "Your father wouldn't approve of me," he said hoarsely. She noticed tears collecting in his eyes.

"Why wouldn't he?" she asked, glancing at his hands, wondering why he kept trying to hide them.

"Because I'm a murderer." His voice cracked. "Every time I'm near you, that fact is so apparent. I try to ignore it, but it's there. Last night, I read that it's not good to kill. That murderers should be put to death."

Her body grew heavy. This was too new and unfamiliar for her to even think properly. She had never met anyone who had taken the life of another person. Her people never chose to do that. Yet, many years ago, the Djorites had been friendly with the Jathenites, and the Jathenites were warriors. Killing was almost a rite of passage for them. They frequently battled the Fashites and Ashites, even killing those who stumbled upon their lands without question if the Jathenites considered them a threat. That had never stopped the Djorites from associating with them. If her ancestors didn't consider killing— No, she realized. Murdering was different, wasn't it? Payden considered himself a murderer.

"But weren't the men you—killed, um, weren't they armed? And didn't they deserve it?" she asked.

Payden's expression grew thoughtful and slightly confused. He looked up at Jordan with eyebrows knit.

"I mean, if you hadn't stopped them, then they would have killed the people in that village. And those men . . ." She couldn't finish the sentence. The men from the other night had laughed in enjoyment of her pain. She shuddered at the memory of them.

His hands made their way back to his lap, and he pensively stared at them.

She shook her head and found her voice again. "There were a lot of men and women in that book who killed, and no one looked down on them because they fought for freedom or in self-defense. I think a murderer is different from a warrior. A murderer just kills someone they don't like or to steal what that person has. You have helped saved lives. And—" She sighed. "And it's just a book, Payden."

"It's not—"

"It is. No one has ever had any reason to think that it could possibly have happened. Someone gave some great advice, and we Djorites have adapted our lives according to the Book's teachings, but it's just a book. Truly."

"It feels like more than that, though."

She scooted as close as she dared. He suddenly seemed nervous.

"What's really wrong?" she asked.

"Honestly, would your father approve of me?"

"It's not his decision."

"Jordan, it's not—"

"Stop," she interrupted. "You're getting yourself all worked up. Stop thinking. Relax. Has anyone here treated you in any way that suggests we don't want you here? Give yourself a little credit."

He nodded, but then his gaze became more intent. Nervous alarms went off in her head and only increased as he pushed himself upright. She swallowed nervously. What was he going to do?

His hand gently cradled her face, and a little fear overcame her. It had been different earlier. She had come to regret kissing him then, but that impulse had been too strong to fight. But now? There were rules of propriety. Certain things had to happen first. She shouldn't have sat on the bed with him. She should have waited and allowed him to ask her father for permission to court her.

As he leaned closer, the flight impulse diminished, which alarmed her. Realizing her inhibitions, she turned away and crossed over to slide off the bed. Nervously running her hands through her hair, she knew she had to leave.

"I'll see you later," she whispered before she quickly left. She paused for a deep breath after closing the door. That had been too close. Why did she feel that she had just made the wrong decision, then?

Chapter 6

The empty study surprised Malkam when he arrived. He expected Samuel to already be there preparing for the meeting. His great concern was David's attendance. Or Lucy's. After the encounter this morning, his worry for her had grown. Zachary wasn't too forthcoming with information either. Just something about her brothers. Malkam left the study in search of David. That man's presence at least was vital.

David watched Malkam leave the room and almost smiled. The old man hadn't seen him, apparently. Sometimes, it was best to hide in plain sight. A tall wingback chair filled the back corner of the room, and David sat inside it. Shadows the thin candlelight couldn't reach draped themselves over the chair, hence the reason for Malkam's oversight. David rested his eyes and waited. Hopefully the others would overlook him as well.

Malkam searched wherever he felt he'd gain the most success, but not even the servants knew David's whereabouts. Frustrated, Malkam returned to the study. This time, there was activity. Two young men were setting up a small bed in the front. They smiled at Malkam when he entered. One of them glanced toward the back corner before returning his attention to his duties. Curious, Malkam's eyes followed the path of the look. He was not amused.

"How long have you been there?"

David smiled again. A hidden smile, for the scarf always covered the lower half of his face, but it still felt good to do it. "For quite some time."

"Couldn't tell me earlier?"

"Well, you didn't ask," David answered.

Malkam stood next to the chair. "You're impossible," he muttered.

David chuckled.

"Oh? Glad to be your entertainment."

"Always are," David quipped.

"How did it go this morning?"

David breathed deeply. "Pretty well. It's not me she hates . . ."

"A first."

"It's who she sees. Did Zachary tell you anything?"

"She had two brothers. Both were killed during a battle several years ago by Fashites."

"That would cause some deep hatred, but there's something else." David leaned his head back. "This chair is very comfortable."

"Shut your mouth," Malkam threatened. He moved away to take up a spot on a settee near the front by the bed. Not much time passed before Payden hobbled through the door. David shook his head in frustration. That boy needed to remain still.

Jordan and Samuel entered next. Jordan pulled a chair beside Payden, which surprised Payden. Her hasty retreat earlier had left him unsettled. He had let himself believe that she didn't want anything to do with him. What had he done wrong that morning? Well, he realized, she couldn't even look at him with his shirt off. Perhaps kissing her was too shocking as well.

Lastly, Zachary and Lucy arrived. She immediately went to a seat in the front, without so much as looking about. Zachary took a place near Malkam, and Samuel stepped in front of everyone, assuming all were ready to hear what needed to be explained.

His nerves captured his voice for a moment. The last time Djorites trusted outsiders, they had been betrayed. The specifics were lost, but the scars remained. None of the oldest generation living in the valley ever wanted to speak with an outsider again. Many of them had expressed their concerns to Samuel since the strangers arrived. They felt that the Fashites attacking the village outside the valley, the arrival of the outsiders, and Jordan's disappearance were not coincidences.

Samuel hesitated for a moment. Then his gaze fell on Jordan. She trusted these strangers.

"I don't think anyone in this valley has properly expressed our gratitude for the help all of you have already provided." He paused. No one moved, so he continued. "In our isolation, we became unattached to the other nations. I know, in the past, my people wanted so much to befriend the Ashites. Even the Fashites, as our efforts with the Jathenites were so successful. But, since we never were friends, please forgive us if we are a bit distant." Samuel's gaze fell upon Malkam. "That part of who the Djorites were died a long time ago. We've not wanted outsiders since. The efforts we've shown this past week have mainly been a shadow of who we once were. I apologize."

David's thoughts drifted. The Djorites of old—over forty years ago—had risked death in their efforts to civilize the Ashites. They tried so many times to help, but the Ashites fought among themselves, fought the Jathenites. And killed any Djorite in the way. Yet the Djorites kept coming down from the mountains. They saw the viciousness as a byproduct of how the Ashites lived—in fear.

David focused on Samuel's words. The Djorites in this valley were a bit standoffish in comparison. Fear had finally settled upon them, it seemed. Yet, though hesitant, they still wanted to trust. David swallowed hard and shut his eyes. The songs. The dancing. The laughter. Memories set aside so long ago emerged. The works of art that the cities used to be. The people who lived in the cities. David understood, more than anyone in that room, exactly what Samuel said. For he had seen it.

"In the records that survived, there is mention of a group of outsiders who came to the Djorites a hundred years ago. We welcomed them. In return for our hospitality, they offered us a gift. The gift was beyond our technology at the time, and though we used it for a few years, eventually it was abandoned. This gift—an instrument, rather, became what you could consider a two-edged sword. It helped make our lives very comfortable. Until the Fashites invaded. In but a few moments, our cities were destroyed." Samuel had been a boy, but he remembered fleeing into the mountains. At the higher elevations, he turned and saw the buildings burning. That was, for many, the last image held of their homeland.

"What exactly is this instrument?" Malkam asked.

Samuel shrugged. "Those records are lost, sadly. Not even the oldest citizen here remembers exactly how they were used."

"They?" Payden inquired.

"Several instruments were built. I haven't found any information regarding the number, but one that we know of still exists. And since they are considered poison to our existence, we didn't try to find it. I don't think it even functions, but if the Fashites are seeking its whereabouts . . ." He left it unsaid.

"So let's go destroy it," Payden said. "If it is so dangerous."

"We don't know exactly where it's located," Samuel confessed. "It is somewhere along the Great Sea. That's it. That's all the information I have."

"It's hardly enough information to capture someone over," Malkam observed. Jordan, already tense, stiffened more. Payden's hand clasped over hers, but she didn't move.

Jordan's thoughts went to her mother's journal. She dared a glance toward her father. He'd never read anything written in that book. The few times Jordan had felt brave enough to peek at the latter half, the words had unveiled some information about the instrument. An old man in the village, ancient in comparison to everyone else, ignored because of his symptoms of psychosis, had told Jordan's mother everything anyone would want to know of it.

Jordan had kept all this to herself over the years. It would break her father's heart if he knew she'd kept a secret, no matter her intentions. Secrets were discouraged, so revealing the truth now was not an option. Her guilt weighed heavily. As her breathing became a bit more labored, it drew more attention than she wanted. Except its meaning was misinterpreted.

"Sorry if that came across as insensitive, Jordan," Malkam said gently. He redirected his attention to Samuel. "Thank you for sharing. I know it's not easy, but we'll do what we can to help. No sense worrying about something when we don't have to, right?"

"Agreed," Samuel consented with a nod. "So, I will leave you to discuss what you want to do for now. You know where I can be reached."

"Thank you." Malkam stood as Samuel exited. He gently patted Jordan's shoulder as he passed her, and then turned to look at everyone.

"Didn't seem like a very good meeting," Zachary muttered.

"It did for him," Malkam said. "I know all of you want to help, but all we can do now is train them how to fight. Without any useful information about this weapon, we can't do anything."

Jordan swallowed nervously and hung her head.

"So how long are we staying?" Zachary asked. "I mean, Lucy and I have these kids out in Tawney City that depend on us. We can't stay here for much longer."

"Noted," Malkam said.

"I'm good for however long you need me," Payden said.

"Not until you're healthy," David said quietly.

Lucy set her jaw and tightened her fists. Payden crossed his arms and sank into the bed. Malkam's eyes went from one to the other. It slightly amused him.

"Fine and good," Malkam said quickly. "I'll get the training started tomorrow. Archery would probably be the best skill for the Djorites. Doubtful they'd fare too well in a full assault. Nevertheless, David, how do you think you'd do with some training? You've only had one pupil—"

"That you know of," David interrupted. His gaze was fixed on the floor. How long could he endure? "I will help as long as I can."

"That's enough for now."

"Excuse me?" Zachary spoke up. "Are Lucy and I getting any jobs?"

Malkam studied the two. She was so different from their first encounter. It didn't seem right forcing her to do anything while in that state. The entire meeting had gone by without a single comment from her. It was unnatural. "How long are you willing to stay?"

Zachary shrugged. "I know we're needed back home. It just doesn't feel right to leave these people just yet."

"What can you contribute?"

"We may not be the experts you are, but I know a bit about fighting. So does Lucy. We teach our kids some basic stuff. We can share that with this lot."

"Very well. First thing in the morning, everyone meet outside."

"Except Payden," David said, more to remind Payden.

"I'll show up if I want to," Payden said impatiently.

"But you're useless to anyone right now," David said gently. "Stay in bed. Rest those injuries."

"Wouldn't have 'em if it weren't for you," Lucy growled under her breath. "Guilt's making you quite bossy."

David rose. "If I'm no longer needed." With that, he left the study.

An uneasy silence filled the void of his departure. It was enough to pull Jordan out of her thoughts. She cast her eyes upon Payden, who seemed a bit sad. Lucy still looked angry, and Malkam was tired. The exhaustion made him seem much older. Jordan quickly tried to come up with something to say, some sort of distraction. Zachary, however, had the same idea.

"Well, since we're all here," he said as he stood. "Could I have everyone's attention?"

"How could you not? Idiot." Lucy rolled her eyes.

"Fine," he said through clenched teeth as he looked down at her. "Since we're going to be here for a while, I want to take advantage of the situation while I can." He swallowed nervously and glanced at everyone. "I don't really think we should spend all our spare time on training and tactics. Most, of course," he said with a nod toward Malkam. "But not all."

"So . . .?" Jordan prodded.

"I think we should have a dance. You know, get some use out of that ballroom."

Jordan and Payden exchanged confused glances. Lucy laughed. "You? Dancing?"

"Why not?" He sat beside her and smiled as he took her hand. "We could have a great big dance to celebrate."

"Celebrate what?" she asked with trepidation, knowing what he was going to say next.

He stared at her confidently. "Well, a wedding, hopefully."

Everyone else froze with shock. Lucy's eyes studied Zachary's face as she processed the request. "Do you realize what you're getting yourself into?" she finally asked.

His smile grew. "I'll love every minute of it."

"All right. Sure. Let's do it."

Chapter 7

The wedding was in six days. The slumbering city came alive. Weddings and births had come and gone before, but everyone understood that the city needed a little life to loosen its rusted joints. Those who frequently worked in the manor descended upon the estate in a flurry of activity. Some created floral arrangements, others rearranged the dining hall, while still others pulled out their sewing boxes to put together new outfits for all who would attend. Above all, the people were excited to dust off their dancing shoes.

The rest, however, prepared for a different dance. Malkam worked with the members of the Djorite army to establish a training area. Many more villagers arrived than he expected. Never before had he witnessed such drive, even in himself. He had to remind himself that these people faced extinction. They would at least be willing to learn every trick. Using those tricks, however, would require a bit more than practice.

During that first day, as much of the time was spent assembling the training stations, David remained out of sight. Malkam hardly noticed. Lucy, however, did. She tried to understand the feelings churning inside her. Zachary had asked to marry her. She had consented. What was she thinking? Getting married, now, amid all this turmoil? It was insanity.

Worse, though, was the lack of excitement. She was getting married, and not a bit of her felt happy about it. She smiled at Zachary whenever he looked her way, but apart from that, she felt empty.

All the blame she set upon David's shoulders. That man had to go. He kept hiding. Part of her wanted to find him, but another part of her feared being around him. As she looked at the subsiding chaos around her, she felt the need to hide as well.

The woman who ran the estate—Salina, was it? Lucy tried to remember the name—provided some type of a distraction. Well, Lucy wanted to ask about wedding plans.

When the camp was finished, Lucy looked about as everyone gradually drifted toward Malkam and Zachary. She returned to the estate. She didn't want to be outside anymore.

Malkam noticed Lucy's departure and breathed a bit easier. He didn't feel like he could handle her on the first day of training. It was daunting enough with all the fearful yet determined faces standing before him.

This was his first encounter with Djorites. He had known of them when the war began, but never had an opportunity to enter their lands. The Fashites kept him busy in his youth. The Djorites were eager. He liked that. Very much.

Lucy entered the estate and immediately wanted to faint. The smell overwhelmed her. Flowers smelled pleasant, yes, but in moderation! They practically filled every square inch of the entrance.

She hurried past the arrangements and ascended the stairwell as fast as she could. The scent was less potent upstairs, yet still stronger than the day before. She crossed to Payden's room, pausing. She suddenly didn't want to see him. The reasons why flashed quickly through her mind. None of them made sense, though. Why did he have to remind her so much of Roscoe? She shook her head and knocked. Payden opened the door.

"Lucy!"

"Hey, Joe," she said weakly. "Mind some company?"

"Nope! Thought I'd actually behave today and stay in bed, but I can't for much longer. Need to get up. Can we go for a walk?"

Lucy shuddered. "Not yet. Downstairs is too overwhelming. Don't think Zachary knew what he was starting with all this wedding stuff. The people in this entire city have gone crazy. I've half a mind to put them out of my misery. But then we wouldn't have a wedding."

"Well, I guess I'll get back in bed. Come on in." He hobbled back to the bed and moaned slightly as he pulled himself back up onto it. Lucy almost wanted to lecture him about staying put, but then David's voice entered her thoughts. She breathed deeply to quell whatever it was she was feeling and walked over to the window.

The training area was far away, but she made out the figures as they lined up for archery lessons. She cringed. She was glad she'd missed that. A tall figure at the end was surrounded by a group of men. Zachary. Shouldn't she smile whenever she thought of him?

Her eyes turned to Payden, who looked a bit helpless lying on the bed. Tears threatened. She'd almost lost—again—almost lost her— She shook her head.

"Excited?" Payden asked.

"Sure. Why not?"

He nodded uncomfortably. For some reason, he didn't know what to say. It seemed weird having Lucy visit. She seemed—different.

A knock at the door interrupted the awkwardness. Lucy quickly crossed the room to open it. "Hello?" she questioned the servant outside the door.

"I'm sorry if I'm interrupting, but I came to bring Payden his dinner. It's very early, but I was told to bring it up now to prevent him from coming down."

"Oh. Okay." Lucy stepped aside to allow the young lady into the room. "Dinner, Payden."

"Really? I'm not that hungry. I mean, what have I done today, right? You hungry, Lucy?"

The young lady set the tray on the table beside the bed and shyly turned to leave.

"Nah. I'll go so you can eat. See you later." She followed the servant out the doors. The girl hurried down the steps, and Lucy didn't know what to do. A flash of black fabric at the bottom of the stairs hurried her heartbeat, and she quickly ran down the hallway to her room, ducking behind her door as the dark figure reached the top of the stairs. For a moment—a brief moment—she thought she saw his eyes burning red.

David heard a door click shut, and he looked up and down the hallway. Nothing else stirred, so he continued his mission and entered Payden's room. At least the boy was in his bed, he noted. With his dinner already? David wondered who had thought to send it up so early. And why. He shook his head and approached.

Payden didn't want to say a word. After their last conversation, he hadn't any desire to speak with David, so he overfocused on the tray of food he suddenly wanted to eat. Deep down, he hated feeling angry toward David. Frustration, however, about a great number of things seemed to justify it.

"Thanks for staying in bed today," David said. "I'm up here to check on those injuries. The doctor here, Roman, lent me what I'll need to take care of you. So, if you could, turn on your side and let me check."

Payden chewed his bite of food for a while, debating on how to acknowledge David. He didn't believe his stalling would work. Whatever little he knew about David, he did know that the man could be patient to the point of aggravation. Payden picked up a vegetable and absentmindedly bit into it. *How did I know that, though?* he wondered. *I haven't been around David that long.*

He glanced up at the figure standing over him. After rolling his eyes, Payden returned the plate of food to the tray before turning onto his side.

David silently redressed the wounds. They didn't seem to be much better, in spite of the day of rest. Payden still showed signs of a fever. David felt the need to say something but didn't feel that his advice would be heeded. "Keep resting, because you should be feeling better by now, and you're not."

"I'm fine," Payden muttered.

"You still have a fever."

Payden shifted his body as a response. He kept his back toward David, who raised his hand to his head as a headache suddenly formed. "Enjoy your dinner," he said before he left. When Payden heard the door open, he turned to watch David depart. After it shut, he sank into the pillows, feeling a slight sensation of guilt. He brushed the feeling aside and turned to stare at the plate of food. He really wasn't hungry.

David stood outside Payden's door for a few minutes. Not to listen for signs of movement. Just to delay his return trip to the gardens. The sounds of dozens of conversations drifted upstairs, and he didn't want to pass through the crowd. One woman's voice cut through the din, and the conversations faded as the people dispersed. David cautiously descended the stairs. A few people passed, carrying chairs. They hurried down the long hall and disappeared into the ballroom. He crossed to the entryway, which was suddenly empty of all the floral arrangements.

"Hello?" someone called. David froze. That voice was familiar. Wasn't it the one he'd just heard ordering everyone about? Either way, he hoped she wasn't addressing him.

"Excuse me, are you David?"

His fingers nervously tapped his thigh. "Yes." He turned about to face the woman.

"Hello. I'm Salina. Pleasure to meet you."

He nodded. "Sure. Do you need something?"

"Actually, with this wedding thing, I need all of our guests for a moment. Not all at once," she said hastily, holding up her hands. "I don't believe any of you have the proper formal attire. We'll need to find each of you a suit that fits. A formal tuxedo, of course. I'm not the best person to guess your size, but I'll introduce you to Easel. She's the head seamstress. If you have a moment?"

David swallowed deeply. "S-sure."

"Thank you. Follow me." She led David down the empty hall and past the ballroom to a corridor on the right. A set of doors stood open, and, to David's dismay, inside sat dozens of women, chatting away as they sewed. Salina studied the man's face, what little of it she could see, and pursed her lips. "Come this way."

She turned and found an empty room a few doors down. It was dark, so she quickly pulled open a few curtains. "Wait here, please."

David grew curious about the change of direction. After a few minutes, Salina returned with another woman in tow.

"Easel, this is David." Salina gestured toward the man. Easel quickly looked him up and down.

"Oh, he's easy," she said. "Wait just a moment. I'll come back with the perfect suit."

David watched the woman disappear and became more confused. As a child, when he first encountered the Djorites, they had fussed over him when it came to clothing. Everything had to be a perfect fit. The seamstresses never approximated. Had they changed so much since then?

"Here," Easel said as she returned. She handed the garments to David. "These will fit you. Try them on beforehand, of course. Let me know of anything that's not right. These will be fine."

"Thank you, Easel," Salina said.

"Not a problem. I'll get to the boy in a minute. If you could, please send the other two in this direction this evening. I think we've already gotten them taken care of as well—just a little tuck here and there, perhaps."

"I'll do what I can," Salina promised. Easel quickly disappeared, and David studied Salina for a moment.

"You're quite perceptive," he observed.

She cast him a quick glance. "So are you, I've gathered. I'm good at what I do. Have a good day." With a curt nod in his direction, she departed.

He carefully handled the clothing given to him before quickly taking it to his room. While there, he decided to watch the training. This was definitely Malkam at his best. That man must feel on top of the world. Tomorrow, David would join him.

Teaching Djorites how to fight—why did that seem familiar? David pinched the bridge of his nose as the headache worsened. This pain felt different. Whenever he had to suppress the programming, it took effort, but this pain felt different. Oddly familiar, but different.

He saw the outline of a figure in the window and turned about, but no one was in the room. The rose garden. He needed to get there quickly.

Chapter 8

The next morning, Jordan paced back and forth in front of the steps with the cup of tea for Payden. She'd entertained a ridiculous thought all day long yesterday, and today it still held her. Part of her wanted to discuss the idea with Payden. The other part didn't want him to know because she feared he would protest. As a servant passed by, Jordan quickly made a decision.

"Addie, could you please take this up to Payden? I really should be elsewhere."

Addie looked a bit taken aback, but she nodded and took the cup. Jordan bolted out the doors and ran to the training area as though fleeing from someone. When she reached the outskirts of the camp, she paused to watch the activity for a moment. On her right were rows of large, round targets. The men fired arrow after arrow at them. Other men were grouped to the side next to piles of branches and barrels of feathers. Malkam stood with a large group, who focused on his every word and mimicked his every gesture with the bow.

Her eyes found Zachary next. The sick feeling in her stomach rose as she watched the Djorites near him spar. Her peaceful village, preparing for war. Tears filled her eyes, and she shook her head. Wasn't that the reason she stood here? After a deep breath, she turned and found David amid another, smaller group of Djorites. The sunlight winked off a few unsheathed swords. She swallowed deeply and summoned a wave of courage so she could cross the field to that group.

David noticed her approach and assumed the worst. He knew Payden seemed better, but when it came to that boy, anything could go wrong. He quickly excused himself and crossed to intercept her.

"What is it, Jordan?" he asked.

She halted and stared at him with wide eyes. "Um," she stammered. "Could you—could you teach me something about swordplay?"

David was taken aback. "I can't do that," he said abruptly, not believing she would even think to ask.

"Please, David," she said and grabbed his arm to prevent his leaving. "I didn't ask you if you think I should learn. I asked you to teach me. When Payden leaves this place, I know I'll want to go with him. And after—after what happened, I realized that I need to do what I can so as not to be a burden. Please."

David's eyes drifted down to her wrists. Bandages still covered the rope burns, and he shook his head. "I understand why you want to, but you must understand why I don't want to teach you. You're an innocent young—woman." David paused. He should have said what he wanted to say: *innocent young girl.* He continued, "I don't believe that there is any part of you that would be willing to kill a man."

She bowed her head and thought. Could she?

"Maybe," she said, looking back up at him, squinting against the sunlight. "I won't know until I'm in that type of a situation. I will be, if I understand Payden at all. Those men who took me—honestly, if they all had been killed, I don't think I would have cared."

For such an innocent person to say such a thing cut through David to the core. Was there any good, unspoiled thing left on the planet, he wondered. Or had the Pendtars managed to poison everyone?

David had to pull himself from those thoughts. He considered Jordan for a moment. She was going to fight with or without his consent. He might as well ensure her a chance of surviving.

"All right," he said. "Everything I teach, you must practice for hours every day. It'll be very hard at first, but given time, your muscles will get used to it. The first thing I want you to learn is the bow. That's where Malkam is the better teacher. He's over there. Make sure he knows that I sent you to him, okay?"

She nodded her head firmly before running to Malkam. He too was surprised to see her there.

"Hi, Jordan," he called.

"David told me to come over to you," she said hastily.

Confused, Malkam looked past her and saw David standing in the middle of the field, looking at him. David then returned to the men he had been instructing. Malkam returned his attention to Jordan. "All right. What can I do for you?"

"I want to learn how to use the bow."

"Oh," he said. "Then let's get you one."

After some instruction, he left her alone to practice, knowing it was the only way she would truly learn.

Later in the day when he noticed David by himself, he approached him to ascertain why David seemed to feel no misgivings about her presence there. He crossed the field, wiping the sweat from his brow. The coolness of the morning had finally vanished. The sun warmed the midmorning air to what would have been a comfortable temperature if they hadn't been exerting themselves. Several of the men in David's training circle had already removed their shirts. It seemed David was a merciless teacher. Malkam saw most of the men doubled over to catch their breaths.

In contrast, David remained fully clothed and breathed easily. It was another trait of David's that Malkam envied. In every battle where they'd fought side by side, David had escaped both injury and exhaustion. Malkam always seemed to suffer at least one, sometimes both.

"David!" Malkam shouted. Some of the men looked his way, but David ignored him. His eyes were focused on a pair jousting with blunted blades.

"Watch the thrust—don't overreach!" David snapped. One competitor hesitated and barely dodged the downward swipe of his opponent. The boy backed away, and David stepped between them. "You're both sloppy! Go! Thirty sprints, now!"

The young men's shoulders dropped, and they placed the blunt blades into a wooden stand before they jogged to a small slope. There, others raced up and down the incline, and Malkam raised his eyebrows in surprise. Apparently, David had taught others besides Payden.

David continued to ignore Malkam as he turned toward the remaining men. "Pair up and practice the attacking routine. Get it flawless! Most of you keep overreaching. Attack with precision. Stop guessing!"

As the men moved about, Malkam drew closer to David, who stood with arms crossed, eyes shifting from one set of men to the other.

"Are you even going to acknowledge me?" Malkam asked.

"Okay. You've been acknowledged," David said flatly before he released a low growl of frustration. "Paul—put that arm down and stop flinching! The sword's sheathed. Be a convincing opponent, or you'll handicap everyone! Got it?"

A very frightened-looking young man nodded and swallowed deeply. He moved his arm down and grasped the hilt of his sheathed sword with both hands.

"Is there a reason you're being so difficult with me?" Malkam felt irritated at being ignored for so long.

"No. It's just who I am."

Malkam spit. "Well, that helps me none. Even after all these years, I still don't know who you are because you're so stubborn about staying silent about yourself."

David glanced at him out of the corner of his eye before he returned his full attention to the men. "Even for civilians, these are the worst group of people I've ever trained," he said.

"Aw, will you shut up!" Malkam snapped. "You know I didn't come over here to talk about their training. Jordan? Really? A girl like that shouldn't be out here."

"She reminds you of Leislie too, huh?"

Malkam was taken aback. He looked over at her. "Great. So that's why."

"Yup."

"Is she half as stubborn or completely?"

"Completely."

Malkam rubbed the back of his neck. "Who'd have thought that Henry's boy would be so much like him that he'd fall for a girl just like his mother without even remembering her?"

"The soul remembers," David said softly.

"Sole? What are you muttering about now? You're always pulling things out of thin air that no one in their right mind knows about, you know that?"

"Forget I mentioned it then."

"Already have," Malkam chuckled. "Sole. That's the bottom of my shoe, you know? Where do you come up with this stuff?"

"If you were to blame one person, blame Henry. Now, if you'll excuse me." David walked toward a man who stepped aside to empty his gut, as several had already done that morning.

Malkam shook his head. "You're going to explain things to me one day," he shouted at David's back. "Sole," he muttered. "Henry never said anything like that to me."

When the sun reached its zenith, Malkam excused the men for a midday break. He thought he'd see relief on their faces, especially those with David, but the Djorites continued to surprise him. They seemed to want to continue, no matter how grueling the work was. As he watched them file past, he thought back to his youth. Hadn't his anger toward the warlords forced him to take action? The frustration—the desire not to feel one more day of fear—turned to determination and countless hours of work.

His eyes drifted to Jordan, who remained where she'd planted herself hours ago. *Determination.* Malkam mulled over that word.

David stopped beside Malkam, eyes on Jordan as well. Between each shot, she looked down at her hands before shaking them and flexing her fingers. A few times, she wiped at her face before continuing.

"Think she's developed blisters?" David ventured.

"Those hands aren't used to this kind of work," Malkam said. "Nor is she."

"They're awful soldiers," David said as he turned to watch the men disappear into the buildings.

"They'll get better."

"Oh, yes," David said softly, "but I don't want them to."

Malkam cast his friend a confused glance. David removed his hat and ran a hand through his hair.

"Why not?" Malkam finally asked.

"This isn't them. I'm training them harder than anyone else because they'll take it. But I really would prefer if they just fled. Because if they do go to war—if they face open battle—then the Djorites are gone forever. This may save their lives, but it won't save them."

"And you know the Djorites so well?"

David nodded, pensive. The pauses between Jordan's shots were growing longer.

"How?"

David turned toward his friend. The old friend who never truly knew him. "I lived with them for a while. Long before you met Henry. The shadows of who there were live in this valley. But by doing what we're doing—they're fading away."

"That's not true. Once they're safe, they can always go back."

"No, Malkam." David's eyes misted as he focused fully on Jordan. "You're never the same after that first kill."

Malkam remained silent, unable to argue. He left David and crossed to the shooting range. Jordan's sniffling was audible, and he approached slowly, for she had another arrow set to fire. When she released it, it went wide of the target, and she hung her head. Her hands hurt too much to hold the bow steady anymore. At first, it had seemed easy, but she just couldn't come near the bull's-eye, and she didn't want to leave until she did.

"Jordan?"

"I'm fine," she said quickly and reached for another arrow. Malkam put his hands on her shoulders.

"It's time to rest. You can pick up again tomorrow."

"Was this part of David's plan?"

"What?"

"Make me come over here and learn firsthand just how much I'm not going to be able to do this."

Malkam chuckled. "Giving up on your first day?"

She shook her head. "No. Never."

Malkam gave her shoulders a quick squeeze before he reached for the bow, gently removing it from her. "Come on. Let's get someone to look at those hands."

She fought to keep her tears from falling, angrily erasing the few that escaped.

"Hey, blisters are good," he said. "In time, you'll develop calluses and won't get any more blisters. See?" He held his hand open to her, and she saw the rough skin on his fingers and palms.

"Okay, but—I'm a terrible shot."

"Yeah. Or did you expect to be an expert your first day?"

She laughed softly.

"Come on. Let's get you fixed. Then come back tomorrow and do it again." He smiled, and she lifted her head and returned one.

"Thank you."

"Don't mention it. Let's go. I'm hungry."

When they arrived at the estate, Jordan parted company with Malkam and headed to the infirmary that stood behind it. Malkam waited until she was out of sight before he ascended the wide, white marble steps. A woman paced in front of the entrance, and he cautiously approached lest he startle her. Also, he hoped to pass her unnoticed, for reasons he didn't want to think. She seemed engrossed in her thoughts, scratching her head before using a quill to write on the parchment she carried. Just as Malkam crossed behind her, she turned and gasped.

"Sir!"

"Sorry," Malkam said quickly. "I was trying not to scare you." Salina, he thought. Hadn't heard her name too much, but he found himself thinking of that name often.

"No. I just thought everyone was inside."

"Not yet." Malkam smiled broadly at her. *What are you doing, you old fool?* Malkam thought. His smile quickly faded. Except he didn't want to take his eyes off the woman. He'd encountered her only a few times, but he'd enjoyed every brief moment.

Salina hesitated, vacillating between addressing him further and returning to her duties, which were always present. This man never stayed still.

"Would you mind a walk? This wedding has me running in circles, and I need a few minutes in the fresh air."

And there it was. Malkam had recognized his attraction immediately but not hers. He didn't know if he should feel any comfort in knowing he hadn't changed much in twenty years. Except Salina's eyes were blue, not brown.

"I—would normally love to," Malkam began. His eyes drifted to his hands. This endless war was not yet over, and he knew he'd make the same choice he had years ago. He was a soldier first, and he didn't want to feel that pain again.

Salina smiled and dared to touch the man, resting her hand on his forearm. "It's just a walk. Maybe some other time."

He raised his eyes in time to catch her smile before she departed. The image of a woman standing beside her cottage, watching him and his army march away, burned vividly in Malkam's mind. He hadn't been able to resist that one last look. Why had he had to sacrifice so much over the years?

Salina reached the pathway and turned toward the rose gardens. Malkam didn't want to watch her disappear from sight, so he quickly entered the building and headed for the loud ruckus of the dining hall. The 'Curse of the Thirst' began to creep into his thoughts. He hoped this place held no strong drinks, for he had no will to resist at the moment.

Chapter 9

David lay on the ground in his grotto, staring at the clouds drifting across the azure behind them. Thoughts cascaded through his awareness, but he wouldn't chase any of them. A sensation had captured him not long ago, and it was very unfamiliar.

The morning of training felt so familiar. If that had been the oddity of the situation, he could have dismissed it. Many Ashites over the years had learned from him. Payden had mentioned Patrick. David had encountered that man many times after severe battles or before Fashite ambushes. Except while he trained these Djorites, it seemed like he was reliving a dream. The motions and speeches were so natural that he felt no nervousness about being around them, no fear of losing ground in his battle against the programming. The sensation was as close to freedom as he'd ever felt. Odder still was the comfort that feeling gave him.

The thicker clouds drifted from sight, leaving some wisps in their wake. David tilted his head. Why did it all seem so familiar?

A shadow fell over him, and he turned to discover the source. An older man stood over him, eyeing him with an impatient scowl.

"It's my week to prune the gardens, and you're in my way," the old man said.

"Sorry," David mumbled as he rolled to his feet. "I've never seen anyone in this area."

"Well, you've only been here a week. How did you expect the gardens stayed so pretty?" The old man walked over to a bench, where a wide broom leaned. "We sweep up the fallen leaves and petals every week, after all the weeding and pruning. I finish with this garden on my week. 'Cept when I got here, you were in the way. Had to wake ya."

"I wasn't sleeping."

"You weren't? Seemed like it. Cleared my throat a couple times after I got in here."

"Really?" David glanced about the garden. By one of the exits sat a pile of fallen greenery, and David curiously stared at it for a moment. How had this man entered without David's awareness? His eyes turned to the man. "I didn't hear you."

"Lost in your thoughts, I take it. No matter. Kindly leave so I may finish and get back to the estate. Have work to do there too. Some of us keep busy, you know."

David nodded and stooped to collect his hat. "I'll get out of your way then."

"Sure, sure. Take your time. Wouldn't want to rush you."

The older man put his hand on his hip and tapped his foot. David narrowed his eyes at him as he walked past. When he got to the archway that was the exit, he paused before he turned to stand and wait. The old man didn't need his absence, so why was he kicking him out of the garden?

"Go on. Go on!" the man ordered tersely.

"I'm out of your way," David said lightly.

"Oh, I see. Fine. Fine. Can't give an old man the privacy he wants, I see. Bet you like to watch people work while you don't."

"Or . . . you could ask for help."

The old man sighed and released his grip on the broomstick. "Fine. You sweep. I'll prune. And weed. Can't expect an outsider to know the difference between a plant and a weed."

David chuckled. "I know the difference."

"Doubtful." The old man muttered other sentences to himself as he turned to the nearest section of flowers and bent to pull out the offending vegetation. After coming up with a handful of weeds, he tossed them over his shoulder with a huff and moved to collect more. David stood amused for a moment before he crossed to the bench where the broom stood, propped against the back. He gripped the handle of it thoughtfully.

The Djorites and their gardening. Once again, his mind wandered back through the dense forest of time to earlier memories. When he lost his family as a child, life had taken him to the unknown world of the Djorites. They were so different in comparison to the way of life the Ashites had at that time. Ashites lived in small villages, open and vulnerable to wildlife and the dark side of humanity. The Djorites had large cities with thousands of residents, though a few dwelled in humble hovels in the foothills. In the center of each city grew an elaborate garden. Some were crafted as this one was, with many different species of flowers in their own sections arranged in a labyrinth of pathways and squares. In other cities, the floral detailing was more subtle in that the features were the beautiful marble and granite statues gleaming under the sun with a myriad of fountains accenting the beauty. The waters flowed at all times, tumbling over generous bowls or shooting out of spouts in various directions. Dozens of gardeners, craftsmen, and even artists tended the gardens. This man was the first Djorite he'd seen actually caring for the plant life.

"Are you the only gardener here?" David asked the old man.

"You weren't really listening to me earlier, were you?" the old man snapped, ripping up another handful.

"I was."

"I told you that this was my week. Implying, to any able-minded halfwit, that there are others."

David felt more amused at the man's grumpiness than offended. Age sometimes had that effect. "Of course. How many others?"

"Two."

The answer surprised David. "Two?"

"Hard of hearing, eh? Yes, two. Only two. No one else wanted the gardens. We can only get the kids to help in the estate, or else we'd be the only ones taking care of that as well."

David thought back to the Djorites he'd encountered in the building. All those who served in the dining hall were very young, he realized. The only other person he'd encountered was a woman probably just a few years older than himself. Salina, he remembered. No, he recanted. The seamstress was about that age as well. Could they be the other two? What had she called the seamstress? Etna? Ester?

"Are the other two the women I had met? I recall the one is Salina . . ."

"That's one, yes, but the other is not a woman. Of course, Easel has come a long way these past ten years and started helping out more often, but she's more likely to be found making dresses or pants for the kids in the village."

"She didn't seem to do her job correctly."

At that, the old man stopped pulling the plants in his hands and stood, turning sharply. "Don't you insult that woman," he snapped. "She does her job properly!"

"Not as I remember."

The old man paused before he replied. Finally, he seemed curious about his intruder. "Remember? What does that mean?"

"Djorites never handed you a suit. Ever. They were all handmade after the seamstress or tailor took every measurement you had the patience for them to take. Then you got your suit a few days later. She just looked at me and handed me one. It was very—odd."

The old man approached David, finally analyzing the Slave before him. In his younger years, he believed that any human being deserved a chance to be treated hospitably and with courtesy, but that had changed after his entire civilization crumbled to the ground. All that had once stood, proudly displaying the existence of his peaceful people, could no longer be found. It was buried under the ground. Not even the evidence of rubble remained. After all he'd suffered, he no longer felt that everyone deserved to be treated with patience or kindness. Some, most especially those Slaves, deserved nothing. And this man dared to stand before him and recount the procedures of his long-deceased countrymen.

"I don't want to have a conversation with you about *my* people, understand? The memories I have, I will not let you tarnish. You cannot take *that* away from me!"

David nodded solemnly. Then he exited the garden. That encounter had erased all the feelings he'd had when he entered the garden. He'd been a fool to think he could possibly belong anywhere.

Jordan left the infirmary and stared at her hands. The rope burns were healing nicely but still needed bandages. Now they had wrapped a few of her fingers as well. At this rate, she'd be covered from head to toe in no time. Such was life, she supposed. With a shrug to no one, she followed the path that wound around the large building, wondering what she should do for the rest of the day.

Her first impulse went to Payden. Why did she have to struggle with herself every time she thought of him? She wanted so much to stay with him, and she knew she'd have support in that decision. If her father ever discovered her visiting him without all the proper protocols being met first, he would certainly not be pleased.

Her feet stopped moving. What if he asked her why she thought it was acceptable behavior? Could she have the courage to reveal her mother's journal? Surely he would accept that she felt her mother would approve, but at what cost? He would no longer trust her. A secret revealed to him after so many years . . .

She shook the thoughts away and continued forward. She began to feel hungry, so she went to the dining hall. As she climbed the steps, her eyes found David leaving the gardens. He hurried toward the village and quickly disappeared between some of the houses. She paused in curiosity for a moment before she crossed the portico, went down the steps on the other side, and continued into the gardens. Of course, as soon as she entered, she wondered why she had the impulse to do so. Someone's singing filtered through the air, and she instantly recognized the voice. Old Ralf must be pruning. As a sour note shuddered her spine, she assumed that David had fled because of the irritating commotion. She spun on her heel and returned to her original course. The scent from the afternoon meal strengthened. She hurried inside to the dining hall.

The smells overwhelmed her, and her mouth watered. Solomon had prepared a special midday meal because the men were training. He wanted them to eat well on this first official day. One of the fattest pigs had been slaughtered the day before and the meat cooked since. Solomon called it his blackened pork masterpiece. Jordan had only tasted the meal once before, and as her nose recognized the smell, she hurried to the kitchen.

"Solomon!" she called as she entered. "I want the best piece!"

Laughter greeted her. Solomon was at his usual place in the back of the kitchen, near the fire pits. She wove through the others busy deep-frying flour-covered vegetables or arranging salads. A few cooks decorated small cakes with various berries, but her nose only wanted the meat. When she reached Solomon's side, she quickly wrapped her arms around his wide waist.

"How's my beautiful Jordan today?" he said jovially.

"Hungry!"

"Go sit down and wait for the kids to bring it out then!"

"No!" she cried loudly in good humor. "I want to eat now!"

Solomon released his trademark bellow, generating curious glances and grins from the others in the kitchen. He gestured to a small pile of meat chunks. Jordan grabbed a piece and tossed it into her mouth. The tender meat almost melted. She could taste all the spices and fruits Solomon had used on it, for the beast's belly was stuffed prior to entering the hot coals. Some parts of the meat tasted sweet while others had a tart hint. Jordan swallowed the bite and beamed at Solomon. "Thank you!"

"Now get out of my kitchen!"

The drumming sound of his laughter followed her out, and she hurried to a seat. News of Solomon's treat trickled through the village, and Jordan sat at the table, watching more people enter the doors than normal. Some faces she didn't recognize, and wondered if this was their first time in the estate, or at least their first in a long time. She wondered if this was what life had been like many years ago. Solomon and Salina were the only ones she knew who weren't afraid to laugh loudly. Some of the younger girls who worked on the estate most often were beginning to pick up that trait, but those two were the exceptions for the moment.

Then her heart dropped. Payden entered. Though she was excited to see him, she hated seeing him walking in his condition, especially since she felt partially responsible. He saw her and his face glowed with a broad smile. She quickly got to her feet in order to help him walk to a nearby chair.

"Hello!" he said warmly.

"You're a dunderhead, you know that?"

"A what?"

Jordan placed her arm around his waist. "I wish you would stop all this wandering about for a while. That's all. Get some rest."

"How could I? Have you been stuck in this building all day with that smell? They brought me some food earlier, but I'm still hungry because of it!"

"Poor pitiful creature."

"I'm glad you recognize that!"

They reached a seat, and she pulled out the chair for him. His face betrayed a wince as he tenderly lowered himself onto the padded wood frame. She shut her eyes and breathed deeply before she sat next to him. If he didn't succumb to her pleas for rest, then whose? She knew Salina had the servers bringing his food early in hopes of preventing him coming down, but he still had that wanderlust that, at present, wasn't healthy. His face still glowed, his cheeks were red, and his eyes had dark circles under them.

"Would you like a plate with everything?" asked a server with a large grin on his face. Jordan glanced up at him, not feeling as good-humored as she had in the kitchen. She forced a large smile and nodded.

"Me, too!" Payden said quickly, and the server turned to retrieve their meals.

Jordan pushed her hair behind her ears and reached for her glass of water. Payden intercepted the reach and grasped her hand.

"Um, what did you do to your fingers?" he asked.

"Oh, uh—it's nothing, really," she said defensively. Then she sighed. "Well, I, uh, I asked Malkam to teach me a bit of archery. It's just a few blisters, that's all."

"And why do you want to learn that?"

Jordan shrugged. "Why not? The opportunity is there, and I just think it would be wise to take advantage of it."

Payden nodded thoughtfully, wondering what to ask or say. Jordan seemed apprehensive, so he decided to drop the subject. Taking everything into consideration, he didn't blame her for wanting to learn ways to defend herself.

Dozens of people trickled through the doors. Extra tables, large and round, flanked the long dining table to accommodate the large crowd. Payden watched, intrigued. Since his arrival, the building had welcomed only a few guests who ate here. Most of the people he'd seen were kids his age, dusting and scrubbing everything on the estate. At this moment, the table was completely full, as was the air with conversations and even laughter.

"Why do you think so many people are here today?" he asked before taking a drink of water.

Jordan thought, looking about the large room. "Mostly Solomon's pig."

Payden chuckled.

"Also, I think this is who we were, you know, before the Pendtars and the Slaves. Back when we had cities and towns and—a civilization. I've read my mother's journal so many times. Well, the first part mostly. She described the Djorites as people who never passed up the opportunity to enjoy life.

There were occasions in these types of estates all the time." She lifted her eyes to the chandelier overhead. The lit candles settled in the arms of the chandelier were surrounded by clear gems that refracted the light onto the ceiling. The lights flickered and shifted in a dance about the room. It was so peaceful.

The server returned with their plates, and Jordan's eyes widened at the beautiful arrangement in front of her.

"Wow," Payden said.

"Solomon's gotten fancy on us, hasn't he?" Jordan asked before thanking the young man who'd brought out their dinners.

"Sure has," Payden agreed. "The dish I got earlier wasn't like this."

"I think it's been a while since Solomon's had an opportunity to show off his presentation skills." She picked up the fork and knife to dig in to the dish, slightly hesitant. Solomon had the meat in the center of the plate, chunks piled atop caramelized carrots. A deep purple sauce covered the meat, and there was a small piece of decorative green on the top. Around the stack, he'd drizzled a light brown sauce in a spiral to complete the masterpiece. "I have a feeling more dishes are going to follow."

"What do you mean? This isn't all we're going to be served?"

"Nope. If I remember correctly from my mother's journal, we'll see plate after plate until we either ask for dessert or leave."

"So I'll be here all day," Payden quipped with a wink before he finally placed a forkful of food into his mouth. "Mmm . . . That's so good."

Jordan finally followed suit and sighed after she swallowed her first bite. "Yup, that's good."

Payden chuckled before finally ignoring all around him to shovel the food into his mouth. Jordan ate slowly, savoring the tastes and aromas as well as the events around her. For the first time in her life, she finally understood the stories Salina and Solomon had told her of who her people really were. Who they could be again.

Chapter 10

Lucy hadn't slept. She sat at the foot of her bed and stared at the locked door. Zachary had tried several times to enter, but gave up when the door wouldn't give. Nor would the person who'd locked herself inside. The smells that filled the building did not affect her as they had the others. Her mind was so far removed from the present that nothing interceded. Why was this happening now? It had been years since she last felt this helpless. She thought she had overcome. When she saw how close she'd come to losing Payden, something inside her had crumpled, as though a fragile dam suddenly could endure no more pressure.

Another knock echoed through the room, loud and persistent. She lifted her eyes to the crack beneath the door. More than one set of shadows blocked the threshold.

"Luce?"

That was Zachary. Why did he have to be so determined? Always questioning and digging for things she didn't want to discuss.

"Lucy? Are you in there?"

That voice chilled her blood and captured her breath. Not him. Zachary better not have brought him.

"Her door's been locked all day," Zachary said, his voice faint through the thick wood. "But I haven't seen her anywhere else. No one has."

"Do you want me to unlock the door, then?" The third speaker she didn't recognize. Probably one of those annoying, perky Djorites. She shuddered. How could anyone be that happy?

"Please." The answer came from that man. She looked about the room, thinking to hide in the washroom, but they'd easily find her. Her feet touched the floor as she next thought of the wardrobe. But the lock turned, and she wouldn't make it in time, so she dropped to her belly and rolled under the bed. She hoped she was out of sight before they entered.

"Luce?" Zachary came in first and quickly walked about the room, checking the washroom. After a few minutes, he sighed in frustration. "Where could she be?"

Lucy saw Zachary's boots by the wardrobe. The gray shoes the servant wore stayed by the door. The third pair stopped in front of the bed. The black boots. She swallowed deeply.

"You said she's been acting different lately?"

She could almost see Zachary nodding. "Yeah. Kind of defensive. She snaps at anything I say."

"How's that different?"

Zachary inhaled deeply. "Okay, sure, but it's not her. I know it had something to do with Payden, but I've never seen her so on edge. Like she's scared of something. She's never been scared of anything."

"I'll talk to Malkam. We'll keep an eye out for her. Don't worry. You two are getting married in a few days. For a lot of people, it's pretty terrifying."

"Sure, I guess. I've never witnessed a wedding before, so I guess you're right. It's probably really me who's feeling a bit nervous."

"Probably."

Zachary chuckled. "Well, I guess I'll get something to eat. Sorry to bother you. Thought I'd talk to you about my concerns before anyone else. Of course, isn't it weird that I found you before finding Lucy? If I didn't know any better, I'd say you were hiding, too."

"Got chased out of the garden. That's all."

Zachary took another deep breath before he headed for the door. "Coming down?"

"Not yet. I think I'll wait here a few minutes for her, you know. In case she's just hiding from you. I'll tell her you're worried."

"Sure. Thanks."

The pair of brown boots disappeared. So did the gray shoes. The black boots remained at the foot of the bed, and she quit breathing. He wasn't moving though. What was he doing? Finally, he walked to the wardrobe and opened it. After a few minutes, he shut the doors and crossed the room to the vanity table. As more of his legs came into view, she scooted farther from him, knowing that it would be easier to see her from that far point in the room if she remained still. Her movements were slow, but she made it to the other side of the bed, unaware that being closer to that side of the bed provided the intruder confirmation to his suspicions. A large mirror hung on that side of the room. Pairing that with the mirror above the vanity allowed him to see the movement under the bed. He tapped his fingers on the table. Upon entering, he had noticed that the blankets at the foot of bed were rumpled, meaning someone had sat on the bed after the Djorite servants made it that morning. So she didn't want anyone to find her at the moment. For whatever reason. And he didn't want to be a hypocrite by forcing her out of her solitude before she was ready.

The black boots returned to the doorway and vanished. The door closed. She felt relieved and pressed her face into the thick rug before rolling out from under the bed. When she stood, she noticed the mirror. In the mirror's reflection was the vanity table. She saw under the bed perfectly at this angle. Her shoulders slumped, and she felt her chest tighten as she tried to heave in gulps of air. So he'd known. She tried to swallow, but her throat was dry. The walls suddenly became very confining.

After she exited the room, she looked about but found no more witnesses to her deception. Without a plan or care to form one, she traversed the hall to the stairwell but paused. To where could she flee?

The image of Zachary filled her mind. He had sounded so concerned.

After several deep breaths, she descended the stairs, pausing again to compose herself more. A few perky Djorites passed her as they exited the building, and she clenched her fists before realizing it. How could these people be in the situation they were in and still be so cheerful? It angered her more than she knew was reasonable.

The sounds coming from the dining hall were much louder than normal. It might distract her, she realized. Maybe she could relax and lose herself in the commotion. She knew herself well enough to know it wouldn't work, but she had to find Zachary. It wasn't right to let him worry. After another deep breath, she moved her feet.

Zachary sat at the table beside Malkam. Payden and Jordan were farther down the table, but seemed to be finishing their meal.

"Hi!"

Lucy turned toward the speaker.

"Lucy, right?" asked the young girl.

"Yes."

The girl grinned. "Do you remember me?"

Lucy's eyes widened. How could she have known anyone in this valley?

The girl giggled. "It does seem like forever ago, I guess. I'm Mary. I gave you my brother's clothes."

"Oh, yes, you're from that village. Wow. That does seem like a while ago."

"Uh-huh. And I see you're still wearing his clothes."

"Yeah." Lucy looked down at the pants that hung awkwardly from her hips. They were just too short as well, exposing the tops of her ankle-high boots. "Haven't taken the time to do any shopping, I guess."

"Well, there's always Easel. She can make anything in a hurry."

"I bet," Lucy said slowly, feeling very awkward around this short, perky person wearing a perfectly fitted violet dress that stopped midcalf. Its cap sleeves and the ribbon tied around Mary's waist just reeked of sweetness. Lucy almost shuddered. Then she had to remind herself of the circumstances in which she first met this girl. "I hope to meet Easel soon. I guess it would be nice to finally have a pair of pants that actually fit me around the waist. I've always been too tall for the pants I could get back home. It seems only menswear is long enough."

Mary giggled. "Well, you'll be seeing Easel soon enough with the wedding and all."

"I will?"

"Yup." Mary smiled. "I mean, you do know that they plan on making you a dress?"

"A—what?" Lucy felt the blood drain from her face.

"A dress. I've never heard of a bride wearing men's trousers."

"Mary, hurry up!" An older woman who looked very similar to Mary stood in the hall, closer to the exit.

"Oh, that's my mom. Got to go. Bye!" With a wave, Mary spun and trotted down the hall to her mother, curls bouncing off her shoulders the whole way.

Lucy stood frozen for a while. *A dress,* she thought in disgust. *I didn't realize I'd have to wear a dress.*

An arm crossed her shoulders, and she yelped as she turned, swinging at the intruder.

Zachary ducked and blocked the blow. "Lucy! It's me."

"Oh! Zachary, I'm sorry," she said awkwardly, covering her head in her arms. "Grr. Why do you do that? You just sneak up on me all the time."

"I said your name a dozen times, Lucy. What's wrong with you?"

"Nothing's wrong with me!" she snapped.

Zachary glanced about at the few witnesses to the altercation. "O-kay," he said slowly. "Then how about something to eat? Food's going quickly today, and there's not much of the pig left. Malkam said it's pretty good. Do you want to eat?"

"Um . . ." she stammered and looked about, noticing a few pairs of eyes looking at them. "Sure, but can we sit away from everyone? I'm a little overwhelmed right now."

"I noticed."

"Oh, you did, did you?"

Zachary tightened his mouth and narrowed his eyes. Then he turned and walked to an empty table near the library doors, unconcerned if she followed or not. She did, though her anger at herself for her outbursts kept her quiet. This man might not arrive at the wedding.

Lucy sat down as another unsettling thought crossed her mind. *Will I arrive at the wedding?* She stared at the empty table in front of her as all the commotion faded. Could she do that to Zachary? On the other hand, considering how she felt at the moment, would it be wise to parade herself around a roomful of strangers? She knew the irritation she currently felt about the Djorites could quickly turn into vile hatred. Enough to give them regrets about the occasion.

A plate of food appeared before her. She blinked and looked up, but saw only Zachary sitting a few chairs away, concentrating on filling his mouth. Her eyes studied the meat and vegetables before her, yet she neither smelled any aroma nor felt any hunger. When had she last eaten?

With a deep breath, she grasped the utensils and cut into the food. She knew she should eat, in spite of no appetite. Zachary would only worry more if she didn't.

When Zachary entered the dining hall, Jordan noticed he didn't appear to be happy. As Lucy followed, looking equally grim, Jordan watched, concerned. The couple sat alone at a table, but didn't seem to be sitting there together.

Jordan couldn't let this distract her too much as she helped Payden leave the dining hall. He leaned a bit too much against her, and must have been in more pain than his pride would admit, she reasoned. She gripped his waist tightly and continued down the hall. They paused for a moment at the bottom of the stairs, and Jordan took in their height. She didn't feel like carrying Payden up them.

"Do you need some help?"

Jordan turned to see Malkam.

"Sure, Watcher," Payden answered. "Thanks."

Malkam nodded and took Jordan's place beside Payden. Malkam dwarfed him considerably and made it seem easy as he half carried Payden up the steps. Jordan slowly followed them up and held the bedroom door open as Malkam led Payden into the room.

"Have a good day," Malkam said as he departed. Jordan shut the door.

"You all right?" Payden asked from the bed as he rubbed his leg.

"No," she said softly.

"What?"

She turned and narrowed her eyes. After a few minutes, he stopped his movements as he realized she wasn't happy, though he couldn't figure out why.

"What?" he asked again, concern thick in his voice.

She shrugged and stepped toward the bed. "Nothing. It's been a long day already. I don't think I'm going to return for the rest of the training today. Or maybe I should. I don't think I could injure my hands any more."

Payden looked at her suspiciously, though his eyes betrayed his disbelief that that was what really concerned her at the moment. He wanted to change the subject before it was even brought up for discussion, so he quickly asked, "Do you think you could show me a few dance moves for the wedding?"

Jordan sat on the end of the bed and stared at him in disbelief.

"Okay, fine. I won't dance at the wedding." Wrong subject. "Um, what am I to wear?"

"Easel hasn't brought you the tuxedo yet?"

He shook his head.

"I suppose she has been busy. I'll remind her. Maybe I should go tell her now. Dinner's almost done, so she may not be busy now, but she will be later. I think. I don't know." She shook her head. "I'll come back tonight with your supper. Bye."

"Bye," he said weakly, feeling that he wouldn't be able to convince her to stay. She'd been standoffish from the moment he saw her in the dining hall. He rubbed again at his leg. He knew the reason why she'd be mad or upset with him, but he couldn't help feeling trapped in this room. He hated it and wanted to get out as often as he could.

After Zachary finished eating, he leaned back in the chair and waited. It didn't seem as though Lucy had eaten much. At present, she was poking her food with the fork and pushing it around her plate. Finally, she noticed it was too quiet in the dining hall, and she looked about the room. Just a few servants remained, cleaning or dismantling the extra tables. Someone whistled in the kitchen as dishes clanged together, but overall, it was calm. She noticed Zachary, sitting back with crossed arms and a patient expression. She loved and hated that about him. He was so tolerant. It frustrated her at that point beyond containment.

"Why don't you leave me alone right now?"

He stood. "I'll be outside. I'm sure everyone's back out for training. Feel free to join us. These guys could use your help." He left, and she sat alone, staring at her half-eaten food. The servants continued their work, keeping their conversations and laughter low. Lucy debated what she should do. Perhaps if she went outside to help, she could shake off this heavy cloud that seemed to ensnare her.

"Well, well, now. I didn't think it was possible, but it is. How about that?"

Lucy looked up at the round man beside her.

"See, the kids told me not everyone was gone. But when they told me your plate was still full, I had to see it for myself. No one has ever not eaten my pork." The chef sat in the chair beside her. "Why don't you like it? Too sweet? Or did you get some sour? I try to mix both together. People like the combination."

Lucy picked up her fork and poked at the meat. She still wasn't hungry. "It's fine, I guess. Not up for eating right now."

"You sick?"

She pondered. She felt ill, but not in the normal way.

"Oh. I see it now. You're soul-sick. Yeah, that takes some time to heal. I know."

"And how would you know?" she snapped, not intending to be so harsh, but she didn't seem to be in much control of herself.

His demeanor changed. Lucy braced herself for the inevitable speech, but then he laughed. "Come with me." He stood and gestured for her to follow suit. "Come on. Get up," he urged. She sighed and complied, following him into the kitchen.

"Step aside!" he shouted heartily. The young men and women in the kitchen, washing dishes or prepping food for the evening supper, turned to the side, adjusting themselves without interrupting their duties. Lucy stopped when he did, in front of several large slabs of beef. He picked up something that looked to Lucy like a mallet made of wood.

"Here," he said, handing it to her. "This meat needs to be tenderized before I cook it."

"Tenderized?"

"Yup. Just beat it to death, please." Then he laughed. She hoped he would explain the joke, but he just shook his head and laughed to himself. She glanced down at the meat. Maybe he laughed because the meat was already dead.

"How do I use it?"

"You figure it out." He went back to the fryers and began whistling. The kids in the kitchen stole a glance her way now and again, but they refocused. The mallet wasn't heavy, and she analyzed it. Wide spikes were carved on both sides. She looked down at the meat. There was only one way to tenderize that she knew. So she pulled the instrument back and brought it down hard again and again.

Chapter 11

Early the next morning, Jordan was once again at the shooting range. Fitted with a new pair of gloves, she settled into a comfortable routine. After finishing off a quiver of arrows, she retrieved them, then glanced about the grounds. To her surprise, Lucy was coming her way.

"Hi, Lucy," she called and waved. *Idiot, why did you wave?* she chided herself. She was hardly unnoticeable, being the only one out there wearing a dress. That included Lucy and the other women practicing. Jordan wondered when she would be forced to wear trousers as her training continued. She couldn't imagine ever preferring to wear them.

Her eyes remained on Lucy, who looked as though she was wearing men's trousers. And they were still too short. Jordan pondered. Perhaps she could make Lucy a pair of pants that actually fit. As a wedding present.

"Hey, Jordan, what brings you out here?" Lucy asked.

"Oh, well, I just wanted to learn how to do this. What about you?"

"Those women are driving me insane," Lucy snapped so vehemently that Jordan flinched. "They keep asking me about this and about that. As if I care what the color scheme is! And I heard someone mention a dress, so I bolted. I need to blow off some steam before I strangle one of them."

She huffed a little before noticing the look on Jordan's face. "Sorry. So, are you any good at this? Because I'm terrible."

"Um, sure. Just – I'm still new, so be kind with your critiques."

"You won't hear any from me," Lucy said, though distantly. Her eyes stayed fixed across the field. Jordan cast a glance and saw David with the men he was training. Lucy fidgeted with the hilt of the dagger strapped to her thigh. Jordan turned and nocked the arrow, feeling Lucy was just bored. Her presence kindled some nervous energy, so Jordan took a few deep breaths before she drew back the arrow and aimed it. Lining everything up just as Malkam had explained, she let it loose. It landed several centimeters to the left of the bull's-eye.

"Well," she said. "Eventually I'll get better."

"Better?" Lucy asked. Her reaction startled Jordan. "I've been trying to shoot that thing for years and can't even get that close. Jordan, you're good. I mean, in a few days, you'll be downright perfect. How do you people do it?"

Jordan smiled larger than she ever had. "Really? I'm good?"

"Here, let me show you how bad I am."

Lucy took the bow, grabbed an arrow, and carefully took aim. She let loose, and the arrow stuck on the outer rim.

"There, you see?" she asked, gesturing with her hand.

"You're just holding it wrong, that's all," Jordan said. "Your back elbow needs to be higher, and you need to drop your shoulders. And turn your body more so you can just look down the shaft to aim the arrow."

"Okay." Lucy set up again. "Where does my elbow go?"

"Higher." Jordan moved it to the correct position. "Then tilt your head and look down the shaft. That's it. Breathe out, then shoot. It helps."

Lucy released her breath, then let go of the arrow. It hit the bull's-eye, just to the right of center. She stared. Seeing it wasn't helping her believe it.

"Good job," Jordan said. "Want to try again to make sure it wasn't a fluke?"

"Uh-huh." Lucy was barely out of shock. She set up and shot again. It landed a little farther away, but she still couldn't believe it.

"Gee, in just a few days, you'll be perfect," Jordan said.

Lucy looked down at her and then gave her a little shove. "Don't tease me," she warned.

Jordan giggled. At that time, Malkam arrived.

"Good morning, ladies," he said cheerfully. Lucy tensed and quickly handed the bow to Jordan. Without another word, she left, heading for the estate. Jordan stared after her before shrugging. When her gaze turned to Malkam, he seemed worried. He kept his eyes on Lucy's retreat.

"Is something wrong?" she asked.

"Huh?" Malkam turned to her. "Oh, nothing. So, how does this thing feel today?"

"Pretty good," she said.

"Very good," Malkam said. "But that's the easy part. What will save you in a battle is getting the arrow out and in its target in seconds."

"Seconds?" Jordan exclaimed. It took more than a minute for her to nock the arrow in the string.

"Yup. When dozens of men are charging you, you need to drop them as fast as you can. Let's get to it. We'll start by getting you used to aiming quicker. Now, set your arrow. When I say shoot, I'll count to five. By that time, I want that arrow in its target. Ready?"

Her wide eyes met his, and he suppressed a chuckle. When she had an arrow set, she looked at him.

"Now, shoot. One . . . two . . . three . . . four . . ."

The arrow bounced off the wall behind the target.

"Good," Malkam said. "Now you know the drill. Keep at it. Come get me when you get ten in a row in the bull's-eye, consistently. We'll get to the next step after that."

He patted her back and left. The defeat settled. That's why David had had her come here first, to show her how difficult the easier stuff was. She pulled out all her arrows and stuck them into the ground in front of her. Setting the quiver aside, she nocked one and paused. She vowed to become perfect at this and show David just how determined she was.

Payden was growing restless from being inside so long. He got up and looked out his windows. The view was filled with the houses that sat in front of the manor and then the mountains beyond that. People were coming in and out, carrying armloads of flowers. He hoped they left some in the gardens.

He dressed himself in loose-fitting trousers and a lightweight, button-up shirt. He was hot, probably from a fever, so he let it remain unbuttoned. No one would notice, he figured. With all the hustle and bustle, one would think royalty was coming.

That last thought caused Payden to pause. Where did the word "royalty" come from? It seemed familiar, but he couldn't pinpoint where he'd heard it. Then the book caught his eye. Oh, he remembered. It spoke of royalty. They were the kings and queens—the rulers. He still couldn't completely understand why such people were awe-inspiring. No, he checked himself. He could understand why people felt that way about the Solomon fellow, but he wasn't finished reading that story yet.

He didn't have any desire to read, and he knew that walking around on his leg wasn't helping it heal, but Payden didn't want to stay in one spot while everyone else ran helter-skelter about him. When he opened the door, he saw David ascending the steps. He quickly shut it.

"Great," he muttered. Hardly a sentence had passed between David and him for the past few days. Payden tried to avoid him at every opportunity, but couldn't when David had it in mind to continue changing the bandages. The knock came at the door, and Payden was forced to open it.

"Yes?" he asked dryly, staring past David.

"Zachary said something to me this afternoon," David said, entering the room.

"Come in," Payden muttered and shut the door.

"Thank you. I will." David sat on the couch. David stared at him intently. Payden shifted under the gaze and finally sighed.

"What did Zachary say to you?"

"It was in passing, really. I don't think he understood its significance."

"And?"

David stared at him again. "Perhaps it was a mistake to come."

"You realize that now?"

David stood. "Could you please stay off that leg as much as possible? I've been sore tempted to put something in your food. Maybe I should, but then I'd have to apologize to the couple for causing your absence at the wedding. Zachary would have to find another best man."

"What did he say?" Payden snapped angrily.

David grabbed him by his neck and shoved him against the door. In the next heartbeat, he pulled Payden roughly away from the door. Payden stumbled and fell, barely able to catch himself. Pain from his wounds erupted, sending many tendrils of raw fire throughout his body.

"He said that he wanted your skills in battle so that he could defeat more enemies. Do you even realize what you have? You have absolutely no idea that people want to have half of what you have. You need to appreciate things that come easily. That's not the case for everyone else. You have been moping around feeling sorry for yourself, but you won't even take care of yourself. I bet you're in a lot of pain right now, aren't you?"

He paused. When Payden didn't answer, he yelled, "Aren't you?"

Payden swallowed nervously and nodded.

"Do you think you could even defend yourself?"

Payden shook his head.

"That would have been different had you just remained in bed. Understand this: if you don't let those wounds heal properly by resting, you won't be able to fight again like you once did. If that wound on your back doesn't heal right, you won't be able to achieve the same range of motion with your arm. I'm not even going to talk about your leg. That fever you still have should be gone by now. The tea and the herbs are helping a lot, but rest will heal everything perfectly. Now, I've let you mope around like a two-year-old for too many days. You always talked about growing up. Well, grow up! There are too many people around you, Payden, who care about you. Show them you care by listening to them and allowing them to help you, okay?"

Payden could do nothing but nod.

"Good. Now I've tried asking you nicely, but you wouldn't listen. So I figured if I scared you to death, that hard head of yours would soften up enough for you to listen."

David reached out his arm to help Payden to his feet. Payden hesitated but took the offered hand. Once he was up, David surprised him again by hugging him.

"I hope you know that I would never hurt you," David said. He let go and gripped Payden by the shoulders. "My dad would call this 'tough love.' Now go lie down. It's time to freshen up those bandages."

Too stunned to argue, Payden went to the bed. His thoughts were running too fast for him to catch any, and the attempts generated a headache.

David removed the cloth. The cut on the leg still looked fresh. He applied the salve and rewrapped it. The wound on the back had begun to fester. David retrieved a bowl of water and a rag.

"The infection's almost out of this one," he said. "It's at the surface now, which is good. The herbs can kill it quicker. Hopefully by tomorrow it'll be better."

He cleansed the wound and thickly covered it with the salve before he wrapped the bandage around Payden, pulling it under the armpit across his chest and around the opposite side of the neck several times until the wound was properly covered.

"Done," he said. "I'll send up some tea and your dinner tonight."

Payden just stared, and David grinned right before he left the room. Finally, something had gotten through to that boy. David threw away the old bandages and went to the gardens.

Payden's eyes remained locked on the closed door for quite some time. What had just happened? His head hurt, but before he moved an arm to rub it, he wondered which one he should use. As he debated, he thought about Solomon and finishing that story. The book was on the table by the bed, and he would have to move to get it. Was it okay for him to move? He didn't know.

Hours later, when Jordan came up with his food and tea, she found him sitting in the same position.

"Hi," Jordan said.

"Hi," Payden returned weakly.

She turned to hide her smile. David had warned her that Payden might act differently.

"David said you can use your arms to eat and stuff," she said. "I'll stay up here and read for a while if you'd like."

"Sure," he said.

"Hungry?"

He nodded.

She set the tray on the table and then set the plate on his lap. Once he was ready, she picked up the book and made her way around the bed to join him, careful to keep some distance between them. His gaze was fixed on the food, but he made no movement. Was he scared to move, she wondered. She leaned her head down so she could see his face. He didn't look scared, just hopelessly lost. She giggled. Whatever David had done had certainly left an impression. Poor Payden. What could she do to regain his presence?

Summoning every ounce of courage within her, she crept closer to him until she was in reach and kissed his cheek. Then she hurried back and sank into the pillows with the book propped open on her lap.

The kiss snapped him out of his stupor, and he looked at her.

"Eat up," she ordered. "I want to read to you a story about a woman."

"What's her name?"

"Ruth."

He listened silently as she read. He ate as quietly as he could so he would be able to hear her. The meal tasted wonderful, and he teased himself that it was only that good because it came from where freedom was, while he was trapped in this prison. He finished off the last few bites of the salad when she finished.

"Is that it?" he asked.

"Yes. It's not very long, but it's one of my favorites."

"Why?" He drank the cup of tea and quickly followed it with a chunk of bread.

"Well, it seems that where she lived, the people— Well, it's like the Jathenites and us. See, we read and love the arts. We like the more creative side of life. The beautiful side. But the Jathenites are methodical. Life's all about warfare and precision. Nothing outside the routine. I'm not sure if that was the difference between the two groups of people in the story, but that's how I see it. Years ago, whenever Jathenites visited one of our villages, they never wanted to leave. They said that we have something that was missing from their people."

"What was that?"

Jordan thought for a moment. "Spirit. This book talks about spirit and how it gives life. See, we live. We don't just prepare ourselves to avoid death."

"Until now."

"No. Though some are training, everyone's attention is on the wedding. It's on the life side. The Pendtars have not killed us yet."

"I love you," Payden blurted out. Wondering why he did, he blushed and focused on his unfinished meal.

Jordan couldn't move. She watched him closely, hoping to read something about him that she had missed. Everyone had said he loved her, but how did he know? She didn't know. The only examples she had ever had were in books. They weren't any real help.

She could tell Payden was berating himself by the expressions on his face. Her heart reached out to him. She wanted to hold him and— She turned to face the window. No. She couldn't kiss him. She hadn't enough bravery. And of course, there were the rules.

She noticed the change of light. It was sunset, which meant it would become darker. She needed to leave.

She slid off the bed, tempted to head for the door, but she needed to take the empty tray with her. Swallowing hard and steeling herself against her own desires, she collected the empty dishes, grateful his eyes avoided her.

"I'm sorry," he said. "I didn't mean to say it. It just came out."

"How do you know, though?" She looked at him, hoping she wasn't shaking.

"When those men—" He looked away, thinking deeply. "I don't understand this feeling, but I honestly didn't want to face another day without you. I really don't know if that's love. I really want to remember everything. Sometimes it seems as though everything would be easier if I could just remember."

She set the tray down and stepped forward to gently put her hand on his face. He lifted his chin to look at her. Her heart raced. Why was she suddenly so afraid now that everything could suddenly be spoken?

The nervousness heightened. She remembered something her mother had written to her in the journal she had left behind. It was the only thing Jordan had that enabled her to know her mother, if only just in part. In one of the poems, her mother had spoken of love. It was the most terrifying thing to do because it could potentially cause the most harm. However, if the birds never flew for fear of falling, or trees never grew for fear of being cut down, or fish never swam for fear of drowning, or stars never shone for fear of being compared to the sun, then nothing on the planet would exist as it should. They would all be too afraid to live as they were supposed to live. People were meant to love, she had written, as surely as they were meant to dance. Life offered fear and love. Only one made life worth living.

"I love you too," she whispered.

His eyes lit up, and a small smile touched his face.

"I need to confess something," she continued. "I want to always be beside you. Wherever you go, I want to be with you."

He reached out to pull her closer. She sat on the bed next to him and leaned down to rest against his shoulder.

"What if I want to stay here?" he asked.

"It won't happen," she said. "You're a wanderer. You can't stay in one place for too long."

"Well, as long as you understand."

"I do. These past few days have proven it. That, and you're dangerously stubborn."

He laughed lightly and rested his hand on her head, caressing her hair, grateful to have her close so he could breathe her scent. Just like those flowers.

"I'm tired," she said. "I did some more training today, and I need to rest."

"Okay. How are you doing?"

"I'm awful." She sat upright and pouted. "Malkam had me work on shooting faster, and I can't hit a thing now. It's so hard."

"Don't try so hard," Payden said. "Don't think about what you're doing. Just relax and do it."

"It sounds so easy."

"Well, it is easy," he said. "I never think about what I'm doing. I just know what to do."

"All I can do is try, I guess," she said.

"You guess? It's easy to not think."

"Perhaps for you," she teased, eyes twinkling.

"Oh." He playfully pushed her and shook his head. "You know what I mean."

"No, I don't. Truly. I've never had to live by instinct."

"I get it. But maybe you could learn to."

"I'm glad you're optimistic. I really want to go to bed. I plan on getting up early to start as soon as I can. I'm determined to get this thing right."

"Don't be too upset if it takes time."

She leaned forward. "I will. That's why I have to work hard."

When she realized how close she was, she froze. Before she allowed herself to get too nervous, she stood and pushed her hair from her face.

"Why do you do that?" he asked, taking her hand. "What's got you so scared?"

"I don't know."

She felt him release her. "Will you ever be comfortable around me?"

There was a hint of sorrow in his voice. *Does he think I don't love him?* She let herself look at him again, but he was elsewhere. His head was resting back on the pillow, and he stared up at the ceiling. When she saw his hands were hidden under the covers, she wondered what he was thinking.

"I do love you," she said and placed her hand to his face. "It's not that I'm uncomfortable around you. I'm just nervous. This is all new to me. And there are rules. Like, you're supposed to get my father's permission to even see me."

"Permission?"

"Yes. But what I really want to know is, why doesn't it scare you?" she asked.

"Why should it?"

She retreated. She didn't know, but it still terrified her. "Good night. David told me to tell you not to get up and not to make any large movements."

He caught her and pulled her close. "You're not running this time. Answer me. What's got you so scared?"

"I don't know."

"Yes, you do."

"Just let me go," she said and tried to push away from him.

"Talk to me. I may actually understand."

She turned her head away and set her jaw. *She's just as stubborn as I am*, Payden observed. Maybe she would come around in time.

"Fine. Maybe you'll tell me when you can trust me."

She quickly turned her eyes to him. "I'm sorry."

He let her escape, and she forgot the tray as she fled.

Chapter 12

Before Jordan left her house the next morning, she had to entertain her favorite guest. Salina arrived just after dawn, eager to enlist Jordan's aid. Lucy proved too hard to find at the moment, and the ladies needed her for a dress fitting.

"She has seemed a bit distant lately," Jordan observed.

"There's rumors she's even avoiding her fiancé," Salina muttered over a cup of coffee.

"Maybe that's just what Ashites do, though."

"True." Salina pondered and leaned back in the chair. "But her companions aren't acting as though her behavior is normal."

"So we should go find her, then—"

"I'll see what I can do first. Don't worry yet, though. It may be nothing."

"All right." Jordan sighed. "Well, I'm going to do some archery for a bit and find Easel later. I hope you get Lucy ready."

"Me too." Salina stood. "Have a good day in the meantime." She patted Jordan's hand and departed. Jordan hurried outside, fitted her gloves, and fired a few shots before she remembered Malkam's new instructions. She stared at the target for a while before her insecurities got the better of her, and she left. She went to the infirmary first. They removed the bandages from her wrists and determined she didn't need them anymore. Nor were they concerned about her blisters.

She skipped back to the estate, gleeful to be freed of all the fuss. The wounds were still pink, but definitely healed. The business of everyone inside the estate caused her to pause. So many of the older Djorites were inside helping now. The wedding was definitely a good thing.

She finally continued her quest to Easel's sewing room. It seemed Salina had found Lucy—but Lucy didn't seem happy about that.

"I don't want a dress," she protested, red faced as she stood on a short stool, hands in fists at her side.

"You can't get married in trousers, dear," said the elderly lady who was pinning up the seams.

"I've done everything in trousers," Lucy snapped. She crossed her arms and blew the hair from her face.

Jordan giggled at the sight of her. She then saw Easel in the back and crept over to her, out of Lucy's line of sight.

"Hi, Easel," Jordan said quietly.

"Well, how are you?" Easel hugged Jordan tightly. "What brings you over to me today?"

"I'm on a quest."

"Oh? Can you share any details?" Easel raised her eyebrows.

"I was hoping you could share some. I need Lucy's measurements because I want to make her a decent pair of trousers that would look better on her than those awful men's pants she wears."

"Poor lass. That fabric she's got pinned to her now is the first dress she's ever worn."

"From what I've gathered in the few talks we've had, where she's from, they fight to survive every day. The city's roads are full of rubble, and food is scarce. A dress would hardly be useful."

"Well, when we're done with her, she's going to be the most beautiful bride." Easel looked up at Lucy, who continued to scowl. "If she smiles, of course."

She and Jordan shared a laugh.

"Ow," Lucy screamed. She turned her head to look behind her. "I didn't expect this event to draw blood!"

"Sorry, miss," the old lady said. "You could blame my old hands or your fidgeting. Either way, the seam will still get pinned."

"Grr," Lucy growled. She lowered her arms to her side and froze.

"Here are her measurements, dear," Easel whispered to Jordan and handed her a piece of paper.

"Thank you so much."

Jordan tucked the paper into her pocket and scurried out of the room. Lucy watched her leave.

"What did she want?" she asked. "Where is she going?"

"Never mind," Easel said. "Stay still or Beth will stick you again."

Lucy crossed her arms. "I'd rather be tortured," she muttered. "Ow!"

"Sorry," Beth said.

Jordan ran to her house and into the sewing room. She had picked out the material before she left the estate, and she was eager to begin. Knowing Lucy's life had helped the selection process. It was a heavier, dark-brown fabric. Jordan quickly measured the length of the leg, then the width. She cut the pieces and began stitching. Sacrificing her practice time was worth it, she knew.

After several hours, more than half the work was finished. The sun peeked through some clouds, daring her to come outside, but she hesitated. She'd done nothing this morning. A fear of failure kept her filled with a desire to forgo the pursuit. Was it really so easy to quit so soon? She felt frustrated. The sewing had to wait.

Malkam saw Jordan running to the archery grounds, and he cut across the yard to intercept her. He had noted her lack of attempt that morning and wondered if he'd lost a student.

"Jordan," he called. She paused and waited for him.

"Yeah?" she asked.

"How's practice?"

"Oh, uh, okay. It's challenging. I'm a bit distracted today. I'm making a new pair of pants for Lucy as a wedding present. I was just going to take a short break from that and practice. I know I need it."

"Oh, I'm glad to hear that," he said. "I was worried that you had given up."

"No, I'm not going to give up on this. Never."

"That's good to hear. I'll leave you to it then."

She continued to her destination. Once her gloves were on and the arrow set, she paused and slowly released her breath, recalling Payden's advice. *"Don't think. Just do."*

She pulled the string and shot. The arrow hit the wall, like all the shots from the day before. She lowered the bow.

"Easier said than done." She grabbed another arrow. "Don't think. Just do. Do what? How can you do something you don't know how to do? Or do men just automatically know how to do all this stuff?"

She sighed.

"Why am I even fretting? Just don't think. Don't think."

She shot again. Another miss.

"I'm still thinking!" she cried. Those nearby glanced her way, but she was oblivious to them.

"Of all the idiotic things to say. Thanks, Payden." She angrily pulled out another arrow. "Don't think. Just do," she mocked. She let out her breath and shot again. Still, no arrow hit the target.

"What am I doing wrong?" she muttered. "Oh. That's it. I'm thinking about not thinking. Brilliant."

She laughed at herself and set another arrow. The bull's-eye came into focus, and then the tip of the arrow.

"Okay," she said to it. "If you do not hit the mark this time, I am going to give you a very stern lecture."

She shook her body to loosen the tension and focused on the bull's-eye again. How was she supposed to be able to do this without taking the time to aim? Maybe she was supposed to just know, she thought mockingly. Or— She lifted the bow, pulled back the string, and looked down the arrow to her target. She held that position until she was sure she knew what it felt like.

But then she lowered the bow. If men were charging her, that idea wouldn't work. What had she been doing wrong? What had Payden said? He just knew what to do. What did he mean by that? She shut her eyes and saw the target in front of her. Then she visualized herself hitting the target. It was so easy.

She opened her eyes and stared at the target. Perhaps that had been her mistake. Her target had changed from the actual bull's-eye to shooting correctly. She needed to readjust. Staring intently at the mark, she raised the bow and fired. It didn't hit the bull's-eye, but it did hit the target finally. She smiled. It was easy.

By the end of the hour, every arrow was hitting the target. None had hit close to the center, but that would come in time. She gathered all the arrows and the equipment and returned them to where they belonged. Tomorrow, she was going to get those ten. She knew.

When she returned to the estate, she saw her father coming down the stairs, and she stiffened. What had he been doing up there, she wondered.

"Hi, Father," she said, pulling him out of his thoughts.

"Jordan!" He approached her. "I haven't seen you yet today. How are you?"

She hugged him. When his arms gave her a loose squeeze, she fought to keep her composure. Their guests gave her warmer hugs. She stepped back, careful not to look up at him.

"I'm fine. I was going to visit Payden for a few minutes. I'm sure he's bored."

"Yes, he did complain about that," Samuel said.

That comment brought her eyes to his face. "You just spoke with him?"

"Yes. Salina told me that he wanted to talk with me." He crossed his arms and looked down at her. "Why didn't he come to me days ago?"

"He didn't know," she said defensively. "I'm sorry. I've just informed him."

He nodded, considering her. "All right. I've given him permission to court you, but I expected proper behavior from you. Like this visiting him unaccompanied. You know it isn't appropriate."

Disappointment filled her, and she lowered her head.

"I'm going to be busy for the rest of the day. You'll have to eat here again." He walked past her, and she watched him exit through the doors before she let the tears fall. When didn't she eat here? She sat on the couch and hugged herself, trying to regain composure. Three days ago, he had been so much warmer. That was only because he thought he had lost her. Now it was back to normal. Propriety. Formality. But absolutely no relationship.

Salina approached and quickly wrapped her arms around Jordan. "Calm down, there," she said soothingly. "I stuck around to hear his verdict. Honey, don't get so upset. He'll come around one day; don't lose hope yet."

"I just want to know what I've done," Jordan choked out. "I'm sorry for being around Payden without an escort, but—he wants to be around me. He loves me."

"Shh. Go on up and be with him then. Don't be afraid. I'll handle your father. He'll never know."

Jordan looked up at her. "But we can't keep this secret!"

"Why not? Have you told your father about your mother's journal yet?" Salina asked, raising an eyebrow.

Jordan bit her lip and looked at the floor.

"I thought so. Some things are better kept. Besides, it's a secret you are sharing, so I don't think it really counts. Now go on up and see that boy. Give him a great big kiss, okay?"

"Salina! I can't—"

"Yes, you can. You have too much of your mother's passion inside of you to keep it stifled any longer. Be who you are, and don't apologize for it. All your dad has are the rules and responsibilities. You've got a handsome young man who loves you. Don't let the past kill that chance for happiness too, okay?"

Salina kissed Jordan on the forehead and straightened her hair.

"Smile."

Jordan smiled, and Salina was happy to see that it was genuine.

"Good. Go, and don't worry anymore. Follow your heart, right? Isn't that what your mother told you to do?"

Jordan nodded and hugged Salina. She wiped her face clean of the tears before she rushed up the steps.

Payden was on the bed reading when she entered. He quickly set the book aside, seeming alarmed to see her.

"What's wrong?" he asked. "What did your father say?"

"Nothing. He's not why I'm here." She shut the doors and went to the bed, climbing up to sit next to him. "I'm here because of my mother."

"Your mother? I thought—isn't she—"

"Yeah, some time ago. She left me many letters of advice in a journal. I don't want to be scared anymore. I love you. And she would have hated me being scared of—" Taking a deep breath, she leaned forward and kissed him.

Payden was shocked. What had happened, he wondered. When she sat upright to look at him, he couldn't help but remain confused.

"So, uh, um—" He stared at her. Why couldn't he say anything? She looked so much more beautiful that day.

"I just wanted to say, hi," she said. "But I have to go now. I'm making Lucy some pants."

She left, and he couldn't get his thoughts together enough to think coherently. Was Jordan just in a really good mood, or was this how things were going to be from now on? His first question came back: what had happened?

The next day, it rained. Jordan sat in her room with Lucy's nearly completed trousers on her lap and stared out the window. She could barely see past the frame, it was raining so hard. This was the day she had planned to perfect her archery skills, she lamented.

Sighing, she finally accepted her circumstances and got to work finishing the trousers. Once they were finished, she held them up against herself. Lucy was certainly tall, but Jordan hadn't realized just how much until then. Setting them down, she thought about stitching some detailing in them, like a flower on the thigh. That wasn't Lucy. Daggers on the side were more suitable. It had been a passing thought, but as Jordan picked up its trail, she thought it might not be such a bad idea. Lucy might actually love it. She opted not to put them up high. Lower would look better. The outside seam, she decided, was the best spot.

Knowing it would take the better part of the day, she didn't feel so glum anymore. Perhaps she could shoot better when her hands weren't so stiff from the blisters. They certainly hampered her ability to sew a quick seam, never a problem before. What was done could not be undone, as David would probably say.

She smiled. David. She was so grateful that he had finally persuaded Payden to stay put. She giggled thinking about Payden the other night, too scared to move. She paused her stitching. Should she go visit him? Easel had her helping with the dress last night, so she hadn't gotten a chance to see him again. Should she go visit him now?

No, she quickly reasoned. These pants could not wait. Her heart ached to go, but her head won a compromise—once the pants were complete, then Payden could receive a visit. She wasn't going to be able to sew fast enough.

Payden stared at the window, watching the water run down the glass. At least the rain ensured no more temptation to go outside that day. Tomorrow would be sunny and clear, he was sure. Of course, it was also the day of the wedding. Everything was supposed to happen inside. He hoped he would be able to leave the room, but David hadn't said anything yet.

The book sat open on his lap, and he flipped through the pages before setting it aside. He had done nothing but read since finally remaining on bed rest, and that morning his head had begun to hurt.

A knock at the door signaled a distraction to his present mundane existence.

"Come in," he called.

David entered with Zachary close behind.

"Hi, Payden. It's been a few days," Zachary said. "You're looking better, though."

"It's the tea," Payden said. "I'm glad you're here. The monotony is getting to me. Where have you been?"

"David's training camp, where else? The women are going nuts here."

"Even so, I'd do anything to get out of this bed."

"It's only been two days," David said.

"Only two?" Payden groaned. "How many more?"

"It would have been less had you stayed put in the first place. But those are the consequences."

"Yeah, yeah. I know," Payden muttered. "Why are you two here?"

"I'm merely here to check on you. Zachary, on the other hand, has been following me around all day."

Payden cast a questioning look at Zachary. "Why's that?"

"Lucy," he said heavily. "The ladies are making her wear a dress tomorrow, and she's this close to blowing fire out of her mouth. I've never seen her like this, ever. It's scaring me."

Payden thought for a moment. "I can't picture her wearing a dress."

"Neither can I! But the ladies are insisting, and Lucy's furious. I honestly think she's going to kill one of them. I'm tempted to hide her weapons. Of course, that would mean I would have to get close to her, but she's snapped every time I've tried to touch her today. I've decided that I need to avoid her at all costs so that I don't change my mind about this. She seems to be avoiding David, so I figure if I'm around him, then I'm safe."

"People feel that way about me a lot," David said.

"Safe around you?" Zachary asked.

"No. That I should be avoided. I can never understand why, though." He winked at Payden.

"I bet. Why would anyone want to avoid a Slave?" Zachary asked sarcastically.

"Well, I didn't choose the uniform."

"I don't want to avoid you, David. I like hanging out with you."

"That's only because you're wanting something to do right now. Let's get a look at those injuries."

Before Payden rolled over, he looked at Zachary again.

"What's happened to your hair?" he asked.

Zachary smiled sheepishly and rubbed his newly cropped mane. "Does it look awful? I haven't had the courage to look yet."

"No, it . . . uh . . . is different," Payden said. "I thought you hated having short hair."

"I do, but Lucy hates long hair, so I figured I'd get it cut off—just for the wedding," Zachary said. "But just for the wedding. She hasn't really noticed yet, but maybe tomorrow she will. I hope she likes it." He paused to pout. "That would make one of us."

Payden finished turning onto his stomach. He relaxed as David checked on the stitches. At that point, Payden had to admit that the pain was finally gone. So was the illness. His leg had stopped throbbing, and sleeping was easier. Still, he felt it too small a gain compared to his loss of freedom.

Once David was finished, Payden returned to his former position, grateful to see David and Zachary sit on his bed too. Zachary crawled over Payden and parked himself in the center.

"I guess I should be grateful that those Fashites were bad shots," Payden said. "Instead of being caged in this room, I could be dead."

David shook his head. "Payden, they're Fashites. No one has better aim. Those were blind shots in the dark. They hit their target."

Zachary pulled Payden into a headlock and rubbed the top of his head with his knuckle. "I would have missed you, kid."

Payden managed to push him away, and Zachary laughed. He looked down at the bed and saw something he had never before seen. He picked it up and inspected it.

"What's this?" he asked.

"A book," Payden answered.

"Wait—this is a book?" Zachary almost exclaimed.

"Yeah. Why?"

"I thought a book was a great weapon or bomb or something. But it's this? What's in it? Why are the Pendtars bent on destroying them?"

Payden shrugged, and both he and Zachary looked at David, who held out his hand.

"Give it here, and I'll show you."

Zachary quickly obliged and got comfortable for the lesson. He had heard about books his whole life, knowing that anyone who possessed one was killed. The Fashite army always searched for them wherever it went. He had never seen one nor known anyone who could explain to him what they were. Finally, he did. He chuckled inwardly at the irony of a Slave having that knowledge. No, he corrected himself. David really couldn't be considered a Slave.

David slowly flipped through the pages, looking for a particular part. As he searched, he decided to begin his teaching.

"Not all books are the same, Zachary. You know the stories you tell your friends?"

Zachary nodded.

"Each is different, right?"

"Yes," Zachary answered.

"Books just tell stories written by people. Most of them came from the Djorites. Some came from the Jathenites. And I think there are actually a few written by Ashites, but I doubt any of them exist anymore. Not many Ashites ever needed to know how to read. Some, those who had contact with the Djorites, learned and wanted to teach others. Then there were those who became doctors and found that their jobs were easier when they wrote things down, so learning became standard for them. Malkam knows only because of your father," David said to Payden, who smiled.

"My dad taught him how to read?"

"It took some time, but yes. And he taught me. But that's a story for another day. Anyway, this book is different from all of the others."

"How?" Zachary asked, leaning forward to peek at it.

"It doesn't entertain. It teaches," David explained. "I want to read this part to you, and hopefully you two will be able to understand why this book is so threatening that the Pendtars want all books destroyed."

"They were really after just one?" Zachary asked. "That one?"

David nodded.

"Huh."

David lifted the book and began to read.

> Jesus turned to those who followed him in order to hear his teachings and said, "If you keep listening to my teachings and actually do what I teach you and show you to do, then you are truly my friends. Then you will know the Truth, and the Truth will give you freedom."
>
> But those who followed him were confused, and they said, "We come from the seed of Abraham. No one owns us. We are not slaves. How can we be set free? We are already free."
>
> Jesus answered, "Do you not understand that when you commit sin, you become a slave to sin and its wickedness? You are then unable to do anything as you choose, but only what sin controls you to do. Indeed, you become a slave. But I am here to set you free from the master Sin. Who I set free is free completely."

David paused and read silently for a moment.

> Jesus explained, "You may say the Creator of All is your father, but if He really were, then you would listen to me and not be offended, because He sent me, and I do all that He asks. You are offended by me because you have a different father, the one who spreads lies and copies all that the true Creator made. That liar is your father. I tell you the Truth to set you free from his lies, but you are not capable

> of listening because you've chosen the lies as better than the Truth."

David stopped and shut the book.

"I don't get it," Zachary immediately confessed.

"The book encourages people to be free, think for themselves, and cast out everything that is wicked. That's the exact opposite of what the Pendtars want. They want—" David paused and rubbed his wrist. "They want slaves. They want everyone to be a slave." He sighed.

"I'm still not understanding this," Zachary said.

"It's easier to rule people who don't know they have a choice," Payden said. "So, to the Pendtars, the most dangerous weapons are things that teach people that they have a choice. Like this book—and my father."

David looked up to find Payden staring at him.

"That's right, isn't it?" Payden asked. "It has to be. My father fought for peace while the Pendtars brought war and control. My father offered a choice, a different way. That's what this Jesus talked about. Freedom." Payden turned to face Zachary. "Zachary, think about it. Do you think you and Lucy were free in Tawney City?"

Zachary didn't have to think. "No. We weren't."

"Why didn't you guys ever choose to leave?"

"I don't know," Zachary said. "I guess we never thought we could. Wherever we went, we saw war."

"That's why they killed the Djorites first and haven't attacked the Jathenites. The Djorites offered a choice. The Jathenites, if they've been explained to me correctly, are a warlike people. Jordan told me that they're stuck, not living—just avoiding death. In a way, they're already in bondage. We Ashites are in the middle. But we're slowly dying, aren't we?" He looked at David.

David had to pause a moment. A few times in the past he had felt a swell of emotion in his chest too unfamiliar to bear. The feeling always caused him to want to cry, yet he knew he was pleased. Each instance had been the result of something

Payden had done or said. David once again felt difficulty breathing and tried to quell the emotion.

"Are you okay?" Payden asked him.

David closed his eyes and breathed. "I'm fine," he whispered. "It's just—hard to say. You're right, Payden. It's amazing, but you get it. You're right. The Pendtars fear most a people who know what they have. They're more likely to fight to keep it."

"That makes sense," Zachary said.

He took the book from David and flipped through it.

"How do you guys understand this?" he asked.

"You learn how," Payden said. "Want me to teach you?"

"How long will it take?"

"All day. Or longer. I don't know. David?"

"It takes a long time for some people, especially when they're older. I taught you when you were very young. You loved to read."

"I did?" Payden asked, the childlike glow returning to his eyes.

"Yeah. I brought you stacks of books that I saved from the fires. I couldn't bring them fast enough."

Payden leaned back and grinned. David watched him fall deeper into his thoughts.

"Well, Mr. Zachary, I must leave," David said.

Payden broke free from his thoughts. "Why?" he asked.

David stood. "No reason. I thought I would leave you two be."

"You don't have to go," Payden said.

"Yeah, stay and talk with us," Zachary insisted. "Tell us some stories or anything that comes to mind."

"Tell me more about my mother and my brother. What was his name?"

"Egan. His name was Egan. And the funny thing about Egan was that he never called you Payden. He called you Egan. And I'm sure that if he had had another brother, he would have called him Egan too."

"Why did he do that?" Payden asked.

"Why did you never want to wear a stitch of clothing until you were four?"

Payden turned bright red, and Zachary hooted with laughter. David chuckled and sat back down. He could stay, he decided. He could stay.

When Jordan brought Payden's tray of food, she heard laughter while she was still on the steps. Curious about the commotion, she slowly opened the door and peeked inside. Payden was sitting on top of Zachary, pinning both his arms down with his leg and tickling him with his free hand.

"Stop it!" Zachary cried. "Get off me."

Jordan heard a deep chuckle to her left. She had to enter all the way to discover the owner.

"Hi, David," she said.

"Hi." He took the tray from her. "Payden, dinner."

"Really?"

The distraction cost him the advantage. Zachary quickly pinned him in no time.

"No! Stop!" Payden howled as Zachary commenced the torture. "Okay, I yield! I give up."

Zachary released him and jumped off the bed. "I won," he said triumphantly. "Hi, Jordan."

He quickly hugged her, picking her up to spin her around. He set her down and headed for the door. "I'm going to eat. Then I'll come back up, okay?"

"Bye," Payden said.

David set the tray on the side table. "I must join him. He may need backup when Lucy arrives."

Once the door was shut, Jordan just stood in the center of the room, smiling but bewildered at what she had just witnessed.

"Thanks for the food," Payden said. "And the tea."

"Oh? You like the tea now?"

He quickly swallowed it all down. "Ah," he said, but then screwed up his face. "Never mind. I can't fake it."

Jordan approached him slowly as he ate a few bites. The moment she was within reach, he grabbed her and pulled her onto the bed.

"Payden!" she cried.

He laughed and hit her with a pillow. "Surprise. I win," he said.

She pushed him away, and he returned to the food. Her reaction made him somewhat leery, so he quickly drank the juice. She was on her knees, piling the pillows together by the headboard; he wasn't fooled, so he turned his back to her a little more. Just as he suspected, she hit him with a pillow. He quickly grabbed it, and she squealed, rolling to the other side of the bed.

"I won!" she cried and giggled.

"Uh-uh," he said, grabbing another pillow. "It's only just begun."

"Then I give up! I know I won't win."

"Oh." He set the pillows down and dejectedly said, "Fine."

He turned and scooted back to the food. She quickly slid over to him and wrapped her arms around him. He looked at her.

"What is it?" he asked.

"I don't know," she said. "I just wanted to hold you, that's all."

He lifted his arm around her and pulled her onto his lap. She nestled her head against his chest and let herself enjoy being in his arms.

"I'm glad to see that you're better and able to be more active," she said. "A few days ago, I know it would have hurt too much for you to wrestle Zachary."

"Oh, he was letting me win," Payden said. "He's twice my size. There's no way I could truly hold him down."

"I was more happy to see David laughing," she said. "He's always seemed so sad and distant."

"He holds himself back a lot, but maybe someday he'll let himself free. It's funny, but I don't understand why I prefer David's presence. Watcher is too— I can't really say, but there's just something there. Something about him."

"Who's Watcher?" she asked.

"Hm? Oh—Malkam."

"Why do you call him Watcher?"

"Well, he told me that's what I used to call him. He said he raised me, but that's just it. David seems to know and understand me more. Watcher just—there's something missing."

"Love?" she offered.

"Why would you say that?"

She sat upright and knelt next to him. "David obviously loves you. He's proven that in so many ways since you've been here. Even when you were being hardheaded and weren't talking to him, he still took care of you. Malkam, well, he may love you, but he seems content to let you do things on your own."

"Why is that bad?"

"A parent has to teach the child. A child left to his own devices won't turn out right. Malkam thought it was just fine to let you hobble around, but David didn't. He knew it would cause you greater harm in the end. He risked isolating you more in hopes of getting you to rest so your injuries could heal. Malkam may love you, but perhaps not as much."

"Huh. I never would have thought that way."

"Of course not. That's why you need me." She smiled and coyly tipped her head. He surprised her with a strong embrace and a long, passionate kiss that made her go limp. She wrapped her arms around his neck, mostly to hold herself up. When he released her, she stared into his eyes in search of something that would help her understand him.

"What brought that on?" she asked softly, slightly breathless.

"At the hospital, the doctor kissed Dawn that way. I didn't understand why until I met you. I've wanted to do it ever since."

"Well, let's not do that again anytime soon."

"Was it that bad?" he asked.

"Oh, no. No. To the contrary, actually. But, uh, I'm afraid I'm not ready for those kind of kisses yet."

"Oh. Sorry."

The look in his eyes revealed his disappointment. She could feel hers growing, not because of his, but because she had once again buried the part of her that was her mother. She lowered her eyes so she wouldn't have to look at his anymore, but he lifted her chin, and she bit her lip, hoping to turn back the tears.

"I love you," he said softly.

A small smile graced her face. He nuzzled his face against her neck and pulled her close. She giggled.

"That tickles," she said.

"Oh?" He moved his arm and tickled her side. She tried to push away as she began to squeal with laughter, but he held her close.

"Stop it, Payden!" she cried.

He laughed and stopped, wrapping both arms around her again. "Fine," he said in as pitiful a voice as he could muster.

She hit his arm with her fist, and he jerked back to look at her. "Hey!"

"You deserve that and more," she snapped, hoping her face remained steeled. "Don't do that."

He obviously saw through the ruse. A mischievous twinkle lit up his eyes, and he smiled.

"Payden, don't," she warned.

"Fine," he said lightly and turned aside so that he could finally eat his food. She moved as far away as she could. He was in too mischievous a mood to be trusted.

After he finished eating, he lifted the tray and set it on the table. Her suspicions rose as he remained distant. Then the light began to change, and she saw his eyes go to the window. Sunset. Her brows knit; she eyed him curiously as he looked longingly to the fading light. What was going through his mind?

Hoping he wasn't playing a trick, she approached him cautiously. He wasn't. She knelt in front of him and placed her hands on his face, and he finally looked at her.

"Hi," she said.

"I must be getting tired. For some reason, I'm more tired now that I'm forced to lie around than when I was up walking all day long."

She breathed deeply as she studied his face. "I love you, too, you know?"

He nodded and pressed his forehead to hers. "Yeah. I guess. Even though you won't let me tickle you."

She hit his arm again, and he hugged her.

A commotion outside the room suddenly drew their attention. Someone was yelling loudly, and they heard the tinkling of shattered fragments sliding across to the floor. Jordan and Payden looked at each other.

"I bet it's Lucy," Payden said. "Don't open the door."

"How do you know for sure?"

"I just know."

"Well, I want to find out," she said.

"I'm not getting out of bed."

"Fine." She hopped down and went to the door. It was definitely a female voice coming from the other side. She opened the door slowly and saw Lucy pacing through the hallway, biting her nails. Zachary stood on the steps, pale and silent. A small vase that once stood on the table beside Lucy's room was broken, water and flowers scattered all over the tile floor.

"Hey," Jordan said.

Lucy jumped and spun to face her.

"Don't scare me like that!" she shouted.

Jordan stepped into the hallway. "What's going on?"

Lucy went back to pacing. Jordan looked at Zachary for an answer, but he could only shrug.

"Zachary, why don't you go and talk with Payden, okay?"

Zachary quickly obeyed. Jordan approached Lucy, full of trepidation, and gently touched Lucy's arm. Lucy jumped again.

"I said don't scare me," Lucy snapped.

"What's got you so scared?" Jordan asked.

"I don't want to get married," Lucy answered loudly. "I don't want everyone looking at me. I don't want to wear that stupid dress. I don't want to make promises I can't keep. And I most certainly never want to have children!"

"Why's that?" someone asked. They turned to find David and Malkam coming up the stairs. "Why do you not want to have children?" David asked.

"Don't you dare talk to me!" Lucy screamed. "You leave me alone, you murderer. Stay away from me. Stay away!"

David took a few steps toward her. "You want to hit me?" he asked. He unbelted his sword and dropped it to the floor before he kicked it aside. "Come on, hit me."

"I don't want to touch you!"

"Come on, hit me," he snapped. "Hit me. I'm the one you see when you think of those who've been killed? I'm the one who made your life a nightmare, right? So hit me!"

"Stop it! Stop it!" she screamed.

David walked closer to her, and his voice grew louder. "What? Do you think you can hurt me? You can't hurt me. I never stop coming. I'm always there. So just take out your vengeance now and hit me!"

Payden's door opened. He and Zachary were both watching.

Lucy drew her sword, and David slapped it out of her hands. He kept walking toward her, and she retreated. She pulled out a knife and rushed him, but he twisted around and knocked that out of her hand too, removing the last two knives from her holster and tossing them on the floor.

"Looks like you have no more options now but to use your fists, so hit me!" he growled.

Malkam grabbed Jordan and pulled her into Payden's room. "Zachary, you need to stay out here. I'm coming inside."

Zachary swallowed and stepped outside. Malkam shut the door behind him.

"What's going on?" Payden asked.

"She's about to break," Malkam said. "David's trying to get her to release that rage. It might calm her down enough for us to help her. If not—who knows?"

"What?" Jordan asked. "I thought she was fine."

"No. The signs were all there. I've been waiting for this to happen. If someone never deals with things that happen in life and tries to push those feelings away, it gets to be too much over time. Weddings have a funny way of exposing those raw emotions. Now be quiet. I have to listen if David needs me out there, in case things don't go the way we hope they'll go."

On the other side of the door, Lucy stood a few feet from David, trembling with fear and rage.

"Hit me, Lucy," he snarled. She shook her head and backed up a few more steps. "Hit me!" he shouted.

With a scream, she ran at him, dropped her shoulder, and knocked him back several feet. He regained his footing.

"Is that all you've got?" he barked.

She charged him again with her hands clasped together and hit him square on the chest with her fists. Her foot slammed against his leg, and she spun to elbow him in the stomach. A punch crossed his face, and her other fist hooked him in the stomach. She threw a right hook into his stomach and another left. The torrents of tears running from her eyes blinded her, and she began to shake uncontrollably. Her body, ravaged from the explosion of hysterics, was drained of strength, and she sank. David caught her in time and kept her on her feet.

"Speak," he said.

She only continued to cry.

"Speak," he snapped loudly.

"Why?" she cried. "Why did they have to die? Why wasn't it me? They were little kids! My Roscoe—why didn't my parents take us away? Why didn't we just leave? We didn't have to stay. We didn't have to fight. They wouldn't have been killed. Those soldiers wouldn't have hurt me. They hurt me! They hurt me! I don't want to get married. I don't. My wedding night was ruined by those wicked men!" she screamed.

Zachary almost collapsed. He leaned against the wall for support. That had been . . . ten years ago. Why hadn't she said anything? A fierce anger rose in him as his hands curled into fists. If those soldiers were still alive—

"I watched them kill my parents. They thought that I was dead. Little Tate saw the whole thing. He was only two years old and saw the whole thing. I couldn't help him. I was never able to help him."

She fell silent, overwhelmed by her tears.

David motioned for Zachary to come over. When he reached them, David whispered in his ear, "Protect her."

Zachary nodded. He carefully wrapped his arms around her shaking body.

"It's me, Zachary," he said softly. "I'm here. No matter what, I'm here. Let me help you."

She clung to him, wetting his shirt with her tears. Zachary stroked her hair and held her tightly.

David gently rapped on the bedroom door.

"Yeah," Malkam asked, looking about to see where everyone was.

"Tell everyone to go to bed," David said. "You go too. Tell Jordan to calm the servants down. Send someone up in a couple hours to clean the mess out here."

"Okay." Malkam ducked into the room to relay the message. Then he exited and silently went to his room. Jordan left without so much as glancing at Lucy. David closed the door and leaned against it, keeping his attention on the couple.

"Keep crying. Let it out," Zachary said soothingly. He gently swayed back and forth, humming softly. Within a few moments, Lucy's sobbing ceased. She turned her head and rested her ear against his heart. It took some time for her breathing to regulate, but once it did, she held on to Zachary even tighter.

David noticed a look of peace upon her face, and he relaxed. He closed his eyes and leaned his head back against the door. His whole heart had hoped and begged for her to pull through. Seeing that she seemed calmer allowed a flood of relief.

He thought of one of the stories from the Book about a man with many spirits inside him. When they left, he was of a sound mind again. Lucy might not have had spirits inside her, but with all the horrors she had seen—faces and images played over and over again—he supposed it was the same thing. He bowed his head thoughtfully. From his own experience, he knew it to be the same thing.

He took off his hat, cloak, and gloves, gathered up all the weapons, and set them outside his room. Zachary looked at him, and David shook his head. Zachary returned his attention to Lucy. He began to stroke her hair again as they continued to sway. He hummed some more, which seemed to have the most calming effect on her.

Another half hour passed before she opened her eyes. David made sure he was out of her range of sight. He was sitting on the steps but still observing. The first thing she did would let him know whether she had broken or if she was stable. Her eyes darted around before they finally found Zachary's face.

"I saw myself floating on a cloud," she said softly. "And I was being pushed around by the winds. Then suddenly, I was on a mountain, and the winds couldn't push me around anymore."

She gently caressed his face and then kissed his lips. "Thank you," she whispered. "Thank you for pulling me out of it."

Tears flowed again, but she didn't try to stop them.

"I really do want to marry you, and I really do want to have babies with you. I'm just so sorry for never telling you anything. I'm so sorry."

He pushed the hair from her face and kissed her forehead. "Lucy, promise me that from now on, you'll tell me everything."

"I promise."

"I still want to marry you."

She laughed softly. "You sure?"

"More than ever. What a strong woman I've found."

She grinned. He hugged her tightly.

David closed his eyes. It was over. And it had turned out all right. He didn't want to intrude, so he stood to head down the steps.

"Where's David?" Lucy asked.

"Over there," Zachary said, indicating with his chin.

Lucy turned, and David froze. She walked over to him, kissed his forehead, and hugged him around the neck. He used one arm to loosely hug her back, but she remained even then, so he used his other arm and hugged her properly.

"Thank you," she whispered. She released him, and he walked up the few steps before gently wiping away her tears. With a brief nod of his head, he headed to his room.

"David," she said. "You're not going to say anything?"

He turned. "No," he said before returning to his previous course.

"I was expecting you to say something like, 'You hit like a girl' or something."

He gathered up the bundle in front of his door, waved his hand to them, and went inside his room. He deposited the items on the couch before going to his spot on the floor. He knew there would be bruises in the morning. No one in her condition ever hit lightly.

Chapter 13

Those who had been on the estate the previous night were surprised to discover that the wedding was still going to happen. They happily retained their secret and busied themselves like everyone else with the cooking and decorating.

Jordan cautiously entered Lucy's room where all the ladies, oblivious to the previous night's drama, fretted over her. Jordan felt a surge of relief upon seeing a smile on Lucy's face.

Easel noticed Jordan enter and walked over to her.

"She is a beautiful bride," she said. "I don't think the women have ever made a wedding dress more stunning."

The dress did seem to suit Lucy, Jordan decided. It was white, with a thick green ribbon woven through the fabric just below the bust. From there, the satin fabric flowed to her feet, with delicate lace woven in patterns on the otherwise solid material. It hung over the layers of underskirt that gave the dress a slight bell shape. At the bottom border, painstakingly embroidered in off-white thread, were what the older ladies called "happy bursts." Jordan had never heard the story behind them, but she did know that every wedding dress carried at least one. They looked like spiraling stars. The long train that began at the green ribbon was buttoned to the dress where it journeyed to the floor, extending for almost a meter. Many flowers covered it, and Jordan knew that each woman who had worked on the dress had chosen a favorite flower to stitch onto the train. Jordan's rose was at the bottom. With a veil almost as long as the dress to top it all off, Jordan couldn't help but marvel at the handiwork.

"It is certainly extravagant," she said. "I didn't expect it to look like that even when I was helping. It took hours, I know."

"It was worth every one. She seems really happy today."

"Yeah," Jordan agreed. "There's finally some color to her skin."

"She's not even complained once," Easel bragged. "She said she loves the dress, and the hair, and the veil. I don't know what happened to change her mind, but I'm glad for it."

Jordan smiled weakly, not thinking last night had been at all pleasant. She crossed the room.

"Hi, Jordan," Lucy said.

"Hi. Uh—how are you?" Jordan asked hesitantly.

Lucy beamed. "I feel as if I'm a whole person lighter. I'm floating. If I had known that I would feel this good, I would have said something long ago. I thought I was saving myself from feeling the pain all this time, but man, I feel so—free. I'm never holding back again."

"Well, you certainly look much better."

"Oh, yeah? Great. I'm so happy. It's my wedding day! I'm finally excited. I can't wait. I am ready to marry Zachary. I have loved him for years. He's been my one constant. I can completely trust him. You know, I think for the first time, I'm full. Does that make sense?"

"No," Jordan confessed, feeling amazed at how Lucy was gushing.

"Well, before, whenever I was happy, it was empty. It was a passing feeling. Now, I can't stop smiling. I've never smiled so much in all my life. I'm full. I'm carrying the happiness instead of letting it pass me by."

"Oh, I understand. I know that feeling."

"It's great." Lucy sighed contentedly. "How do I look?"

"Absolutely beautiful."

"Thanks."

Jordan held out the pants she had made. "This is my wedding gift to you."

"Really? I get gifts?" She took the pants and held them up. "These are amazing! And I love this." She looked at the bottom and ran her fingers over the detailing.

"At least they'll fit better than what you have been wearing."

"Thank you. I love them."

"Good," Jordan said. "Now I have to go and do a million things with only an hour to do them. I'll see you later."

She hugged Lucy good-bye and ran down to Payden's room. Knocking first, she entered but didn't see him.

"Payden?" she called.

"I'm hiding because I'm not dressed."

"I'll wait outside then."

"But I don't know how to put this stuff on."

She giggled. "What do you have on?"

"Just my undergarments because I don't know if these pants are backward or not. They look funny."

"Put them on, and I'll let you know."

After a few minutes, he poked his head around the wardrobe. "Just to warn you, I hurried behind here as fast as I could, but I didn't grab a shirt."

"Okay. Just show me the pants."

He stepped out, holding up the pants because they fell when he didn't.

"That's the right way," she said, feeling her cheeks burn red at the sight of him shirtless. She quickly went to the bed and retrieved his shirt. "Put this on."

He did as he was told, but the pants fell. With one arm halfway in his sleeve, he grabbed for the pants with his free hand, but the movement only resulted in a torn shoulder seam. Jordan, with an even redder face, was forced to help him into his shirt.

"I've ruined it," he moaned.

"The jacket will cover it, so don't fret. Now hold up those pants."

"They're too big."

"No; you just don't have everything on yet." She grabbed the suspenders and handed them to him. He held them in his hand and stared at them for a moment before looking up at her. She shook her head. Might as well. She took them and buttoned them at their proper places, pulling the straps over his shoulders. Carefully, he released his grip on the pants, grateful they remained in place.

Next, she retrieved the cummerbund. "This goes around your waist, and the jacket goes on last."

"I hate the jacket," Payden said.

"It's just one night."

"Yes, but who said that we had to wear this stuff? I look like some sort of bird."

"And a very cute one at that," she said coyly, smiling up at him.

"What if I don't want to look cute?" he asked, fumbling with the cummerbund. She pulled it from him and wrapped her arms around him to button it.

"How about handsome?"

He was too frustrated to think romantically. He stayed in place, waiting for her to move so he could finish the costume off with the jacket and the hat.

Not understanding his frustration, and thinking he looked more handsome at that moment than ever, she stood on her tiptoes to kiss him.

"Not now, Jordan," he said and walked away. His leg only bothered him enough to cause him to limp to the bed, where he snatched up the jacket. He held it up to inspect, finding it every bit as silly looking as before, so he tossed it back down and sat on the bed, unaware of the tears Jordan was trying to hold back. He ran his hands over his face and through his hair. When he finally looked at her, he immediately saw that she was upset; however, he couldn't imagine why.

"What is it?" he asked.

"You don't have to be so mean," she said.

"What did I do?"

"How can you not know?" The tears began to win the battle.

"I don't know. You tell me. Everyone else seems to know why I do things anyway."

"I'm not everyone else," she snapped.

"Then what is it?"

"You just callously tossed me aside—"

"I didn't toss you aside," he interrupted.

"So now you won't listen to me?"

"What is wrong with you today?"

"What is wrong with *you* today?" she shot back. She wanted to run from the room, but something kept her feet planted. "It's just a suit that men traditionally wear at weddings. Everyone's going to look equally ridiculous, so what's the problem? Why are you so frustrated?"

"I can't remember anything, so how am I supposed to know?"

"Because it's going on in your head," she cried. "Surely you can figure out what's going on inside your own mind. It has nothing to do with your memory."

"Maybe it does! Maybe I just can't function properly because I don't know who I am!"

"Knowing who you are has nothing to do with your past."

"It has everything to do with my past!" he yelled as he shot to his feet. "Lucy almost had a complete breakdown because of her past. And David—he's running from his, and it does affect him now. The past affects who all of us are now, and I'm tired of not knowing. I was up all night trying to remember something. Don't treat this situation so lightly. I would kill to get back my memories."

"Well, we already know you can kill." The moment it was said, she wanted to erase it. Her hand went to her mouth as if trying to stop the words.

Payden's face fell, and he narrowed his eyes to glare at her. "Yeah, I can," he snapped. "You're the only one who knows how hard that is on me. I want to wash off all the blood. And you told me it didn't matter, that I shouldn't be ashamed. But now you can stand there and say—say that—"

He turned his back to her. Once again, his hands became crimson before him, and he clenched his fists and held them to his sides.

Jordan didn't know what to do. She'd had a rough night's sleep as well, worrying about Lucy. She certainly hadn't known she was capable of saying something so cruel to the one she loved. What was wrong with her? She wept silently and stared at his back.

"I'm sorry," she whispered. "I'm so very sorry. I'll leave if you ask me to, but I really don't want to leave while you're angry with me. I could blame it on my weariness, but it was still said. That's not how I feel. I was hurt, and I knew what to say to hurt you back. But it was so wrong, and I'm sorry."

Payden was trembling, but he remained silent.

"Payden, please say something."

"Do you love me? Really?"

"Yes," she said without hesitation.

"I love you, too," he said softly. "I was stuck in my head all night trying to figure things out—to remember. I guess I can't deal with anything outside my own thoughts right now. I'm sorry too."

She wiped away her tears and wondered what she should do. She wanted to stay as much as she wanted to leave. With Payden still turned away from her, and Jordan unsure of his thoughts, she decided to leave. Not wanting to disturb him, she quietly went to the door and tried to open it as carefully as possible.

"Jordan, wait," Payden said. "Don't leave thinking I'm mad at you."

"I'm not," she said. "Just keep thinking until you figure out what you need to figure out. Just think more positively. I mean—if it weren't for what happened to you, do you think you would have ended up here?"

She exited, and he sat down heavily upon the bed. Did he have to drive everyone away? Ever since he left the hospital, he seemed to have been mad at someone for some reason or another.

He paced, limping slightly. The anger was still there. Maybe it wasn't anger. Maybe it was envy. No one else had the problem of continually hitting a wall with no hope of that wall coming down. He the Book, flipping it open to read whatever his eyes first saw.

'Don't talk about the things you're going to do tomorrow because tomorrow is a day you do not own, and what happens therein the day will determine, not you,' he read. He paused. With this book, he rarely understood the things he read. The stories he liked, but some of the words seemed like a bunch of random thoughts, most which he couldn't understand.

"Tomorrow," he said aloud, musing. Until last night, today was supposed to have been a happy day, he realized. But it wasn't. "So that's true, I guess. I certainly wasn't planning on fighting with Jordan," he muttered. "Ever."

He stared at the letters again. Should he keep reading? Sure. He had nothing else to do for a while, and he welcomed any delay to putting on that ridiculous jacket. So he continued, to read. 'Don't boast about what you've done, but let others boast about your talents.' Hmm—okay.

'Carrying a large stone is heavy, or much sand that's shifting is hard, but carrying resentment toward a fool is harder.'

He furrowed his brows and talked to himself again. "Resentment toward a fool? Hating a fool?" He released a small laugh. "Hating me."

He shook his head. He'd been acting like a fool. Did Jordan hate him now? No. She hadn't seemed mad when she left.

'Anger can be grueling and wicked; rage drowns and overwhelms like a flood, but envy is worse, more dangerous and destructive than both.'

Tell me about it, he thought.

'For one to reprimand you shows how they love you, and it's better than someone loving you secretly.'

He rubbed the wound on the back of his leg. It felt better now that he was resting more. Jordan had made sense about David's "tough love." But here it was, written down by someone hundreds of years ago, saying roughly the same thing. David had shown more love by reprimanding him than by doing nothing.

"It's good to know these things happen to other people," he said thoughtfully.

He rolled onto his stomach, and read more.

'Wounds given by a lover in sincerity can be trusted . . .'

He shut the book, set it aside and said, "Okay, now this is getting too scary."

He shrank back as he stared at the Book. He had read barely a paragraph, but everything addressed the events that had happened just that week.

"I think I should finish getting dressed."

He slid off the bed and pulled on the jacket. With the hat on, he went to the mirror to get a good look.

"I can't believe I am going to let other people see me like this."

He tugged at the front of the jacket, not understanding why it had to be so much shorter than the back. For that matter, why was the back hanging down in two pieces instead of one? At least he wasn't going to be the only one.

Finally accepting his fate, he grabbed the cane and headed out to find Zachary. Checking Zachary's bedroom first, yet seeing no sign of him, Payden went downstairs. For a moment, he thought he was walking into one of the gardens. The scent greeted him as he came down the steps. Colors leaped from the petals; the flowers seemed eager to celebrate with everyone else. Purples and whites filled the scenery, though he also spotted red. He forgot his hideous costume.

"'Even the great King Solomon wearing all his glorious robes could not compare to the beauty of flowers,'" Payden heard someone say. He knew that voice.

"David?"

David walked around the large vase of flowers that sat on the bottom step into Payden's view.

"You look good," David said.

Payden tugged at the jacket and hoped he didn't look embarrassed. "Do you think so?"

"Yeah. A fine gentleman. I'm sure Jordan will think that you look nice."

"I don't know about that," Payden muttered.

"Why not?"

"We just had a fight. I was being a jerk."

"At least you're man enough to own up to it," David said in jest.

"Ha ha." Payden fidgeted with his sleeves.

"Why are you messing with it?" David asked.

"I hate it and want it off, that's why. Where's yours? Why aren't you wearing your costume?"

"Costume?"

"Oh, what did they call this thing? Tuxedo?"

"I didn't get one," David answered.

"Liar."

David laughed. "Okay, I've been caught, but I'm not going to attend, so it doesn't really matter, does it?"

Payden finished his descent and stood in front of David. "Why not?" he asked, alarmed. Why did he always feel as though David was about to leave for good?

"I'm sure you can figure it out."

"What's the excuse now? Not feeling like anyone wants you here?"

"I've never heard of a Slave attending a wedding before," David said.

"This could be the first. Besides, I know at least two people who will be severely disappointed if you don't come."

"I know hundreds who will be if I do."

"Does what they think really matter? Come on, David. You need to be there."

David lifted Payden's hat to ruffle his hair. "I'll think about it." Then he went outside.

"Please come. Please," he whispered. Then he headed for the ballroom. Still no sign of Zachary.

Payden sat for a moment. He could think of nowhere else Zachary could be. Well, there was the dining hall. That's exactly where Payden found him, sitting with his head on the table, sound asleep. Payden sat next to him and felt more comfortable with Zachary in his tuxedo, too.

Payden rested his head on his hands and watched everyone going through the room, carrying one thing or another, setting up tables and decorating them. He wanted to help but knew he would only be a hindrance.

After some time had passed, the deadline drew near. Payden picked up his cane and nudged Zachary with it.

"Hm?" Zachary sat upright and rubbed his eyes with the palms of his hand. "What?"

He blinked and looked around before he saw Payden.

"What?" he asked again.

"It's almost time."

"What?" Zachary jumped to his feet. He quickly walked toward the exit before realizing he was missing his hat, and returned to retrieve it.

"Calm down there, Zachary. It's not time yet. It's just almost time," Payden said, suppressing a chuckle.

"Oh." Zachary sat down with relief. "Okay. Okay."

"Are you sure?"

"Hm?"

"Not awake yet, huh?" Payden asked.

"Huh?"

"Guess not. Come on, let's get to the ballroom, okay?" Payden suggested.

"Now?"

"Yes. Let's go."

Zachary followed Payden. It took him a few minutes to completely shake off the grogginess. Once the deadline finally arrived, he was alert and ready but feeling more nervous than he had ever felt in his entire life, even in the worst and most hopeless battles he'd experienced.

Payden sat down as they waited for everyone to arrive and take a seat. Every man arrived wearing a tuxedo. He began to feel more comfortable in his. He thought about how Malkam would look, and he chuckled. It was a sight he searched for eagerly: Malkam going from breastplate and helmet to a frilly tuxedo. When Malkam finally entered, Payden turned and laughed silently. Malkam looked as out of place as Payden felt. Like a fox wearing a squirrel's suit—the tuxedo didn't suit Malkam.

When Malkam noticed Payden, he cleared his throat and tugged at the jacket before he made his way up front and sat next to him. Payden was still laughing, so Malkam smacked him in the back of the head.

"Shut up," he growled and pulled at the jacket.

"Sorry," Payden sputtered. "Really, I am." But he only laughed harder.

Malkam ignored him and looked around, continually tugging at the front of the jacket. He saw Jordan enter and nudged Payden.

"What?" Payden turned to him. Malkam tilted his chin toward the entrance, and Payden looked in that direction. His breath was stolen away. She was stunning.

"I think the flowers lost," he whispered.

"Hm?" Malkam asked, but Payden didn't hear him. He stood and went over to Jordan.

"Hi," he said, unable to blink.

Understanding his look completely, she blushed and ducked her head. "Hi," she said shyly.

"You look so beautiful," he said.

"Thanks. You look nice, too."

He held out his arm, and she giggled before she placed her arm in his. Then she lifted her dress with her free hand, as was customary, and walked with him to their seats. Malkam scooted to make room.

"You look beautiful, Jordan," he said.

Payden nodded. "You really do."

She blushed and concentrated on smoothing the fabric of the dress. She did like the dress. It had been her mother's. The deep blue color exaggerated the ivory shade of her skin. A thin red ribbon laced up the back of the simple dress. Salina had helped lace it up for her so that it would fit just right. Her favorite feature was the sleeves. The dress had thick straps, but sheer, light-blue fabric fell loosely from them, covering her upper arms. An emerald hung from a thin gold chain and rested against her chest, and she reached up to touch it, another item of her mother's. Jordan wasn't used to wearing jewelry, so it felt different against her skin.

They sat and waited for Easel's signal. Jordan and Payden were supposed to stand up front with the bride and groom, but only when it was time.

Payden watched Zachary as he pulled at the high collar and swallowed a lot. The events of last night had not yet been discussed, and Payden wanted to know everything that had happened. He wasn't sure why the wedding was still going to happen, and since he hadn't seen Lucy yet, he didn't know how she was. He assumed she was fine. At least, he hoped she was.

Easel approached and crouched in front of Jordan.

"Jordan, I need your help," she whispered.

"What is it?"

"Lucy isn't going to come out."

"What?" Jordan exclaimed as silently as she could. "I thought she was fine."

"She is, but when I asked her who was going to escort her down the aisle, she looked confused. So I explained things to her. You know, she's never seen a wedding before! So I asked her if she wanted to skip that part, but she said, 'No.' She knew exactly who she wanted. To my surprise, she said it was the Slave, David. She was insistent, so I looked for him and couldn't find him. She's not coming out until I do, but I've looked everywhere."

"Even in the gardens?" Payden asked.

"Why would he be there?" Easel asked.

"I know where he is," Jordan said. "But he won't be wearing the tuxedo."

Easel paled, but forced a smile. "Really? We've delayed the wedding so much as it is. I'll have to ask Lucy if it's okay to wait for him to change. Come on."

Jordan and Easel left the ballroom through the side door and walked around to the back where Lucy stood.

"Did you find him?" Lucy asked.

"Jordan says she knows where he is, but he won't be dressed, so—"

"It doesn't matter," Lucy interrupted.

"No, see, we could—" Easel continued.

"It doesn't matter," Lucy said. "I'm comfortable with David how he is. I won't have him be anything else. Everyone will have to deal with it. We'll start as soon as he gets here."

"I'll be right back," Jordan said.

She hurried as quickly as she could to the garden where David and Payden had spoken in what seemed like so many days ago. David was sitting on the bench, leaning forward with his head down, when she arrived.

"Jordan!" he said as he stood. "What's wrong?"

She grabbed his hand. "You're needed at the wedding."

"I'm not attending."

"Oh, but you have to. Lucy's orders. Without you, the wedding won't even start. If you don't want to disappoint those two, then you had better come with me."

Touched, yet unable to speak, David allowed Jordan to lead him to the ballroom. He didn't understand why she took him to the back doors, but he didn't want to question her.

"Here he is," she said. "I'll see you up front."

The confusion deepened as he watched her leave. He looked at Lucy for an answer.

"Shouldn't I go inside?" he asked.

She smiled and wrapped her arm around his. "We're about to."

He looked down at her arm, then up at her face. "I don't understand. What's going on?"

"Have you ever been to a wedding before?" she asked.

"Once."

"Well, I found out today that a gentleman has to escort the bride down the aisle."

David withdrew his arm and stepped back. "No, Lucy."

"Yes," she said. "I've made up my mind. It's you, or I'm not getting married."

"At least let me change."

"Listen," she said. "The music has started. We have to go in now."

"Lucy, please. No," David pleaded. "Not like this. Not as a Slave."

"You're not a Slave, David," she said softly. "You're the man I want to stand in place of my father. Easel, please open the doors." Lucy held out her hand. "David, please."

He swallowed and stepped forward, slowly lifting his arm. She hooked hers though his. "Thank you," she said, and tears threatened to fall. "Thank you for everything."

Hearing the heaviness in her voice and feeling her hand squeeze his arm helped David release his fears, if only just a little. Easel nodded to her assistant, and they opened the doors.

David felt as if he were about to do the most frightening thing he had ever done. All eyes would see him now. He wouldn't be able to hide this time. As Lucy moved forward, he hesitated but finally fell in step with her. When he felt the eyes on him, he realized that this was the most terrifying thing he had ever experienced. Sweat collected on his brow, and his heart beat faster.

Just don't look at the faces, he thought. He saw them anyway. He saw shock and some confusion. Then his eyes fell upon one of the guards he recognized, one who had helped him in the cave. The leader. He wore a huge smile. David looked at him for as long as he could, completely confused. His eyes found another face. One of the young men in training. David remembered that he had had to take that boy aside many times for more specific instructions. Fighting wasn't easy for that young man. He too was smiling broadly.

David stopped looking around. He looked up at Zachary, whose eyes were fixed on Lucy. He was smiling, but his smile fell as he fought back tears until he could smile again. Seeing his emotion made David want to chuckle. Though Henry hadn't known he was there, David had been able to see his wedding. Henry had done something similar while Leislie was coming down the aisle with her adoptive father.

Her father. The man she had said she most respected and admired. David looked at Lucy. She only saw Zachary. There was an actual light in her eyes. Why had she insisted that he give her away? A few days ago, she had hated him, hadn't she?

They reached the front and stopped. The small orchestra finished the song while everyone remained standing, eyes fixed on the beautiful bride covered in clean, white material, and the Slave covered in dingy, faded black. The corner of the room looked tantalizing; David wanted to be there, tucked away, far from every pair of eyes he felt on him.

The orchestra had to finish first. He knew that much. As sweat continued to gather, threatening to fall into his eyes, the music finally stopped. He closed his eyes and slowly exhaled. Samuel stepped forward. He looked a little piqued, but his voice was steady and strong.

"Who gives this woman in marriage?" he asked loudly, following protocol, despite his inclination to do otherwise. The Slave still made him uncomfortable.

With tears in his eyes, David lifted his head.

"I do," he said, but his voice broke. He cleared his throat. "I do," he said again.

Once Lucy was successfully handed over to Zachary, David made his way to the vacant seat next to Malkam, who simply grinned and rested his hand on David's shoulder.

The rest of the service went smoothly. David was careful to observe Payden, who didn't seem at all uncomfortable standing the whole time. When David finally looked at Jordan, he almost didn't recognize her. He was amazed how beautiful she looked with curly hair. He wondered how she was able to do that with such naturally straight hair.

Mr. and Mrs. Zachary Taylor were presented, and everyone stood and applauded. The ballroom quickly emptied as everyone piled into the dining hall, lacking the long table but filled with many circular tables to better use the space.

The number of people able to fit in there astounded Zachary. Every time he turned, he bumped into a new face of someone giving congratulations. He kept thinking about how difficult it was to breathe; that is, everywhere except next to Lucy. She took his breath away for sure, but at least in a calming way. He had never realized before just how beautiful she was, perhaps because she was smiling.

He took another drink of water and set out to find her once again. The crowd kept pulling them apart, and he wanted to scream at everyone to leave them alone. Pulling at his collar once again, he plowed ahead until he saw a familiar figure. David was standing in the corner, arms across his chest, out of everyone's way. Zachary sighed. When would that guy ever get it?

"Hey," he said once he reached David's side. "Why aren't you out mingling? Everyone knows you're here. In fact, you stand out more than anything."

"I need to confess something," David said just loudly enough for Zachary to hear over the noise of the conversations around them.

"All right."

"I'm not used to crowds. I don't know what to say to anyone, and I'm actually completely terrified that someone will come talk with me."

"This is how you look when you're terrified?" Zachary asked.

David nodded, keeping his eyes on the crowd while avoiding eye contact.

"You're teasing me."

"No, I'm not," David said. "If I could do it without anyone noticing me, I would leave right now. But like you said, everyone knows I'm here."

A young woman passed by and grinned. Zachary smiled at her. David inclined his head. Once she was gone, David slowly exhaled.

"I'm about to pop," David said. "This is too much for me."

Zachary laughed. "You're actually serious?"

"Deadly so."

"Wow. That amazes me."

"I have fears too, you know."

"Yeah, but, you're so—steady. I'm sweating and fidgeting, but you–gosh, how do you do it?"

David lowered his head. "It's just from years and years of zoning out in order to—" He paused and rubbed his wrist. "Never mind."

"Oh." Zachary looked at his cup. "Oh."

"I haven't said congratulations yet."

"Thanks." Zachary beamed. "I just want everyone to let us be. I'm tired of having to hunt her down in here."

"This town hasn't had this much life in it for a long time. They're going to soak it up as long as they can."

"Yeah," Zachary said thoughtfully. "I want to ask you something."

"What's that?"

"Last night, when you—you know—had me come over to help Lucy, why did you say, 'Protect her'?"

"What should I have said?" David asked.

"I don't know. Hold her, take care of her. Something like that."

"Yeah, I could have, but you would have only done that."

"I don't understand," Zachary said.

"Payden's father, Henry, explained to me many, many years ago that a man doesn't use every bit of himself until he's protecting something or fighting for someone he loves. If I take care of someone, I'll clean their wounds, bring them food, and wipe their brow. But if I'm protecting them, they wouldn't have gotten wounded in the first place. Fighting for someone stirs your heart more. I mean, how did you feel last night?"

"I wanted to find those men and kill them," Zachary said flatly.

"And?" David prodded.

"She will never suffer again."

"Isn't that different from just taking care of her?"

"Yeah. Yeah, it is."

David put his hand on Zachary's shoulder. "Good. Lesson learned. It's hot in here. I need something to drink. Dare I even attempt to get something?"

"Well, I've learned that people are quite content if you just nod and smile at them. But in your case, you can nod and wave. Have fun."

"You're not coming with me?"

"I need to find my wife!" Zachary laughed and plunged into the crowd. David watched him depart and gulped. A large group of warriors he could handle, but ordinary people? He crossed his arms again and leaned against the wall. The drink could wait.

Chapter 14

When Zachary found Lucy again, she was with Jordan and a few other women he hadn't met or didn't remember meeting. He figured he had met hundreds of people that day. If he had known the hassle this wedding would cause, he might have waited for a more private place to have it. He was grateful it was over. Their lifestyle hadn't offered them much of an existence. Now that they could have a life and an option other than Tawney City, he wanted to share that life with her for as long as he lived. The kids still in Tawney City would love this city, or even Landar. They might adjust better to Landar.

"Hi," Zachary said, placing his arm around Lucy. "How's my wife?"

She blushed and leaned her head against his shoulder. "Fine. I'm tired."

Jordan giggled.

"I wonder why," said one of the older women.

Zachary extended his hand. "I'm Zachary."

With a small grin, she took it. "We've met, but I know you don't remember. I'm Easel, the one in charge of putting all this together."

"Ah," Zachary said. "Sorry. I've met everyone these past few days, and every face looks alike."

"I understand. These other ladies you haven't met. This is Salina. She's in charge of running the manor. She schedules the workers for their shifts and the like. You know Jordan. This young lady is Mary."

"Hello, Salina, Mary." Zachary inclined his head to each as he said their names.

Mary smiled. "We've met briefly before. I was living in that village you helped save. I was happy that Lucy remembered me."

"Without you, I would have come here naked," Lucy said with a small laugh.

Mary ducked her head and blushed, which made Lucy roll her eyes. The girl was younger than Jordan, so she didn't hold her shyness against her too much.

"Well," Lucy said. "When do we eat?"

Salina raised an eyebrow. "Are you sure you're ready?"

Slightly nervous, Lucy looked up at Zachary. When he realized she was looking at him, he shrugged.

"Now's fine to me," he said.

Salina chuckled. "I'll tell the servers to prepare. Easel can try to get everyone seated."

"Why should I be ready for that?" Lucy asked. "That doesn't seem so hard."

"Yes, but this is the first dress you've ever worn," Salina said. "Sitting and eating will be different. Why don't you head to your table, and we'll get to work?"

Zachary led Lucy to their table. Payden and Jordan were assigned to sit there as well. When everyone noticed them take their spots, the tables quickly filled. At that moment, David saw an opportunity to leave. Before he reached his goal, a strong hand grabbed him by the shoulder.

"Not so fast, old friend," Malkam said. "If I have to stay, you have to stay."

"Or we could both leave?"

"Tempting, but I am hungry. Come on; we've got a nice spot in the corner."

Malkam led David to the table. A few other people were sitting there already. It was going from bad to worse for David.

He usually ate alone or far enough away to safely lower his scarf. Everyone was too close.

The plates were set before them. The first course was a small salad. Though David's stomach ached for some attention, he ignored it and stared at the food, unable to look at anyone else.

"Have you eaten yet?" Malkam asked him. "I tried to fill up on the appetizers they had, but there weren't enough. They were good, though. Did you have any?"

"No. I'm really not hungry."

"Really? Have you eaten since last night?"

"No," David answered.

"Then you're hungry. Eat up."

David watched Malkam shovel in the leaves, but he himself just couldn't do it. The other people at the table talked among themselves, for which David was grateful. He glanced up and noticed one lady staring at him, so he tried nodding and waving, but immediately felt ridiculous.

"Are you not going to eat?" she asked. Suddenly, everyone except Malkam was looking at him.

"I'm not used to eating in front of people, that's all."

"Do you eat differently from the rest of us?" she asked. "Are you trying to spare us that sight?"

He stared at her intently. "I am trying to spare you from something, but it's not how I eat."

She leaned back and met his gaze. "Why? Do you think yourself an ugly man?"

David laughed, albeit more out of nervousness. "At one point in my life I wasn't," he said.

"Then why are you hiding? Certainly you've realized that no one has any harsh feelings toward you. You've earned the admiration of many people here. We're not like the rest of the world, you know."

"Maybe," he said.

"So?"

"So what?"

"Are you going to remove your scarf and eat?"

"No," David answered firmly.

"Until you give me a legitimate reason why not, I will persist in my interrogation."

David glanced at the other diners, who looked away once they were caught staring. After he was sure they weren't going to look his way, he held up his wrist and exposed a small area. When her face fell, he quickly covered it.

"I hope that is a satisfactory answer," he said softly.

She shifted in her chair and stared at him more intently. David felt more comfortable under that kind of scrutiny. He was familiar with it.

"I'm sure you could at least—"

"I appreciate your concern," David interrupted her, "but I am quite fine. Thank you."

After a few moments, she turned her attention to her salad. David relaxed slightly but still felt alert, ready for another attack. His eyes remained on the plate of greens until he noticed some movement. The servers came around with the next course, which David refused.

Once dessert was finished, everyone was invited back into the ballroom for dancing. The seats that previously occupied the space had been removed to clear the dance floor. The orchestra began playing before everyone arrived. Malkam and David, however, remained in their seats in the dining hall.

"Here," Malkam said. "I saved you a roll."

"Thanks." David took it and pulled the scarf down far enough to be able to eat, unconcerned if Malkam saw anything at that moment. His hunger allowed him to drop his guard at least that much. The relief of finally being, for the most part, alone threw off his caution.

Malkam, ever curious about what his friend insisted on hiding, looked enough to notice a few scars that peeked from the top.

"So that's why you insist on wearing it."

David froze. His mouth was too full to speak, but he slowly pulled the scarf up more as he nodded.

Malkam shook his head. "I'll go get us something to drink."

David swallowed. "Heading for the wine?"

"They don't have any wine. Just water and several types of juice."

David knit his brows. "No, I've smelled wine before, you know. It's very distinct . . ."

"There's just juice. And I hate juice. But I'll get you some while I get water."

David narrowed his eyes. "You hate juice? I have never heard you say that before. So I'll ask, why do you hate juice?"

"Because it's just a teasing reminder that it's not wine." Malkam left the table for the drink cart. David took another bite. He was glad to see that Malkam's no-drinking resolve was once again active. With a contemplative sigh, he recalled the past few years of successful sobriety tainted with periods of complete, debilitating drunkenness.

Malkam returned with two full glasses of water, and David quickly downed half of his. He finished eating the bread before he drank the rest of it.

"I'll get you another one," Malkam said.

"No, I can—"

"I'll get it for you. Sit down, stubborn."

Malkam returned with two more glasses and set them both in front of David, who laughed.

"Thanks."

"I don't know why you insist on torturing yourself," Malkam said after he sat down, stretching to get into a comfortable position.

"Maybe because I'm used to it."

"That's not funny," Malkam said.

David laughed.

"No, I'm serious. That's not funny. I saw your arm. Why'd you do it, David?"

"The lady said she wasn't going to shut up. You know I hate talking to people I don't know."

"Not that. David—" Malkam set his hat aside and rubbed his head. "Please, just—one day, tell me why."

"Fine." David pensively took another long drink.

"I would love it if that day were today."

"Nope. Not likely." He swirled the glass around and studied the liquid.

Malkam, silently accepting his defeat, drank some of his water.

"Hmm . . ." David said thoughtfully. "Something just occurred to me. This wedding has gotten me to thinking about Henry and Leislie a lot, but I just thought of—" He paused, studying the glass.

"What?" Malkam prodded, hoping his friend would open up at least a little.

"Henry's brother, William. When I got to him, he'd been awake for only a month. That's when the one Slave was sent to retrieve William. I followed the Slave, killed him, gave William the antidote, and brought him back home. Two days after I left, the Jathenites invaded and killed everyone in that village. I think that part always bothered me."

"What part?"

"Just the timing of it all. William had been bait for Henry to come out of hiding. We knew the Pendtars wanted both of them dead. Why William, though? Wasn't the threat just Henry? William was a doctor. He wasn't the visionary Henry was. But I just realized—the timing. What if—I mean, could I have been—" He paused, looking beyond the glass, deep in thought.

"What is it, David?"

"Was I programmed? Did I do what they wanted me to do?"

"David—"

"They had to have known," David said thoughtfully. "The Pendtars are a lot of things, but they're not stupid. Could they have known who I was and used a different way of programming on me? They've had thirty years to perfect it. I wouldn't even know."

"That's ridiculous, David," Malkam snapped.

"Is it? I still want to kill the Pendtars. I still want to take off this uniform. That programming is still in me. There are other things. Like today. There's so much programming that I'm aware of, and that's the only reason I can fight it. But it's still in me. It's not gone. I know I've forgotten things that I once knew. There's so much to fight now that it's hard to think straight sometimes. Years are missing. I try sometimes, but the memories won't come."

"David, we all want to kill the Pendtars, and we all hate your ugly uniform."

David sighed in frustration and finished off the second glass of water. Suddenly very weary, he rubbed his temples.

"Do you remember the day I first met you?" Malkam asked, hoping a change in conversation would lighten his friend's mood. "I had come to Landar, the small, small, small town—well, couple houses that it was back then."

He laughed slightly, hoping David would, too. He couldn't tell if David was even smiling anymore, as the scarf had found its original place again. Malkam continued.

"I came because I had heard about the vision of a man named Henry Carpenter. Was I surprised to find a boy, though. But he didn't act like a boy. It didn't take me long to realize that he was more a man than anyone I knew. That's what impressed me. He knew what he was talking about. He knew how to do what he wanted to do. If it weren't for that, I would have left immediately. Everyone else would have, too. I think I stayed because I knew he had started a few years before, and he was twenty-two when I met him. A boy couldn't have done that much already. Henry Carpenter." Malkam chuckled. "He was the Carpenter who wanted to build a city. Man, we were so busy back then. I had started to put together an army. That was even before the Pendtars attacked the Djorites, I believe."

"It was so long ago," David said softly.

"Yeah. I had entered the town. Henry was there. That was where it all had to begin, he said. He wanted to unite the Ashites so much. He told me why once, but I still don't understand. When I saw him, I was just going to leave, but then he opened his mouth. Boy, could he speak."

David nodded. "'Got that from my father,' he'd say."

"You were this scrawny little kid following him everywhere. I remember thinking, 'Who is that pathetic creature?'"

David laughed. Malkam tried not to but eventually joined him.

"I won't tell you what I first thought when I saw you," David said.

"You probably thought, 'My goodness, what a blockhead.'"

"Pretty much. You were definitely the cockiest of the group."

"Henry got up and delivered this stirring speech about unity and freedom to me and this band of soldiers I had led there. It struck me as very odd, if not downright ridiculous when he said, 'If any of you would like to get to know me better—'"

"'I'll let you if you can beat this kid with a sword,'" David finished. "He hated the idea of me fighting, but he thought it was the funniest thing in the world. All these big men would step forward—"

"And you'd beat them."

"Yeah. Yeah." David chuckled at the memory. "Then you stepped forward."

"I was going to beat you."

"I knew I had you beat the moment I saw you."

"Did not," Malkam protested.

"Did too. The cockiest always fell the fastest."

"I didn't get a swing in—"

"You were my fastest kill," David interjected.

"—and I wanted to kill you."

"You were also the fastest back on his feet, though."

"I bet I was blowing steam," Malkam said.

"Well, there was a lot of hot air coming out."

"Before I killed you, I had a brilliant idea."

"Oh, so it's brilliant now?" David asked.

Malkam ignored him and continued. "Why had this man insisted on us going through this pathetic creature? I figured it out right then."

"Henry was going to use the unlikely to bring about the impossible."

"And it almost worked."

"But then William disappeared," David mused.

"Henry wasn't the same after that."

"Until he met Leislie."

"Until he met Leislie," Malkam agreed.

David picked up the third glass and stared at it. "Did you put rushwood or davenleaf in here or something?"

Malkam chuckled. "No. What you're feeling right now is what we normal people call 'being relaxed.'"

"Oh." David thought for a moment. "I'm relaxed. Well, I think I should go to bed and sleep it off, because if I get used to it, I won't survive a day once I leave."

"Good night, then."

"Good night." David headed for the exit.

"It's still early evening!" Malkam called out to him. David ignored him, and Malkam chuckled. "Too long away from your training, huh? Oh, well. I was glad to see you relax finally. Man, it feels pretty good to be relaxed—so good, you can even talk to yourself. Ah, I should go see what this dancing is all about."

He strolled to the ballroom, glancing at the few couples who lingered in the corridor, whispering to themselves, barely aware of anyone else. Young love, he thought, smiling to himself. How foolish youth could be. His thoughts wandered. In his youth, love eluded him. It found him eventually, but the wear of life had encrusted him beyond the reach of such a tenderizing emotion.

His footsteps paused as he found himself by the exit. Laughter and music tiptoed from the other side of the hall. It would either be a pleasant distraction or salt in a freshly opened wound he'd been trying for days to ignore. The training this past week had been a blissful distraction. He loved nothing more than encouraging young men to meet their full potential. Love was never mentioned in thoughts or actions. On this day . . .

He glanced at the exit. Escape? He'd just chided David for his flight. David always ran. Malkam did his best not to. "Stand and fight." His own personal motto. So, with a deep breath, he swallowed his fear and trod softly forward. He hoped the crowd remained large, because he did not want to encounter Salina. He'd been trying hard not to dwell on her, as he felt his focus needed to be on war preparations.

Once Malkam entered the organized chaos of the ballroom, he relaxed. A lot of people filled the space. Chairs lined the walls, and the orchestra remained in the same spot where it had played during the wedding—in the front corner of the room. Or the back, he reconsidered, if the front was at the entrance. Many couples filled the center, moving about the dance floor like butterflies over a field of flowers. Lucy and Zachary were in the middle of it all, oblivious to everyone around them. Malkam marveled at the glowing beauty before him. She looked so different from the way she had looked in the short time he'd known her.

As his eyes surveyed the room, he spotted another beauty sitting on one of chairs along the far wall. Jordan was certainly much younger than Lucy, and looked even younger than that, but her mannerisms and mentality would convince anyone she was much older. Exactly like Leislie, he mused. Payden had found a woman to keep close.

Malkam's gaze fell to the floor. Perhaps it would be better for him to leave. Too many happy couples were proving to be a more painful reminder than he had expected. Best to depart before he endured the pain it would cause to cross paths with the captivating Salina. As he turned, a lady approached him.

"Sir, would you care to dance?" she asked.

"Uh, I don't dance," he said, sputtering out the first excuse that came to mind.

"I don't really accept that as an excuse. Come with me." She grabbed his hand and led him to the floor, with Malkam at a loss as to how to escape.

Payden quickly spotted Malkam on the dance floor, and he nudged Jordan beside him and pointed. "Look. Watcher's on the dance floor," he said.

"He looks positively ashen." Jordan giggled.

"I wanted to dance more."

"Oh, someday. It's better if you rest."

"Yeah. It is feeling better today," Payden said, rubbing his leg. "I think I'll be all healed in a week."

"You are a pretty fast healer, I must say."

"I think it's the tea," Payden confessed. "When I first came out of my coma, I was lightheaded and weak a lot. Then this guy named Patrick gave some to me, and in a few days, I was feeling much better."

"Oh, so that's where you had it before."

"Mm-hmm."

She leaned against him and rested her head on his shoulder. He put his arm around her and relaxed. He hummed softly.

"Did they play that song today?" she asked after listening to him for a few minutes.

"Uh—was I humming a song?"

"Yeah." She sat upright. "Didn't you know?"

"I thought I was just humming," he said. "It was a song?"

"An old one, yeah. I don't recall them playing it today."

"Huh." He sat upright, and she saw that she was losing him to his thoughts.

"Hey." She nudged him. "Why don't you stay with me until the night's over, okay?"

He kissed her forehead. "Okay."

The sun had long set when the festivities finally ended. Most of the city had already gone before it was officially over, though. Jordan, wanting to help Salina as much as she could, bid farewell to the Djorite citizens who weren't staying the night while making sure those who were found the correct rooms.

When the entryway was finally vacant, Salina approached.

"Everyone where they should be?" she asked Jordan.

"Yes."

"Even our guests from out of town?"

Jordan nodded as she tried to stifle a yawn. "Mostly. David and Malkam left the festivities early. I think the newlyweds are still dancing."

Salina shook her head. "Let them enjoy it as much as they wish. It's their right. But now the fun part. Since I let everyone join in the dancing, we now have to clean up the kitchen and the dining hall. A new set of people will be here tomorrow, so no one's too worried about staying late."

"Do you want some help?" Jordan asked.

"Oh no, sweetie; go get some sleep. We're fine. It won't take too long. Besides, tomorrow we can do a deeper cleaning job. Good night." She hugged Jordan.

"And you, too," she said, squeezing Payden tightly.

"It was wonderful to meet you today," Payden said.

"Oh, I think it was more enjoyable for me." She winked at Jordan before she turned to disappear into the dining hall.

"What did she mean by that?" Payden asked Jordan. She shrugged and sat on the couch. With Salina, she could only suspect but never know for sure. Before Payden could drill her with more questions, Lucy and Zachary came waltzing down the hallway—the very last to leave the ballroom.

"Hi," Jordan said. The two finally stopped, laughing riotously.

"Oh, goodness," Lucy said once she was calm enough. "I love that room."

Zachary hugged her tightly. "Well, wife, I think it's time for bed."

"Good. I'm exhausted." She leaned against him. "I think I'm going to fall asleep as soon as my head hits my pillow."

"Or my pillow."

"Your pillow?"

"Yeah, in my room," Zachary said.

"No, we're going to my room."

"Actually," Jordan said, standing in front of them. "A different room has already been prepared for you two. You'll find it at the end of the hall, and your things are already in there."

"Well, that settles that," Zachary said, smiling at Lucy. He quickly picked her up and headed for the stairs.

"Will you put me down!" she ordered, squirming.

"Hey, will you just let me do something kind of romantic just this once? I promise to never do it again."

"Promise?"

"Yes. All day I kept hearing everyone talking about carrying your new bride across some threshold—" His voice faded as they disappeared up the steps.

Payden reached for Jordan's hand and pulled her back to the couch. "Great save," he said.

She sat down wearily. "There will never be peace in that relationship."

"Oh yeah, there will. When they're both silent."

She giggled.

"What are you thinking?" Payden asked.

"Oh, nothing."

"Liar."

"I want to marry you."

He released her hand and sat back.

"Not now, but in a few years perhaps," she said.

"You do?"

"Yeah. Why wouldn't I?"

"After this morning, I thought—"

"If my feelings for you couldn't survive that, then I never really did love you to begin with." Her face fell. "Or do you not feel that way about me anymore?"

He leaned forward and stared at his hands. "Jordan, there's nothing I want to do without you, but do you really want to marry me? Or is it, you know, being caught up in the moment with Lucy and Zachary and this day?"

She wrapped her arms around him and kissed his cheek. "It's not that. I'm sure of it. I've known since right after—"

He turned to look at her. "After what?"

"When you saved me that day. I know I won't meet anyone who could ever replace you. I want to be with you wherever you go. That's not something I feel. That's something I know."

"What if, when I finally get my memory back, I'm different? What if things change in two years?"

"Then they change. We can't stop that from happening. Why agonize over it? What are you so afraid of losing? I love you. That won't ever change. If you do love me, why worry? Things are going to happen that neither of us can control. Let's just worry about what we can control, okay?"

"How did you get so smart?" he asked teasingly.

"From reading my mom's journal."

"What's a journal?"

"It's a book, but a blank one so you can write in it whatever you want. My mom wrote a lot of songs and short stories. It mostly had her thoughts or events that happened in her life. She even wrote some letters to me when she was pregnant. It helps me get to know her."

"Was it your mom who wanted to name you Jordan?"

"It was my dad," she said, turning away to stare at the floor. She crossed her arms and bit her lip, not wanting to say any more, hoping Payden wouldn't pry.

"What is it?" he asked, scooting closer to her. "What's wrong?"

She felt the tears come despite her efforts. "My dad always used to call my mom his 'Promised Land.' She was his Promised Land, the greatest thing to ever happen to him. She wrote about that, when he started calling her that. She loved it."

"Why are you so upset?"

"The day I was born was the day she died," Jordan answered. "My dad was so angry. I think it was the last emotion he ever felt. So he named me Jordan. The Jordan River stood between the Israelites and their Promised Land."

The tears drowned out her words, and she covered her face, hoping to hide her shame. He pulled her close, and she buried her face in his chest.

"He loves me, I know," she struggled to say. "I think I know. He never says. I just— I'm so tired, Payden. I'm so tired."

"Shh," he said softly. "I'm sorry. I didn't mean to upset you. I'll sit here with you all night if I have to."

"Why do you love me?" She sat up and looked him in the eyes, earnestly searching for an answer.

The question did not deserve a light or a hesitant answer, Payden knew, especially at this moment, but he had been caught off guard. Without even a moment of thought, he said, "Because you set me free."

Clearly not understanding his answer, she studied him more. Grateful for the opportunity to think, Payden took her hands into his.

"I don't want to act around you," he explained. "Around everyone else, I feel that there's some way I should act, and I try to do it. But I'm comfortable around you. When you're not by me, I want you to be by me. You help me focus on what's outside instead of the mess that's inside my head. That makes you the most valuable person to me right now."

There were no words she could say, so she simply hugged him. "Thank you."

"You know, they had to cross the Jordan River in order to get to the Promised Land. The Jordan carried them there. What if your dad doesn't blame you? What if he's just scared because he doesn't want to lose you too? You didn't see what happened to him when we found out you were missing, you know."

"Maybe," she said and sniffed. She sat back and wiped away her tears. "I am tired. I can barely hold my head up, and I still have to make it to my house."

"Why don't you stay here for the night? Others are."

"There are no more free rooms. Even Lucy and Zachary's old rooms are taken."

"You could stay in my room," he offered. "I can sleep on the floor. It actually doesn't bother me."

"No. My father would not approve, trust me." She stood and headed for the door. "Good night."

"Hey, Jordan, can I ask you one more thing?"

"Yeah?" She turned to face him, hoping he wasn't going to keep trying to get her to stay. She only had the strength to refuse him so many times. Her house seemed so far away at that moment.

"About those journals you mentioned. Do you think you could bring me one? If there are any left, that is."

"Sure," she said. "There are several in my house. My dad likes to keep records of our history, just in case."

"Great. Thanks. I'll see you tomorrow, right?"

"Sure."

He watched her leave, amazed that she could even think that someone couldn't love her.

Even though the trip to his room wasn't too far, the steps appeared to taunt him, challenging him to try and conquer them. He took a deep breath. Just one at a time. Suddenly, resting on the bed for a few days didn't seem like such a bad idea.

Chapter 15

Jordan woke before dawn but remained in bed, wondering what had caused her to wake so early. She listened intently, but no sound came from anywhere. Still feeling as if something was out of place, she quickly dressed and went outside.

A few lamps were winking, fighting for life as they drained the last of their oil. She was able to hear something, the sound of someone breathing heavily with some grunts every so often. There was another sound, a swishing sound, but she couldn't place what it could be. Somewhat alarmed, she silently crept through the gardens toward the sound.

As she drew closer, she was able to determine that it was someone doing some sword work. The sounds were exactly as she had heard them from swordsmen nearby while practicing with the bow.

She half dreaded finding Payden. Prepared, she stepped even more gingerly to avoid making the slightest sound. She paused after she passed a bush and spotted the culprit. Darkness shielded the figure, so Jordan moved closer. The motions mesmerized her. She felt as if she were watching a woman using a weaving loom—piece by piece, the work culminating in an exquisite work of art. Barely breathing, she drew closer, staying behind the shrubbery.

Dawn suddenly awakened the valley. The hint of light eased the strain on her eyes but made her more cautious in her slow approach. She remained in the shadows, hypnotized. Enough light had not entered the small garden, so she still could not see the man's face. He was only wearing pants. Though her modesty would have normally caused her to look away, the dance so enraptured her that she hardly noticed his lack of clothing.

The sun climbed higher, and its first rays touched the treetops. Birds took to flight to herald the new day. The man finally stopped. Despite the rigorous workout, he didn't seem out of breath. In fact, he had no trouble breathing at all. Jordan suddenly came to her senses and knew she should reveal herself and apologize for spying. She stepped into his view.

"Sir, I—"

"Jordan!" he exclaimed. She recognized the voice.

"David?"

"Don't come any closer." He stepped back, then swore to himself. The rest of his clothing lay right beside her.

"I didn't mean to startle you, but what you were doing was so beautiful that I couldn't stop myself from watching. I'm sorry."

"That's okay. Just go back to your house now."

"What's wrong?" she asked, stepping toward him.

"Jordan, please," he cried desperately, taking several more steps away from her until he ran into a rose bush. He ignored the thorns as though they didn't exist.

She stepped back and glanced down at his shirt. She looked at him again and squinted. "Why do you do this?" she asked. "Why do you act as if we would be repulsed by you?"

He was silent.

She picked up his shirt and examined it. It was worn thin in some places, torn in others.

"You want this?" she asked. "Here."

She held it out to him.

"Come and get it," she ordered.

He couldn't move. Even if he had wanted his feet to move, they wouldn't have obeyed.

"Jordan—don't."

"Come and get your shirt," she said, punching every word.

"Leave, please."

"Hypocrite," she said. "You tell others to face their terrors when you won't face yours! Now come and get your shirt."

He swallowed and wiped his brow with a trembling hand. He focused on moving his foot to make the first step. It would all be easier after making that first step. When his foot scooted forward, he concentrated on the next step. Then the next. When he was within reach of the shirt, he stopped and held out his trembling hand to grab it, but Jordan pulled it away and held it behind her back, staring him in the eyes.

"Jordan, you don't understand."

"Then make me. Explain it to me. Why are you more terrified of people seeing you like this, completely exposed, than you are of death?"

He began shaking like the trees from the winds coming down the mountains.

"I don't want them to know the truth," he said.

"Why?"

"You can't see it?" he cried and held out his arms, taking another step toward her. "Isn't it obvious why I hide?"

In her stomach, she felt like vomiting, but her will was set against it. It hardly looked like a body, so much flesh had been scarred or burned. She looked back at his pleading eyes. The light that remained amazed her.

"You're beautiful, David," she whispered, choking back the tears. "You're so completely beautiful."

Stunned would not accurately describe how he felt. He had been a hard, black rock suddenly exposed to the hottest flame, and he began to melt. He sank to his knees, then farther still as he curled up and wept.

She knelt beside him and gently placed her hand on his shoulder. He shuddered as he sobbed. The sunlight drew her attention as its rays ran through the trees, trickling ever so lightly to houses far below. The rays began to hit the city, drop by drop. They were in a secluded area of the garden, more isolated than where David had previously ventured, she knew, and was grateful. No one would come by for hours.

She began to sing the same song she had caught Payden humming the night before. It came out before she knew she was singing.

Birds stoop to the brooks
And sing their songs
Then fly up to the skies
Their songs ever flowing
Ever filling the air
Bringing peace, oh, peace to the winds.

But the winds, they roar
They shout, they rush
Angry with the peace
To them clinging.
But that little peace,
The song from the bird,
Began at the brook—it rambling.

And the brook is full
Of Heaven's tears.
The brook is full
Of Heaven's tears.
For she cries and weeps
Over all her kin.
For she cries and weeps
O'er her little ones.

So the wind it roars
And the brook, it whispers
And the bird sings songs of peace.
But the winds will die
And the brook turn to ocean,
And the bird will teach her little ones.

And the songs she sings
Are of Heaven's tears
That she cries o'er
Her beloved ones.
How she wishes her kisses
Would dry our tears.
And her tears would cleanse
Her little ones.

She closed her eyes. David had stopped crying. He seemed to be asleep, so deeply was he breathing. He must have been exhausted, she thought. She looked at his back for a moment before gently touching his skin. It felt so smooth despite its appearance. Her fingers followed the lines of his scars. She stopped and simply placed her palm against his back.

"David," she whispered. "David."

"Sing that song again."

She sang it again. When she finished, he moved a little.

"I always loved that song," he said.

"Where have you heard it before?" she asked.

"Payden's mother, Leislie. It was her favorite song. She sang it all the time, especially at bedtime. Payden and Egan would fall straight to sleep without a fuss."

"How did she come to know that song? It's not even one we Djorites sing too often."

"She was a Djorite, just like Henry, and just like Henry's parents. They all came down the mountains to help us Ashites."

"You mean, Payden—he's a Djorite?"

"Mm-hmm. No one knows. Henry didn't want anyone to know. Malkam doesn't even know. Just me. No Ashite would have listened to him if they had known. He kept it a secret, and they listened, and we finally came together. It saved us. The Fashites won't ever attack Landar, or if they do, they'll all die trying. Unity. Banding together. Made us strong."

"What else can you tell me about Payden?" she asked.

"What do you want to know?"

"How old is he?"

"Sixteen. He'll be seventeen very soon, though."

"Hm." *Same age as me*, she thought. Remembering Payden's fears from the previous night, the next question was obvious.

"Is Payden the same now as he was before he lost his memory?"

"Exactly the same. Of course, it's been about five years since I last saw him, but he's the same."

"That's good to know."

David sat upright, but hung his head to rub his neck. That's when Jordan saw the brand upon his jaw.

"What's this?" she asked, touching the burn.

"The mark of a Slave," he said.

"Like they couldn't put enough on you."

He snorted. "Of course not." He finally looked at her. "Are you going to tell anyone?"

"No. It's not my secret to tell," she answered. "But you should share. There are people who do truly care about you, and it hurts them more when you hold back than when you share. I think you know that, but I can't understand why you hold it all back."

"These scars just cover a darker secret, one I'm not ready to share just yet."

"Well, get yourself ready soon, okay?"

"I can only promise that I'll try," he said.

"I suppose I'll have to settle for that then."

"Can I have my shirt now?"

"Oh, yeah."

He took it from her but paused for a moment and stared at it.

"What is it?" she asked.

"I absolutely hate this shirt," he said.

"Well, if you let me, I can make you a new one. It would be easy."

"No. Maybe someday, though. Thank you anyway." He pulled the shirt over his head and slowly exhaled.

They sat silently in each other's presence, watching the sunrise. Once the last traces of the morning fog were burned away and the chattering birds swooped into the gardens, Jordan allowed herself to think about her greatest secret.

"Um, I guess since you've just shared something personal with me, I'd like to tell you something I haven't really talked about with anyone."

"You don't have to," David said.

"I know. I think I just want to talk to someone who I know will understand, if that's all right?"

David reclined, leaning back into the shade. He clasped his hands under his head. "It's fine."

She inhaled deeply before she began. "It's about my mom."

David shut his eyes. His mother's face came to mind. He swallowed deeply to bury the rising emotions. Hypocrite indeed, he thought.

"She, uh, well, she was wonderful." Jordan smiled warmly as her eyes focused on the nearest bunch of roses. "When she was pregnant with me, she wrote so many things. One of the things she wrote told me that I was the source of her inspiration. There were many beautiful poems and short stories. Some small pictures that she drew in the margins. I think she was just a really optimistic person. And Salina always talks about how full of life she was."

She glanced at David, who seemed to have a sorrowful look on his face. "Are you okay?"

"No. Your mom sounds like Leislie—Payden's mom. She was always laughing or singing. I never met anyone like her."

Jordan hugged her knees to her chest. "My father never mentions my mother. I would love to ask him dozens of questions, but the pain is intolerable. It's like he no longer feels anything."

"Yeah. We all have our demons."

"That's a concept from the Book. I'm sorry to say that I'm surprised to find any Ashite with a book, let alone that one. Of course, if Payden's father—" She shook her head, trying to grasp the new information. "A Djorite," she said softly, not fully believing.

"He told me to pick a book that inspired me and read it daily. Out of all the books that were around at that time, that was the only one that fit the prescription."

"And why would he tell you to do that?"

"I was young—ten or eleven years old—and dealing with a lot for my age. Of course, so was Henry. The situation was new to him, too. When had an Ashite ever lived with Djorites? And Djorites were naturally optimistic people. Ashites aren't. He was seventeen." David paused as the memory became clear. "I think he was hoping something he said would work to calm me down."

"Calm you down?"

David nodded. "I was living with him in a Djorite city called Siantcho. Coming from a very humble Ashite town made it a difficult transition for me. Henry didn't stay there long – less than a year. I know he had a life there, a life that he left in order to make mine a bit easier, but—" David opened his eyes and studied the clouds. "I could live for another hundred years and still not be close to repaying Henry for all he did for me."

"All that he did for you?"

"I thought we were talking about you."

She smiled and pushed her hair from her face. "When my mom was four months pregnant, she began to—to lose her mind. So I've been told. The things she wrote up until then were so beautiful . . . I have this image of her in my mind, and I don't want it tainted." She rested her chin on her knees. A soft breeze pushed a fallen leaf across the ground. Jordan watched it tumble along until it became caught in a tuft of grass. It seemed like the right time to end the topic. She felt the need to do something else.

"When will you teach me the sword?" she asked.

"Right now if you'd like."

"Sure."

He stood first, then helped her to her feet. She lost herself in thought for a moment.

"Since Payden is a Djorite, and his father being one too, would his father have approved of Payden's—"

"Killing?"

She sighed heavily. "Yeah. That."

"No. Henry hated the idea of it, but Payden was born a warrior. He knew it before he could understand anything. Henry recognized that warrior spirit, and it grieved him. Henry was a peacemaker. He was effective at it."

"But Henry began his work when there were no wars, right? He began before the Pendtars marched against even the Djorites."

"He did. And I think that is why Payden's a warrior, like David in the Book. You either fight against the evil that's growing, or you let it come where it can overwhelm you and eventually destroy everything."

"I understand that," she said. "It bothered me at first, but after my experience with the Fashites—there's no good left in them, is there? They won't stop until we're all dead, will they?"

David didn't reply. He retrieved the rest of his uniform and donned it, unwilling to speculate. "Okay, let's get to work."

Chapter 16

The sun climbed higher, warming the air. The valley, finally aroused from its slumber, filled with the sounds of life.

Jordan began to tire from the small amount of training she was receiving. David focused only on teaching her how to hold the sword and move it about with her hand and wrist to begin strengthening her muscles.

"It doesn't seem like I've done a lot," she said, "but I'm tired. I think I may need some food."

"Water, actually. Besides, I think that's enough for now."

"A large tub of water sounds like a good idea to me," she said and wiped the sweat from her brow. "It might be a hot day, which would be a wonderful break."

"Mm-hm. It has been oddly cold. I'll teach you more tomorrow, so work on what I've shown you for today."

"Okay. I'm going to my house then. I'll see you at breakfast."

He nodded, his only response. She left and bathed before hurrying to the estate with an empty journal in hand for Payden. Upon discovering that Payden had already received his breakfast tray, she ran up the steps to his room and burst through the door without thinking. At that moment she remembered her previous experiences doing so, and she immediately backed out of the room and shut the door. She took a deep breath and knocked. Hearing no response, she knocked again and waited. Then she slowly opened the door.

"Payden?" she called. She saw him on the bed, and he waved his hand at her, but she could see nothing else. As she drew closer to the bed, she realized what he was doing with his head buried under his pillow.

"Don't laugh at me," she demanded and grabbed a pillow to throw at him.

He still could not respond but removed the pillow and let his laughter fill the room. She crossed her arms and tried her best not to look embarrassed, but she knew her face was red. She felt it burning.

"All right, enough already." She sat down next to him.

"Sorry," he choked. "If you could have seen the look on your face." His laughter strengthened again, and he rolled over to press his head into the mattress.

She allowed herself a small laugh, but the excitement that had driven her there was gone. As Payden did his best to calm down, she thought about what she wanted to tell him. Should she tell him everything that David had said to her? Suddenly grateful for the delay Payden's laughter had caused, she decided to let David tell him.

"Are you done?" she asked.

"Oh—yeah," he said. "I think I am."

"Good." She handed him the journal.

"That was funny. Now my stomach hurts."

"I'm happy to hear that," she said.

He finally noticed the journal. "What's this?"

"The journal you wanted. You'll find an inkwell and a quill in the desk over there."

She went to the desk and collected the items.

"Here," she said, climbing back onto the bed.

"Thanks," he said. "Oh, I slept so good last night. I woke up later than I usually do."

"Humph. I woke up hours earlier."

"Why?"

"Well, something just wasn't right. I couldn't understand it. So I got up and wandered around until I discovered what it was."

"What was it?" he asked, propping himself up with his elbow as he turned toward her.

"David was in the gardens, working with his sword."

Payden sat up all the way. "How were you able to hear that?"

She shrugged. "I don't know, but it was a good thing. We had a good talk."

"Oh? What did you talk about?"

"You. Oh, and you are sixteen, by the way. He said that you would be seventeen soon."

"And?"

"And what?" she asked with a smile.

"You didn't have a good talk about me and only learn my age."

She leaned closer to him. "I made a promise."

She kissed his cheek and hopped off the bed. Grabbing his empty tray, she headed for the door.

"I'll see you later," she said.

"Jordan!" he cried.

"Bye!" She left. He threw up his hands, not believing she wouldn't tell him. She ran to the kitchen and dropped off the empty tray.

"Hello again!" she said. "I can carry my own plate if that's not a problem."

"That's all right, Miss Jordan. Thank you."

She piled some fruit onto her plate and went out of the kitchen to eat. When she sat down, all her energy suddenly disappeared. She put her head down, thinking she would just rest for a while. Until she felt someone nudge her shoulder, she didn't realized she had fallen asleep.

"It puts less strain on your back if you sleep on a bed," Malkam said. "Are you coming out to practice today?"

She yawned. "Yes, as soon as I'm done eating."

"It helps if you start." He patted her back before leaving.

Jordan took her time eating. She drank a lot of water, and she did feel some energy return. Hoping to have seen David by then, she looked around the room. Saddened by his absence but not too concerned by it, she stood to go outside.

She found a fresh quiver waiting next to her bow and decided to shoot a few arrows the normal way just to get back into the shooting mood. After several shots, she felt relaxed, and set up to do the newer exercise again. Not expecting to hit the target, she pulled the string and fired. When she saw the feathers shaking by the bull's-eye, she almost dropped the bow. She looked around to see if someone else had shot from behind her, but she was relatively alone in her part of the grounds.

Not wanting to lose the momentum, she set another arrow, breathed, and fired again. This one landed farther away, but closer than on any previous day.

"Don't think, just do," she whispered.

Staring at the bull's-eye, she knew that all of her shots were going to hit it. She took off the quiver and pulled out the arrows, sticking them into the ground, and got right to work firing one after another, pausing only between shots to set the arrow on the string. No longer was she worried about hitting the mark. She knew they would.

Once every arrow had been shot, she was finally able to stop. Most of them were where she wanted them to be. She hopped up and down with excitement before she ran to the target to replace it with a fresh one.

She returned the quiver to her back with just ten arrows inside. The rest lay on the ground. She went through three more targets before achieving Malkam's request of ten in a row in the bull's-eye. At that moment, she wanted to shout and scream with joy, but she contained it all with a triumphant smile. She shot a couple more perfect rounds of ten before hunting for Malkam.

When she found him, he could tell by her face what news she brought.

"You finally did it?" he asked.

"More than ten even," she said.

"Good. Give me a few more minutes, and I'll be right there."

She returned to her spot. Too excited not to shoot, she passed the time filling the target.

"You're almost perfect," Malkam said when he reached her.

"Thanks."

"It's rare to find someone who's a natural."

"What do you mean?" she asked.

"It took me weeks to achieve what you've done in days. It's a gift. You with your arrows, given some more time and training, will be as good as Payden with his swords."

"I haven't really seen how good he is."

"That's a shame," Malkam said. "Perhaps next week he'll find his way out here. It's hard to keep that boy away from his sword fighting. If you ever see David in action, know that Payden's his shadow."

"David is positively captivating with the sword."

"How did you manage to see him? He's always so keen to work where no one can watch. I don't know exactly why, but I suspect he doesn't want anyone to see his tricks. You must have had a great show. I've only seen him in battle, so I never really get a chance to actually watch. I've only seen Payden, and David taught Payden a lot."

"Oh."

"Anyway, let's focus on what we're really out here to do. The next step is setting the arrow from the quiver, onto the line, and in the target in five seconds. Watch."

She watched as he pulled out the arrow, set it, and fired. She hadn't even counted to five.

"I like to hold the bow down as I get another arrow. I've seen others keep it up. Find whatever way is more natural for you. I'd stay longer, but I'm overwhelmed today. I don't think you need my help much more anyway. Let me know when you've reached twenty in a row."

He trotted away before she could ask a question. The process didn't seem too hard. She repeated the steps in slow motion and didn't run into any trouble, so she set up, ready to begin.

For the first attempt, it took her five seconds just to grasp an arrow.

"Goodness, Jordan," she said angrily. She adjusted the quiver and focused on pulling out the arrow with speed. Once the motion became more natural, she tried again; by ten, she had the arrow set.

"Great. This could take all day, and I still haven't worked with the sword." She continued to practice the motions of setting the arrow over and over until it too felt more natural.

"One step at a time," she muttered.

Then she fired one off. Then another and another. The counting didn't matter until everything flowed right. The quiver was empty, so she paused and glanced up at the sun. It was well past noon, she noted. Resigning for the day, she went to the kitchen.

"Has Payden been fed yet?" she asked the head cook.

"No, Miss Jordan. Salina suggested that we should wait for you."

"Thank you." She made a plate for herself too and went upstairs. To avoid more embarrassing moments, she knocked loudly before entering.

"Hi!" She set the tray on the table and approached the bed.

Payden was visibly upset.

"What is it?" she asked.

He held up the Book. "I hate this book," he said and angrily tossed it onto the bed. It bounced and fell off the side.

"Payden!" She ran around the bed to retrieve it.

"They killed Jesus," he said. "All he wanted to do was help them, and they killed him."

"Did you finish the story?"

"I stopped reading."

"Well, maybe you should continue, because he's alive," she said.

"But it said, 'He died.' How can he be alive if he died?"

"In the next chapter, his grave is empty."

"They took his body too?" he asked.

She laughed. "You could finish before you get angry."

He ran his hands down his face. "I don't understand. It said, 'He died.' He can't be alive if he died."

"I don't know," she said. "A lot of people in this book died and were brought back to life."

"It just doesn't make sense."

"It's not real anyway, silly." She set the book onto the nightstand and crawled onto the bed to sit next to him.

"But what if it is real?" he asked. "What if everything in this book really did happen?"

She allowed herself to entertain the idea for a moment. As a child, she had wanted it to be true, she remembered.

"It would be nice to know that someone I loved could come back to life, but that's never happened. No one has ever heard of that happening anywhere."

He crossed his arms and stared at the book. She crept up next to him and sank into the pillows, drifting back in time.

"I used to hope so much for my mother to come back. I used to," she said softly.

Her tone told Payden that she was far away, and he moved so he could look at her. A slow smile crossed her face, and she looked at him. He rested his head on her shoulder.

"Do you think that if that Jesus were here, he could heal my memory?"

"Sure. He healed a lot of people," she answered, lifting her hand to let it run through his hair.

"And David—"

Her hand stopped moving. "What about David?"

"I've seen his face," Payden said, "and he's shown me his arm. I would love for all those scars to—to go away. I'd love for him to have the past thirty years back so he could get married and have kids, or at least be happy. Do you think that could happen?"

She lifted his head and kissed him. She couldn't stop herself. An ache had grown inside her while he spoke that overwhelmed her. It was as if this was a moment when her love for him had grown. She didn't want to stop kissing him.

"Jordan, what is it?" He wiped tears from her cheek, concerned.

"I promised not to tell," she said, then placed her head on his chest.

"You said you saw David this morning."

She nodded.

"What did you see?" he asked.

She shook her head. He moved to lift her up so he could see her eyes.

"What did you see?" he asked again.

"He was practicing. He had his shirt off. I—it was horrible, Payden. He was so scared of me seeing him. How could anyone do something like that to another human being? How can anyone be so evil? But he—how can he be such a good man after going through all that? I don't understand. For thirty years? And why? He won't tell anyone why."

"I know. I know." He kissed her forehead. "Maybe he will someday. Maybe." He wanted her to stop crying. She wrapped her arms around him, and he held her close. After a few moments, she fell asleep. When he realized she was gone, he chuckled softly and kissed her head, inhaling deeply. He was happy that she still smelled like roses.

On the nightstand was the journal with the writing utensils. He carefully pulled them to his side. For some reason, he wanted to write. He had already written his first entry. But he wanted to record what he was feeling at that moment. Jordan sighed and shifted, and he smiled, seeing the peaceful look on her face. He suddenly knew exactly what to write.

Chapter 17

Over the next two days, Jordan grew more skilled at the bow, though the sword required more effort. David could tell that she would never be great with it, so he concentrated on helping her use it to survive.

During that time, no one saw much of Lucy and Zachary. Jordan would glance down the hall to their room and shake her head. Sometimes she heard yelling, and sometimes no sound at all. Finally, Lucy decided to leave the confines of the bedroom and reconnect to the outside world. Jordan was walking down the hall after having breakfast with Payden when she almost ran into her.

"Hey Jordan," Lucy said, catching the tray. "How are you?"

"Fine," Jordan said, noticing that Zachary was nowhere to be seen. "How are you?"

"Great. I need a break today. I love Zachary, but I need some space and time. Don't tell him you saw me. He's still asleep."

"Oh. Do you want to come with me? Actually, Salina wants to talk to you. She's asked if I've seen you every day since the wedding."

Lucy looked suspicious. "Why? Women talk?"

"I don't know. I can rarely guess Salina's plans despite how well I know her. She's harmless, trust me. She has a gift of being able to say exactly what needs to be said when it needs to be said. I would actually be excited to hear what she has to say if I were you."

"Okay," Lucy said, unconvinced. "The moment it gets weird, I'm out of there. Training camp is actually the primary motivation for me to leave that room. No, it's secondary. Zachary's been—really clingy. I'm not used to that yet."

"That's fine. I'll take you straight to her so that we can get it over with, then. I'll even join you for some sword training today."

"Why would you want to learn how to use a sword?" Lucy asked, placing her hands on her hips.

"Payden, obviously," Jordan said. "We'd better hurry, in case Zachary wakes up soon."

"Good point."

They went to the kitchen, and the cook informed them that Salina was in the rose garden, pruning. As they went to find her, Jordan shook her head.

"I should have known," she said. "Salina loves to be in the rose gardens more than in any other place, even the other gardens."

"Why? I mean, they're beautiful, but I actually like some of the others better."

"Maybe we should ask her," Jordan suggested, "because I honestly don't know."

Salina was humming loudly when they found her next to the largest bush of pink blooms. The light made her blonde hair seem lighter, covering the gray, and her weathered face didn't seem to look as old.

"Hi, Salina," Jordan said, causing the older woman to turn to them, a smile readily finding its way onto her face.

"Hello, you two pretty girls," she said. "How's my favorite one?" Salina hugged Jordan tightly.

"Great."

"And the blushing bride."

Lucy smiled and felt silly as she felt her face flush red. "I'm fine."

"Still blushing," Salina said, raising her hand to Lucy's cheek for a gentle pat. "It makes you look even prettier, so I'd watch that if I were you. That poor boy seemed too smitten to me already."

"Goodness, that poor boy won't stop touching me."

"All the more reason for you not to blush." Salina took their hands and led them to a shaded area under a small tree with large branches full of leaves. The bit of grass there provided a comfortable area to rest.

"Sit. Let's talk," she said.

Lucy reluctantly obliged, greatly suspicious of Salina's intentions. Even when her parents were alive, she had gravitated toward her father. Female stuff had never interested her.

"Don't worry. This won't hurt," Salina said, expertly knowing what Lucy was thinking.

Jordan sat close to Salina, who put her arm around Jordan's shoulder. "So, Miss Jordan, do you think that Lucy can survive a few minutes with a couple of women?"

"She will," Jordan said. "We may not."

"Don't tease," Lucy warned, crossing her arms as she suppressed a smile.

"I won't leave you wondering what this is about," Salina said. "I heard what happened the night before the wedding. As respectful as we Djorites try to be, we've had no visitors in many, many years, so we are greatly hindered by our curiosity. A couple of the younger girls regrettably heard every word. Expect them to hunt you down in order to apologize."

Lucy had turned away and focused on the flowers. Though she had felt better afterward, she couldn't deny that the pain was still present. Another reason she hadn't emerged earlier was that Zachary wanted her to talk more. She had promised not to hide anything else from him again.

"I'm sure your husband will fulfill his duty of taking care of you," Salina said, "but some things a man can't do. Right now, I am here to offer what only a woman can offer to another woman."

Lucy looked at her. "What's that?"

"Friendship," Salina answered. "A shoulder to cry on. An ear to hear. Tears to cry with you."

"I honestly don't know how that is appealing," Lucy replied skeptically.

Salina reached out and took Lucy's hand. "I need to explain something to you, child. Here, there are many children who have lost a father, a mother, or both, but there are no orphans in this city. Every woman is a mother. Every man is a father. I took Miss Jordan under my wing after her grandmother left us. Though you are a grown woman, married and all, a part of you is still a lost little orphan who needs to be mothered. You can scoff all you want and disbelieve me, but I know what I am talking about. No one makes it through life without guidance. Without a mother to teach you how to be a mother, you won't be able to truly be one. Without a father to teach you how to be treated by a man, you won't know how you're supposed to be treated. That Zachary is rare. I can tell he still needs to be fathered and mothered. I've caught him hanging around some of our older men, standing there, not really saying anything. He needs it. He's just not aware of it."

"Why would you care enough to want to do that for me?" Lucy asked. "You don't even know me. On top of that, I'm an Ashite."

"Doesn't matter," Salina said. "A real woman only sees the need of a child and nothing more. I don't have to know you in order to love you."

Lucy eyed her curiously. "So—what do you want me to do for you, then?"

Salina laughed. "Oh, child. I must remember that you are an Ashite. A Djorite is raised to understand that when someone offers you something, you accept it graciously. In time, that child wants to offer things to others. They get so excited when those others accept. We enjoy serving. We serve one another. No one is in want or need. Giving and gaining happen naturally here. I'm offering what I do best to you. What do I want you to do? Accept it. When you see someone who needs help, and you can help him—do it. Then you'll take the best of us with you wherever you go. Does that sound like a deal you can accept?"

Lucy's eyes narrowed as she considered the older woman. "All right," she said slowly. "It's a deal."

"Wonderful," Salina said. "I want to see you tonight after dinner. Meet me in the ballroom. Alone. The first talk will have to be private. Afterward, bring your husband. Now I need to get back to the roses. They're missing my attention. Have a wonderful day, girls."

They stood, and Salina hugged them before they left. Humming followed them, gently fading once they left the garden. Lucy was still reeling, though; no adult had ever wanted to help her, even when she was still young and trying to survive while taking care of her two younger brothers.

"Is this how all of you are all the time?" Lucy asked.

"No," Jordan said, giggling at the reaction her answer drew from Lucy. She seemed more than surprised. "We fight and argue. My father has his position for a reason. People get angry or scared. He settles the disputes according to our laws. We've been blessed to have the other nations, in a way. Years ago, many of the Djorites wanted to reach out to you Ashites, but—it was as if you thought we just wanted to kill you or something. So much suspicion. It made us grateful for our way of life. But I'm glad to have met you, and David, and Malkam. Even Zachary."

"And of course Payden. Who would have thought you two would like each other? I've never heard of any Ashite marrying a Djorite. That's not saying much. It's not like I got any news out in Tawney City."

Jordan had fallen silent. When it continued for too long, Lucy nudged her. "What?"

"Hm? Oh, sorry. I was just thinking," Jordan said.

"About what?"

"Could you really see me marrying Payden?" Jordan had to ask something, not wanting to tell Lucy the truth about Payden. For some reason, she didn't feel that anyone should know yet. Perhaps not until Payden knew first that he was really a Djorite.

Lucy chuckled and placed her arm around Jordan. "If you don't, I will certainly wonder about your sanity."

Jordan smiled and wrapped an arm around Lucy's waist, feeling terribly short and envious. Height was something she had never worried about until then. She wouldn't have minded being a little taller.

As the days continued to drag by, Payden grew increasingly restless. He begged David for walking rights, and after some time, he was allowed a few hours. The outdoors embraced him, and his first day out found him standing on the steps for a long while, hugging the sunlight that kissed his face. The wind, too, rushed to greet him, pulling at the hair that had begun to lengthen again. When he felt it move, he rubbed his head and thought about a haircut. Perhaps Zachary could direct him to the barber. Whenever he had seen Zachary the past few days, Zachary would often absentmindedly rub his own head, as if the very act would stimulate hair growth.

The day David took out the stitches, Payden felt as if shackles had been removed. Payden eagerly got to work easing movement into those injured areas to get them back into shape. They were only a little tender, and Payden did listen to David's advice, taking it slowly and performing the exercises he was told to do. Experience told him that David knew what he was talking about, so Payden decided to be obedient lest he incur another episode of "tough love."

"Ready to fight yet?" David asked him three weeks after the wedding.

Payden had just finished jogging around the estate, and he froze. "Am I ready?"

David chuckled. "Of course you're ready. You've been ready for weeks, but your body is finally ready, too. Muscles do heal quickly. You didn't screw up too much for you to have not healed completely. Do you think you can get your swords out and let me see how you do with them? I want to be sure before I let you go completely."

Payden's eyes lit up, and he ran up to his room to collect his things. The harness had not gotten dusty, as Payden was sure to keep it cleaned and the swords polished. Just touching them had helped as each day he hoped to use them again. As he burst through the doorway, harness in place, he caught a glimmer out of the corner of his eye; instinct brought a sword out to meet it.

"Good," David said, sheathing his sword. "Reflexes are fine. Let's go to our garden spot so no one can see us. I have a surprise in store for these students, and I don't want them to see you yet."

Payden beamed. "I'm going to help teach?"

"Sure. Or would you rather do something else?"

"No! Where are we going?"

"My usual spot. We've been there before."

Payden followed him because he had forgotten how to get there. Unintentionally, the gardens formed something of a maze behind the estate and then on through several of the nearby houses until they ended outside of the city. David wove through one walkway to another, and Payden didn't see anything familiar, until a certain scent reached his nostrils. It was Jordan's scent.

"What am I smelling?" he asked.

David chuckled. "Flowers."

"What kind?"

"Roses, I'd guess. We're going to the rose garden. It's right by Jordan's house, incidentally, though the house can't be seen over the bushes. The vines that are there cover the fences. It keeps the area secluded, so we'll be hidden for a while."

"They're by Jordan's house?" Payden asked.

"Hasn't she told you?"

"I haven't asked, I guess. That's why."

"Okay," David said with a small laugh.

"She smells like them."

"Ah. Her whole house smells like them. They keep the windows open. It's nice in there. Maybe we will visit when we're done."

Payden inhaled deeply.

"You seem happier than usual today," David observed, finally stopping in an open area where he had spent hours alone, practicing or focusing to fight the unwanted intrusions to his thoughts.

"I like it here," Payden said. "I couldn't live here, but I like it. This whole time, we've been worried about the Fashites coming, but you wouldn't even know it the way these people act. There's no fear, really. Their focus isn't on what might happen, but on what's happening now. I don't know. It just feels different than the other two cities I've visited."

"Yeah. It's helped me, too. You know, this is the longest I've ever stayed in one place since I was ten."

"Really?" Payden pulled out his swords and swung his arms to loosen them.

"Yeah. I was with your father, and he traveled around a lot. Then I spent some time with the Jathenites. They taught me so much." David laughed softly. "You should have seen your father when I returned, though. He had a temper. I couldn't sit for days."

"He spanked you?"

David shrugged. "He was more a father to me than a friend anyway. I never left his side after that. That's when the dreams began."

"Dreams?"

"I saw myself fighting in battle. I would wake up and still remember every move. I thought it wouldn't hurt to work on them. When I realized those moves gave me the advantage in many duels, I couldn't wait until the next dream. I would have an idea as I was walking or practicing. Now it's like the vision doesn't need to happen first anymore. I'm already doing it, which is nice. I never worry in battle."

"I'm like that too," Payden said. "It's weird."

David nodded. "Okay, kid, let's get started. Small movements and nothing too taxing. I just want to see where you are."

Payden nodded, ready to move. He had been having dreams the past few weeks too, of himself fighting others. Though some of the dreams seemed more tangible – like memories. He didn't want to discuss it with David just yet. It didn't seem important. And with David's unprompted explanation of how he learned to use the sword, Payden didn't find his dreams unusual anymore. Just another thing he had in common with David. For some reason, Payden loved that discovery.

When they finished a few hours later, David took him to Jordan's house. He watched as Payden took deep breath after deep breath. That boy was too smitten by that girl. An image of a young woman's smiling face passed through his memory briefly, and David flinched. Who was that? The door opened before he had a chance to mull it over, and he had to compose himself.

"Hello, David," Samuel said. "What brings you here?"

"You've met Payden, right?" David asked.

"Yes. It's good to see you up and about. How are you today?"

"Wonderful," Payden said. "Is Jordan here?"

Samuel smiled briefly and sorrowfully. "No. She usually spends her time on the estate. I rarely catch her here, except when it's time for bed or if she oversleeps in the mornings."

"Oh."

"I actually wanted to show Payden your house, if that's okay," David said.

"Why?" Samuel asked.

"I told him your house smells like the roses, and he wants more evidence than my word."

"I believe you," Payden said. "I just love the smell. I would love to live in a house that smelled like that all the time."

"You did," David said.

Payden looked up at him. "Really? My mother grew roses?"

"Among others, but the roses filled the kitchen."

"Come in," Samuel said, stepping aside. "I was just writing, so if you'll excuse me. Feel free to go wherever and let yourself out when you're done. You know where my office is if you need me."

"Thank you," David said. Samuel ascended some stairs to their right. Payden leaned over to look up them. They were steep and seemed to vanish into the floor above them.

"Let's go to the living room and kitchen, okay?" David suggested.

"Sure."

David led him through a short entryway into a decent-size living room. It was half the size of Payden's room in the manor, which for some reason surprised him. An overstuffed couch rested in front of a large open window. A rocking chair with a colorful quilt draped over it and a small round table next to it sat across from the couch.

"Why did I expect it to look different?" Payden asked.

"The manor is deceptive, but every house seems to be simply furnished."

"How many houses have you been into?"

"Well, just this one at Jordan's insistence a few times. Malkam's been getting to know everyone, and he feels the need to report to me everything he sees and does."

"Why?"

David shrugged and went through the living room to the connected kitchen.

"If they ate here, they would dine at that table in the corner." David pointed to a small table with two chairs that sat in the corner. "That's if they ate here."

"I can smell the roses," Payden said. "Well, I guess I should go back. Jordan may be looking for me."

"You two need to go on an official date," David said, heading for the exit.

"How do we have one of those?"

David laughed and went out the door.

"What?" Payden asked, closing the door behind him.

"Nothing. Just go back to the estate. I've got something to do."

"What's that?"

David rubbed Payden's head. "Never you mind. I don't have to tell you everything."

Payden crossed his arms and glared at him.

"That won't work either. Have a good day." David left, and Payden was tempted to follow him, but smelling those flowers for the past few hours had only made him miss the person attached in his memory to the scent.

When he entered the estate, he went up to his room to deposit the harness by the couch. Then he went in search of Jordan, which could take the rest of the day, he knew. For some reason, especially since he had gotten well enough to be more active, she had kept herself busier than ever.

Payden bounded down the steps, and the first thing he noticed was the riotous laughter that tickled his attention. He glanced in its direction and saw the ballroom doors wide open. Lucy and Zachary, no doubt. Determined to avoid distraction, he went to the kitchen. The cooks always seemed to know Jordan's whereabouts. They and Salina. Payden had finally had an audience with Salina, and he couldn't help but instantly fall in love with her. Jordan seemed happier around her, which had helped Payden like her even more.

"Hi, Solomon!" Payden called.

"Mister Payden, how are you on this beautiful day?" Solomon asked, drying off his hands. A pile of freshly cleaned dishes rested on the counter.

"Desperately seeking Jordan, actually."

Solomon laughed. "Last I heard she was in the library. Dusting."

"What? Why is she so busy?"

"Go ask her. I bet she'll give you an answer."

"I bet it's 'I don't know.'" Payden smiled. "Have a good day."

"Always."

Jordan was standing by the Book in the glass case, staring intently at it when Payden entered. She didn't seem to notice him, so he sneaked behind her. She jumped when he hugged her, and he pulled her close.

"Hi," he said.

"You scared me."

"I know." He nuzzled his face next to hers. "What are you doing?"

"Reading."

"Okay."

"This is the oldest book anyone knows about," she explained. "I can barely read it."

"How old is it?"

"Very old."

"How did it get here?" he asked, craning his neck to get a better look.

"I told you that my people lived in the mountains, remember?"

"Yes."

"In that first year the Fashites attacked, our most valuable books and artwork were hidden in the mountains and eventually brought here. Everything that didn't make it has probably been destroyed. Others brought paintings and personal belongings as they came here, and we've been able to make replacements for so much, too. They really wanted to ensure this book's survival. It's the first one."

"It's huge."

"Yeah, and very used."

"What should we do today?"

"I'm not done dusting."

"Someone else can do that, you know," he said.

"Sorry." She bowed her head. "I know. You're probably wondering what I'm running from, huh?"

"Pretty much."

"I've been shooting the bow a lot. Apparently I'm really good at it. Lucy and I have been practicing together with the sword. Apparently I'm really bad. Nothing seems to help, and David keeps trying to encourage me. I guess I've just let my frustrations get to me, and I haven't wanted to vent on you."

"Hey, you know, I'd prefer you yelling at me than not talking to me."

"I'm sorry. I'm just—" She paused.

"Yes?" he prodded.

"I'm scared. One of these days, you'll leave here. I have to go with you. I can't stay here by myself. Despite all this training, I wonder, could I—" She tried to walk away, but he kept a firm grip.

"I'm not letting you run today."

Trapped, she placed her hands over her face. He pulled all her hair to just one side of her head so he could try to see what little of her face remained exposed.

"Let it out," he said.

"I can't even imagine myself killing someone. All this work is useless."

"No, it's not. You don't have to kill anyone, you know? Let's go do something fun so you can stop thinking like this for a while."

She nodded. "Okay."

They found a group of the younger kids outside kicking a ball around, and they joined them. It didn't take long for Jordan to squeal with laughter. Payden pretended he needed to rest so he could sit on the grass and watch her, captivated by every bounce of her hair and movement of her body as she held up her dress to run after the ball, kicking it away from the kids who weren't on her team. Despite his contentment, he knew that he could never live in one place for the rest of his life. His eyes went up to the mountains. Something was out there, and he needed to get to it.

Chapter 18

Though David never could sleep restfully, that night seemed more difficult. He finally gave up trying and got off the floor to look out the window. The moon shone brightly, as was typical during that time of the year, and he watched it for a while as clouds lazily drifted by, covering the moon, causing darkness to dominate the night in those brief, fleeting moments. He turned and rubbed his neck, wondering if he should even attempt to figure out what was keeping him awake.

The woman's face came to mind. Unable to properly think in the confines of a room, no matter how large, David gathered up his items and went to his garden, careful to take the route that didn't pass Jordan's window so he wouldn't wake her. Since the day after the wedding, he'd been paranoid about her catching him again. If she hadn't reminded him so much of Leislie, he probably would have left the valley after that. He had been sorely tempted but eventually talked himself out of it, though it had taken hours.

When he reached his spot, he sat on his favorite bench and breathed deeply. Like Payden, he too had a special attachment to the scent of roses. Whenever he had visited Henry and Leislie, she could always tell if he was upset, and she'd steal him away to the kitchen for a long, healing talk. Ever since, roses had helped him heal.

This spot had become a place to think whenever he needed to be alone, which was often, or whenever he needed to battle some impulse that had been programmed into him. As he sat mulling over his thoughts, the woman's face appeared again for just a moment. He sat upright, half expecting her to be standing right in front of him. Was she someone he knew? It wasn't Leislie. Leislie had light-brown hair. This woman's hair was black, and she had brown eyes.

Had the Pendtars made him forget her, or had he made himself forget? If it was the latter, then perhaps he shouldn't try to bring the memory back to life. He had a hard enough time managing the memories he already had. Any more might be too much.

If the Pendtars had made him forget, what was their motivation? Could they have known who he was? Surely they did. But how? David thought back through the years, once again reaching some that he couldn't remember. Those were the few years in the beginning.

David scratched his head. He would have to get back to the castle soon, he realized. The only time the Pendtars didn't worry about a Slave's delay was if he was sent to spy on the Jathenites. Most Slaves came back, but some were caught and killed by the Jathenites.

David made sure never to delay his check-in—but wait. David's thoughts caught something he had missed. The Jathenites. Once a Slave reached a certain rank, he was sent to gather information about the Jathenites. Every Slave was, except David had reached that rank years ago, and he hadn't been sent north. His eyes studied the ground as his thoughts deepened. They knew. He was certain of it. So William was—

Unwilling to dredge up an unwanted crisis, he tore off his hat, cloak, scarf, shirt, and gloves. The cool air felt soothing to his skin and eased his mind as he meditated for a moment. Everything flowed out of him. As he felt more grounded, he closed his eyes and began to practice. Nothing new came to mind, so he settled into several older routines and focused on pouring out his frustrations through the sword and into the air.

Once he realized dawn had broken, he stopped and watched the sun rise. He grimaced and quickly pulled on his attire to protect himself from the light. As much as he tried to fight it, at that moment he seemed weak, and the little light that touched him caused his skin to burn. Why he felt that way, he couldn't remember. Whenever he tried, nothing came to mind. Perhaps it was another sensation he wanted to forget. If so, why did it bother him? He managed to return to his room unseen and scrubbed himself down. He hated water too, but he did remember why. He shuddered as he felt cold hands on his shoulders and quickly got ready for a day of training.

He went down to grab a quick breakfast, hoping to get to the grounds before making contact with anyone. His thoughts were not completely reined in yet. The cook came out, smiling, and David steeled himself for the inevitable greeting.

"Hi, Mister David," Solomon said. "You're up earlier than the help. I haven't started breakfast yet, but what do you have a taste for this morning?"

"Just some berries or something easy."

"Not in the mood to talk yet. All right. I'll get you something." Solomon disappeared into the kitchen while David paced, almost deciding to forget the food entirely and leave. Solomon came back before David made a decision.

"Here you go," Solomon said. "I hope one day you talk to someone. I hate to see people so miserable."

David nodded, taking the bag in which Solomon had wrapped everything. Solomon grabbed him and gave him a big hug. He held David by his shoulders and looked him in the eye.

"I can tell being around people really bothers you. I want to thank you for staying and helping us anyway. What you do does not go unnoticed. We all try to give you your space. It's very hard, but we do it. I sincerely do hope you talk with someone one day." Solomon smiled. "Have a good day, Mister David. I have work to begin."

David quickly left and made it to the end of the grounds before he began hyperventilating. He sat on the grass and set the bag of food aside so he could bury his face in his hands as he fought to breathe. Tears poured out of his eyes, and he wondered why. His mind was clear. Everything had been caged, hadn't it?

Once his breathing became normal, he finally ate, though his appetite was completely gone, and watched as the young guards began to trickle onto the field. Jordan waved at him as she made her way to her archery lessons. Malkam had made her smaller targets to work with in diverse areas in order to challenge her aiming skills. She seemed more content with the difficulty than she had with prior drills. The time quickly approached for them to begin, and he hoped Payden wouldn't be late.

Payden came out of the estate, fidgeting with his shirt as he also adjusted his harness. David observed that Payden tried his best to appear casual and calm. A smile finally formed on David's face, unobserved by anyone else due to the scarf. Payden was the one thing that helped David focus. David knew how much he loved that boy. As he watched the approaching figure, he wondered how he could keep Payden safe. If the Pendtars knew who David was, how would he be able to?

For the past thirty years, David had wanted to achieve the rank that ensured him a place in the inner circle, where he would finally be able to stand before the Pendtars. His hand gripped his sword tightly as he thought of what he had planned to do on that day. He was just a few ranks away, but if they knew—he'd never make it. They wouldn't let David without several dozen other Slaves between him and them. The deep-seated anger that he had locked away began to bubble out of the cell.

Focus, David, he thought and looked up at Payden. *Focus. The Djorites need you here now. Payden needs you here now.*

"Hey, Payden, are you ready?" David asked.

"I can't believe you have to ask," Payden said.

"Everyone," David said loudly. "Gather around in a large circle. I bet this young man thinks he can defeat me."

A chuckle coursed through the group. Most of the men had watched Payden approach and wondered what he was doing there. The youngest of the Djorites there was twenty-one, and they were all large in stature. A few suspected that he was in need of as much training as they were.

"Let's see if he can," David finished. He winked at Payden.

The men busied themselves finding a good position. Payden noticed that he was the smallest man in the group. Then he saw Zachary. Zachary was certainly the largest. Payden shook his head. How had Zachary managed to get that tall? When Payden saw Lucy, he smiled at her. She laughed and rolled her eyes. David approached him.

"These men have been learning how to dodge a blow lately, but they're still swinging their swords about wildly. I want them to see that they can survive a fight unarmed, so don't draw your sword until I tell you, okay?"

Payden nodded, eyes twinkling with excitement. David stepped away and waited until everyone was settled, keeping an eye on Payden. Though David shied away from crowds, Payden loved them. He was comfortable around people, especially when he was teaching or leading anyone. That was a characteristic inherited from Henry. Payden was certainly meant to be a leader.

Everyone settled, so David channeled his energy into his role as a teacher. "Okay, men. I know what you're thinking. This scrawny little kid is going to be dead in thirty seconds. I know I've told you time and again that what you see and think you know always work against you in a battle. I've been trying to teach you how to think differently. I hope you will after today. Payden."

"David."

David drew his sword, and he and Payden began to move in a circle. They drew closer to each other, and the men immediately murmured, wondering why Payden hadn't unsheathed his weapons yet. When David was in range, he attacked. Payden twisted, dodged, ducked, and rolled, successfully avoiding each thrust or swipe. When he rolled out of range once again, David charged him and struck while he was still on the ground. Payden twisted from side to side, then quickly grabbed David's arms with his legs and rolled, leaping to his feet as David hit the ground.

"That one's new," David said as he got to his feet.

Payden merely grinned.

David attacked again, but instead of dodging, Payden stepped into the blow, and David's arm hit his shoulder. David grabbed Payden's shirt, but Payden locked his hands over David's before he dropped to his knees to dive forward, which sent David head over heels. David, back on his feet in an instant, smirked.

"This is the Payden I was expecting a month ago," he said.

"I've had a lot of time to think lately."

"Okay. Now."

Payden pulled out his swords. A larger crowd had gathered when those at the archery range saw what was happening. Jordan had quickly pushed to the front, and even Malkam allowed the distraction because he, too, wanted to see this fight.

"You've got your crowd now, Payden," David said. "Don't disappoint them."

"At least this time I won't be cocky."

"So that's what happened. I have honestly lost sleep wondering why you had gotten so bad."

David then leaped forward, and the men watched in awe, barely able to make a sound. The blades moved so quickly, a few had a hard time following them. When David began a series of leaps and other aerial maneuvers, the silence grew. Payden withdrew his attack and went on the defense at that moment, unsure exactly how to work against him.

"That was a mistake," David said.

He completely disarmed Payden in seconds.

"Never plan," David said for only Payden to hear. "You're at your weakest when you plan."

The men were quickly in an uproar, hooting and whistling. Payden picked up his swords and bowed to David.

"Today I have been humbled," he said and stepped back to join the crowd.

David's face fell, and he stared intently at Payden, but no one noticed. Except Jordan. David looked as though he was lost in old thoughts, and she wondered why Payden's reply had triggered such a reaction.

"Okay, okay," David yelled, and the group grew silent. "How unusual that he could survive so long without drawing his sword. Better still, when he was in trouble, he didn't just swing his sword, hoping to hit something. He made every strike count. I hope you finally understand that in a battle, you can be doing this for hours. You can be as strong or as physically fit as you can possibly be, but it doesn't really matter. After just an hour, you can barely lift your arm, and they're still coming. Save your energy. Make every motion count. Strike only when you see an opportunity. Most importantly, exhaust the enemy. That's when they're easier to kill."

The men instantly sobered. Though they knew why they were training, the thought of killing someone had never really materialized. David was keenly aware of this. Not a single one of these men was a warrior in heart or in action. It didn't sadden David. He was actually envious. His own life decisions had brought him to where he was. A Slave. He shook his head.

"For today, I want you to have Payden help you," he said. "He dodges blows better than even me. Get to work."

As the men dispersed, Payden pulled David aside. "Why didn't you point out my retreat? What about the not planning bit?"

"That's just for you, Payden," David answered. "They have to strategize, concentrate, and think. That's how they'll survive. You're the opposite. You're like me. Whatever pops into your head to do, do it. It'll be the right thing. Keep that in mind when you're helping these guys, all right?"

Payden nodded. "Oh—but I have a request," he said.

"Yeah?"

"Those last moves—I want them."

David rubbed Payden's head. "Maybe. Go teach. They're all yours."

When Payden stepped away, a group of men quickly approached him, and the day went on as planned. The guards were clearly excited about learning new moves, especially defense. They still had great fear of killing.

David eventually eased from everyone's sight before going for a long walk. The guards outside the walls greeted him but remained vigilant otherwise. David was grateful for that.

He was also grateful that Malkam's suggestions were being used. The men were branching out through the three tunnels that remained unblocked to keep a better eye on their surroundings rather than staying in the valley. They even discovered old telegraph equipment in some of the tunnels that still worked. Immediately, they learned how to send and receive messages, rerunning some of the wires through the tunnels that were not sealed.

The scouts hadn't reported any activity, which didn't make David feel comfortable at all. The Djorites took the news with great relief, but David knew better. There was always a calm before the storm. The longer the calm remained, the larger the storm. He was grateful for the time, though. It had allowed the boys to become men.

A ledge jutted out of the trees halfway up the slope, and David climbed up to it. As he sat, looking over the city below, watching the tiny dots of moving men, he wondered if it was finally time to leave. The Djorites could learn from Payden and Malkam everything they would need to know.

Some rocks tumbled past him on his right, and he looked up to see a couple guards hurrying down.

"What is it?" David asked.

One of the men yelped in surprise while the other stumbled and fell as he tried to stop. David quickly got up to catch him.

"They're here," the man said.

"What do you mean?"

The other man reached his side. "The Fashites are in sight. They're coming up the river. Andrew sent a message from his post at the other end of the tunnel overlooking the river. The Fashites should land tonight."

"Stay calm," David said. "Let's go tell everyone to prepare."

They went down the slope, telling every guard they met, who in turn relayed the message to others. As panic spread,

David became frustrated. Had the Fashites really known the location of the instrument all this time? There'd been no talk of it at all in the Pendtar castle. Another reason for David to believe they'd suspected him. If the instrument was near, why hadn't any of the Djorites seen it? Or should they have spent the past weeks searching for it in order to destroy it? David had been so worried about getting these men in the proper mind-set that the tool hadn't even crossed his mind. He hoped it wasn't too late.

By the time he reached the manor, a crowd had gathered consisting of all the nervous men who suddenly had to face reality. Their preparations for the past few weeks were about to be tested.

Samuel ran from the direction of his house straight to David.

"What should we do?" he asked breathlessly.

David looked about him. Why was everyone staring at him? Malkam pushed his way through and placed a strong hand on David's shoulder.

"Let's go, David," Malkam said. "Just us. Let's go and see exactly what we're up against. Get a quick count of the numbers or, at the very least, try to determine what they know."

"Okay," David said softly.

"But what of the instrument?" Samuel asked. "That's what they're after. Does this mean they know its location? We have to destroy it if it does indeed still exist."

"But how do we destroy it?" Malkam asked. "No one knows this information, so what would be the point?"

"If the Fashites use that tool, then we're all dead," Samuel explained. "History has shown that. Entire cities leveled in one day!"

"Except we don't have the information. And I really don't believe the Fashites do either. Why else would they have taken Jordan? The first thing they're going to try to do is get information out of everyone in this valley. So the first thing we concern ourselves with is keeping them out. David and I will go through the tunnel to check out the Fashites. Then we'll have all the archers set up in that tunnel in case the Fashites discover it. Any Fashite who tries to get through will be an easy target. Keep the scouts at the other entrances, too."

Jordan ran her hands down her dress and thought of the little bit she had read in her mother's journal about the instrument. The information her mother had gotten from the only man in the valley who'd actually used one. Should she reveal it now? Could she?

"And if they do find the instrument? If it is there? What can we do?" a soldier asked nervously.

"Then we'll destroy it," Malkam answered. "But I don't want to worry about anything we don't know. Right now, they're on the river. And I have a good group of archers. Let's go."

"Wait," Jordan said loudly. The men turned to look at her, and she nervously approached Malkam.

"I know—I know something about the instrument," she said, glancing at her father before ducking her head in shame.

"What?" Samuel asked. "How?"

She swallowed. "Mother."

Samuel's face paled. Jordan couldn't look at him. She could only imagine what he was thinking.

"What do you mean?" Malkam asked, suddenly feeling greatly frustrated. If she'd had helpful information all this time, why hadn't she shared it?

"My mother wrote about the instrument. She spoke to a man who had used and destroyed many of them. They're camouflaged. It's hard to see them if you don't know what to look for." She swallowed deeply and hung her head even more. "I can help you find it. I know how to destroy it."

Malkam clenched his teeth and kept his mouth shut. He'd tried hard his whole life to keep anger at bay so it wouldn't be the cause of his words or actions. Payden had been the only person spared from that self-control, but Malkam felt it difficult at the moment to not feel anger over this child's silence. There was no excuse for it.

David noticed the upsurge of emotions from Malkam, Samuel, and Jordan and knew something had to happen quickly before any of them erupted. David first approached Jordan, bending forward to ask quietly, "Are you sure?"

She nodded, eyes never leaving the ground.

He then stood and faced Samuel. "How much do you trust me?"

Samuel narrowed his eyes in confusion.

"If I take her with me, do you believe that I will bring her back unharmed?"

Samuel inhaled sharply before his eyes quickly searched David's. "You promise?"

"On my life, she will return," David swore.

Samuel studied Jordan, who continued to stand frozen in her shame. "Keep her safe."

Jordan raised her head and focused wide eyes on her father.

"Why didn't you tell me before?" Samuel asked her.

"I didn't want to hurt you. You never talk of Mother. I thought any mention of her would—would push you further away."

Samuel nodded as he weighed her words. "I'm sorry I made you feel that way." She rushed to his side, and he held her tightly.

David approached Malkam and merely held his old friend's gaze for a moment. Malkam nodded, almost imperceptibly, and David turned to Samuel and Jordan. "We'll go now. Have your captain ready the archers. And make more arrows. And Jordan—go put on some pants. If we need to get somewhere in a hurry, that dress will surely snag everything and slow us down."

She nodded and hurried to the one house she knew would have trousers her size. As she ran off, Payden stepped forward. "I have to go, then, if she's going. You know you can't stop me."

"We don't need a lot of people to go, Payden," Malkam snapped. "It'll be easier with just a few."

"I don't care. I'm going."

Malkam crossed his arms and glowered at Payden, who defiantly held his stare. "Still the same stubborn kid," Malkam muttered before he turned and spit, still seething inside. In all these years, he hadn't learned how to tame Payden.

"And if we don't return come tomorrow morning, fill up the tunnel with archers. Kill anyone moving," Malkam stated flatly, trying to keep his emotions out of his voice.

Samuel's eyes became empty. The thought of them not returning was the only sentence he had not wanted to contemplate. His gaze drifted in the direction Jordan had departed. Once again, and so soon after the first time, he had to feel the agony of worry that his daughter would never be seen again.

"You know you're not leaving us out of the action!" Lucy shouted from the crowd.

"Oh, no!" Malkam lamented, throwing up his hands. "Girl, if you think I am going to put up with your hotheadedness, then you have another think coming."

"She'll be good," Zachary said loudly. "I promise."

"No!" Malkam asserted. "You two stay here. It's bad enough Payden's going—"

"That's why I have to go," Lucy interrupted as she approached. "Last time, you didn't let me go with him. I swear, if you do that to me again, you will never be able to sleep soundly."

Malkam knew he would gain no more ground. "Fine. Anyone else care to join us?" He shouted. The rest of the group remained silent, too petrified at the reality crashing down around them to understand a seasoned veteran's act of whimsy. Zachary, however, raised his hand.

"Can I at least go to make sure my wife doesn't act like a hothead and get everyone else killed?"

Malkam glared at Zachary with an icy ferocity that made Zachary take a deep, nervous gulp. David did his best not to chuckle. If there was one thing Malkam hated the most, it was when he lost control over a situation he believed he had under control. Those situations had always amused David.

Jordan arrived presently, having donned a shirt and trousers, tying her hair back as she arrived. "I'm ready," she announced breathlessly.

"Give her your equipment," Malkam said to the nearest archer. The young man quickly handed the quiver and bow to Jordan, who nervously accepted the items. "Let's get this over with."

The path to the cave was new, freshly created in the past weeks like so many other things. The changes—paths, scouts, telegraph lines—mixed with the training had changed life in the valley.

Lucy remembered the route, and her palms began to sweat. She'd forgotten the first trek already, as so much had happened since them. If it weren't for her pride, she would have changed her mind and stayed instead of entering those dark, confining tunnels again. Since she had fought to go, she remained silent. Perhaps there was something she could focus on in order to distract herself.

Zachary trailed behind her, and Payden was ahead with Jordan. Her eyes locked on to her little Joe. That helped. She knew the reason she wanted to go was to make sure he remained safe.

Malkam reached the entrance and glanced inside. The post was abandoned. The telegraph machine sat unchanged. His brows knit as he approached it, quickly sending a message. A few minutes passed, but no reply came.

"Who's on the other end?" Malkam looked to David for the answer.

"Andrew, I believe."

"Andrew?" Lucy asked.

David nodded.

"I like him. He's one of the few who can actually fight."

"He's not replying," Malkam said softly.

"The ships were still too far off, though," David pointed out.

"Maybe he's out of the cave," Lucy offered. "There's a lot of trees that block the view."

"Or we'll pass him on the way. Let's go." Malkam lifted the nearest torch and lit it from the flames that filled the fire pit nearby. "Payden, Zachary, grab a few more, please. Everyone keep up. I'm not slowing down."

His long strides were hard for Jordan to match. She trotted along, trying to keep the torch's light in view. Lucy and Zachary kept their march slow to not overrun Jordan, who seemed out of breath when they reached the open cavern with multiple exits.

"The third opening," Jordan said breathlessly, as soon as they entered. When Malkam stopped ahead, relief flooded her system. She bent forward to catch her breath. Malkam slowly approached the exit. Zachary rushed past her while Lucy and Payden quickly flanked her. The tension finally became obvious to her as everyone kept completely silent, eyes darting around the room. Malkam tossed his dying torch onto the pile of wood in the center fire pit. Jordan stood upright, cautiously casting her eyes about, wondering why everyone seemed so alert. David knelt on the other side, and she finally saw why everyone was frozen.

"He's dead," David said quietly, rising to his feet beside Andrew. Jordan covered her mouth to stifle a gasp. "This was a Slave's doing."

"So where is he?" Malkam hissed.

David shook his head. "The body's been dragged here. Slave's don't do that. They stalk their victims and kill them where they want to leave them."

"Unless Andrew went the wrong way," Zachary whispered. He gestured to the floor. "He was dragged through here."

"Give me a torch," David ordered.

Zachary tossed him one, which David lit from the fires before holding the light closer to the floor. David followed the tracks in the dirt. They continued into the tunnel they'd just exited. "Andrew was on his way back when the Slave caught him. But where was he taking him?"

"Back to the exit?" Malkam asked.

"But why?" David handed the torch off to Zachary as he went to the third tunnel. "I guess he's this way. I'll lead. Malkam, open your shield. Zachary, follow him. Payden, take the rear. Lucy, you'll keep an eye on Jordan, right?"

Lucy nodded, tight lipped. Her apprehension over the confined space morphed into fear of an unseen Slave. Jordan stepped closer to Lucy, and they lined up behind David. Light glinted off Malkam's shield, and he and Zachary crouched as they moved forward. The slower pace was easier for Jordan, but the conditions that necessitated it made her wish for their former speed.

At the end of the tunnel, David held up his hand for everyone to stop. Then, slowly, he drew his sword and delicately ascended the ladder. Malkam held out his arms to keep everyone back as he craned his neck to watch David's progress.

Jordan's heart beat so rapidly, she thought everyone could hear it. She dared to look at everyone else, whose eyes focused intently on the now-vacant ladder. Lucy gripped the hilt of her sheathed sword, ready to release it if needed. Payden's breaths sounded deep and relaxed behind Jordan, and she wished to feel that calm. Her eyes slid shut as the worry overwhelmed her.

Above, David nearly crawled out of the porthole, staying low to the ground until his feet were planted. He listened, knowing his unseen opponent had the advantage and could strike from anywhere. No one stood near the opening, and David angled toward it, keeping most of his back toward the sunlight. When he finally reached the wall, he returned to the cave, back against the rock as his eyes sought any nuance of the intruder. Deeper in the cave, the light decreased greatly. Before his eyes could fully readjust, the flicker of a blade appeared, which David barely parried.

The Slave's attack was fast, the sword flickering from seemingly all directions. David retreated to the light, drawing his opponent to more even ground, but the man did not fall for the ploy. So David surged forward, eyes closed as they were useless in the unaccustomed darkness, and relied on his instincts. He chased his prey deeper into the cave, hearing the hiss of each swipe, knowing its source and direction of arc with precision and experience his opponent didn't seem to have. Judging by the man's speed, David guessed him to be much younger.

When David opened his eyes, he faintly made out the shape of his opponent. The Slave would not even know when the duel was over. David feigned a low blow, switched hands midthrust, and struck high. The body fell to the ground, and David checked to see if the man had survived. As expected, it had been a quick death. David returned to the opening.

"Come on up," he said.

Malkam, shield retracted, exited first. "You found the Slave?"

"His body's in the back."

Malkam nodded solemnly, yet said nothing as the rest of them emerged. Lucy breathed deeply several times once she was topside and ran her hands down her pants legs. Jordan, feeling too stunned to stand still, staggered toward the sunlight. Payden followed, catching her in his arms before she left the cave.

"It's over," he whispered.

"No, it's not," she said hoarsely. "The Fashites are here. Now. We can't pretend anymore. Poor Andrew. And his family . . ." She buried her face in Payden's chest and tried to breathe. He pulled her close, unable to think of anything else to say.

"Jordan, we do need to hurry," David said gently. "We'll go out to see exactly where the Fashites are. If you could recognize exactly where this . . . weapon is, then please do. Soon."

She pulled away from Payden and nodded. "Yes. All I know is only a Djorite can find it. I can't say for certain what that means, but we'll find out."

Malkam passed Jordan and Payden as he walked into the thick growth of trees. Everyone followed, up until the trees grew farther apart, exposing them to the view of the Great Sea. Malkam held up his hand for everyone to freeze.

"There they are," Malkam said with a hushed voice.

Zachary released a low whistle.

"David, you were right," Lucy breathed. "That looks like their entire army."

Dozens of large ships dotted the waters, anchored in the deeper waters offshore. Smaller boats surrounded them, while dinghies laden with men and machinery were being lowered to the waters below. Some of those boats were already ashore.

"Do you think they can see us?" Payden asked.

"I don't want to give them the chance," Malkam answered. "Stay low. If they've landed here, then they think this instrument is nearby."

"I didn't see anything when I was here," Lucy said. "Not up here, anyway. Just a pile of boulders at the edge of the cliff. Didn't look that threatening to me."

Malkam moved the group closer to the tree line and paused again. This time, he glanced about with a puzzled expression on his face.

"What's wrong?" David asked him.

"I think I've been here before."

"Can you figure it out while we walk?"

"Of course I can," Malkam snapped. "I just saw something familiar and had to look about."

"And that was?"

Malkam gestured to a large, leaf-laden tree not far from them. "It's got an insignia carved into it. It was the symbol an old fighting buddy of mine used to distinguish his troop. Haven't thought about him in years."

"Must have been a good friend."

Malkam glared at David, who chuckled softly.

"I'm glad you two are enjoying this," Lucy hissed.

Malkam glanced at her before he inched forward, crouching low among the shrubbery as the trees grew scarce. Zachary flattened himself onto the ground and crawled. Jordan wanted to stay in the rear, nervously watching the ships. Payden wanted to keep close to her, but he pulled away to reach Malkam and David at the front. When he got to their side, Lucy gasped. Everyone turned to her, but her eyes were focused on the edge of the cliff. There stood a short tower, topped with encased windows. No one moved for a moment.

"That wasn't there," she said in alarm. "That wasn't there before!"

"Why didn't we see it when we got out?" Malkam asked. "Where did it come from?"

"That's not all we need to worry about," Zachary said, his eyes on the water. The men on the shore had noticed the tower too, and the men moved more quickly, turning themselves toward the cliff.

"What do we do now?" Payden asked.

"Let's take a look," David said. "Jordan, you sure you know how to destroy it?"

She remained frozen, eyes unblinking as they centered on the tower.

"Jordan," David said sharply, gaining her attention.

"Y-yes," she stammered. "We need to go inside."

"Let's go," Malkam ordered, nearly crawling toward the building. As David followed Malkam's advance, he studied the structure more thoroughly. It protruded from the ground like a stoic watchtower. Why did it seem so familiar? The location wasn't, just the machine. He shuddered. Something deep inside him felt desperate to destroy it.

A rock wall on their right bordered a stairway that curved down to the bottom of the tower. Another stairway curved up around the tower to a higher level. Malkam led them behind the wall before he stopped. "We're out of sight here, but if those soldiers get any closer, they'll see us for sure. We don't have much time. I'll stay here with Payden and Lucy. The rest of you go down and see if you can get the door open."

David led them down, ducking low to keep the wall between him and the Fashites' line of sight. At the bottom, a rusted metal door covered the entrance. David pulled at the handle, but it didn't budge. Zachary slid beside him, staying low, and pulled with David. It remained stuck.

Jordan sat on the step and watched, feeling unable to help in any way. She tried to remember all her mother had said about the instrument. Something about a key. The tower, built of rocks and mortar, was covered in moss and climbing vines on this side. The steps were stone, but covered in dirt and patches of weeds. But that key . . .

She stood and inspected the wall, unaware of the plans being hatched and executed by David and Zachary. Her hand traced the stones of the wall until she found a loose one. With a trepid breath, she pulled at it, amazed at how easily it slid from its roost. She set it aside and reached into the hole.

At first, all she felt was dirt and spiderwebs. Then her fingers found a small, thin object, and with relief, she clasped her fingers around it.

"Here!" she whispered excitedly, carrying the item to David. "This is the key to unlock the door."

David stared at the small object in her hand. "This whole time, the door's just been locked?"

Zachary chuckled and grabbed the key. "Let's get inside."

The door creaked and moaned many protests as they slid it open. Jordan's fingers curled at each sound. She was frightened to peek over the wall to see if they'd been heard by those down the cliff. They entered the dark, dank room. Zachary coughed at the stench.

"Something died in here a long time ago," he muttered, desperately trying to figure out how to breathe.

Jordan pulled her shirt over her mouth and pressed forward. "We should find some sort of controls."

Zachary followed grudgingly, hand over his mouth as he felt along the wall for anything to help. David walked straight to the back, where several cylindrical tanks lined the wall. Wires and hoses spun out from them to many areas of the room, many snaking up the wall through the ceiling. The word written on each tank was unknown to him: *hydrogen*. He narrowed his eyes as the feeling of unease increased. The entire place felt familiar, but he was certain he'd never before seen one of these instruments. As the eerie familiarity increased, he began to doubt.

"I don't see anything," Jordan said after searching. "There's just wires and cables."

"And they all lead to the floor above us," David pointed out. "So what we're looking for must be up there."

"Can't we just hack away at the stuff down here?" Zachary asked. "You know, like cutting the electricity wires in Tawney City? Cut a few, and no one gets power in the building."

"Maybe," David said slowly, looking about. "But I have a feeling that that would be dangerous. Really dangerous. Let's get up top."

"They'll see us up there," Zachary said. "That door's exposed. And I recall you mentioning the great accuracy the Fashite archers have."

David nodded. "But Malkam's got a shield."

"Oh yeah. I keep forgetting."

David led them out, remembering the key after he locked the door. He handed the key to Jordan. When they reached the others, Malkam had only bad news.

"There's already four to five hundred on the ground. And they're beginning to climb uphill."

"It's a steep climb," Payden said. "Any way they get up here will only corral them to a narrow path. We can easily keep them at bay long enough, you think?"

Suddenly, a loud boom came from the direction of the ship. They ducked and wondered where the bomb would hit. The blast shook the mountain from whence they came, and an avalanche of rocks tumbled to the ground.

"Our exit," Jordan whispered. "It's gone."

"Why did they do that?" Lucy asked. Hers eyes darted from face to face. "Why did they do that?"

"The Slave," David said. "Must have told them about the cave."

"Which would lead them to the Djorites, so why would they cut off their access?" Lucy asked.

"With this tool, the Fashites won't need it. But no Djorites can exit that cave to destroy the tool, can they?"

"Why do they hate us so much?" Jordan asked softly.

The group sobered, and Malkam risked another look. "If we run to the trees now, we'll make it before they get a chance to shoot."

"With their arrows, sure," Lucy said. "They'll get us with another bomb."

"But we'll be safe by then," Malkam shot at her. "There's another exit here. Many years ago, I fought with a guy named Oscar. I think the Djorites made more tunnels in this mountain than they know of, because he made his way around through them. Don't know if he's still alive, but I do know there's another exit over there by his insignia. We'll have time to find it before they launch another bomb."

"If they don't find us first," David said. "They're too close. A few of us should go down and distract them while Jordan goes up to the top and figures out how to destroy this thing." He stood and jumped over the wall, sliding down the cliff's side until he grabbed a short bush. Once his momentum was halted, he pushed against the rock with his feet and landed on a shelf, which connected the cliff to the steep, sloping landscape the Fashites were trying to navigate.

His appearance didn't surprise them, as they probably suspected a Slave was there. But once he encountered the men in front and their bodies fell, rolling down the terrain to the advancing soldiers behind them, the other Fashites realized the need to defend themselves. David felled at least a dozen men before anyone could react, but once they did, Malkam knew he had to help.

"Jordan, here." He unclasped the sleeve of his armor that covered his left arm and quickly adjusted it to fit hers. "Flick this switch when you're standing. It activates the shield. Use it to get up into that instrument. We'll give you time. Got that?"

She nodded.

"Zachary, let's empty our quivers first, then head downhill. Payden, hurry. Cover David."

Without a word, Payden leaped over the wall, rushing down the hillside as David had, unsheathing his swords as soon as his feet hit level ground. He and David immediately found a rhythm, pushing the advancing army back to unsteady ground, where they spent most of their time slipping or tumbling down the hill.

Zachary pushed a few rocks off the top of the wall and settled in, nocking arrow after arrow as he expertly targeted the Fashite archers within range. Lucy's hand gripped her knife handle. "Where do you want me, General?" she asked, eyes focused on Malkam. For a moment, he remained speechless. Then he risked another survey of the battle.

"Head for the trees. Use them as cover. See those men trying to flank David?"

She peeked out and looked where he pointed. "Got 'em." Then she took a few deep breaths before sprinting to the trees.

"And Jordan, if you can't destroy this thing, then we're going to need your help," Malkam said as he removed his bow. "Use those new skills of yours. You'll only be able to get a few areas because of their armor. Their throats are the most that's exposed, but that's a hard shot; it'll only be presented for a moment. Maybe try to get their arms—elbows or hands. It doesn't matter. You'll be helping us out either way, understand?"

She gulped and nodded again. Malkam moved farther down the wall and knocked several rocks off the top, following Zachary's example. Within minutes, he was shooting arrow after arrow.

With everyone performing their assigned tasks, Jordan knew she had to get to work. It all depended on her. She stood and flicked the switch, trying not to gasp as the shield formed in front of her. It looked like glass, but it didn't seem to be the same. She saw the thin lines throughout where the pieces snapped together seamlessly. She shook her head, knowing she was wasting precious time, and quickly followed the steps to the top of the cliff.

The shield proved useful as she broke free from the cover the wall had provided. Arrows clanged against the clear surface, and she yelped, crouching in fear. A few more arrows hit the shield, and Jordan felt grateful for it as she remained untouched. Her breathing quickened as the shafts scattered around her.

Determination finally set in. The battle raged before her from that vantage point. David and Payden seemed overwhelmed, but were moving so fast and with so much precision that she didn't fear for them. Lucy, on the other hand, looked to be in trouble. Zachary, out of arrows, sprinted toward her location, but several arrows rained upon him, and he dove behind the nearest tree, pinned down.

Jordan acted before she realized what she was doing. She unclasped the shield and set it on the ground, leaning the top against the tower. Then she gripped the bow and removed an arrow. Zachary advanced to another tree, but it was not close enough yet. Lucy scrambled uphill and tripped. A Fashite rushed her, raising his hand to strike.

"Don't think. Just do," Jordan whispered. She aimed, but then shut her eyes before she released the arrow and tried not to vomit. If the arrow struck, she didn't know. When she finally opened her eyes, she saw Lucy was back on her feet, heading uphill. Three more men charged her, and Jordan reset her bow. One man lunged, and Lucy drove her sword into his abdomen, but she couldn't remove it in time to block a blow from another. He hit her on the head, and she fell to the ground. The man lifted his arm to finish her. Jordan aimed at his knee, then his hand. He lifted his head and exposed the throat. She released the arrow, not wanting to see it strike. She quickly doubled over and finally heaved. Wiping her mouth with the back of her hand, she looked up to see Zachary finish off the third before he turned to attend to Lucy.

Zachary carried Lucy uphill and set her carefully beside a tree. A half dozen men made it up to him, but they met a savage man protecting his injured bride. In spite of receiving several blows, Zachary managed to subdue them all before he fell to his knees, clutching his side. Malkam, out of arrows, made it over to him.

"You all right?" Malkam asked.

Zachary shook with rage and pain, unable to say anything. Blood poured from his side, upper thigh, and back. Malkam removed the cloak he always wore and pressed it against Zachary's side. Then he picked up Lucy and motioned for Zachary to follow. It took some time, but Malkam found the tree with Oscar's insignia carved into it. Malkam dragged his foot through the brush that covered the area until he felt something that wasn't dirt. He laid Lucy gently on the ground and uncovered the trapdoor.

"Can you get this open?" he asked Zachary. Zachary nodded.

"Get in and shut it behind you."

Malkam left quickly, hurrying to cover David and Payden. Though David still seemed to be faring well, Payden displayed signs of fatigue. Malkam saw a large boulder perched precariously near the edge, and he looked downhill to determine the best direction it should tumble. When satisfied, he squatted beside it and pushed with all his might. It finally rolled.

"David!" he shouted.

David dared a quick glance. When he saw the tumbling rock, he pulled Payden to the side, out of its path. As the boulder rolled, sending Fashites scrambling, David ran uphill with Payden in tow.

"It's good that this hill is as steep as it is," Malkam said, "but we can't do this much longer."

Payden noticed Jordan cowering behind Malkam's shield beside the tower and ran up to her side. David let him go and addressed Malkam. "He's done for a while, but we still need to keep fighting."

"To the end, old friend." Malkam unsheathed his sword, and he and David returned downhill, staying among the trees to give the archers a harder target. The rock had bought them several minutes to catch their breaths before another wave surged uphill.

"Let's have some fun," Malkam shouted and laughed. David shook his head at his battle-hungry friend.

"I miss the old days."

"Me too!" Malkam lashed at the first unfortunate man, and David engaged the next.

Payden dodged the arrows until he was safely behind the shield. Jordan sat there, sobbing hysterically. Payden wrapped her in his arms.

"Shh. Jordan, just breathe. It's going to be fine."

"I can't do it, Payden. I can't." She sniffed. "We're going to die—and I—can't . . ."

"No, we're not. We're all going to get out of this."

She looked downhill and watched as the men began overwhelming David and Malkam.

"Payden, look, we *are* going to die," she said.

More men were coming up the hill. The boats on the river were full of thousands more. Payden looked up at the weapon. It needed to be destroyed fast.

"How do you use it?" he asked.

"I don't know." She looked at it. "Mother said it's controlled by your thoughts. Whatever you think it can do, it will."

He sheathed his swords. "Stay here." He stood and turned uphill.

"Payden, no, you can't!" she cried.

"I'm going to try."

"Wait!" She stood. "The key." She pulled it from her pocket. "I'm sorry I can't do this, Payden. I'm not like you. I thought I could be, but I can't."

He took the key. "I love you because you're not like me." Then he ran uphill to the door, keeping close to the wall. The door opened inward, and Payden used his whole body to force it open.

Inside were two levels: the main floor, and a short metal stairway that curved up to an open area surrounded by windows. Many panels covered with buttons and switches filled the walls, and he approached one.

One switch was larger than the rest, and he gripped the handle, moving the arm up. A click sounded, and suddenly lights filled the space. Beeps and whirring sounds surrounded him.

He turned and rushed up the steps. In the center of the room stood a raised platform, over which hung a helmet covered in wires. Two stands beside it held what looked like metal sleeves. A thick layer of dust blanketed everything, and Payden left footprints across the floor as he stepped forward and placed the helmet on his head. He slid his arms through the sleeves and gripped the bars at the end of each.

An electric current passed through his body, and all he saw was a blinding light, which caused him to squeeze his eye shut, grimacing at the painful surge of energy. Payden imagined the light wrapping itself around him. Images, sounds, smells, and emotions flooded his system, and he became overwhelmed, shaking slightly. With a deep breath, he calmed before he opened his eyes.

David almost lost his footing again. He swung his sword around him to open up a small clearing. As he did, a bright light passed him, pushing every single Fashite soldier down the slope and into the water, generating waves that rocked the boats.

He and Malkam turned to look up at the machine. Two large arms protruded from empty sockets on the side of it, and light shone out of the ends of them. David and Malkam stared for a moment, trying to comprehend what had just happened.

Malkam turned back toward the shore, grimacing as pain shot through him. His left arm, slashed when he forgot his shield no longer covered that appendage, dangled at his side. The Fashites tried to press forward, but they couldn't.

"A shield," he said quietly. "That light is a shield. That gives us time." He hurried uphill. David remained frozen for a while, eyes locked on the machine at use before him. That sight he knew he'd seen before. The doubt did not plague him at that moment. The fact that he couldn't conjure up the memory terrified him.

"David!" Malkam shouted. David emerged from his trance and followed his friend. Malkam sat beside Jordan, who was still crying in shock.

"Payden's in there," Jordan said. "He's in there. He may need help. It's not good to use the machine. My mom said it's not good for anyone to use the machine. I didn't think he would use it. I wouldn't have said— Get him out!"

"Shh," Malkam said soothingly. "Come with me." He collapsed the shield and lifted it. "Jordan, hurry. We need to get into the woods. David, get Payden. I found the trapdoor so we can get out of here."

Jordan, finally numb, followed Malkam. They easily found the door, as Zachary had not yet descended. He leaned against a tree, one hand holding the cloak against his side while the other rested on Lucy's head. Malkam gathered Lucy into his arms and carried her down the rickety ladder.

"Where's—where's Payden?" Zachary asked, his voice drawn.

"Inside the machine. David's getting him."

Zachary nodded and his eyes slid shut. Jordan couldn't look at him, as so much of his own blood covered him. She turned and kept her eyes on the tower, worry saturating her.

David stepped lightly to the tower's open door. He paused again as the knowledge of the machine filled his mind. He knew that he'd find a platform inside and panels with lights and strange sounds. The low humming. He heard it before he even entered the room.

Once inside, his eyes went up the steps and found Payden. What he saw wasn't comforting. Payden was on his knees, shaking.

"Payden," David called and hurried up to him. When he touched him, electricity zapped his hand, and he jerked it back. "Payden, we're safe. Let's go."

Payden relaxed and struggled to his feet. The mental exertion was overwhelming. Image after image passed through his mind, and he couldn't understand everything he was seeing. Thoughts and emotions made it hard to focus. But the memories. All the memories he had been trying to regain were there, as well as other images he couldn't understand. Maintaining the bright light shield was becoming difficult to imagine. Talking would be difficult. Payden shut his eyes tightly and worked to clear his thoughts in order to speak. "I have to destroy it."

"We'll do that, but right now, I want you out of there."

"Is everyone safe?" Payden gasped as a heavy weight seemed to hit him, and he struggled to stand. Whenever he thought about destroying the machine, he had more difficulty controlling it.

"Yes. Malkam can get us out of here."

"Good." Payden took a deep breath. "I'm going to destroy it." A fire coursed through his system, deep to the bone. The muscles in his body began to quiver, and he moaned, bending forward.

David, growing more alarmed at each passing breath, tried to touch Payden again. But his hand was repelled. “Come on, Payden. Get out of there. Let’s go.”

“It has to be destroyed now!”

“How?”

Suddenly, Payden knew how. He focused on that image. But—

“Why are you so determined to destroy it?” David asked. “Get out of it, and I’ll use it to annihilate their entire army right now!”

Thoughts and words began coursing through Payden’s mind, feelings, causing his skin to shiver and his insides to quake. “This thing is evil. I have to destroy it now.”

“What?” David asked. Payden sounded far away.

“If this machine was given to the Djorites to help life, why did they stop using it? What happened here all those years ago?”

David was dumbfounded for a moment. These machines hadn’t helped to bring life, he wanted to say. As if correcting Payden’s assumption. David shook his head. Why was he thinking that? No—how did he know that? “I don’t know,” he finally answered.

“The machine is evil and should never have been built.” The task began to take its toll. Payden felt faint. It was growing difficult to breathe. David had to leave. How could he make David leave?

David noticed how white Payden had become in such a short amount of time. “Payden, please. Don’t you dare—”

“I know how to destroy it now. Hurry and go.”

“How? Tell me how, and I’ll do it,” David begged. A deep desperation filled him. Something wasn’t right. He recognized the look on Payden’s face. David couldn’t place it, but he knew that look. He remembered enough to know that it wasn’t a good thing.

“Use its arms to smash it.”

David glanced out the window. The light that was surrounding them, providing a protective barrier, began to dim, with holes appearing in some places. Sounds from outside told him that the Fashites were firing their bombs upon the shield. "I don't understand, Payden. How do we use the arms? Won't someone have to be—inside?"

Payden lifted his head, high and focused. He channeled his thoughts and steeled his resolve. As tears formed in his eyes, he softly said, "Tell Jordan I love her. So much."

David's eyes widened. That look on Payden's face—the memories surfaced. David knew where he had seen that look before. As the emotions erupted, David reached out and grabbed Payden's shoulders, but a pulse of hot energy sent him back several feet. David rolled, but quickly clambered to his feet, stumbling forward as he regained feeling in his legs. "Don't you do it!" he screamed. "Get out of there. Let me do it."

"You promised to take Jordan back. I don't want you to break your promise."

"If you die, you'll cause me to break a promise I made years ago. This is stupid! Let's find another way. Don't do this. Please!" David fell to his knees beside Payden as his legs still hadn't regained their proper use. "Boy, please," David choked. "Think of something else to do. Tell me how to do it. Don't you dare—"

"I can't—I can't—" Payden moaned and doubled over, and the light shield fell for a moment. Payden inhaled and it returned, but sweat poured from his skin, and he could no longer control his shaking.

"Don't you do this to me, boy," David said with a trembling voice. "Don't you dare try to die on me. I won't be able to live if you die, do you understand that? Why do you want to do this?"

"I can't keep the light up much longer, David. Go. My strength is leaving. I can feel it."

"Why, Payden?" David shouted.

"'A man can show no greater love to his friends than to die in order to save them,'" Payden said.

"That's just something you read in a book! It doesn't mean anything."

"Yes, it does," Payden said. "I know that it does."

"Payden—" David reached for him again, determined to hold on this time.

Payden backed up and raised his arms, lifting the machine's arms over it. "Go now, or I'll bring these down on both of us!"

"Let me do it!"

"I love you, David," Payden whispered. How could he make David leave? An idea crossed his mind. It could work. "I remember everything now. I remember everything you've done for me. Protect Jordan. Please. Now get out of here," Payden said.

David was outside by the trees before he knew what had happened. How had he gotten there? He looked at the machine, and its arms rose higher.

"Payden!" he screamed. David sprinted toward the weapon. "No!"

Inside, Payden paused. "Please may I survive this," he whispered. "For David's sake." Then he pulled down the arms.

Rock and steel collapsed into the room below, breaking open the tanks. A spark ignited the gas. The explosion sent David flying back into the woods, and he rolled until his body struck a tree.

Jordan watched and fell to her knees.

"What the—" Zachary breathed.

Malkam quickly exited and looked at the smoke and fire that covered the hillside. The whine of bombs en route filled the air as well. They had to hurry.

"Jordan, get inside, quickly."

She remained.

"Jordan!"

Her body shook, and he grabbed her arm to pull her to her feet. "Get down there, now!"

A bomb struck the hillside, below the tower, while another soared overhead, landing on the other side of the ridge. Both sent up rocks and more dust. Malkam searched for David and Payden, but he only saw David nearby, struggling to get to his feet. Malkam didn't even want to comprehend what that meant as he looked at the pile of stone that had once been the tower.

David rose, dizzy from hitting his head on something. He stumbled toward the rubble.

"David, come on!" Malkam yelled.

David stopped moving.

"Hurry, before we all get killed," Malkam said.

David turned and watched Malkam struggle to get Zachary to his feet. He turned back to the smoking rubble before him. The boom of another of the ships' cannons sounded. David took a few slow steps backward, unwilling to believe the sight before him.

"David, now!" Malkam screamed.

David finally turned and hurried toward Malkam, who helped ease Zachary down the steps. The bomb landed on the cliff near the trees, and Malkam and David ducked as tree fragments burst through the area. Malkam hurried down next with David right behind him, locking the door. When he reached the bottom, Malkam handed Lucy to him.

"Okay," Malkam said, knowing he didn't have time to think about what had just happened. "These tunnels are designed so that if you stop for too long, you'll trigger a booby trap. We need to keep moving. Zachary, hold on to me. Jordan, hold on to Zachary. You okay with Lucy, David?"

There was no response.

Malkam sighed. "There will be a place for us to rest; don't worry. I'll stop when we get there. Come on."

He kept them moving at a steady pace, mindful of Zachary's injuries. He could only wonder what everyone was thinking. *Stupid kid*, he thought. Payden had always been too stubborn.

In the rear, David was numb. He didn't feel anything. He shifted the weight in his arms and thought back to several weeks ago when he had carried a different limp body. The shock wore off, and tears finally flowed.

Chapter 19

It was some time before they reached an opening. A large fire was ablaze in the middle. Other tunnel entrances opened to the same room. David laid Lucy beside the fire and stood, staring at it.

"What happened up there?" Zachary yelled, pushing away from Jordan. He shoved David back. "What happened?" He pushed David again, and David backed up until he hit the wall. "Why wasn't it you?" Zachary continued. "Why didn't you die? Was it your idea? Was it? Too big a coward to do it? Had to let a kid do it?"

"Zachary, that's enough," Malkam snapped. Jordan wanted to say something too, but she was on her knees, hyperventilating.

Zachary clenched his fists. "What happened?" he screamed, but David only stared at him. "You jerk! You coward! Why?" he screamed and slammed his fists onto David's chest. "Why?" he sobbed and finally sank to his knees. "Why?"

He clung to David's shirt with one hand and held his head in the other, sobbing. David slowly moved his hand and placed it on Zachary's head, but he offered no other movement or sound. He stared blankly at the wall in front of him.

Malkam, feeling pain throughout his body, decided to settle. He sat and leaned against the wall by the opening they had just come through. He placed his helmet to the side and studied his friend. Zachary was only releasing his grief, and Malkam understood. Did David?

Malkam stared at David's eyes—the only part of David he had seen for twenty years. Those eyes had always been filled with intensity. Ever since Malkam had met David, he had been amazed by the life and animation of his eyes. For all that David had done or seen or been through, he had never allowed it to destroy him. As Malkam looked at his friend's eyes now, he knew. He knew that David had died with Payden. He grieved that loss a little more.

Hours later, after Malkam had dressed everyone's wounds and Zachary had fallen asleep, Malkam went over and sat beside David, whose only movement since they arrived had been when he slid down the wall to sit. Malkam looked over to Jordan. She appeared to be sleeping too.

"Talk to me, David, please," Malkam said in a low voice.

David slowly shook his head from side to side.

Malkam hung his head. "Give me something, David. I loved that boy, too."

Tears fell down David's face. "After we sparred today, he said, 'Today I have been humbled.' Henry used to say that. Whenever he met someone who impressed him, he'd tell them he was humbled by them. The person was always touched. Here was this great, famous man saying he was humbled to be in their presence."

"You added a saying to that too. Remember? 'When in the presence of someone greater than yourself, be humbled and not humiliated.' I teach that one to my soldiers."

David continued as if he hadn't heard him. "When Payden said that, he even bowed. I thought I was seeing Henry again. Henry was seventeen when I met him. Seventeen. Payden will be seventeen tomorrow."

Jordan began to cry—deep, loud, aching sobs that shook her body. David immediately went to her, and she wrapped her arms around him, shaking with each sob. He cried with her as he rocked her back and forth.

"Jordan, he loves you," he said. "He loves you."

"Why?" she asked. "Why did he do it?"

"I don't know."

"What did he say?"

"Greater—greater love," David stammered. He couldn't speak. "No greater love—than to save his friends."

"I don't understand."

"It's in the Book—in that book," David whispered.

Jordan grew silent and eventually ceased crying. When David knew for certain that she had fallen asleep, he gently laid her down and covered her with his cloak. He stayed by her for some time, gently stroking her hair. His mind was blank. For the first time since Henry's death, he felt empty.

Malkam eventually approached David. "Come on," he said and pulled his friend to his feet. "Come sit with me by the fire."

David sank heavily to the dirt where Malkam stopped him. Malkam took a seat beside him and stared at the flames.

"They use a special type of oil for these fires," Malkam said, "to keep them going longer."

"I don't care," David said.

"You've got to care about something."

"I have nothing left to care about."

"Really?" Malkam asked. "I'm your brother, remember?"

"My brother was murdered years ago."

"Mine, too. I miss Henry—"

"I meant my real brother," David interrupted. "Before I even met Henry. Same day they took my father. They even—" David stopped. "I forgot my brother's name."

"How'd he die?"

"I don't want to talk about it."

Malkam grabbed David and pulled him face-to-face with him. "You're going to say something because I am not going to watch you do this to yourself. Not again. Tell me something, or I will beat you half to death, wait for you to heal, and then do it again!"

David chuckled.

"Why are you laughing?" Malkam asked.

"I don't know," David said and pushed away Malkam. "That just struck me as funny."

"You've lost your mind."

"Not just yet. But it's the last thing I have left to lose." David took off his hat and tossed it aside. His gloves quickly joined it. Then he stretched out his legs and leaned back onto his elbows.

"All right, let's talk," he said.

"Why do you do this to yourself?" Malkam asked. "You act like a child sometimes."

"I think a part of me is still ten years old," David confessed. "I keep trying to kill that part, but it always comes back to life."

"Why ten?"

"That's when my punishment began."

"What do you mean by that?" Malkam asked. He wanted to get more comfortable, so he took off his sword and breastplate.

David noticed blood on Malkam's shirt. "Why didn't you mention that?"

"Huh?" Malkam pulled up his shirt to reveal the wound. "I didn't know about it."

"Let me get a look at that." David leaned closer, using Malkam's shirt to cleanse the blood. "You're going to need some stitches." His eyes finally noticed Malkam's arm as well and he shook his head. "I don't have the proper tools with me, just some herbs."

"Not really," Malkam said. "I've used a lot for Lucy and Zachary."

"We can use what's left." David quietly approached Jordan and removed the pack of herbs stashed in a pocket of his cloak. He opened it to take inventory.

"Well," he said when he sat back down beside Malkam. "We'll have to improvise, but we'll manage."

After he had the injuries wrapped tightly, he leaned back, propping himself up with his elbows again. "You know, you wonder why I never say anything, but then you go and hide these injuries from those you fight with. Why do you never let your men know when you're wounded?"

"Because I know I can last until I get to someone who can help," Malkam explained. "Besides, it's not good for morale for my men to see their general fall."

"Keep that in mind when you wonder why I hold things back."

"I get help, David. Where's yours? How do you heal your wounds?"

"I read," David answered. "I read from that book Henry gave me. Of course, that one's so old and worn that my eyes can barely make out half of it anymore, but I promised Henry I would read it. In a way, it's as though I'm talking with him again. It's uncanny, but I always seem to get what I need to hear."

"Why didn't Henry ever share this book with me?"

"You wouldn't have listened."

"How do you know?"

"First of all, it was a Djorite book. That alone would have deterred you. And second, you were a warrior. As much as you wanted peace, you wanted to fight for it."

"So?" Malkam reclined and folded his hands behind his head.

"Okay." David went over to Jordan again and retrieved his book from another pocket of the cloak. He dropped it onto Malkam's chest and sat down again. "Read it. Then let me know. I'm going to sleep now. Good night."

David curled up and shut his eyes. If he at least pretended to be asleep, Malkam might let him be. He sighed and rehearsed some of his favorite parts of the Book to himself, hoping to keep his thoughts from what really bothered him.

Malkam sat upright and flipped through the pages. David was right; much of it was faded, and many of the pages threatened to fall out. He turned to the first page. "In the beginning," he read. That seemed like a good place to start, he reasoned.

Chapter 20

Voices raised in terror filled the night. David's eyes twitched. The voices fell away, one by one, until it was just the screaming of a woman. Then her voice was abruptly cut off. Light flashed, followed by a low, steady rumbling. David was standing with a group of men, and all eyes were on a rising cloud in the distance.

"That was the last one," someone said.

"Are you certain?" another person asked.

"Even if it wasn't, I ensured that it would be."

"What do you mean?" David asked.

"If any more of the instruments are out there, they would only be visible if a Djorite were present. Otherwise, they would just appear to be part of the landscape surrounding them."

An older man nodded. "That was a good thought."

"We need to hurry. The Fashites will be here in a few hours. There's still much to do."

David watched the men turn to leave. His eyes went back to that distant pile of rubble. The man who had destroyed it placed his hand on David's shoulder.

"Come on, Brother. My sister will not be happy if I return without you."

David smiled. "*I* wouldn't be happy if I didn't return to her."

They hurried to catch the others.

Then the image faded to a woman's face, crying, her eyes filled with terror.

The fire snapped and popped. David's eyes flew open and he sat upright. Then he looked about the manmade cave. For a brief moment, he didn't know who he was or where he was. The haze of the dream still lingered—or was it more than that? A memory?

A hiss from the fire pulled him completely from his dreams and back into reality. Payden. David ran his hand over his head. The explosion. He silently rose to his feet and crept to the tunnel that led back to the machine. They had left too soon, he realized. Somewhere back there, Payden was alive. He had to be.

Part One: Ashites

154. "There was a man who had great . . ." Luke 15:11–17
155. "He would tell his father that . . ." Luke 15:18–24
155. "Your brother was lost . . ." Luke 15:32.

Part Two: Djorites

242. "Like water turning to blood." Exodus 7:20
242. "It said that he would be strong . . ." Psalms 21:10–11
242. "But then it spoke of him . . ." Psalms 22:6–8
242. "Well, I flipped some pages . . ." John 15:13
243. "Last night, I read that . . ." Exodus 20:13
243. "That murderers should be put to death." Exodus 21:12
308. "Jesus turned to those who . . ." John 8:31–38
308. "Jesus explained, "You may . . ." John 8:42–47
318. "He thought of one of the stories . . ." Mark 5:2
318. "When they left, he was of . . ." Mark 5:15
327. "Don't talk about the things . . ." Proverbs 27:1
327. "Don't boast about what . . ." Proverbs 27:2
327. "Carrying a large stone . . ." Proverbs 27:3
327. "Anger can be grueling . . ." Proverbs 27:4
327. "For one to reprimand you . . ." Proverbs 27:5
328. "Wounds given by a lover . . ." Proverbs 27:6
328. "Even the great King Solomon . . ." Matthew 6:29
413. "A man can show no greater . . ." John 15:13

CPSIA information can be obtained at www.ICGtesting.com
Printed in the USA
LVOW13s0556240114

370711LV00001B/2/P

9 781490 820446